TIME'S ASSASSIN

TIME'S ASSASSIN

BOOK III OF THE ISLEVALE CYCLE

D.B. JACKSON

Cover Design by Robyne Pomroy

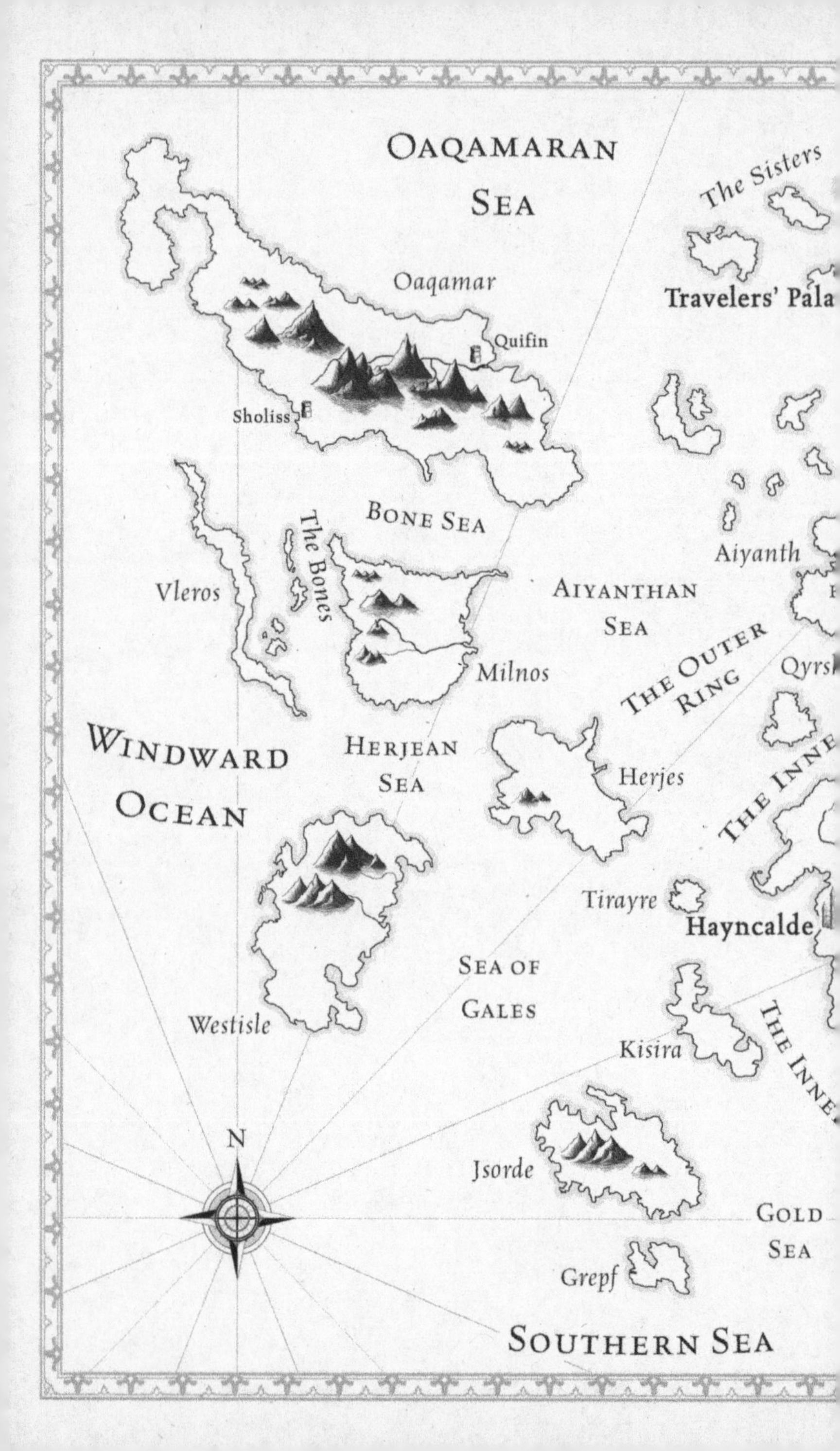
Oaqamaran Sea
The Sisters
Travelers' Pala
Oaqamar
Quifin
Sholiss
Bone Sea
The Bones
Vleros
Aiyanth
Aiyanthan Sea
Milnos
The Outer Ring
Qyrs
Windward Ocean
Herjean Sea
Herjes
The Inne
Tirayre
Hayncalde
Sea of Gales
Westisle
Kisira
The Inne
N
Jsorde
Gold Sea
Grepf
Southern Sea

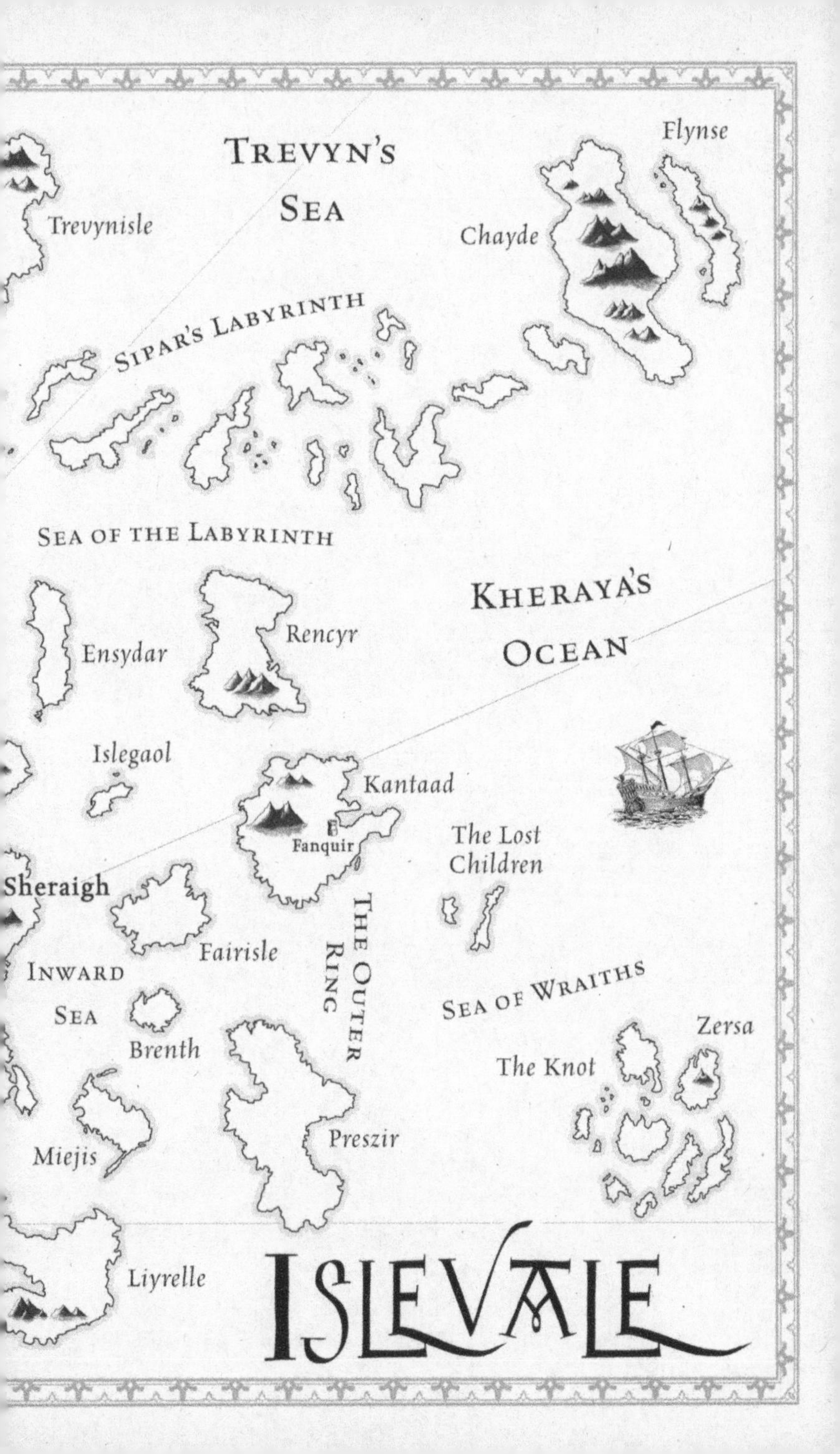
Trevyn's Sea
Flynse
Trevynisle
Chayde
Sipar's Labyrinth
Sea of the Labyrinth
Kheraya's Ocean
Rencyr
Ensydar
Islegaol
Kantaad
Fanquir
The Lost Children
Sheraigh
The Outer Ring
Fairisle
Inward Sea
Sea of Wraiths
Brenth
Zersa
The Knot
Preszir
Miejis
Liyrelle
Islevale

To Alex and Erin
With all the love in all the worlds I know

WHAT HAS COME BEFORE

TIME'S CHILDREN: Tobias Doljan, a Walker, born with the ability to journey back through time, is summoned from the Travelers' Palace in Windhome, where he has lived since he was a boy, to the court of Sovereign Mearlan IV on the island of Daerjen.

The chancellor of the palace arranges passage for him to the royal city of Hayncalde aboard a merchant ship captained by Seris Larr. The night before he sails, his friend Mara, who is a Spanner, capable of crossing great distances in mere moments, speaks of wanting to follow him to Daerjen and then kisses him passionately before fleeing to the girls' dormitory.

Droë, a Tirribin, has been watching. Tirribin, or time demons, appear as children but are lethal predators who feed on human years and live for centuries. Because Walkers' years are tainted by journeys through time, time demons do not prey on them. Droë and Tobias have developed an awkward friendship. But when Droë threatens to feed on Mara's years, Tobias forbids her to do so, despite being powerless to stop her. They argue and part on poor terms. The following morning, after surviving an attack by a Belvora demon, Tobias sails for Daerjen.

His new home country fights dual wars with Oaqamar and

Westisle privateers, and these wars go poorly. The sovereign, Mearlan, wants Tobias to go back in time to keep him from committing to the conflicts. This requires a Walk of nearly fourteen years, and, as Tobias explains to Mearlan, for every day he journeys through time, he ages that amount. After considering the stakes, however, Tobias agrees to make the Walk.

Quinnel Orzili and his beloved wife, Lenna, are Travelers—he a Spanner, she a Walker. They are also assassins employed by Pemin, the autarch of Oaqamar. They arranged the failed Belvora attack before Tobias's journey, and a second unsuccessful attack on the boy the night he arrives in Daerjen. Now, Lenna follows Tobias back through the years and conspires with a younger Orzili to assassinate the sovereign.

The assassins who strike at Mearlan's castle can Travel like Spanners, but do so clothed and bearing weapons, which shouldn't be possible. They kill all of Mearlan's family and ministers except Sofya and Tobias, who fights his way free and spirits the princess away from the castle. During the fight, his chronofor is broken. He cannot Walk to another time until he replaces or repairs it. The castle has been taken by soldiers of Sheraigh, Hayncalde's bitter rival. And Tobias and Sofya are alone and helpless in the streets of Hayncalde.

Back at the Travelers' Palace in Windhome, Mara wakes sensing that something with the world is not right. And, indeed, the palace is a bleaker place, patrolled now by Belvora demons and soldiers of Oaqamar. A different set of wars rage throughout Islevale. Spanners and Crossers are now the most valued Travelers; using what are called "tri- devices," modified sextants and apertures, they can now Travel in groups, clothed and armed.

Droë, who has feelings for Tobias as well, approaches Mara and confirms that the disruption she senses is real. Time has changed because of what Tobias has done. In this new "misfuture," Mara has no memory of Tobias, but though she is a Spanner, she also possesses abilities common to Walkers. Droë tells her that she and the boy were friends and more. Mara has to help him. She secures a chronofor and travels back fourteen years, intent on finding and aiding Tobias.

Tobias and Sofya are taken in by an older couple, who shelter the fugitives and treat Tobias's injuries. But Orzili captures Tobias, takes him to the castle dungeon, and tortures him, hoping to learn Sofya's whereabouts. Agents of the Temple free Tobias from the dungeon and arrange passage for him and Sofya away from Daerjen. When assassins in Orzili's employ thwart these plans, Tobias calls on two Tirribin, Maeli and Teelo, who help him kill the assailants. They lead Tobias and the princess to the Notch, a shadow city located along the shoreline.

Mara finds Droë in the past and confirms that she is in the right time, before Spanning to Daerjen seeking Tobias. After their conversation, Droë is intrigued by the idea that she might love Tobias, whom she has yet to meet. She seeks out Tresz, a Shonla, or mist demon, who carries her toward Daerjen.

Tobias seeks help from the Arrokad, Ujie. Like all of her kind, she is beautiful, capricious, and dangerous. She agrees to help Tobias in the future, for a price: an undetermined boon. Mara is taken hostage by Gillian Ainfor, a traitorous minister from Mearlan's court, and her husband, the Binder, Bexler Filt. Tobias then encounters Gillian. Relieved to find her alive, he follows her to her shelter, where she and Filt turn weapons on him and demand that he hand over the princess. Tobias refuses. With help from Mara, he overpowers and disarms the couple. Gillian escapes and tells Orzili that Tobias and Sofya are in the Notch.

Tobias and Mara seek passage on a ship leaving Daerjen. Orzili and his trained assassins find them, and in the ensuing battle, Mara and Tobias wound Orzili, though not before he shoots Tobias and nearly kills Sofya.

Tobias survives and locates a younger Seris Larr, the captain who transported him from Windhome to Daerjen. She agrees to transport Tobias, Mara, and Sofya from Daerjen. As book I ends, they sail from the isle, knowing that Orzili and Sheraigh forces hunt for them.

TIME'S DEMON: The second Islevale book opens nearly two decades before the action described in book I.

Cresten Padkar, newly arrived in the Travelers' Palace, is bullied into a fight with a group of older novitiates led by Jaer Tache. Tache beats the new boy bloody, but Cresten catches the older boy with a solid punch. Before Tache can retaliate, Cresten is rescued by Wink Wenikai, a senior novitiate whom everyone fears. She befriends Cresten.

Cresten meets Lenna Doen, who is a year ahead of him at the palace. The two of them spend much time together, and Cresten develops feelings for her. One night, they encounter Droë, the Tirribin, who is drawn by Lenna's Walking ability. Droë, always fascinated by love, embarrasses Lenna and Cresten with a remark, undermining their budding romance.

Tache and Cresten have built a friendship, though Tache remains moody and strong-willed. When Cresten tells him of the Tirribin who ruined his romance, Tache, eager to treat with an Ancient, demands that Cresten arrange a meeting with Droë. Soon after, Tache spots Lenna and Droë speaking in the palace courtyard and forces Cresten to take him to them. Tache's boorish behavior and poor treatment of Lenna offends Droë. The Tirribin attacks and kills Tache.

Twenty years later, Orzili returns to Hayncalde Castle bearing wounds from his fight with Tobias and Mara. He convinces the older Lenna Stenci to remain in this time and help him track Tobias. She has Walked back fourteen years and has refused Orzili's romantic advances knowing that a younger version of herself waits for him in their home in Fanquir.

Orzili calls on Binder Filt to build him more tri-sextants. Filt's wife, Gillian, goes to see Orzili under the pretext of negotiating payment and delivery of the devices. She is desperate to be useful again, and to be independent of Filt. She offers her services to Orzili as a spy.

Lenna interrupts Orzili's conversation with Gillian. She realizes it was the minister whose missive in her proper time ordered her back in time. The encounter disturbs her, and she decides abruptly to Walk back a few days more, to warn Orzili of Tobias's escape from the dungeon. Preventing the boy's escape, she reasons, will free her to return to her time, and to the older Orzili she loves. But upon Walking back this short time, she meets herself, and her thoughts shatter like glass.

Droë separates from Tresz. She feels restless and remains intrigued with the notion of human love and passion. She calls for Ujie and asks the Arrokad to bring her to adulthood. Ujie refuses, warning her of the dangers of what she contemplates, but she suggests that what Droë wants is possible.

Droë calls for another Arrokad, seeking a boon. Qiyed answers her summons and agrees to bring her to maturity with his magick. As payment, she will share her time sense with him and help him with commerce. Their arrangement remains vague. Though she questions his motives, she is impatient and desperate to change herself. Over the next turn, Qiyed transforms her into a grown woman, but he withholds desire from her until she is indebted to him. He has bargained in bad faith, and she has submitted to an arrangement that will control her for years to come.

Back in Cresten's time, blame for Tache's death falls on Cresten and Lenna. Because Lenna is a Walker, valuable beyond measure to the palace, she largely escapes punishment. Cresten offers to leave in order to deflect blame from Lenna, about whom he still cares deeply. He convinces the chancellor to give him coin, a weapon, and a Bound sextant, and he finds shelter and work in the city of Windhome. There he comes under the tutelage of a scheming old innkeeper named Quinn, short for Quinnel Orzili.

Quinn puts Cresten to work Spanning for a smuggling ring. During one assignment, Cresten has a harrowing run-in with cut-throats. Droë helps him, and they develop an unlikely friendship. When the smugglers murder Quinn and attack Cresten, the two of them kill the men. Cresten flees Windhome, taking Quinnel Orzili's name as his own and seeking asylum in Milnos, where Wink has become the court Spanner.

Twenty years later, the crazed Lenna escapes Orzili and the

other Lenna. Drawing on instincts she has honed over years, she kills a man and takes his money and blade. Orzili and his men search for her, but she evades the soldiers and bests Orzili in a fight on the strand. She returns to the castle and strikes a bargain with the other Lenna. She will remain with Orzili, whom neither of them loves. The other Lenna will return to her proper time fourteen years in the future.

After Sofya is nearly lost to slavers, Tobias, Mara, and the crew of Seris Larr's *Sea Dove* sail Islevale's seas seeking Bound chronofors to help them combat Orzili and his assassins. Belvora demons follow the ship to the Ring Isles where Tobias and Mara enlist the aid of a Shonla. Gillian Ainfor, now a spy for Orzili, hears of their search for devices and sends word to the assassin, suggesting a trap that will end their pursuit.

Still harried to Belvora, Tobias and Mara finally hear of Bound devices available near Westisle, where pirates are known to deal in such items. The *Sea Dove* heads in that direction.

Droë and Qiyed voyage together but their relationship is fraught with conflict. Qiyed controls her with threats, violence, and magick. Droë tests the limits of his power, and learns to combat it, though while they are at sea, she cannot risk fighting him. When they sense Walkers nearby, she knows they have found Tobias, and sees an opportunity to escape the Arrokad.

Orzili, his assassins, and the Belvora attack the *Sea Dove*. Mara is shot. Tobias and Orzili fight to a stalemate. Mara calls for aid from the Shonla, but one of Orzili's men kills the creature. Its death cry draws Qiyed and Droë to the ship.

Qiyed wishes only to avenge the Shonla; Droë seeks to intervene in the larger battle. She overpowers him and throws off his control, taming and humiliating him. She still loves Tobias and considers harming Mara. She chooses instead to help them. She has Qiyed take Orzili far away so that he can't hurt Tobias. But Qiyed and Orzili scheme together to defeat the boy and punish Droë.

Sad and jealous, Droë cannot face Tobias for long. She leaves him and calls for Ujie. Tobias and Mara know they must leave the *Sea Dove*; Orzili knows of the ship and of Captain Larr. They will find a new home, strike at the assassin, and end this conflict. All they have is each other, and Sofya, whom they both love. But that may well be enough.

30th Day of Sipar's Settling, Year 633

They fall out of the gap onto a strand south of the Notch, flame-lit, the sand firmed by rain. Twelve of them in all. Orzili and his assassins, and eight uniformed Sheraighs from Hayncalde Castle.

Lenna has come from the future to warn him that he failed once at this. Hence the extra soldiers. Surely twelve should be enough to overpower a Walker and a princess. Tobias will not—cannot—escape him again.

The boy and a woman Orzili doesn't know stand before them, grim and drenched. The woman raises a musket to her shoulder. Tobias trains his pistol on Orzili, his other arm cradling the infant princess to his chest. Firelight warms Tobias's scarred face and glimmers in his eyes. Orzili senses that men and women gather around the fire behind him, closer than he would prefer. He doesn't care.

"Good evening, Tobias," he says, baring his teeth in a smile. "We've been looking for you." He raises his pistol. "Put down your weapons, or I'll kill the princess." He glances at the woman but senses that she won't act without leave from Tobias.

"We won't," Tobias says. "Drop yours or we'll kill you where you stand."

"Brave words, but you're outnumbered."

"That doesn't matter. We're leaving here tonight, and I won't let you stop us."

Orzili laughs. "Leaving? Why should I care if you leave? I can track you anywhere. Don't you understand that by now?" He gestures at the golden tri-sextants wielded by his assassins. "With these devices, I can go anywhere I wish, armed and accompanied by soldiers. You won't escape me again." He flashes another grin at the woman. "He isn't as pretty as he once was. I'm sorry for that. Couldn't be helped. Shall I tell you how he wept at the mere thought of being subjected to more torture? Shall I tell you how he screamed and begged us for mercy?"

She casts a pitying look at Tobias but holds her musket steady.

"Give me the princess," Orzili says to this boy in a man's body. "Or die. Those are your choices."

Tobias says nothing.

"I can spare your companion. She need not die. The two of you can go free. Just give me the child. Everything else is negotiable."

"No."

"What do you think to gain?" Orzili asks. "As I've already said, we can find you anywhere."

The woman's musket booms. Tobias staggers, and the princess screams, flailing in his arms. Orzili can't help but flinch as well.

Yet, only when he sees what she has shot does he recognize the danger. One of the tri-sextants lies on the wet sand, gleaming with firelight, dented, bent, useless. The assassin who held it rubs his hand. The woman has dropped her musket and produced from within her overshirt two pistols.

"You can't follow us anywhere now," she says.

Orzili levels his pistol at Tobias again. "That was foolish!"

"Actually," the boy says with a grin, "I think it was bloody brilliant."

The Sheraighs grip their weapons. Men and women near the fire shout. Orzili peers back at them. Many hurry in their direction. Perhaps bringing uniformed soldiers was a mistake. This can't end badly again.

"What are you waiting for?" he demands of the soldiers.

Before he can say more, the woman fires both her weapons. Two soldiers drop to the sand, both bleeding from chest wounds. She's good.

Reports echo from the crowd behind him, and bullets whistle past. The surviving soldiers dive to the sand, as do Orzili's men. Orzili roars his frustration.

Seeing Tobias hesitate, he raises his own pistol again and fires.

At the same time, Tobias wrenches away, seeking to shield the princess. The babe's screams spiral into the night. Tobias cries out as well and collapses, still clutching her to him. Blood glistens on his sleeve.

Orzili's assassins and the soldiers will fight off the rest. Or not. He is intent on killing the princess. He draws his dagger and throws himself onto Tobias and the child.

The woman screams a warning. More pistol fire crackles.

Orzili drives his blade toward Tobias's face. The boy catches him by the wrist, fights him off. He's stronger than Orzili would have guessed, but Orzili has the advantage. He forces the point of the knife closer to the boy's eye. Tobias's arms shake. He gives way, grudgingly, but inexorably.

Orzili hammers his free fist into the bloody bullet wound on Tobias's arm.

The boy bellows but still holds fast to Orzili's blade hand.

Orzili feels him reaching for something, pounds at the wound yet again. He pushes himself up and punches the boy in the face. Tobias's eyes glaze.

Orzili rears back for one final, killing thrust of his knife.

And agony sears his leg. The boy's blade. Orzili roars, rolls away, the blade ripping his flesh. The pain redoubles, and he howls again. Tobias grabs for his pistol.

Blood gushes from the gash in Orzili's thigh. He's already fired his weapon. People from across the strand converge on them, some loading weapons, others aiming. Most of the Sheraighs lie dead, as do two of his men. Three soldiers flee northward, back to the city.

Orzili has little choice but to do the same. He hobbles away as fast as he can, discards his weapon, clutches his sextant. He expects at any moment to be shot in the back.

A pistol thunders. Anguish explodes below his shoulder. He stumbles, rights himself, runs on. As he limps over the wet sand, he sheds clothing, his shoulder and leg screaming in protest, until, at last, he is naked. He aims his sextant and with a twitch of his thumb activates the device. The familiar tug jerks him forward, out of firelight, beyond the crash and retreat of the surf and the cries of the princess, still alive. Another failure.

The gap swallows him.

CHAPTER ONE

11th day of Sipar's Waking, Year 619

The bells tolling in the ward outside her shuttered window were a summons to the king's court. They had been every day since her arrival in Herjes. They should have roused her from her bed today.

Lenna remained where she was, buried beneath woven blankets, curled in a tight ball, her face damp with tears.

Her entire body hurt: her jaw tender and tight where he had hit her, her back and hips and thighs aching from her vain attempts to fight him off, her most private places abused. Her spirit was broken as well; she was too humiliated to call for the castle's healer, too ravaged to stand before the king and his court, too weak to kill the bloody fiend. She loathed herself.

Yet, that wasn't even the worst of it.

Eight turns had passed since she arrived in Herjes from Windhome—Jispar IV's new Walker, celebrated throughout the royal city of Vondehm, feted with a dizzying ceremony in the king's throne room and a sumptuous feast afterward. She tripped through that day in a haze, overwhelmed, brimming with pride and excitement. If only her parents and sisters could see her!

Soldiers in green and silver livery, their faces marked with the intricate black etchings for which Herjes was known, bowed to her as they would to royalty. Ministers welcomed her as an equal.

The twin doors outside the king's chamber stole her breath: carved in the form of a great serpent, coiled, head reared to strike, inset pearls for eyes. And yet this was nothing compared to the interior. The walls were curved, the chamber a great circle. Glazed windows looked out over an enormous garden, and a thick, woven rug covered a floor of pink marble. As in the chancellor's chamber in Windhome, colorful tapestries hung along the walls and a pigeon cage rested by the window to the right of the door, the birds it held cooing softly. There was a standing desk beside it, broader than the chancellor's, and far less neat. These common furnishings, though, were the only similarities Lenna could see between this chamber and the one she remembered from Windhome palace. Comparing the two rooms was akin to equating a common Kant to an Oaqamaran Marauder.

Directly in front of her, a throne gilded in silver rested on a raised dais made of some dark, finely grained wood. And upon the throne sat her king, the man who had paid to bring her here.

Jispar accepted her obeisance—three prostrations, as was expected of newcomers to the court—with a smile and a lingering gaze that warmed her cheeks. He stood then and walked to her, a welcome on his lips. She heard none of what he said.

She was barely fifteen years old, an innocent in matters of the heart and the body. If asked, she would have said that she'd never had a romance with a boy in Windhome. Yes, she had cared for Cresten, before their encounter with the Tirribin, Droë, before Tache's death and all that followed. But they had been children, she and Cresten both.

This king, Jispar—he was something entirely different. He was... He was stunning. He stood at least three hands taller than she, and she had long considered herself tall for a girl her age. His chest and shoulders were broad, powerful. She thought him relatively young—late twenties, or perhaps—*perhaps*—early thirties. Flowing black hair, full lips, dark eyes, and a complexion somewhere between the blanched pinks of the Inner Ring, and the dark browns of Lenna's fellow novitiates in Windhome. Black etchings spiraled around his right eye and down over his cheek and jawline, giving him a fearsome aspect. His smile, however, revealed perfect white teeth and crinkles around his eyes and mouth. With every change in expression, every raised eyebrow and quirk of his lips, the markings on his face shifted so that they seemed alive.

He wore a loose ivory tunic and satin breeches of green and silver. A silver crown rested on an emerald cushion beside the throne, along with a scepter of silver and crystal.

Throughout that first day, he was so intent upon her that she might as well have been the only person in his court. He walked her through his gardens and down one wondrous corridor of his palace after another, acting as chaperone and guide and companion. Women in the court, those wearing diaphanous gowns rather than ministerial robes, followed her with their glares, or gazed possessively at their liege. At the time, Lenna hardly cared. She basked in his attentions, in his words of welcome, in his recitation of her pedigree and the words of praise he read from the letter of introduction sent by Windhome's chancellor.

She blushed when he took her arm and hung on his every word as he spoke of art and history, of Herjean customs and luminaries and conquests. At the banquet, he had her sit at his right hand, and after the stewards filled their cups with Brenthian white, he and all his guests rose in tribute to her. Later, when the platters had been cleared and musicians began to play in the hall, he danced with her, his warm, strong hand pressed to her back, his eyes holding hers.

Lenna retired to her chamber that night breathless and smitten. But still naïve.

When she was summoned to Jispar's chamber five nights hence, she assumed he wished to speak with her of a Walk he needed her to complete or—dare she think it?—wanted to include her in a discussion with his most trusted ministers.

A guard, silent and severe, steered her through torchlit corridors to the king's quarters and ushered her inside. There, she found Jispar alone, dressed in satin sleeping garments, the chamber lit by the hearth fire and candles that smelled of bay and musk.

His eyes glinted like onyx, and the smile with which he greeted her was harder than the one she recalled from the day she arrived. The writhing of those marks around his eye put her in mind of snakes. She shrank from him and his grin sharpened.

She turned from the memory then, burrowed deeper beneath her blanket. He had sent guards for her many times since. Too often. Once, when she refused his summons, he came to her chamber, beat her, and took what he wanted anyway.

That should have ended her resistance. Surely, the king expected it would.

But Lenna was not one to surrender. She was a Walker of Windhome, raised by parents who possessed next to nothing but lived and loved and thrived anyway. Jispar's assaults awakened the pride her mother and father had instilled in her when she was little more than an infant.

Lenna continued to resist, to endure the beatings, the violations. He wouldn't kill her. She knew this. He had paid handsomely to bring her to Vondehm, in part because having a Windhome-trained Walker enhanced the standing of his court. He also wouldn't back down. She knew this as well, steeled herself to whatever would come.

So she believed.

He had brutalized her again just last night. That, however, was not why she hid beneath her blankets, why she shed tears and ached deep in her chest. She had put up with his cruelty for nearly eight turns and would for as long as she had to until she could escape this place, or rid herself of the king.

No, it was a different exigency of time that kept her huddled in the warmth of her bed—equally stark, as immutable as the tide.

Two turns had passed since her last bleeding.

Each day for some time now, she had awakened feeling queasy, a sour coating on her tongue. This morning, upon waking, she vomited until her stomach was empty and her throat ached.

Innocent though she might have been not so long ago, she had never been a fool. She carried Jispar's child in her womb. Pride was one thing, but this... She wanted to die.

On the thought, her mood shifted subtly. Why not die?

If she could have killed the king, she would have, but she knew that was next to impossible. He was guarded night and day by the fiercest warriors in all Herjes. He had tasters for each meal, even for his midday tea and his evening wine. And even if she managed to evade the soldiers and attack him, using the skills she had honed in the lower courtyard of the Travelers' Palace, Jispar himself was said to be a skilled swordsman. He was canny, cruel, as strong as a Presziri horse.

That said, he did have a weakness: All in his court knew that he wanted a son. Desperately.

For the first time since this nightmare began, she considered taking her own life. Not out of despair, but as an act of defiance. She would tell the king that she carried his child—she might even claim she knew it to be a boy. Walker magick could tell her such things, she would say. She doubted he would know enough to question this. And then she would kill herself, and the babe with her.

Grim purpose, but purpose nevertheless. Lenna stretched, winced, threw off her blanket, and swung herself out of bed. She splashed cold water on herself, rinsed her mouth, and spat into her chamber pot. She dragged a comb through her bronze hair and perfumed it. Last, she donned her ministerial robe. Green and silver, of course. In those first days, she had worn Herjes' colors with pride. Now they reeked of him, like everything else. Like her.

She could not hide the bruising on her face, and she would not go to the healer, even now, having come to this decision. She would enter the king's hall with her chin raised. Strength. Pride. Folly, perhaps. One did what was required to endure.

Lenna followed the maze of corridors to the hall, swept past the guards who opened the twin doors for her, and entered the hall. It was crowded. A blessing. Some by the doors marked her entrance. A few stared at her bruised jaw. Most in the grand chamber took no notice of her. She skirted the edge of the throng, making her way to the cluster of ministers flanking the throne. As she walked, she tried to hear what was being said. She gathered that Jispar had consented to an audience with subjects of his kingdom who wished to petition the crown for some small boon or mercy.

Another stroke of fortune. None would presume to ask a favor of the king that involved his Walker. Perhaps Jispar was unaware of her absence and late arrival.

She reached the rear of the hall, slipped in behind the Minister of Protocol, offered a weak smile when he glanced back at her. His gaze dipped to her chin before he faced front again. He had served in this court long enough to know how she had come by the bruise.

She heard little of what was said to or by the king. Periodically, polite applause rippled through the hall, acknowledging Jispar's magnanimity. Each time, of course, Lenna clapped with the rest. The morning crawled by. Her stomach remained unsettled, but now discomfort warred with hunger.

At last, a sharp noise echoed through the chamber—the rapping of a staff butt on the marble floor. A guard announced that the audience was over, and men and women began to shuffle out of the hall. When the citizenry was gone, the king's ministers exited the chamber as well. Before long, Lenna, a few guards, the king's page, and Jispar himself were the only ones left in the hall.

The king regarded her, his expression revealing nothing, the etching quiescent for now.

"You wish to speak with me?"

Her gaze flicked to the guards.

"Leave us," Jispar told them. "Close the door." He eyed her jaw. When they were alone, he said, "You should see the healer about that."

"Are you concerned for me, or for your reputation?"

Jispar laughed, not kindly. "Neither. What is it you want?"

Bastard. "I thought you should know. I'm..." She swallowed. "I'm with child."

"It's about bloody time, isn't it?"

She felt like she'd been slapped. "What?"

"I'd been wondering how long it would take. With the others, it happened a good deal sooner. How far along?"

"Um..." She gave a small shake of her head, racing to catch up with the exchange. "A turn or two. No more."

"I see." He considered her, eyes narrowing, the black lines on his face stirring. "I've wondered if a child of ours might someday become a Walker. Do you think that's possible?"

Only if it lives.

"I wouldn't know."

"My liege," he said, his tone pointed.

Lenna dropped her gaze. "My liege."

"Well, I'm grateful to you for letting me know. I will inform the palace stewards. Anything you need will be provided, of course. I will expect you to fulfill your responsibilities to this court, until such time as you no longer can."

"Yes, my liege."

He picked up the silver bell from beside the crystal scepter and gave it a sharp shake. Before the sound of it died away, several guards, the page, and a pair of stewards had entered the hall once more.

"Is that all?" Jispar asked, in a tone that made clear he had already dismissed her.

What could she say? "Yes, my liege." She curtsied, straightened, and hurried from the chamber, her breath coming in shallow gasps.

Rage, shame, contempt for herself—these followed her through the corridors and out into bright sun and a cool northerly wind.

Once in the gardens, away from the scrutiny of others, she allowed herself to cry, tears burning like acid.

It's about bloody time...

Demons take him!

She hadn't told him it was a boy, as she had intended. Not that he would care.

Why—*why!*—when he asked whether their child might be a Walker, hadn't she said yes? If she couldn't deprive him of the son he so fervently wanted, she could dangle before him the possibility of bearing him a Walker before she ripped away his hope.

With the others it happened sooner...

How many others? Did this child matter to him at all? Did she, beyond the expenditure of gold that brought her here?

Would he care when she killed herself?

This question she could answer with confidence. He wouldn't care in the slightest. She was no more to him than a whore who could Walk through time. He would enter her death into a ledger, an asset lost, gold spent and wasted, akin to a ship lost at sea, or a horse gone lame. Except she was reasonably certain that he loved his mounts.

So why die for him?

She heard the question in her father's voice, a remnant of a childhood forever lost.

Why spend your own life when he is the one who ought to die?

"I could be killed in the attempt," she whispered, as if in conversation.

Wouldn't that be a better death?

Lenna placed a splayed hand on her belly. Wasn't her child more deserving of life than Jispar? If nothing else, didn't she owe herself and the babe the possibility of a future beyond this castle?

So be it then. She would kill the king or die making the attempt. But how?

She could Walk back in time, of course. That was her greatest gift, her most valuable talent.

Yet, as with all else, Jispar exercised strict control over her, over all his Travelers. He kept their Bound devices—her chronofor, the Spanners' sextants, the Crossers' apertures—which, in fairness, were purchased for them with Herjean gold, always locked away in his treasury. Only when the king wished for one of the Travelers to Walk or Span or Cross did he allow them access to the devices. From all she had been taught in Windhome, and all she had heard from her fellow Travelers in the castle, this was highly unusual. Most royals bestowed the devices on their Travelers, and thereafter, they were treated as the property of those who could use them.

Even if she could think of a way to kill him that involved Walking back through time, she would need to request that he give her the chronofor, or she would have to steal it from the treasury. Impossible.

In truth, she didn't see how a Walk would help her anyway. Traveling to any time since her arrival in Vondehm would leave her with the same obstacles she faced now: his constant vigilance, his guards, and his own prowess as a fighter. Going back farther, to a day before her arrival in his court, would only compound her disadvantages, make him that much harder to reach.

It occurred to her that if she offered freely what he had taken thus far, she might get close enough.

"No," she whispered in the sunlight.

She would kill him or fail, survive or die. She would not abase herself by insinuating herself into his bed. Better to make no attempt at all.

Lenna wandered the gardens for some time before returning to her chamber, no closer to a plan, but fully resolved to see her dark ambitions through to their conclusion. She had been a victim of Jispar's depredation for long enough. From this time forth, he was her prey, even if he didn't know it.

Days passed, measured by mornings of sickness, pointless audiences with the king and his court, and nights of fruitless plotting. To her relief, Jispar no longer summoned her to his bed or forced himself into hers. It seemed his goal had been to get her with child. No doubt he had moved on to some new conquest, someone more compliant than she. Lenna was certain there were plenty of women in the court who would have welcomed the king's advances.

She had yet to decide how to kill him, despite considering the problem day and night. He did like to hunt, usually in the forest lands north of Vondehm, leagues from the castle and his army. Guards accompanied him, of course, but a small contingent.

Lenna hadn't yet decided what to do with this information, but his hunts struck her as the best opportunities she might have to carry out his assassination.

She wondered if she might ride out to the woodland on her own—she did have some time to herself—to scout the terrain and find a place where she might ambush Jispar. During her years in Windhome, she had been more skilled with a sword than a bow, but she was competent with both. If she learned beforehand where he planned to ride, she could lie in wait for the king, slay him with an arrow, and escape the forest unnoticed.

Or maybe she could simply sprout wings and carry him off like a Belvora.

Her scheming consumed her thoughts. Notions of how she might murder the king accompanied her everywhere she went, including Jispar's hall. She knew the danger, but she couldn't help herself. Each time she saw the man, each time she heard him speak, or recalled once again his brutal assaults, her hunger for his death deepened.

So it was this day, as she took her place with the other ministers at the edges of the hall near his throne. So close that she could have killed him with a thrown blade.

She barely heard when the king's herald announced the morning's visitors to the Herjean court. Something about emissaries from Milnos. The names given by the herald meant little to her, and she paid little heed to Jispar as he greeted his visitors with platitudes and meaningless niceties.

When she paused to study the delegation from Milnos, however—eight guards in uniforms of blue and vibrant green, the minister who appeared to lead the delegacy, and one other figure standing beside the minister—her knees nearly gave out. That last one already watched her, recognition in the intensity of his gaze.

Surely she would have noted his name, had she heard it. Could she be mistaken? At this distance it was possible. But see how he watched her, how he communicated with the most minute shake of his head that she should pretend not to know him, how he pointedly shifted his attention back to Jispar—who still spoke—indicating that she should do the same.

She did, but only for an instant. Her eyes found him again. What name had he used? And why?

And what was he doing here, really? Was it chance, or the Two, or some darker purpose that had brought Cresten Padkar back into her life?

CHAPTER TWO

19th day of Sipar's Waking, Year 619

His face was much as she remembered: his chin square, his eyes widely spaced, his lips full. Time had sharpened his cheekbones, melted the softness that once rounded his jaw. He wasn't a boy anymore. He was taller than she recalled, his body now tapered and lean. Enough remained of the lad she had called her friend that she had no doubt as to his identity. Enough had changed to make her stare and stare again.

She had always thought him nice-looking. Kind hazel eyes and a boyish smile in an open, friendly face. Now he was more. Hardened in some way. She saw in his mien and bearing less trust, less welcome. His features, chiseled, the color of the finest dark woods from the Labyrinth, gave away nothing. His gaze—keen, intelligent—shifted constantly, seeming to assess risk and opportunity. It occurred to her that living in the streets of Windhome would have forced such changes upon him. He would have had no choice but to become a creature of the lanes. Did he blame her? He had shouldered responsibility for the events leading to Tache's death, leaving the palace so that she might have a future as a Walker. Had he come to exact some measure of revenge or recompense?

And how had he found his way to the court of Milnos? He wore robes of emerald and blue, and he clutched a golden sextant in his right hand. He had done better for himself than she had imagined he could as an exile from the palace. He had a tale to tell, and she longed to hear it.

Where a tencount before Lenna had been content in her oblivion, largely unaware of what was said in the hall, now she hung on every word, trying to make up for what she had missed.

The older man with Cresten—black-haired, short, and rotund, also dressed in ministerial robes—was Milnos's minister of protocol. According to those around her, they had come to continue negotiations on a new treaty of trade between Herjes and the Shield. Lenna guessed that Cresten had accompanied the minister so that he might Span back and forth between the isles to facilitate the minister's consultations with his king. The Milnosian guards joined the soldiers of Herjes in a tight cluster at the far end of the hall.

Cresten's glance flicked her way again, both guarded and avid. She reconsidered. Milnos's king might have sent him as a courier, but Cresten had come for reasons of his own.

Jispar had arranged for a midday feast to welcome his guests, and now he called forth musicians and dancers for their entertainment. Cresten and the minister of protocol took seats near the throne, their backs to Lenna and the rest of the Herjean court. She had little patience for such diversions. Questions burned in her chest, demanding answers.

More than mere curiosity fueled her impatience. How long had it been since last she spoke with anyone she considered a friend? The other ministers and Travelers in Jispar's court treated her as they would a child. Other women in the court had viewed her as a rival; now, she guessed, they pitied her, called her a fool. So many nights she had lain in her bed, longing for the simple pleasure of companionship, much less the luxury of a confidant. Vahn. The Tirribin, Droë. And, yes, Cresten. She had missed them all. Too much to have to endure this pointless squandering of valuable time. Who knew how long Cresten would be here before he had to Span back to his court?

After three songs, she was ready to tear out her hair. When the musicians started their sixth, she had to bite her hand to keep from screaming her frustration.

After more than a bell of meaningless song and dance, Jispar rose, clapping his hands. Of course, every person in the hall followed his example.

"Splendid," he said in his rich baritone. "A fine prelude to our banquet. We shall now make our way to the West Hall, where we shall share our bounty with our good friends from Milnos."

He stepped off the dais and, as the gathered men and women parted to allow him through, made his way to the door.

The minister of protocol fell in step behind the king and to his right. Cresten, Lenna saw, followed but lagged.

She slipped through the crowd until she had nearly pulled even with him.

"Is it really you?" she whispered.

If he was surprised to find her so close, he gave no indication of it. "Wouldn't the answer be the same no matter who I am?"

A breath of laughter escaped her.

"It's good to see you again, Walker."

Yes, caution called for formality. "And you, Spanner." She hesitated. "I...I didn't know you had been called to the court of Milnos. Congratulations."

"Called is not really accurate. But that story can wait for another time. You don't look well, Walker. Forgive me for saying so."

That nearly broke her. Tears stung her eyes, threatening to pour over her cheeks.

"I'm well enough," she said, her voice less steady than she would have liked.

He chanced a quick look her way. Facing forward again, he said, "The minister and I are to stay here for at least this one night. When might you and I speak in private?"

"After the banquet?"

Cresten shook his head. "We'll be in negotiations for much of the day."

"Tonight, then. There will be an evening meal when you're done. I don't know if His Majesty will expect the rest of his court to attend, but either way, we can speak after."

"Very well," he said. "I'll look forward to that."

He continued apace. She fell back a few strides. Upon reaching the West Hall, he joined the Milnosian minister near Jispar. Lenna took her place among the other ministers and Travelers.

She ate a bit of bread and slices of apple with honey, but felt too queasy to think of eating meats and cheeses and stews. She allowed herself a cup of watered wine. Conversations buzzed around her like flies in a stable, but she kept silent, and as surreptitiously as possible, watched Cresten.

She remembered him as quiet, watchful, and she saw the same qualities here in Jispar's castle. He seemed intent on the king's conversation with Milnos's minister. When others in the Herjean court offered observations, he listened to them as well, attentive, solemn. On a few occasions, he inserted himself into the discussion. Jispar appeared to think Cresten's contributions sound.

Not surprising, really. He had always been smart. Still, she saw in him other attributes she hadn't noticed in Windhome. She remembered him as timid, unsure of himself. The Spanner sitting with her king and the Milnosian minister, however, struck her as poised and confident. She had to admit that she found this new Cresten compelling.

Not Cresten. Not here, not right now. What name had he used, and why?

Did the minister know his real name? Was this a deception designed for this visit to Herjes? In which case, did she owe it to her king to reveal the truth?

Or had Cresten taken on an alias before ever reaching Milnos? Was that how he had gained a position in the court?

Again, her curiosity threatened to overmaster her judgment. She wanted to claim him from the table, drag him from the hall, and demand that he tell her all. And she wanted as well to tell him her tale, dark though it was. She hadn't realized until now how much she had missed her friend.

At length, the king declared an end to the banquet and dismissed all those in attendance except his two guests and a few of his most trusted counselors: the ministers of protocol and arms, as well as his Seer.

Lenna retreated to her chamber.

As darkness fell, she approached the West Hall, only to be confronted by a pair of Herjean guards. The soldiers of Milnos stood nearby as well.

"Is there something you need, Walker?" asked the older of the two, a lanky, yellow-haired man with angular etchings around his eye.

"They're still negotiating?"

"They're still inside," he said. "Do you need to speak with His Majesty?"

"No, I..."

They both watched her, the older man with a colder mien.

"The Walker—from Milnos—he was a friend in Windhome. I wish to speak with him."

Neither of the guards spoke.

"Perhaps tomorrow, then." She hurried away without hearing their reply, feeling that she had done wrong. She couldn't say how.

On her way back to her quarters, she passed one of the pages who served the ministerial corridors. She halted, called the girl's name. The page approached her and bowed.

"The king is speaking with the minister and Spanner from Milnos," she said. "I would like you to keep watch on the West Hall and let me know when their discussions have ended."

"Yes, my lady."

The page bowed. Lenna nodded to her and walked on.

Less than half a bell later, there came a knock on her door—the page informing her that the king's audience with his guests had ended, and the two emissaries from Milnos had gone to their quarters.

A problem, that. Lenna couldn't request the location of Cresten's chamber without raising suspicions. She thanked the girl, gave her a few treys, and closed her door once more.

She barely had time to cross back to her hearth when another knock drew her gaze.

"Who is it?" she called approaching the door again.

"A friend."

Lenna smiled. Opened the door.

Cresten stood in the corridor, torch fire flickering in his eyes. This close he struck her as taller, broader. "Your king kept us later than I had hoped. Would you prefer I found you in the morning?"

"No, this is fine."

"The moon is up. Shall we walk? I've seen little of your castle."

Not at all the Cresten she remembered.

"Yes, all right."

She retrieved a cloak from her wardrobe and led him through the hallways and down into the gardens. The air had chilled, and high haze wreathed a gibbous moon. Lenna pulled the cloak tight around her shoulders and exhaled, vapor billowing before her.

Cresten spoke lightly of the day's discussions, of the two Spans he was commanded to undertake back to Milnos so that he might confer with his king. Somehow the boy she had known, the one sent forever from Windhome Palace, had managed to place himself at the center of his isle's affairs, and those of Herjes as well.

"What happened to you?" she asked. "How did you find your way to a court?"

He smiled, eyes trained on the stone path in front of them. "That's a long story."

"A good one, I hope."

Cresten cast a look her way. "Yes, a good one."

He began his tale with the day he left the Travelers' Palace, the last time Lenna saw him before this morning. He spoke of *gaaz* cutting and smugglers, the Tirribin Droë and an innkeeper who took him in and befriended him, and finally of surviving a battle with armed criminals and discovering a gem that had been stolen from Milnos.

"By that time, I had taught myself to Span," he said, "and I remembered that Wink was called to the court in Caszuvaar. I hoped that by returning the gem to the king there, I might earn a position in his court."

"That was clever," she said, stealing another glance at him. He was beautiful. How had she not known this?

"Thank you."

"Why are you not using your real name?"

He faltered mid-step, quickly scanned the courtyard. "The smugglers. They knew me as Cresten Padkar, and they knew that Quinn was dead. I used his name to get to Milnos, and Wink introduced me to her king that way. At the time, it seemed like a good idea. I'm not sure it's necessary anymore, but I'm also not sure I can change back to being Cresten." He shrugged. "And I sort of like it now."

"So you call yourself Quinn?"

"Quinnel. Quinnel Orzili."

She halted, considered him. "I'll need some time to get used to that."

He smiled. They walked on.

"What about you?" he said. "What is it like serving the king of Herjes?"

Her turn to stumble. Her heart, which had been dancing only an instant before, now seized like a fist.

"Lenna?"

Tears spilled down her cheeks. She spun away from him, took a step, fully intending to bolt back to her chamber.

"Please!"

She halted, her body poised to flee.

"I'm sorry," he said. "I didn't mean to offend you."

A harsh laugh escaped her. "Offend me. Is that what you think?"

"I don't know what to think. I only know that I upset you. That wasn't—"

She raised a hand, silencing him. Yes, she had longed for a friend, was desperate for someone—anyone—with whom she could unburden herself. Now that the moment was here, though, she couldn't bring herself to reveal her humiliation. She swiped at her tears and made herself face him, a smile pasted on her lips.

"Forgive me," she said. "I've... Sometimes I miss the palace and Windhome. That's all. My emotions are... I'm fine."

He didn't answer. They had been close not so long ago. It felt as distant as another lifetime, but it was less than two years. Apparently he still knew her. Too well to be fooled by her denials. He stared at her, waiting.

Her chin quivered. Fresh tears ran down her face. When would she have this chance again? When would another friend come to these shores?

"I'm carrying his child," she whispered. "He...he rapes me."

Cresten looked stricken. "Oh, Lenna." He took a step toward her.

"Don't. Please."

He stopped, nodded.

She took a long, hicupping breath. She felt better for having spoken the words. She glanced around, as he had earlier, and at her gesture, they resumed their walk.

"I hate him," she said, still in a whisper. "More than I've ever hated anyone or anything. I even—" She stopped herself before she could give voice to her desire to kill the king. She couldn't share that, not even alone with this man, far from others. "I've even thought about killing myself," she said instead, because it was also true. "Just to spite him."

"Can't you leave this place?"

"You know how commerce with Windhome works, how it is for Walkers and Spanners and Crossers. The palace paid for me when I was young. They paid my parents. They sheltered me, and fed me, and raised me to be a Walker in a royal court. And then, once I'd been trained, Jispar paid them for me. A lot I would imagine, since I'm a Walker. He may not own me, but...well, he does own me in a way."

Cresten stared straight ahead, the muscles in his jaw rigid, his fist clenched. "What he's done to you... He signed a contract with the palace, and he has abrogated that contract."

"Do you know that?"

He didn't answer right away. "The contracts say that Walkers and other Travelers can't be forced to do certain things—"

"Those clauses are about our talents. Jispar can't make me Walk back ten years. I doubt there's anything in the contract about...about this."

"If the chancellor knew—"

"How would I tell him? Don't you think Jispar has all of my messages read? Not only mine—everyone's."

"I could tell the chancellor. I could go there and speak to him in person."

She shook her head. "No. Thank you, but... That would be humiliating. It would be worse even than taking my own life."

At first he didn't answer. Then he asked, "Why should *you* die?" in a voice almost too soft for Lenna to hear.

A shiver went through her. They walked some distance in silence, their steps like the ticking of a clock. "I've asked myself the same question," she admitted.

They shared a glance, their eyes locking for a fivecount.

"I can help you with this," he said, his voice low, calm.

"Cresten—"

"That's not my name anymore. I can help with this, Lenna. I've...I've taken lives. I'd wager you haven't. I can help you. You shouldn't make the attempt alone."

"Have you ever killed a king?"

He actually grinned. "No, that I haven't done." He sobered. "But he's a man first. A sword will kill him. So will a pistol, or a knife."

His composure both reassured her and chilled her.

"How many men have you killed?"

"That's not—"

"Tell me."

He drew a breath. "Three. And I let Droë kill another for me. His death is on my head as well."

"And you killed them—"

"Because they would have killed me. I give you my word."

"My king wouldn't kill you. Clearly you're willing to murder for other reasons."

He halted again, forcing her to do the same. "I'm willing to murder for you."

Lenna held his gaze, despite being frightened by what she saw there. "Why?"

He hesitated. For the first time since their conversation began, she sensed that he was disconcerted.

"You're my friend," he said.

"Do you kill for all your friends?"

Another laugh escaped him. "No. That's a service I'm offering only to you."

"Then, I'll ask you again. Why?"

His grin faded. "Fine. Because I love you. I have for a very long time, and I never stopped, even after Droë embarrassed us, even after Tache died, even after I was sent from the palace."

He was more handsome than she remembered, more mature than he had any right to be at their age, more daring than she was herself. And, she realized, he was still the best friend she'd ever had. She needed to be honest with him.

"You know that I don't love you. It's not that I can't, or that I won't eventually. I'm not certain about any of that. I just know that I don't love you now, and that I won't be able to while...while he lives."

"I understand."

"We could both be killed."

"I understand that as well. But we won't be. We're Windhome-trained, and I've learned to trust that training and my own instincts. We can do this."

Before she could answer, he said, "There's a guard approaching." His voice had dropped further, so that he barely breathed the words. "From the direction we came. Don't act alarmed, don't startle."

She heard nothing and was about to say so when she caught the faint jangle of a soldier's belt. A fivecount later, a man stepped into the small courtyard in which they stood, his boots scraping on stone. He bowed.

"Forgive me, my lady, my lord. The king wishes a word."

"With me?" Lenna asked.

"With both of you."

Lenna shot a glance at Cresten. He kept his eyes on the guard.

"Very well," he said, with a convincing smile. "Lead the way."

The man pivoted and started back toward the castle. Lenna and Cresten followed two paces behind. They walked in silence for a short while, before Cresten—no, Quinnel—said, "You were telling me about these gardens. Please go on."

Clever.

Lenna launched into a soliloquy on the history of the castle grounds. She tried to remember all that Jispar had told her that first day. When she couldn't remember something, she asked the soldier, drawing a subtle nod of approval from Cr— Quinnel.

All the while, her heart drummed in her chest and her breathing shallowed. At one point, with the guard still facing ahead, Cresten gave her hand a quick squeeze.

Quinnel! *Damn.*

Before long, they neared the twin doors of the king's hall. Torches lit the pearl eyes of the serpent carved into the wood. To Lenna's surprise, they passed by these doors and continued to Jispar's private quarters. Outside that door, they were made to wait in the corridor while a second guard informed the king of their arrival.

Cresten said nothing, kept his gaze trained on the floor. Lenna followed his example. Soon enough, the door opened, and the second guard bade them enter.

They stepped into the chamber and bowed in unison.

Jispar stood at a small table before the hearth, filling a goblet with red wine. He looked up as they straightened, smiled a greeting. He wore breeches and a silk shirt. A sword hung from his belt, but otherwise he was unadorned. Nevertheless, he filled the chamber, candles and the blaze behind him casting hulking shadows around the space. For all the changes Lenna saw in her friend, he appeared slight beside the king.

"Thank you for joining me," Jispar said. He stepped around the table bearing two goblets. He handed one to Lenna and one to...to Quinnel. Then he claimed his own, took a chair by the fire, and waved them to two chairs that had been set opposite his own.

"You honor us, Your Majesty," Quinnel said, lowering himself into his chair.

Lenna sat as well, raised her cup in salute of the king, but held her tongue.

"Will Minister Kraetas be joining us?" Quinnel asked.

The king shook his head. "This is not a matter of trade. This is a social occasion." He smiled again.

"Then you honor me doubly, Your Majesty."

"I believe my Walker has seen to that."

Lenna tensed. Quinnel merely canted his head.

"I'm afraid I don't understand, Your Majesty. Lenna and I are friends from Windhome. Before today we hadn't seen each other for the better part of two years. We were merely resuming an old acquaintance, reminiscing about our time together in the Travelers' Palace. And she was kind enough to give me a tour of your impressive gardens."

"You make it sound quite innocent. Spanner...?"

"Orzili, Your Majesty. Quinnel Orzili. And it was innocent, I assure you."

"Yes, of course. Forgive me, Spanner Orzili." Jispar sipped his wine. "But really: innocent? In the light of that lovely moon, alone in the gardens?"

"Yes, Your Majesty. Innocent. Still, I thank you."

Jispar frowned. "For what?"

"For flattering me that I should be deemed a rival by one such as you. Again, you honor me."

A dangerous game to play with a man like Jispar. Lenna hoped he knew what he was doing. She gulped a bit of wine to mask her fear.

The king appraised Quinnel, faint amusement curving his lips and waking the snake around his eye. "Tell me, how many Spanners does Arlis have in his court now? There's you, of course..."

"And two others, Your Majesty. One is another friend of ours from Windhome: Fesha Wenikai. The other—"

"Yes, thank you. How long have your served him?"

"Less than a year, Your Majesty."

"I see. And you came to his court the usual way?"

"No, I didn't. I was forced to leave Windhome. I trained myself as a Spanner and, when the time came, sought employment in His Majesty's court."

"You trained yourself?"

"That's right."

"And why did you have to leave Windhome's palace?"

"I'd rather not say."

Lenna had raised her goblet to her lips again, but she lowered it now without drinking. She nearly spoke Cresten's name aloud but stopped herself in time.

No one refused Jispar in his court.

"You would rather not," the king repeated, his tone velvet.

"It was a tragedy. I don't like to speak of it."

It occurred to Lenna that Quinnel had yet to take a sip of his wine. Did he suspect poison?

"Of course," the king said. "And yet, I have asked you a direct question." He gestured, a sweep of his hand that encompassed the entire castle. "Within these walls, in this chamber, while you are drinking my wine and presuming to have private conversations with my Walker, my word is law."

"Of course, Your Majesty. A boy I knew died."

"You killed him?"

"No, he was killed by a time demon—a tragedy I might have prevented had I been smarter and stronger."

"You knew of this?" Jispar asked Lenna.

"I was there," she said. "The Tirribin and I were conversing, as we often did. The boy in question was a lout and a bore. He gave offense, and before we could stop her, the Tirribin attacked him."

"Why did blame fall on you?" Jispar asked, facing Quinnel again.

When he didn't answer right away, the king shifted his gaze back to Lenna. "Why was he blamed and not you?"

She gave a thin smile, remembering that day: the fraught discussions in Chancellor Samorij's chamber, and also Cresten's prescience. He'd seen it all, known exactly how it would happen. *You'll be all right,* he'd told her. *You're a Walker. They can't make you leave. I won't be here tomorrow. I'm expendable. They have no reason to think I'm anything special. I'm a Spanner, and not a particularly good one...*

Out of all he said that morning, only this last proved wrong. He was more than all of them had known at the time.

"He was blamed," she said, "because I'm a Walker, and they couldn't afford to blame me. Windhome had many Spanners, and still does. I was the only Walker."

"Why haven't you told me this before?"

Yes, why didn't it come up one of those nights when you were brutalizing me?

"I didn't think it important, my liege." She heard the edge in her own words, was surprised by it.

Perhaps Jispar was as well. He didn't challenge her.

"Well, this is all most interesting," the king said. "Though I'm no less confused as to how you came to be in Arlis's court."

"I promise you, Your Majesty," Quinnel said, unruffled, "there is no more to the story than I've told you. I trained myself, went to Milnos, and offered the king my services. Is it so surprising that His Majesty should welcome a Traveler to his court without having to pay any fee to Windhome?"

Jispar's frown returned, as if he were bothered by the clarity of Quinnel's reasoning. "No, I suppose not."

The king drained his cup. Lenna sipped from hers. Quinnel shifted his from one hand to the other, but to her knowledge had still not lifted the cup to his mouth.

Silence stretched among them, until, at last, the king stood. "It's been a long day," he said. "And you and your minister of protocol begin a long voyage in the morning."

"Yes, Your Majesty." Quinnel set his cup on the table and bowed to Jispar.

Lenna bowed as well.

"Walker, you will remain."

Her pulse stammered, but she nodded.

Jispar escorted Quinnel to the door. "Goodnight, Spanner. This has been a most illuminating conversation. I regret that we won't have more time."

"You're kind, Your Majesty. I hope we'll have occasion to speak again before long. As you know, a Spanner is never too far from anywhere."

He flashed a smile, darted a look at Lenna, and left.

CHAPTER THREE

19th day of Sipar's Waking, Year 619

Jispar closed his door with a soft click and fixed Lenna with an accusatory eye. She resisted the impulse to back away.

"What were you doing with him?"

"Talking," she said, pleased that her voice sounded steady. "As he said, we were friends in Windhome. We spoke of our time as novitiates, and I showed him your gardens. He was most impressed."

He stalked to the hearth. "You walked for some time, and far from the castle. At night."

"I believe he was with you for much of the day."

He glared at her, and she lowered her gaze.

"That story about the Tirribin. It's true?"

"Every word of it."

"And you didn't tell me—"

"Because it was long ago and doesn't matter anymore. C—" She caught herself. "Quinnel left the palace, and I didn't see him again. I all but forgot about him until he showed up in your hall today." She hesitated. If she wanted to kill this man—and she did, desperately—she needed to bridge the divide between them. He wouldn't trust too much goodwill on her part. He would be wary of an attempted seduction, and the idea of it made her want to vomit. But a small gesture on her part, a hint at reconciliation, might allow her to get close enough to kill him later.

She set a hand on her belly. "Besides," she said, "he was never more than a friend, a boy I once knew for a brief time. It goes without saying that I never carried his child."

Jispar scowled at this, and she feared she had miscalculated. After a breath, his expression eased.

"Yes, all right. You may go, Walker." His tone softened the dismissal.

She bowed to him, crossed to the door. Before she could open it, he said, "You're not to see him again."

"Yes, my liege."

"And you should prepare yourself for a journey through time. Now that I know the terms of our agreement with Milnos, I wish to change a few things in preparation for the negotiations we've just completed. I intend to send you back several turns. Later tomorrow, probably. Or the day after."

"Very good, my liege."

"Can you Walk? In your...condition, I mean."

"Yes, my liege. The child will be fine. The same magick that allows me to Walk should protect him."

His gaze sharpened at this—at her use of "him"—but for now he didn't pursue the matter.

She left him and made her way back to her quarters, thoughts swarming through her mind. This would be her first Walk of consequence since arriving in Herjes. Jispar had tested her soon after she joined his court, to assure himself that she could indeed Walk through time as Windhome had promised. He had yet to send her back with a true purpose.

He had other uses for you in the meantime.

Several turns, he said. In all her training in Windhome, she had never Walked as far as a single turn. This would be a challenge for her. She couldn't imagine being in the between for so long, without air, assailed by light and noise, and the tastes and smells of every intervening day. A challenge? More like an ordeal.

An opportunity, as well.

Several turns could mean three, perhaps four. By that time, he had already started violating her, but she wasn't yet carrying the child. She could pretend that in the interval, sometime in his future and her past, they had reached some understanding. She had become more...submissive, he more tender. He might be intrigued with the idea of lying with a woman from his future. She could get him to trust her, to let down his guard long enough to allow her to slit his throat and leave him in his bed, bleeding like a butchered boar.

Moments ago, in his chamber, she had recoiled from the thought of trying to seduce the brute. But if she could go far enough to render him vulnerable, if she could kill him and then Walk back to her own time and thus escape punishment...

Reaching her chamber, she entered and closed her door behind her.

At the sight of a figure on the far side of the room, she gasped, backed against the door, and drew her blade from her bodice. She had her arm cocked to throw the weapon when Cresten—Quinnel—stepped forward into the light of her hearth.

"It's me," he said. "I'm sorry. I didn't mean to frighten you."

"You nearly got yourself killed."

"You're that good with a knife?" He grinned.

A smile tugged at the corners of her mouth. "Yes, I am. You shouldn't be here. Jispar told me he didn't want me to see you again. If his guards see you..."

She trailed off. He had taken another step forward, allowing her to see what she had missed before: He wore one of her robes over, it appeared, nothing at all. He held up his sextant, which she had also missed earlier.

Lenna laughed, covering her mouth with both hands. She couldn't help herself.

"You look ridiculous."

"I know. I wanted to see you again, and I knew better than to walk across the courtyard. So I Spanned to the nearest tower."

"And ran naked through the corridors to my chamber?" she asked, laughing still.

"I believe 'snuck' would be a better word. Perhaps 'stole.' Or even 'slunk.'"

Her laughter crested, died away, leaving her gazing at him. "I wish I'd seen that." Her cheeks warmed as she spoke the words.

Did she imagine it, or did he color as well?

"I think it's best that you didn't."

"He plans to send me back," she said. "Now that your negotiations are done, he wishes to alter certain things, no doubt believing he can extract better terms given the chance to bargain a second time."

"Unfortunately, there's nothing I can do about that."

"I know. My point is, I believe I might be able to...to do in the past what seems impossible in this present."

His eyes widened. He understood her well enough.

"I can't help you if you do this in the past."

"I know that as well. But I can't think of what else to do. I've been trying to figure out how..." She glanced toward the door, afraid of who might be on the other side. "This Walk," she went on in a whisper, "may be the best chance I'll have."

"You'll still be alone," he said. "And..." He trailed off, brow creasing. "When will he send you?"

"Soon. Within the next day or two."

The look of concentration deepened. "I know little about Walking. I know you can go back in time, and then return to this time."

"That's right."

"Do you have to come all the way back?"

Lenna blinked. "Do you mean... Do I have to come back ever?"

"No. I assume you'd want to come back eventually. I'm asking, do you have to make the journey back all in one Walk?"

She shook her head. "No, I can—" Her breath caught in her throat. Possibilities she had never considered flashed through her mind.

"I can come back to this night."

"Yes."

"You'll help me."

"We both will." When she frowned, he said, "The other you and me. There will be three of us in all. Even Jispar won't be prepared for that."

They agreed that she would be better off going back in time as far as the king instructed and doing all that he asked of her in that past. If she were to disappoint him in the past, he would know of it in the altered future and might be more leery of her. They also shared ideas for the assassination, and the precautions necessary to keep Lenna from interacting with the other version of herself and thus risking insanity. They made no firm decisions, though, and didn't speak of these matters for long.

"You should return to your quarters," she said. "It wouldn't do for someone to discover that you're not there."

"You'll accompany me to the top of the tower? That way you can reclaim your robe."

"Yes, all right."

She eased to the door, intending to check the corridor for guards. When Quinnel joined her there, she paused. After a moment's hesitation, she rose onto her toes and kissed him lightly on the lips.

"What was that for?" he whispered.

She lifted a shoulder. "I'm glad you've come back to my life. I've missed you."

"And I you."

They shared a smile. Then she held a finger to her lips, opened the door, and peered out into the torchlight. Seeing no guards, she motioned for him to follow and led him up the nearest tower, back into the cool air and moon glow.

They avoided the soldiers patrolling the ramparts. Quinnel crept a short distance from her and removed the robe. She averted her gaze but couldn't help glancing his way. The moon silvered a body that was lean, muscular. His sextant flashed in that argent light, and she feared guards might see. An instant later, he was gone, tugged into the gap.

Lenna gazed across the courtyard, thought she glimpsed a dark form on the ramparts there. She didn't linger atop the tower but retreated to her chamber. Long after she climbed into her bed and doused the candle beside her, she lay awake, thinking of how she might smuggle a weapon into Jispar's chamber. In a reprise of this night that loomed in her immediate future.

In the morning of the second day after Quinnel's departure, Jispar summoned Lenna to his hall. She was no closer to knowing how they should kill him, but she had resolved to make the attempt no matter the risks. Only the Two knew when he might send her back through time again, and she tired of living with her hatred and her humiliation. She had made what preparations she could. She had decided what to wear on the night in question, once she arrived in the past—a dark blue gown she knew he liked. She would leave her hair down, again knowing that he preferred her this way. She would claim three blades from her wardrobe: one she would hide in her bodice, another she would strap to her calf, the third she could carry at the small of her back. If they were discovered—all three of them, or even just one—he would know what she planned and she would die.

When she reached the king's hall on this morning, he was in discussion with his ministers of protocol, arms, and commerce, as well as the omnipresent Seer. Eyeing the Magi as she entered and approached the throne, she wondered if the old man would know what she had in mind to do. He was said to have the power of divination. Could such powers detect an assassination that would be carried out in the past?

Halfway to the throne, she paused to make obeisance. Then she straightened and walked the rest of the way to the king, stopping before him. Normally, he might have ignored her, kept her waiting as he continued his deliberations with the others. Not today.

"Walker, good morning."

"And to you, my liege."

"The Walk of which we spoke the other night—I'm ready for you to undertake it now."

She bowed again, as he would expect. "Of course, my liege. How far?"

He eyed his Seer, who said, "Three and ten, my liege. I believe that is what we decided."

"Yes. Three and ten."

"To be clear, my liege: three turns and ten days."

"That's right." He canted his head, indicating her chronofor, which rested on a small table near the throne. She took it, the gold cool against her fingers.

"When you arrive in the past, you will tell me the following."

He began a lengthy description of steps he wished to take in establishing trade in the Bone Sea. Some of it was complicated; Lenna asked him to repeat certain phrases several times, saying them after him so as to commit them to memory. Very soon, she hoped, the message would be rendered irrelevant. In the interim, this Jispar expected her to pay close attention, and the Jispar in the past might grow suspicious if the information she delivered didn't sound authentic. Not to mention that if—the Two forbid—her journey into the past went poorly, she would be better off having repeated his instructions exactly as he intended them.

When she had mastered all he wanted her to say, she bowed a third time.

"Very well, my liege. I shall repair to my quarters immediately and—"

"No. You will Walk from here."

Ashes on her tongue, her mouth so dry she could hardly speak. "From here?"

"Of course. Aside from the chronofor, what could you possibly need? Why is it so important that you Walk from your chamber?"

Lenna tightened her hold on the chronofor, peeked down at it. It was more lovely than any jewel she had ever seen, more dear to her than any item she had ever held. The embodiment of her gift, and, now, the key that might unlock this cage Jispar had constructed around her. Burnished gold on the face, an engraved design on its back, which, as it happened, closely resembled the etchings around His Majesty's eye.

Etchings that shifted menacingly now.

"It's not that I need anything, my liege." She fought to keep her voice level, reasonable, devoid of panic. "But in order to Walk, I have to be wearing nothing."

"I know that."

"Of course, my liege. Going back so far, however, I cannot be sure of the exact time I might arrive. I could emerge from the between, naked in your hall, in the middle of an audience." He remained unmoved, and she grasped at another possibility, one that might carry greater weight. "Or at a time when you're speaking with someone who ought not to know of your plans with respect to these negotiations with Milnos."

That reached him. He sent another glance at the Seer, and then looked to his minister of finance. Both of them, she thought, had been persuaded by her argument.

"Yes, all right. You will do this in your quarters then. Upon your arrival in the past, you will come directly to me and you will tell me exactly what I've instructed you to say. Understood?"

She tried not to let her relief show. "Yes, my liege."

He assigned a guard to her, but that didn't trouble her. The man couldn't follow her into the past.

She left Jispar, bowing to him one last time, and walked in silence through the corridors with the king's guard. She told the man to await her return outside her door and, when he hesitated, informed him that she could only Walk when naked. His face burned red and he stammered his acquiescence.

Once inside the chamber, she removed her clothes, set her chronofor for three and ten, and prepared to thumb the central stem of her device. She faltered, wondering if she ought to aim for sometime earlier or later in the day, again fearing a chance encounter with herself in the past.

In the end, she decided that no particular time of day was

more or less safe than another. She took a long breath and pressed the stem.

She tumbled back into a fury of light and clamor. A thousand tastes and smells assailed her, the combinations so foul she couldn't help but gag. Which made her gasp for breath. No air. Panic. The between held her fast, pounding at her senses, choking her. She had believed she could endure such a Walk. She knew others of her kind went back farther. Under the terms of his contract with Windhome, Jispar could have sent her back a full year. Three turns shouldn't have been enough to kill her.

Her chest ached. The pressure on her lungs grew unbearable. The abusive glare of light and shadow went on and on, but now black spots darkened her vision. Not the between this time, but her own mind, shutting down, denied air for too long. An irony that, having chosen not to kill herself, she might die before she had the chance to slay her king.

She fell out of the between onto cool stone, hands and knees throbbing, her chamber dull with the gray light of morning. The window was unshuttered; she had left behind the cool of autumn for a comfortable dawn in the growing turns. The other her did not stir. Perhaps she was sleeping off yet another of Jispar's assaults.

"Who's there?"

Awake after all.

Lenna held perfectly still, afraid, warnings blaring again in her memory.

Linens rustled.

"Stay there," she said, terror tearing the words from her throat.

A pause, and then, "How far?"

"Three turns and ten."

"Something's happened?"

This was dangerous ground as well. How much should she tell herself?

"Nothing of great consequence. He wants his earlier self to have certain knowledge."

"Of course."

Amazing that two words could convey so much: hatred, pain, shame, despair.

"We haven't gone insane," said the other Lenna from her bed. "We haven't looked at each other. I believe that lessens the danger. I need to get dressed and go to the king's hall."

"It's early yet."

"Earlier than I intended. My Walk was less precise than I had hoped."

"Is this the first?"

"Yes." Only after she said this did Lenna pause to wonder how much she ought to reveal to herself.

"This is our first opportunity then."

Lenna went still, unsure of how to answer. Silence stretched, implication hanging between them.

"I suppose it is," she said.

She forced herself to her feet, staggered to the wardrobe. A fivecount later, candlelight bloomed. Lenna resisted the urge to peer back at herself.

"Thank you."

She found undergarments, the blue gown, a robe, a pair of leather shoes. She dressed as quickly as she could, but was slowed by cold fingers and trembling hands. She left her hair unbound.

"I take it he hasn't stopped," said Lenna from the bed.

How to answer? It might be dangerous to reveal the pregnancy, but was it any safer to lie?

"I don't think I should tell you any more than I have to."

"Maybe not. Maybe it's enough to know that we still hate him."

Lenna smiled briefly, even knowing the other her couldn't see. "Yes, we do."

"Then you won't squander this chance."

Again she hesitated. "As I said—"

"I'm not not asking you to tell me your plan. Just... I need..." Her voice broke. A full tencount passed before she could go on. "I need to know that you have one."

Lenna wanted to weep for herself. "You have to trust in us, you and me. And you need to be patient."

"Three and ten."

She wished she hadn't revealed even that much, but she said, "Just so."

The other Lenna took a long, ragged breath. "Yes, all right. Not today then."

"No. Not today. And after I speak with him, I'll need to return here and Walk back." She revealed no more than that.

"Of course. I'll be away, in another part of the castle, or in the city."

"Again, thank you."

A moment later, something slid across the stone floor, stopping a stride short of her. Her small dagger.

"You should be armed," the other her said. "Who knows? If you kill him while people can see me in a tavern or in the gardens, we might get away with it."

She said nothing, stared at the weapon, then stooped for it and hid it in the bodice of her gown.

Lenna stepped to the door, paused there. Did the other her deserve to know of the child? Probably, and she would soon enough. She pushed back against a surge of guilt. "May the Two keep you safe," she said.

"And you."

Lenna slipped out of the chamber, followed corridors to Jispar's hall, where guards stopped her.

"Is he expecting you, Walker?" one of the men asked, both courteous and stern.

"He's not, but he'll want to speak with me as soon as possible."

The guard frowned, even as he gestured to one of his fellow soldiers. This second man entered the hall, only to reemerge a tencount later. He nodded once.

They let her enter.

As she advanced on the throne, she held her head high, her chin raised, her gaze fixed on the king. Jispar spoke with the Seer as she walked and barely spared her a glance. Initially.

He sent a second look her way. At the same time, she opened her hand slightly, allowing light to catch the back of her chronofor. A signal she hoped only he would notice.

He eyed her for another instant, then turned his attention back to Curden Sten. Lenna slid her chronofor into the folds of her gown.

Jispar and the Seer spoke for another spirecount—long enough that Lenna began to question whether he had noticed the golden device.

As Seer Sten withdrew, however, Jispar told his herald, "You will clear the hall."

Sten cast a wary glance at Lenna, but he filed out with the others. Soon Jispar, Lenna, and a pair of guards near the main doors were the only people left in the grand chamber. A lesson there. Even when discussing matters of great sensitivity, Jispar was never anything less than vigilant. He trusted no one, was never alone. Or almost never.

Jispar waved her forward. Lenna walked toward him, struggling to control her heart, her breathing.

"You have come back?" he asked, his voice low.

"Yes, my liege."

"How much time?"

"Three and ten."

He studied her, taking in her hair. His eyes met hers again. "You are...changed."

"Am I?" she said, panic rising.

"You are. For the better, I think. I sense resolve, maturity."

She dropped her gaze, sketched a small bow. "My liege is kind."

"I assume you bear a message from a future me."

"Yes, my liege." She proceeded to relate to him all that he had told her to say about what were, in this time, the impending negotiations with representatives of Milnos's king. He listened, intent upon her the way he had been in those first days, when she thought him beautiful and believed he was taken with her. She understood now that his passions were limited to gold and power and control over everything and everyone in his demesne, and likely beyond.

She finished her recitation, and he asked her to repeat a few points.

When she had answered his questions to his satisfaction, he thanked her, told her how helpful she had been. His gaze lingered on her, making her skin pebble and her stomach crawl. She should have tied back her hair. She endured his attention, though, and even managed to smile back at him. It could behoove her to make him think that in the future they had reached some sort of accommodation.

She bowed to him again. "If that is all, my liege, I will Walk forward to my own time."

Before she could move, he caught her hand in his powerful grip, turned it, and held her wrist to his lips.

She resisted twin urges—to yank her hand from his grasp and pull the knife from her bodice.

"For some reason I find this version of you quite compelling. Perhaps that maturity you mentioned. And your hair. I like your hair this way."

Carefully.

"I must not tarry here, my liege. Walkers are taught to limit the length of our forays into the past, and to encounter as few people as possible. I really must Travel to my time."

She had seen anger in him too often not to recognize the signs: the tensing of his jaw, the twist of the snake around his eye.

"I wish you to stay," he said, still gripping her hand. "Besides, for what I have in mind, there is no need for you to encounter anyone else."

A knock at the hall doors drew his glare. He dropped her hand, allowing her to sidle away from him.

"Find out who it is," he said to one of the guards.

The man opened the door a crack, spoke in a lowered voice to someone in the antechamber before facing Jispar again.

"Your Seer, Your Majesty. He wishes a word."

For once, Sten's mistrust of her served her purposes.

"This is what I mean, my liege," she said in a whisper. "I should leave you, allow you to discuss with your ministers and the Seer the tidings I've brought. This is what the future you wanted."

His expression soured, like a boy denied sweets. "Yes, very well," he said. "Go."

Lenna feared for the other her. He would be in a towering rage tonight, and he might well take it out on her. That couldn't be helped. She needed to be away from this time.

She bowed to him and left the chamber, walking by the Seer without so much as a glance passing between them. She followed the corridors back to her quarters. Finding it empty, she entered, set the knife on her night table, and replaced the gown, garments, and shoes in her wardrobe. She then set her chronofor. Hardly more than a bell had passed since her arrival here, but given the imprecision of her Walk back to this time, she feared that made little difference.

Still, she set the chronofor for three turns, eight days and seven bells, hoping she would arrive near to the time when she and Quinnel commenced their walk through the castle gardens. She inhaled, closed her eyes, and thumbed the central stem of her device.

This journey through the between proved no less harrowing than the previous one. A storm of light and noise and fetor that stretched on and on, until she thought her chest would explode for want of a breath.

Upon her arrival in this new time, she slumped to the floor, sucking greedily at the air, grateful for the steady dim glow of a single candle.

This last reached her. Night?

"Don't look this way."

She could only nod.

"Did you mean to come to this time, this day?"

"Yes," she said, her voice like steel scraped across stone.

"Dare I ask why?"

Lenna would have looked at her then, very nearly did. "By now, you would have seen Cresten."

"Yes," the other her said. "I'm hoping to speak with him soon."

"And you will. The three of us—well, he and I have an idea. Though he actually doesn't know of it yet in this time."

"No wonder others find our kind confounding."

How could she argue? She stood, staggered to the wardrobe, and began to dress. The blue gown again. "What's the time?" she asked.

"It's been dark for no more than half a bell."

Lenna buttoned the bodice, thinking that Quinnel would reach the chamber in another spirecount or two. It could be difficult interacting with both him and herself without making eye contact with the other Lenna. She needed to leave.

A knock at the door drew her glance. The other Lenna crossed to the door, eyes fixed straight ahead. Lenna hid herself behind the wardrobe, listened as the other her spoke to the page about the emissaries from Milnos.

When the other Lenna finished with the girl and closed the door again, Lenna stepped out from hiding, staring at the floor.

"I should go. Please listen carefully. The friend you know as Cresten will be along shortly. Trust him. Confide in him. He can help us. It would be best if this night were to unfold precisely as I remember it. Please don't mention to him that I'm here, not until you absolutely must."

"Yes, all right. Can you tell me...what are you—"

Another knock stopped her.

"It's all right," she said. "Trust me, as well."

She imagined the other Lenna dipping her chin at this, but she didn't look. The other her approached the door again.

"Who's there?"

"A friend."

She hid once more as the other her opened the door, listened as she and Quinnel exchanged remembered pleasantries, kept her gaze lowered as the other Lenna retrieved her cloak from the wardrobe. Then they were gone, leaving her alone in the chamber.

Lenna waited a full spirecount before slipping on a pair of

shoes and retrieving her daggers from the back corner of the wardrobe. She slipped one into a sheath, which she strapped to her calf. The others she hid in the bodice of the gown and at the small of her back. She stole out of the chamber into the shifting shadows of torchlit corridors. She followed a roundabout path to Jispar's chamber, managing to avoid guards and other residents of the castle.

Within sight of the king's door, she tucked herself into a narrow space behind a plinth that supported a bust of Jispar II. There she waited. A strange calm settled over her. She hadn't ever killed before, and she could imagine a thousand different things going wrong before this night was over. Jispar could kill her. So could one of his guards. She could be discovered before she Walked back to her time. Blame could fall on the other her, or, worse, on Cresten. Quinnel.

But she had made her decision. She would not go back to her own time without making the attempt. She would not meekly return her chronofor to that small table in the throne hall and allow Jispar to reclaim control over her life.

A quarter bell passed. Maybe a little more. Finally the door to Jispar's chamber opened, and a single guard, the one who had fetched her and Quinnel from the gardens the first time she lived this night, stepped into the corridor, shut the door quietly, and strode toward the nearest stairway.

It was time.

She left her hiding place and crept to the door, pulling the blade from her bodice as she advanced. She knocked once, lightly. Then she stepped to the side and flattened herself against that wall, so that when the second guard pulled open the door she would remain in shadow.

The door cracked open. Light slanted into the corridor, illuminating the spot where she had been standing.

"Who's there?" she heard Jispar ask.

"I'm not certain, Your Majesty."

The guard opened the door wider, stepped out of the chamber. He was taller than she. He peered down the hallway, swiveled his head in her direction. His eyes widened when he saw her. He opened his mouth to speak or shout a warning.

She gave him no chance.

With all the strength she had, Lenna pounded her blade into the side of the man's neck. Blood spurted. He jerked away, but she maintained her grip on the weapon, tearing his flesh. More blood sprayed. It puddled on the floor, splashed her shoes when he fell. She hadn't expected there would be so much blood.

Her stomach lurched, and her throat seized. She clamped her teeth together to keep from being ill and stooped to pull the man's sword from his belt.

She stepped over his body, entered the chamber, and closed the door behind her.

CHAPTER FOUR

19th day of Sipar's Waking, Year 619

Her heart thudded against her breastbone, making her entire body tremble. Her hands were slick with sweat.

Nevertheless, she faced the king, noting that he already had his sword in hand.

"My liege," she said.

He frowned, confused, but seemingly unafraid. "You were in the gardens. I saw you go there with the Spanner from Milnos. You couldn't..."

He trailed off, taking in her garb.

His laugh was as dry as sand. "The danger of employing a Walker. You've come back through time to kill me."

Lenna said nothing, stalked deeper into the chamber, to an expanse of open floor near the hearth. A better space for combat. She stepped out of her shoes, her bare feet offering a more certain stance.

"Before you die," he said, "I would know who sent you."

She held the sword in her off hand, the knife in her throwing hand. She wished to keep the fire at her back, so that she could see his eyes, and he would see only a silhouette of her.

"Who?" he thundered.

He would expect her to quail. Did she lull him by doing so, or confound him by refusing to? Grenley Albon, the weapons master back in Windhome, would have insisted on the former. It was the safer strategy, the one most likely to succeed.

Lenna refused. Pride, fury, her determination to be free of this man. She would never bow to him again. Not in any way. Not even if it meant her life.

Instead, she laughed at him, and he glowered. "You believe someone had to send me?" she asked, mockery in her tone. "As if you haven't given me cause to want you dead myself?"

"You do this out of vengeance," he said with disbelief. Another laugh escaped him, which only enraged her more. "That, I did not anticipate."

"Then you're a fool."

"Am I? You stand before me, armed for a fight. But you're weak, small, a naïf. You think you can best me? And *you* call *me* a fool?"

He walked toward her, slicing the air with his sword, his confidence daunting.

Lenna feinted a lunge in his direction. He halted, then grinned and started to say something.

She cocked her arm and threw the knife in one smooth motion.

Jispar ducked, allowing the blade to sail over his head. It struck the far wall and clattered to the floor. He glanced back at it.

"A poor throw," he said.

He charged her, surprising her with his speed, his agility.

She backed away, switching the sword to her good hand, stumbling past a chair. He was on her before she could right herself. He hacked at her with his blade. She barely parried. The force of his blow shuddered through her arm and shoulder. She cried out in pain, fell onto her back.

Jispar laughed once more. "You're puny," he said with relish. "You're nothing. I could defeat an army of children like you. You never should have come here."

He kicked her in the gut, and she folded in on herself, even as the force of his blow lifted her off the floor and spun her. She crashed back onto stone, the sword flying from her hand. She nearly retched.

She also reached for the second knife, the one strapped to her lower leg.

Before she could pull it free, he kicked her again. She whimpered. He laughed. Lenna forced herself onto her hands and knees and scrabbled away, positioning herself behind a chair.

Jispar stalked her but seemed in no hurry to kill her off. She grabbed again for the sheath at her calf.

"What I find amusing about this," he said, picking up the chair and throwing it to the side, like it weighed nothing, "is that—"

The second blade struck true, embedding itself in his right eye. His mouth fell open, his sword dropped to the floor. His body swayed like an oak in a storm wind. Blood ran over his face, the beast etched around his eye gutted at last.

His knees buckled, and he collapsed to them. He started to reach for his blade, then toppled onto his side.

Lenna dragged herself to her feet, the lingering agony in her gut keeping her from straightening fully. Every muscle in her body trembled. She stared at Jispar.

His chest rose and fell still. She expected at any moment to see him stand and renew his assault.

She tiptoed around the king's body and across the floor to retrieve the first blade, peering back at him as she did. She left the soldier's sword where it had fallen.

That second knife, however... She couldn't leave that. Someone might know it for hers.

Jispar's hand shifted, and she choked back a scream. It moved in increments, edging toward his face. His eye. Her knife. Blood pooled around him, rippled as he attempted to lift his head off the floor.

Lenna could only gape. He made a sound—something between groan and growl. His fingers brushed the hilt of the knife jutting from his eye. Then his hand fell back to the floor.

She eased closer to him. He didn't move again. Not even to breathe.

A laugh tickled her throat, tipped over into a sob. She bent over him, gripped the blade, and pulled it from his face. It slipped out with a slurping sound that roiled her stomach. She turned away and gagged again, fighting a wave of illness. The pain in her abdomen redoubled.

She wiped blood from the blade on Jispar's robe, retrieved her shoes, and crossed to the door, every step hurting, the taste of bile in her mouth. At the door, she paused, took a long breath, and peeked out into the corridor.

Aside from the dead guard in the hallway, she saw no one. She stepped over the corpse, avoiding the blood around him. After pulling the door closed with as much care as she could, Lenna started back to her chamber.

It seemed farther this time. The stairway was almost too much for her. Twice, she had to hide in shadows to evade patrolling soldiers. Upon reaching her chamber, she removed the chronofor from the folds of her gown and set it on the small table. She stepped to the hearth, studied the killing knife in the light of the fire. Seeing some residue of blood, she used her gown to wipe it clean, going so far as to wet a corner of the hem in the basin by her bed.

Once the knife was clean, she concealed both blades in her wardrobe.

She removed all that she was wearing and threw the clothes and the shoes onto the fire. At first, they merely smoked, and panic bubbled up inside her.

After a fivecount, though, the cloth caught fire with a *whoosh* that startled her.

She reclaimed the chronofor, set it for the Walk to her own time. Pausing, she scanned the chamber. Satisfied that she had done all she could, taken every precaution, she thumbed the release and surged into the frenzy of the between.

The instant she landed in her own time, new memories flooded her mind. While still on her hands and knees, her gut aching, she recalled reaching the king's chamber with Quinnel and Jispar's guard. Seeing his fellow soldier dead in the corridor, the guard drew his weapon and pushed into Jispar's chamber.

Quinnel and Lenna remained in the hall. She had killed both the guard and the king, of course, and she remembered doing so. She also recalled the shock of her other self at seeing the blood, the guard with his neck ravaged.

The soldier ordered her and Quinnel to wait in the corridor and then ran off, raising the alarm. Within a spirecount, bells tolled in the castle courtyards.

She and Quinnel shared a look. The guard had left the king's door ajar, and she ventured nearer, gaped at what she saw in the chamber: the overturned chair and discarded sword, and Jispar with his face a mask of gore.

Quinnel said nothing until, at the sound of footsteps, he whispered her name. She backed away to where she had been standing.

A tencount later, Herjean soldiers swarmed around them, some entering the chamber, others encircling the two of them, swords drawn and leveled.

"They were with me," said the guard who had accompanied them. "They didn't do this."

The castle healer bustled past them and into the chamber. Several ministers and the Seer arrived. Sten inspected the king's chamber and returned to the corridor, where he confronted the two of them.

"What are the two of you doing here?"

"We were summoned by the king," Lenna said. "From the gardens." She pointed at the guard. "He found us there and brought us here. When we arrived, the guard and His Majesty were dead."

"And what were you doing together in the first place?"

"We were friends in Windhome. We were renewing our acquaintance, sharing news of mutual friends."

"I see. And you had nothing to do with His Majesty's death?"

"Of course not. As I say, we were in a different part of the castle, and we were seen there by one of His Majesty's soldiers."

Sten glowered. "Indeed."

"You doubt me?"

"I know you have powers that enable you to slip between times without detection."

"Yes, I do," Lenna said, straight-backed, uncowed. "Do you think I went to His Majesty and asked for my chronofor so that I might go back and murder him? How, precisely, do you imagine that conversation might have gone? And even if he had given me my chronofor, allowing me to Walk, do you honestly believe that I could best His Majesty and one of his trained guards in a contest of blades?"

Risky that. She wondered if Sten understood just how well Windhome Travelers were trained.

To her relief, he twisted his mouth sourly and addressed Quinnel. "And you, Spanner," he said. "I suppose you had nothing to do with this either."

"That's right," Quinnel said, somber, his voice level. "I was with Walker Doen."

"I'm sure. Yet you have powers as well. What would have stopped you from leaving her in the gardens to Span here, kill the king, and go back to her before you were found?"

"With what, Seer?" He spread his arms. "Search me. You will find no sextant. It's in my chamber."

Lenna nearly laughed aloud at the way Sten deflated. Yet, Quinnel wasn't done.

"As long as we're speaking of powers, Seer," he said, his voice rising so those around them could hear, "I wonder why it is you didn't foresee any of this. Isn't that what divination is for? Isn't that why your king brought you to this court in the first place?"

"You forget yourself, Spanner! You are a guest in this court."

"Yes, I am. Do you often accuse your guests of crimes? Or is that only a tactic you employ to distract attention from your own failures? Or betrayals?"

Dangerous words. With the king dead, Curden Sten might well have been the most powerful man in Herjes.

But enough guards looked over when Quinnel said this to discomfit the Seer.

He offered a brittle smile. "Forgive me, Spanner. This is all...a terrible shock." A frown flickered at this echo of Quinnel's accusation. "I spoke out of anger, grief," he forged on. "I ask your forbearance."

Quinnel tipped his head. "Of course, Seer. I accept your most gracious apology. And I know that I speak for Minister Kraetas and my king when I say that Milnos wishes to help our Herjean neighbors in any way we can during this difficult time."

"Yes, indeed," came a voice from down the corridor. Kraetas himself, surrounded by a phalanx of Milnosian soldiers. "My young colleague speaks true," he went on, approaching them and stepping past those at the fore of his guard. "Even if he does so without proper authority."

Quinnel dropped his gaze, but the corners of his mouth twitched into a faint smile.

The healer emerged from Jispar's chamber a short time later to tell all within hearing that the king had been killed by a single knife wound to the head. He was otherwise unhurt. Aside from smears of blood from the guard on the floor beside the door, the healer found no other blood in the chamber and nothing to suggest that the king had wounded his attacker.

Soldiers commenced a sweeping search of the castle. No one in the royal court or the delegation from Milnos slept much that night. Lenna didn't return to her chamber until close to dawn.

The following day, she was summoned to the king's hall, where Seer Sten presided over a gathering of all Jispar's advisors. Talk of successors had burned through the castle like flame across parchment. Jispar had no male heir—only girl bastards—and Herjes had not been ruled by a queen in centuries.

Many mentioned Jispar's younger brother, Urjas, who was

marquis in Silver Rock, on the isle's western shore. Most said he was a wastrel and a brutal leader of his marquisate. Many preferred a distant cousin of the line, who ruled in a viscountcy in the north.

Lenna had little interest in who came after Jispar. It was enough that he was dead, his reign over her ended.

Unfortunately, with the new day came a deepening of Sten's suspicions. Frequently during their discussion, the Seer cast dark glances her way. He had asked Minister Kraetas to stay on in Herjes with the Spanner and their guards, ostensibly because he sought the minister's input on how the kingdom ought to proceed without a leader. Lenna guessed that he wished to keep Quinnel close.

She and Quinnel kept their distance from each other, lest they draw the notice of others. Despite her confidence the night before, Lenna grew more afraid throughout that day. She despaired of ever leaving Vondehm. As the bells passed, word came from Jispar's soldiers. The castle had been searched, as had the city. No assassins had been found.

Late that day, when Sten dismissed her and the other ministers and Travelers from the king's hall, Lenna was too weary from the night before, and too unnerved by the day's events, to do more than retreat to her chamber and take to bed.

On this morning, she was flung from sleep onto her floor. Hands and knees. A crippling pain in her belly, and writhing sickness, akin to the queasiness that had come every day for more than a turn, and nothing like at all. She forced herself up, reeled to her chamber pot, vomited acid as tears streamed.

She felt an ominous warmth between her thighs. Blood ran down her legs, stained her floor.

She cursed, pulled her sleeping gown from her bed and put it on, heedless of the way it clung to the blood streaks. Someone seeing her in this state would expect that.

Lenna hobbled to the door and called for her page. When the girl came, she told her to fetch the healer.

More tears. She knew what this meant. One heard quite often

of women losing pregnancies. How many lost them because of kicks to the stomach by their king?

She crawled back into bed, awaited the healer. She only realized then that she still held the incriminating chronofor. In a different future, Jispar had given it to her freely. Now, with the king dead and history irrevocably altered, no one would remember that. Its presence in her chamber was accusation, evidence, conviction. She buried it deep in her bed linens, pushed it farther down with her foot. Prayed to the Two that no one searched her chamber before she could rid herself of it.

The healer arrived moments later and confirmed what she had feared. The child was lost. The shock of losing her liege, no doubt. She doubted the Seer would believe this.

Sten came to her chamber around midday. She watched him from her bed as he wandered her chamber.

"I'm sorry for the loss you suffered today," he said, his tone unctuous.

What could she say?

"Thank you, Seer."

"The healer blames the trauma of His Majesty's death."

"Yes."

"I wonder if the ordeal of a Walk through time might prove equally disturbing."

"Not this again, Sten."

He responded with a thinning of his lips and the baring of teeth. "I wonder if you might tell me, Walker, where is your chronofor?"

She tried not to react, wasn't certain she succeeded. "Wherever the king keeps it, I would..."

Lenna trailed off, seeing Sten shake his head.

"I looked. It isn't there."

"Then it's been stolen," she said, a tremor in her voice.

"I wondered about that, and then asked myself, why would a thief take the chronofor and leave behind sextants and apertures?"

"I wouldn't know." She fought to steady her voice. "You are

free to search through my belongings. My wardrobe, my desk. Have at it."

"I intend to. Shall I begin now?"

"Begin what?"

Sten turned. Lenna looked to the door, schooled her features against a rush of blessed relief.

Quinnel stood in her doorway. He glared at the Seer, then shifted his gaze to her. "I heard you were ill. I wanted to see you."

"How touching," Sten said.

Quinnel stepped into the chamber, his hand resting lightly on the hilt of his sword.

"Once again, Seer, I question the efficacy of your divination powers. Because surely, if they were as honed as they ought to be, you would know the perils of mocking me, or my friend."

"You threaten me, Spanner?"

"I encourage you to moderate your tone."

Amusement quirked Sten's lips again. "The minister will hear of this."

"Yes," Quinnel said, "he will. As will my king."

The Seer cast another look Lenna's way and crossed to the open door. "I'll be back before long, Walker. In the meantime, I intend to post a guard outside your door. For your safety, of course. In the past day, as our search of the castle and city have proven fruitless, there has been talk of a traitor within these walls. Some have come to question your innocence in this matter. Unjustly, I'm sure. Still, I wouldn't want one of them to take it in their own hands to avenge His Majesty, nor would I want you to suffer any more than you already have."

He exited the chamber, closed the door behind him.

Lenna and Quinnel locked eyes.

"I have my chronofor," she whispered. "Usually Jispar kept it, but he gave it to me in a different time. And Sten knows it's gone."

"Wouldn't it have returned to wherever the king kept it? In this time he never sent you back."

"That could happen with another item—a bauble, a gown, something not tied to my Walking. Chronofors..." She shook her head. "They're subject to their own rules; they're more like Walkers than objects."

He appeared to weigh this: another Traveler, accustomed to the odd phenomena connected with such talents. Before long, he nodded and said, "Give it to me, then."

"You can't—"

"Just until we get you away from here."

She stared, fresh tears spilling. "I don't think I'm ever going to leave this place. Not alive."

"Of course you will." He crossed to the bed and sat beside her. After the briefest of hesitations, he took her hand, laced his fingers through hers. "What happened today?"

"I lost the baby," she said, breathing the words through more tears. She wiped them from her face, angry with herself. "I shouldn't care. It was his child."

"It was your child. Of course you should care. He or she would have been strong and smart and beautiful, like you. And in spite of him."

She regarded their hands. "I should have left the palace in Windhome with you all those years ago. None of this would have happened."

"We can be together now. That's what matters. First, though, you have to give me that chronofor."

"Of course." She reached down to the end of her bed and retrieved the device, eyeing the door as she handed it to him.

Quinnel took it from her and tucked it into his hose, under a sheathed dagger that he wore there. "I expect they'll search me when I leave here. They won't find it."

"It won't matter. It's missing. That's enough to convince everyone that I killed Jispar. I'm the only person in Vondehm who would have any use for a chronofor. Sten knows that. He'll see me beheaded."

"No," Quinnel said. "He won't. Are you well enough to leave here tonight?"

She faltered, dropped her chin.

"Good. Be ready to leave after dark."

"What if they put me in chains before then?"

"If they do, I'll work out a way to free you, but I expect they won't. Not yet. They won't find the chronofor, and without it, they can't prove anything. Most important, they think you're too ill to leave your bed. We can make use of that. Tomorrow might be too late, but we can get you away from here tonight." He held her hand to his lips, which were warm. "Now," he went on, "here is what I need for you to do."

His instructions were simple enough. So simple, in fact, that she doubted his plan would work. But he sounded sure of himself, which was enough for now.

Lenna didn't argue with him or give voice to her fears. As he left her, she tried to look hopeful.

The guards did search him when he left her chamber. They were thorough enough to find the sheath strapped to his thigh. Not so careful that they found the Bound chronofor hidden beneath it.

Orzili—that was how he thought of himself now—knew that he and Lenna could die this night. He was endangering the lives of Minister Kraetas and the Milnosian guards as well, and so his first task after leaving Lenna's chamber was to seek out his minister.

He liked the man, just as he liked most of the people he'd met in the court of Arlis III. He trusted Kraetas. The minister was generous, kind, intelligent. In this case, however, he would be asking a great deal of him. Too much, perhaps.

He found Kraetas in his quarters, the door guarded by four of their soldiers. The guards allowed him entry of course, and the minister greeted him, as ever, with a smile and the offer of tea and a place to sit.

Orzili remained standing.

Kraetas's expression hardened as Quinnel spoke, but the minister kept his silence until he had finished, and for some time after.

"This is why you asked to come with me," he said, disapproval in the words. "Instead of Fesha. You planned this."

"No, sir. I intended only to see Lenna. We were close friends back in Windhome and...and I've been in love with her for a long time. I had no idea that Jispar would be killed, and I never would have guessed that blame would fall on her."

"Did she kill him?"

He wouldn't lie. Not about this, under these circumstances. He was asking too much of the man.

"He violated her. Repeatedly, until she was with child. He was violent and cruel—"

"Jispar was an ass. I know it. Our king knows it. That wasn't my question, but I fear you've answered."

"They'll kill her."

"Yes," the minister said. "That's what is done to assassins who kill kings."

"I intend to help her escape. You should know this."

"You are an emissary of the king of Milnos, a representative of his royal court—"

"Then I hereby resign as royal Spanner and relinquish all privileges conferred by the position."

Kraetas sighed. "Quinnel—"

"And I hereby request asylum within the royal court of Milnos, as provided under the Ring Treaty of 539."

The minister stared, open mouthed. After a fivecount, he began to laugh. "Now that I did not anticipate. Very clever indeed. Sadly, I must refuse, in the name of my liege, Arlis III."

Orzili's turn to be surprised. "But—"

"Requests for asylum are not designed to protect criminals. The treaty specifies that someone guilty of any crime punishable on the isle in which protection is sought cannot be harbored. Murder is as illegal in Milnos as it is in Herjes. And so is aiding a murderer."

Orzili sagged.

"I can't allow you to accompany me back to Caszuvaar. Not if you insist on bringing the Walker with you. In fact, once we're clear of this castle, I can't associate with you in any way."

It took him a moment. "Wait. Once we're—"

Kraetas grinned. "I've always thought Jispar's Seer was a bit of an ass as well. Really, I don't like anyone in this court. And I sense that the agreement we worked out with the king was not as advantageous to our isle as it should have been." He crossed to the door and opened it, motioning Orzili into the corridor. "I don't wish to know any more about this," he said, his voice dropping to a whisper. "Getting her out of this castle is up to you. And after that—well, I'm afraid at that point we will have to part ways. I cannot risk precipitating a war with Herjes."

"I understand." Orzili proffered a hand, which the minister gripped. "It has been my honor to serve with you."

"And mine to serve with you. I fear you're making a terrible error, but I admit I harbor a certain admiration for your passion, your courage."

Orzili left him and went in search of the commander of the small contingent of guards that had accompanied them to Herjes. He would need the woman's help to carry out what he had in mind.

She was reluctant at first; Quinnel's plan was audacious. He assured her, though, that the minister had offered his limited support. And he promised as well that once they were away from the castle, she would never have to see him or the Walker again. She agreed. It seemed no one in the Herjes delegation held Jispar or his court in much esteem.

It helped that Jispar's Walker was tall, and also that she was ailing.

Late in the day, two Milnosian soldiers escorted the Spanner to her chamber. In light of Seer Sten's accusations and obvious hostility, as well as the apparent lack of security in the castle—after all, the Herjean king himself had been killed by an unknown intruder only two nights before—no one in the delegation felt safe wandering the castle unguarded.

While saying his farewell to the ailing Walker, he noticed that she looked even more ill than she had earlier in the day. He called for the Herjean healer, requested on the Walker's behalf a powerful sleeping tonic, which the healer, after examining her briefly, agreed would be a welcome balm for the poor woman.

As the gloaming darkened her chamber and the castle grounds, the healer delivered his elixir, recommending that she only take it when she was ready to sleep. It would work quickly and keep her abed through the night.

The Spanner said his goodbyes to her in the chamber, with the door closed, but with his soldiers present. The Herjean guards thought nothing of this. The woman was distraught, ill. Word was she had been with the king's child and had lost the babe in the aftermath of Jispar's death. Grief, shock, or, some said, a guilty conscience.

While the Spanner spoke with the woman, the commander of the Milnosian guard arrived with three more of her soldiers. It seemed the minister required a word with the Spanner—a matter that couldn't wait.

In the ensuing bustle of soldiers leaving the chamber for a dimly lit corridor, the two Herjean guards could be forgiven if they paid little heed to the one soldier who, while tall, was slight in comparison to others in her company, her bronze hair unevenly shorn, her uniform not quite as snug as it should have been.

Nor would anyone in the courtyards have seen a lone figure in dun clothes climb from a darkened window and jump to the shrubs below before stealing toward the castle gate.

The Herjean guards in the hallway might take a moment to peer into the room of the Walker—she who was said to be a traitor guilty of regicide. All they would see, however, was a shadowed shape bundled in the bed, and a healer's cup—surely empty by now—resting on the small table beside.

The delegation left the castle that night. And if the guards at the castle gate, with those odd etchings around their eyes, failed to notice that the delegation included one more guard than it had when the Milnosians arrived days before—well, who could fault them?

Once the emissaries from the Shield were clear of the gate and on the winding lane that led toward the wharves, two members of the company split off from the others—a soldier and a man in ministerial robes. No one followed. No one saw them.

The following morning, no one could explain how the Walker had managed to escape the castle unnoticed. Though the Seer, Curden Sten, had some idea. After all, he possessed the power of divination.

CHAPTER FIVE

6th Day of Sipar's Ascent, Year 634

From the hilltop perch of the small stone house, Mara had a sweeping view of the Firth of Rime and the rocky shoreline that angled to the south and west away from Duvyn. On a clear day, she might see all the way across the Inward Sea to the pale rise of Liyrelle. Today, a cool, heavy rain fell, a last gasp of autumn before winter's arrival in Daerjen's southern headlands.

Tobias and Sofya had gone to the village of Little Duvyn, a league away from the city proper, along the banks of the river. They sought barrowfruit—or crane fruit if they could find it—and a flask or two of Brenthian white, along with fresh bread and the season's last greens. Soon their choices would be limited to rabbit and fish, tearroot and kelp leaves.

Sofya loved the marketplace in Little Duvyn, and the merchants there seemed taken with her. In Duvyn itself, a father and daughter with dark skin—he with raised scars on his face, she with arresting blue eyes and perfect features befitting royalty—might draw notice and prompt unwanted inquiries. Little Duvyn was, in many ways, like the Notch, the shadow village south and east of Hayncalde in central Daerjen. Most who lived there had escaped or fled or abandoned...something. They didn't ask questions. They didn't betray their fellow residents, or those who came to trade. Tobias and Sofya would be safe. And the princess wouldn't be here.

From the doorway of the house, Mara eyed the firth again, then glanced up into a sky of unremitting gray. She preferred not to Span in a rain this heavy, but if the ship appeared before the rain abated, she would have to.

After fighting off Quinnel Orzili and his band of assassins, the three of them had little choice but to leave Seris Larr's ship, the *Sea Dove*. The ship was known to their enemies, as was the captain herself. Larr gave up her vessel for a new one. Tobias knew the new ship's name before Mara read the captain's message.

The *Gray Skate*.

He had sailed the ship from Windhome as a young Walker of promise, barely more than a boy. And he had done so years from now, in a lost future, a thread of history destroyed by assassination. The implications of Walking through time could befuddle anyone, even those trained in the way of chronofors and Walks and the dreaded between.

Seris Larr piloted her ship to ports on nearly every isle between the oceans, as anyone observing her would expect. Sometimes she lingered in the waters around the Axle, or in the bays of Ensydar. Sometimes she anchored her ship farther south, in the calm waters between Liyrelle and Daerjen, near the mouth of the Firth of Rime. There was nothing so unusual about that.

And no one would see a lone figure flash through the space between the headlands and that lonely ship, lashed by a gap wind, guided by calibrations on a Bound sextant. A sextant that once belonged to Quinnel Orzili.

By now, Mara knew the *Skate* well enough to recognize her from distance, even through rain. She was a three-masted merchant ship, a good deal larger than the Kants that frequented these waters, and a few hands longer than the *Dove* had been. Here, among the Ring Isles and not so far from the Axle, she always flew an Aiyanthan flag.

Thunder rumbled, distant enough that Mara hadn't noticed any lightning. She retreated into the house and added a log to the fire. Tobias and Sofya would be wet and cold when they returned, and at this point, they might reach the house before she Spanned back from the ship. She stirred the coals, buttered a piece of dark bread. When she crossed back to the door to check the firth again, a ship lurked in the gray at the mouth of the inlet.

She watched it carve closer to land, finished eating her bread while it slowed and stopped. Soon its sails were furled. She assumed the crew had lowered her anchor. She couldn't see the flag for the rain, but she knew this was Larr's ship.

She retrieved the sextant from beneath the bed she shared with Tobias, removed her overshirt, and stripped off the rest of her clothes. As always, she took extra care with the calibration of her device. She was an accomplished Spanner, but even a small miscalculation would dump her into the surf rather than onto the deck of the *Gray Skate*. She had no interest in swimming today.

Larr steered her ship to the same spot each time. Mara knew the settings. Still, she checked them twice, set her feet carefully, and, finally, flicked the release.

The gap seized her. A screaming gale. Raindrops as hard as pebbles, as sharp as needles. Water blinded her, filled her mouth and nose, making it so hard to breathe, she might as well have been Walking through the airless between. She wondered if she would drown before she reached the safety of the ship.

On it went. Combined with the gap wind, the rain leeched warmth from her body, leaving her shaking and terrified that even this small motion would throw her off course.

Then it was over, and she dropped into the chill waters of the firth. She slipped under, nearly losing her grip on her sextant, came up sputtering, and turned a quick circle as she treaded water.

She had missed Larr's ship by some distance. Fortunately, sailors on the vessel were watching for her. Already, they had lowered a pinnace to the rain-roiled surface of the inlet and were piloting it in her direction.

Her arms and legs felt leaden, and the cold made breathing difficult. She marked the pinnace's approach, grateful for the urgency with which Larr's crew rowed. Before long, strong hands gripped her arms and pulled her into the small vessel. Someone draped a blanket around her shoulders and wrapped a second around her legs. She set her sextant on the floor of the boat and flexed her cold, cramped fingers.

The blankets smelled of brine and tar, roasted fish, and stale ale. In short, it smelled like the hold of a ship, and it took her back to the turns she had spent with Tobias and Sofya aboard the *Sea Dove*. Their days with Larr's crew had been fraught, perilous, marked by death and pursuit and more than a few sea-roughening storms.

Still, she missed the camaraderie of being part of a crew, the sweet air and freedom of sailing across open sea. She missed the hold, where Tobias and she had consummated their burgeoning love. She was bound to Tobias by vow and passion; she would journey with him wherever chance or purpose took them. And if necessary, she would give her life to keep the princess safe. But if she'd had her way, even after their battle with Orzili in the Sea of Gales, she would have chosen for the three of them to remain with Captain Larr and her sailors. She found life on land...confining.

Rain continued to douse the firth as the sailors oared her back to the *Gray Skate*. Despite the blankets, she shivered uncontrollably, her teeth clacking, her breathing still ragged.

When they reached the vessel, two men she didn't know helped her up the rat lines to the ship's deck. There she was greeted by Bramm and Moth, Jacq and old Yadreg, and, finally, Captain Larr herself. Larr had added new crew after that bloody night west of the Ring Isles. Some of them Mara now recognized, others she didn't. She couldn't help but search the deck for Ermond and Gwinda and some of the others who died helping them protect Sofya. Only three turns had passed; each visit to this ship still felt bittersweet. Tobias couldn't Span, and he didn't dare board the *Skate* on those occasions when she made port in Duvyn.

The truth was, Mara wasn't sure he would have come aboard even had there been no danger. The wounds were too raw.

"I'm glad to see you, Missus Lijar," the captain said, a smile softening the angular face, rain plastering dark hair to her brow. "Can I offer you hot tea, or perhaps hot rum?"

"I'd t-take b-both about now," Mara said through chattering teeth.

Larr put an arm around her shoulders and steered her toward the stern and her quarters. "It's warmer in my cabin, not to mention dry."

Mara didn't argue.

They retreated into her quarters and shut the door. It was comfortable within, the space bright with lamps. Larr presented her with dry clothes and turned her back as Mara dressed.

"Tobias and the princess are well?" Larr asked, speaking to the back wall of the cabin.

"They are, thank you." She pulled on a cotton shirt. "I'm dressed."

The captain took her seat, as did Mara.

"Do you have news?" Larr asked.

"Less than I would like. Duvyn's duke has sent messages to other nobles throughout Daerjen. They say nothing of Sofya, of course. They speak vaguely of opposing the Sheraighs. He's had few replies, and no commitments of aid. So far."

"Even from Trohsden?"

A knock at the door kept Mara from answering. The captain called, "Enter," and a young man stepped into the cabin bearing a cup of steaming tea. He handed it to Mara and left them. She wrapped her hands around the cup, breathed in the steam, which was redolent of black leaf and sweetpine.

"Trohsden is a long way," she said, in answer to Larr's question. "We don't know for certain that the missives have even been delivered yet."

Larr didn't answer, and Mara wasn't sure she believed her own reasoning. Yes, Trohsden was far to the north, but surely by now the letters dispatched by the duke of Duvyn had reached the northern highlands. Trohsden had yet to reply. Myles, the duke there, had been a loyal supporter of the Hayncalde Supremacy, and no friend to Sheraigh. His silence was ominous to say the least.

"Daerjen's nobles are still reeling from the Sheraigh Assertion. They may not be ready to oppose the new supremacy."

"They may entertain ambitions of their own," Larr said.

Mara and Tobias had considered this. One more complication in a plan that remained unformed and dauntingly bold.

"Yes," was all she said.

Larr considered her, sympathy in her gaze. Mara could guess at her thoughts. She and Tobias might have looked like adults—the result of their Walks back through time, which aged them some fourteen years—but they were barely more than children, she a turn or two shy of her seventeenth birthday, and Tobias a few turns past what would have been, in a different future, his sixteenth.

"Who knows of Sofya?" the captain asked. "Forgive me. Nava."

"Only Risch. We're not ready to trust so much in anyone else."

"I believe that's wise."

"Eventually we'll have to tell others."

"Yes, but not yet."

They lapsed into silence. Mara sipped her tea.

"What news from beyond Daerjen?" she asked after some time. "I take it you've found no chronofors."

"I would have told you straight away if I had. No, there are none in the usual places. Belsan, Hayncalde, Fanquir, even Caszuvaar. We've made inquiries—as quietly as possible, naturally. We've found nothing."

"Well, one is bound to show up eventually."

The captain gave a slow shake of her head. "I don't think so. It's been too long. I haven't seen one in more than a year now. That's too unusual to be a coincidence."

Mara's stomach knotted. "What are you saying?"

"I believe your enemies are hoarding them." She laughed, low and dry. "That might be too strong a word. There wouldn't be enough of them to hoard. But I suspect Orzili and his friends are buying up whatever devices appear in the major markets. They don't want you going back in time, and so they're doing the one thing they can to prevent it."

This possibility hadn't occurred to her, though it should have. She wondered if Tobias had considered it.

"Well," she said, voice flat, "keep searching. Please."

"Of course." A pause, and then, "We spotted Belvora over Qyrshen." Larr said this in the same tone she might have used to speak of a change in the weather, or the price of baviseed in the markets. "Others report seeing them over Fairisle."

Mara flinched at the words, recalling too many battles with the winged demons, and thinking again of Ermond, who had died fighting one in the waters near the Knot.

"I assume they'll find us eventually."

"Maybe. They might not think to look on Daerjen. No one would expect you to venture so close to Hayncalde, much less settle there."

"They're hunters," Mara said, "and we possess magick. In time, they'll find us."

"And what will you do?"

Mara shrugged. "We'll run, we'll fight if we have to, and we'll find a new home."

That look again: sympathy shading toward pity.

Mara drank her tea and stared at one of the lamps rather than meet Larr's gaze.

They spoke for another quarter bell, discussing trifles—markets and storms, Sofya's latest exploits, and the people Mara and Tobias had encountered in Little Duvyn. Too soon, it was time for Mara to face another flight through the Spanning gap.

She stood, gripped the captain's proffered hand.

"We'll be back this way in another turn or so," Larr said. "From here we head north and west, to Tirayre and Herjes, perhaps to Milnos." She grimaced. "I usually avoid the Shield, but this time of year they have excellent oils and savory fruits." She shrugged. "Gold is gold."

"Of course," Mara said. "I wish you success."

"Thank you. Should you need help before we return..."

Mara forced a smile. "We have the names you gave us."

Other merchant captains, men and women Larr trusted. Unknown to Tobias and her, however. She doubted they would seek such aid, even in the most dire of circumstances. Orzili's reach was too great, Tobias's fears too deep.

They left the cabin. To Mara's relief, the rain had slowed to a chilling mist. Maybe she wouldn't Span into a tree trunk on the way home.

She faced Larr. "Thank you, Captain. Again, and as always."

The captain embraced her, something she had only done once before, the day Mara and Tobias left the *Sea Dove*.

"May the Two keep you safe," the woman murmured. "All of you."

Touched as Mara was by the display, she was even more alarmed. Did the captain sense perils to which she and Tobias were oblivious?

Larr released her. "We'll leave you to Span back." She motioned her crew toward the bow and pointed to a spot on the aft deck. "Leave the clothes there."

Mara nodded, heaved a breath. Then she removed her clothes, aimed her sextant, and thumbed the release.

The gap swallowed her again.

She stumbled out of the wind and cold onto dried leaves and rich loam.

"Mama!"

Sofya barreled into her, nearly knocking her over.

Tobias enveloped her in a blanket that was softer than those on the ship. It smelled of wood smoke and spruce and him. Home. He kissed her forehead.

"You must be freezing."

She could only nod.

He walked her into the house and sat her beside the hearth. Sofya followed and climbed into Mara's lap, telling her a story about the market that Mara struggled to follow. She gathered that a peddler had given her sweets, over Tobias's objections, and that Sofya had eaten all of them.

"Well, that sounds very exciting," Mara said, when she finished her tale. To Tobias she said, "Did you find fruit?"

"We did. And bread, and fowl for tonight's supper."

He brought her a slice of crane fruit—tart, succulent, crisp. Guilt at her earlier longing for life at sea lanced her heart. Notwithstanding all their precautions, and the constant fear that hung over their home, they were making a good life here in the headlands—a comfortable home, fine food, love and laughter and passion. Many passed all their years without any of these things. Mara had them in abundance.

"Tell me about Larr," Tobias said.

Sofya leaned back against Mara and sang a song Mara had taught her, one she had learned turns ago while at sea.

Mara related her conversation with the captain, skirting some matters so as not to alarm Sofya. She did mention Larr's theory about the chronofors, and she asked Tobias if the possibility had occurred to him.

"No," he said. "It makes sense, though, and it brings me back to an idea I had a qua'turn ago. I should have mentioned it to you sooner."

She raised her brows, questioning.

He shook his head, darted a glance at Sofya. "Later."

Curiosity, and just a touch of fear, prickled her skin. For now, she bit back her questions.

When she was warm, Mara dressed, and together she and Tobias began to prepare their dinner, which promised to be a feast. She was famished from her Spanning, and content for the balance of this day and the evening to think only of herbs and broths, fowl and tubers and greens.

The three of them sang and played and ate. After their meal, Tobias told the princess a story, or rather an installment in a saga he had been spinning for turns. Once she was asleep, Mara and Tobias took to their own bed in the candlelight and quietly, tenderly made love.

After, in the shifting amber glow of that single candle, Tobias revealed to her what he had been considering.

"We've been looking for a chronofor forever it seems," he whispered to her, his breath, warm and scented with wine, tickling her neck. "And for a time, while we were on the *Dove*, and even after we left the ship, doing so made sense."

Mara watched him, tracing the strong profile with her eyes. "But?" she prompted.

"Maybe there's another way to get a chronofor."

She frowned. "I'm not following."

"What if we found a Binder who would be willing to make us one, or to repair mine?"

Mara didn't know what to say. "You want to leave here?"

"Not forever. Not even for that long. But if Larr is right—and you seem to believe she is—we're never going to happen upon a chronofor. We only have the sextant because Droë took it from Orzili and gave it to us."

"The risks—"

"I know."

They lay without speaking for some time, the only noises Sofya's soft snores, the crackle of their fire, and the rustle of wind in trees outside.

"I wouldn't even know where to go," she said at length. She didn't like this idea, but she couldn't deny that it made sense.

"There are three Binders in Daerjen." At her look, he added, "I asked in Little Duvyn."

"Dangerous."

"I was careful. It was a question buried in a lengthy discussion of the isle's most powerful courts in the wake of the Assertion. Which houses have the biggest armies, the most gold, the most Travelers. And which ones have Binders."

"Clever."

He kissed her neck. "Thank you."

"So? Where?"

"Hayncalde and Sheraigh, of course." He paused. "And Trohsden."

"Tobias—"

"We need to know what Myles is thinking," he said. "He hasn't replied to Risch's letter, and we can't possibly move against Sheraigh until he does."

"I know that—"

He raised a hand, stopping her. "Let me finish. The letter from Duvyn could only tell him so much. If I go, if I can have a private audience with him, I can tell him more. Maybe everything. He was an ally of Mearlan. Everyone agrees on that. I'm sure I can convince him. So why not make the journey and, while I'm there, ask if he'll allow his Binder to work on my chronofor?"

Clever. She loved him for so many reasons. This was one. He was not only loving and gentle and kind, he was also smart. And since his fight with Orzili aboard the *Sea Dove*, which could have ended with either one of them dead, he had acted more sure of himself, more willing to come up with notions like this one. He still spoke of the assassin as an enemy, a threat to their lives, particularly Sofya's. Orzili was someone to be respected, even feared.

Still, since that night, Tobias hadn't sounded afraid. Cautious, yes, but the timidity she had seen in him while aboard the *Sea Dove* had vanished, leaving him more willing to take calculated risks. He was no less vigilant in guarding the princess, or Mara herself, she had to admit, but she believed he was a far more dangerous enemy for Orzili.

"So you would go alone?" she asked, after considering his idea.

"I think I have to. On the off chance that things go badly with Myles, I don't want Sofya anywhere near Trohsden."

Mara weighed this, as well. She couldn't fault his reasoning, but she remained reluctant.

"If you think you should be the one to go, instead of me, that would be fine," he said, filling a lengthening silence. "I just thought that because I was Mearlan's Walker—"

"I don't want to go."

"Then what—"

"I don't want you to go either."

He watched her, his expression pained.

"Larr said there were Belvora seen in Qyrshen," she told him.

"That's..." He blew out a breath. "That's alarming."

"It's so close to Trohsden—they'd sense you."

"Maybe. Myles has a Spanner, a Crosser, a Binder. That might be enough magick to shield me."

"If you make it there."

"I've dealt with Belvora before."

"It's not only the Belvora. What if there's a reason Risch hasn't heard back from Trohsden?"

"Trohsden was Hayncalde's ally. Myles and Mearlan were said to be close friends."

"Yes, but Mearlan's dead, and the Sheraighs rule Daerjen, and maybe Myles has decided he can't afford to make an enemy of the new sovereign."

Tobias didn't answer right away.

"He wouldn't be the first noble to abandon loyalty for his own well-being," she said. "And for all he knows, Mearlan's entire line has been wiped out."

"If he's pledged loyalty to the Sheraighs, we need to know that."

"I understand. But until we know for certain one way or another, you probably shouldn't deliver yourself to him."

He shifted onto his back, stared up at the ceiling. "We need a chronofor."

"Yes, we do, and I like the idea of finding a Binder. I'm just not convinced that Trohsden's Binder is the one."

Tobias made a small gesture that might have signaled acquiescence. Mara wasn't certain. He didn't say anything more. In time, he rolled onto his side, his back to her. Mara wanted to say more, but she couldn't find the words.

After a spirecount, he reached back for her, found her hand, and gave it a gentle squeeze.

In time, she fell asleep, only to dream of Belvora—their screams, the rank smell of rotting meat, the pain of a demon claw carving across her cheek.

She woke to darkness, sweating, breath coming in quick gasps. It took her a long time to ease her pulse, and longer still to slumber again. When she woke to daylight, she didn't feel any more rested than she had the night before.

Mara rose, dressed, washed her face with chill water. Somewhere outside, Sofya laughed and Tobias said something Mara couldn't hear. She donned her overshirt and left the house for the damp and cool of morning. The sky had cleared overnight; soft white clouds scudded across an expanse of deep blue, driven by a hard wind.

Sofya and Tobias stood in the open space before their home, both holding wooden swords that Tobias had fashioned from fallen branches in the wood. Sofya's was tiny, of course, but Tobias had insisted that they teach her to wield a weapon as early as possible.

"She's a princess, and she's being hunted. If her father were alive, he would have started training her by now. We should do no less."

Mara wasn't certain she believed this last, but she did see the value in teaching the girl to defend herself. Who could say what perils she would face through her childhood? They would have been fools to wait.

The princess cried, "Mama!" when she saw Mara in the doorway.

"Show her what you learned to do, Nava," Tobias said.

Sofya nodded, set her feet as they had taught her, and held her weapon ready. She looked like a little warrior.

"Ready?" Tobias said.

"Weady!"

Tobias advanced on her slowly and swung his sword at her in a slow, exaggerated arc.

Sofya parried, ducked under his weapon, and swung backhanded, hitting him in the side of the leg. Her movements were deliberate—nothing he couldn't have blocked had he chosen to. That hardly mattered. She was barely more than two years old, and already she was mastering movements third year novitiates in Windhome would have been learning on the training grounds.

Mara clapped. "Wonderful, love!"

Sofya beamed.

"Again, Papa!"

They performed the maneuver three or four times more, always at that same speed, but with precision. She would be a swordswoman by the time she was four.

After one last time, Sofya handed her sword to Tobias and announced that she was hungry. Without waiting for them, she marched into the house.

Tobias walked to the door, leaned the wooden swords against the wall, and kissed Mara.

"You didn't sleep well."

She crossed her arms, shivered despite the overshirt. "Not really, no. Bad dreams."

He kissed her again, wrapped his arms around her. Mara rested her cheek on his chest, savoring his smell, the solid strength of his arms, the brush of his unbound hair over her cheek.

She couldn't have said what made her glance up at that particular moment. Fate? Good fortune? Instinct?

The Belvora soared low, but hadn't yet tucked its wings for a killing stoop.

She shouted Tobias's name, broke away from him. He spun, cursed. They dove into the house. Tobias grabbed a musket. Mara gathered Sofya in her arms.

CHAPTER SIX

7th Day of Sipar's Ascent, Year 634

This was why they kept loaded muskets on a shelf beside the door, beyond Sofya's grasp, but within easy reach for them. The princess cried at the sight of the weapon. Too many times in her short life the presence of muskets and pistols had been harbingers of danger, violence, blaring noise.

Mara whispered to her.

Tobias strode back out into the clearing. The demon had banked, wings splayed, long legs angling in the wing, helping to steer into this turn.

He set his feet, lifted the musket to his shoulder. The Belvora saw, wheeled again, flapped its enormous wings. Tobias pulled the trigger.

The boom of his weapon echoed through the woods. Blue-gray smoke stung his nostrils. The Belvora spasmed, dipped, rose again on labored wingbeats. Flew on.

Tobias ducked back into the house, where Sofya now wailed. He grabbed the other musket and one of the pistols. Outside, he aimed again, but the demon had flown nearly beyond range of the weapon. And before he could aim and fire, it disappeared behind the treetops.

He sprinted into the wood, weaving past trees, searching for another clearing, desperate for another shot at the demon. If it got away, if it reported back to other Belvora, or whoever had sent it...

By the time he found another open spot, the demon was gone. Or it had circled back.

He whirled, raced back toward the house. Only once had he encountered a lone Belvora. Usually they hunted in groups. He tried to scan the sky through the trees but saw no others. He knew that didn't mean anything.

As he emerged into their clearing, he called to Mara.

She appeared in the doorway, still clutching Sofya. Tobias slowed, whispered thanks to the Two.

He and Mara checked the sky at the same time. Blue and clouds—nothing else.

"Did you hit it?" she asked.

"Once, yes. That wasn't enough to stop it." He peered at the sky again, then faced her. He read his own despair in her hazel eyes.

Sofya's face was streaked with tears; both her little hands were fisted in Mara's shirt.

"Why you make noise, Papa?" she demanded, an accusation in the question.

"There was something I had to shoot, love. I'm sorry I scared you."

He walked to them. Sofya buried her face against Mara's shoulder.

Mara patted her back, eyes on Tobias. "We can't stay," she said.

"No, we can't."

They scanned the sky again. Nothing. For the moment. Tobias stepped past her into the house. He reloaded the musket he had left there and leaned it by the door. Then he reconsidered and handed it to Mara. They both carried weapons to their bedroom and began to pack.

Sofya sat on their bed, watching in silence. Her anger at Tobias didn't last long.

"Whewe aww we going?"

"On a new adventure," Mara said, managing to infuse the words with enthusiasm.

"Back on a boat?"

"Maybe."

"I wike boats!"

Tobias almost envied her.

He had no idea where they would go. If only the Belvora had found them the day before, they might have arranged passage with Seris Larr on the *Gray Skate*. Now, the *Skate* was gone—north and west, Mara said. They needed to find a ship. They wouldn't get far on foot if the Belvora returned in numbers.

They had prepared for this day, knowing it would come eventually. All the clothes and items they would need with them they kept accessible. The window shutters could be locked from inside; the door had a heavy lock as well. In case they found a way back here when the danger passed. A dream perhaps, but one he and Mara shared.

In less than half a bell, their travel sacks were packed, the fire banked, the windows closed. Sofya rode on Mara's shoulders, her favorite doll in one hand, a slice of buttered bread in the other. Mara's hair would be a greasy mess in no time.

From her perch, Sofya couldn't see the tears on her mother's face. Tobias grieved for Mara. She had followed him back through time, chasing a dream of love. She had saved his life several times since her arrival in this past. He had considered her his closest friend in the future they had shared, the one she never knew. Now she was his world. Once, on the night of his battle with Orzili, he had made the mistake of suggesting that she should leave him, leave this time, make a life for herself elsewhere.

She'd berated him. They were husband and wife, parents to Sofya, their lives intertwined like fibers in braided rope. Never again would he speak to her of separating. But a part of him wished he could spare her this sadness. He wanted to give her a true, lasting home. He wanted them to live as other families did.

Another dream.

He pulled the door shut, turned the key on that iron lock.

"Say 'Goodbye, house!'"

"Goodbye, house!" Mara and Sofya said in unison.

A new adventure. One that was as likely as not to get all of them killed. The only thing riskier would have been remaining here and waiting for the demons' inevitable attack.

Tobias and Mara were dressed for war. They carried muskets and had two pistols on their belts. They bore blades as well—knives on their belts and in sheaths strapped to their legs. Tobias carried a sword.

Tobias watched the sky, checking behind them every few steps. Mara did the same.

They had done all of this before; it took them no time at all to fall back into old habits.

After a brief discussion, they chose to make their way first to the modest castle of Duvyn's duke, a walk of no more than two leagues.

Seris Larr had introduced them to the duke, Risch. She trusted the man, and it had taken Tobias mere moments to understand why. He was friendly, open, guileless, generous to a fault. And he professed to be an admirer and supporter of Mearlan, the lost sovereign.

"I wouldn't presume to claim a friendship," he told them that first day. "I'm but a minor noble, and he was...what he was. I would like to think, though, that he valued me as an ally."

When, at Larr's urging, they told him who Nava really was, he pledged his aid. "Anything you need, regardless of cost or circumstance—ask, and if it's in my power to give it, you shall have it."

Tobias didn't wish to bring Belvora to any man's door, but he and Mara had few choices.

The walk to Risch's Castle took them through the shadows of Duvyn Wood along the slow, deep river that was also named for the duchy.

They passed peddlers on the road, and a family housed in

canvas tents in the shelter of the wood. Otherwise they had the forest to themselves. No one troubled them.

After a winding descent to open farmland, they spotted Duvyn Castle. It was a simple fortification, square, towers at each corner. The red and white flag of Daerjen snapped in the wind atop her ramparts, just above the blue and red banner of Duvyn. Guards patrolled the walls, helms gleaming in the sun, bows slung over their backs.

Beyond the castle, the waters of the firth glittered with fractured reflections of sunlight. Gulls cried overhead. Smells of salt and fish thickened the air. They glimpsed the walls of the city itself, and the pinelands fronting the nearby shore.

As Tobias, Mara, and Sofya approached the castle's main gate, soldiers shouted from on high. Gate guards emerged from the arched entry and planted themselves in the road.

Tobias raised a hand in greeting. Sofya, who by this time rode on his shoulders, waved as well.

The three of them halted before the soldiers, a few paces shy of the gate, and gave their names. Tobias didn't recognize any of the soldiers from previous visits to the castle, which set him on edge.

"The duke will want to see us," he said.

"I have no doubt. You'll need to leave your weapons—"

Tobias shook his head, and the man broke off. "Please send for your duke. He'll allow us entry as we are."

"We have orders not to allow entry to *any* who are armed as you are. Your weapons will be guarded and returned to you. If you insist on keeping them, you'll need to move on."

Tobias and Mara shared a glance. The unfamiliar soldiers, this strict adherence to a policy from which Risch had exempted them in the past—none of it boded well.

Tobias considered passing the castle by and continuing on their way. The problem was, for now they had nowhere else to go. He nodded to Mara, held out his musket for the guards to take.

Several of those in uniform came forward to take the firearms and blades, including their hidden weapons. They searched their carry sacks as well.

"You have enough here for an army of ten, much less two," the commander said, eyeing the confiscated weapons. "You're expecting trouble?"

"We've complied with your request for our weapons, commander," Tobias said, keeping his tone conversational. "We would see your duke now."

The man's smile could have frosted the grass beneath their feet. "Of course."

The commander and another soldier led them through the gate into the broad central courtyard. Fruit trees and flowering shrubs grew in a simple garden, and three peacock hens scurried across a stone path.

Sofya pointed and twisted, wrenching Tobias's neck. "Biwds, Mama! Did you see the Biwds?"

"I saw them, love."

"She's a lovely girl," the guard said, glancing up at the princess. "I should have checked. Was she carrying arms as well?"

Surely he meant this as a jest, but it only served to deepen Tobias's apprehension.

"The musket was hers," he said, feeling he had to respond. "I was holding it for her."

The man chuckled. They walked on.

Despite the chilly greeting, Tobias noticed nothing alarming within the castle. There were no more soldiers apparent than usual, no fewer laborers in the garden. Indeed, Risch's duchess, Corinne, spotted them from the orchard and called to the guard.

All of them halted as the duchess strode to them. She was tall, elegant, even in the plain garb she wore to tend her fruit trees. She wore her silver and black hair coiled and piled atop her head. A smudge of dirt darkened her brow above deep brown eyes.

"Tobias, Mara! Welcome. What a lovely surprise."

The soldier regarded them anew, fresh appraisal in his stare. It seemed he hadn't placed much faith in Tobias's claim of friendship with the duke.

"Good day, Nava," the duchess said to the princess. "Don't you look pretty today."

"Hi, Cowinne." Sofya reached for the woman. Tobias lifted her off his shoulders and handed her to the duchess.

Sofya gave her a hug and asked to see the birds again.

"I'll take her," Corinne said. "She'll be fine. You go on. Risch will want to speak with you."

This she said pointedly. Tobias's fears spiked again.

"This way," the guard said, with a touch more deference.

It was a measure of how completely Tobias and Mara trusted both Risch and Corinne that they didn't hesitate to leave the princess in that courtyard. Tobias did pause to check the sky over the castle for Belvora, but the demons hunted magickal prey. They would be far more inclined to follow Tobias and Mara than to attack Sofya. He hoped.

As they neared the arched entry to the duke's tower, Tobias halted again, indicating to the soldier that he should do the same.

"I should have told you this earlier, but we spied a Belvora earlier today. I don't believe we were followed, but it is possible. Both my wife and I have...abilities that might draw a Belvora's notice."

"As do the duke's Spanner, Crosser, and healer," the man said. "Thank you for telling me. We'll post additional marksmen on the walls. The demons won't trouble you here."

"Thank you," Tobias said, revising his opinion of the man.

They entered the tower, climbed to the castle's third level, and made their way to Risch's quarters. At the guard's knock, a voice from the chamber called a greeting.

The guard opened the door and stepped aside, allowing Tobias and Mara to enter.

Risch sat before his fire. Seeing them, he set aside the parchment he'd been reading and stood.

He wasn't tall or graceful like his wife, nor was he particularly handsome, as the duke of Trohsden was said to be. His thinning wheaten hair was salted with white. His face was long, his eyes widely spaced, his nose long and crooked—from a fight he'd had as a young man, he explained the first time Tobias and Mara met him.

His gifts, they had learned long ago, were subtle: a nuanced intelligence, a biting wit, patience and wisdom in abundance, and generosity beyond expectation. Tobias had admired Mearlan IV in the brief time he knew the sovereign, and he thought highly of several of the masters and mistresses he knew from Windhome in a lost future. Never, though, had he met anyone more worthy of leading a kingdom than this man. It struck him as unjust that the modest means of House Duvyn would keep Risch from ever ascending to the throne.

The duke greeted Tobias and Mara with embraces and kind words, instructed a steward to bring food and wine, and steered them to chairs by his hearth. Only when they were seated did he ask what had brought them to his castle.

An instant later, he leaned forward, the color draining from his cheeks. "Where is Nava?"

"With the duchess, my lord," Mara said. "She wanted to see the peacocks."

He sat back, clearly relieved. "Good. So, I'll ask again—"

"Belvora," Mara said. "Over our home."

"Blood and bone. How many?"

"Just one," Tobias said. "I shot it, but only managed to wound."

Risch steepled his fingers. "I see."

"I told your new commander. He said he would post more marksmen on the ramparts."

"Yes, good."

Mara glanced Tobias's way. "What's happened here, my lord? The gate guards were...more leery of us than usual."

Risch's expression curdled. "Noak is consolidating Sheraigh rule. We've had companies of Sheraigh soldiers here twice in the last ha'turn. They claim to be searching the wood for bands of Hayncalde sympathizers, but I believe he's trying to intimidate me. And six days ago, while I was out on a hunt, someone tried to kill me."

Risch said this calmly, as if it were as expected as the dawn. Tobias and Mara gaped.

"Were you hurt?" Mara asked.

He shook his head. "I was fortunate. The assassin's arrow struck a tree branch ahead of me and careened off its line."

"And the assassin?"

"He fled, my guards gave chase. When he realized he couldn't get away, he took his own life."

"Did he wear black?" Tobias asked, thinking of Orzili and his men.

The duke frowned. "No. He dressed as a woodsman, and my guards took him for one. Why?"

"The men who killed Mearlan usually appear in black. I thought it possible... It's nothing. I'm glad you're all right."

Risch popped a date in his mouth. "You're welcome here, of course. You know this. But I can't guarantee your safety. I fear what might happen if Sheraigh's men return while you're in the castle. They haven't searched the grounds and towers yet, but that's not to say they won't the next time they're here."

Mara turned back to Tobias, their gazes locking for a five-count. He read weariness in her eyes, and alarm.

"We'd be grateful if you could shelter us tonight," Tobias said, facing the duke once more. "We probably shouldn't stay longer than that."

"Of course. Whatever you need."

"We need a Binder."

Risch's brows lifted. "A chronofor?"

Tobias nodded. "Mine is broken. Perhaps it can be fixed. If not, we have coin. We can have a new one made. Either way, we would be in a better position to fight Mearlan's assassin." He hesitated. "I take it you've still heard nothing from Myles."

The duke glared at the flames in his hearth. "Not a word. I expect he's had encounters with the Sheraighs as well. And he has more to lose than I do."

"I mean no disrespect, my lord," Mara said, "but his house is stronger than yours. He should be able to resist."

"That's not how this works. He *is* stronger—I take no offense at you saying so. And because he's stronger, he's more of a threat to Noak. Sheraigh will be far more aggressive in attempting to control him, and far more generous in rewarding him should he prove willing to profess loyalty to the new supremacy. I don't envy Myles, nor can I blame him for keeping his distance from me."

"It would be easier for you—"

At a glower from the duke, Tobias fell silent.

"Easier has nothing to do with this. I was loyal to Mearlan, and I loved him as my sovereign. I would never... And Noak knows this. He won't trust me no matter what I do or say. Myles is different. Yes, he and Mearlan were like brothers, which means he can't afford to show any lingering loyalty to Hayncalde. His life would be forfeit. It might be anyway. But he's strong, valuable as a potential ally, and dangerous as an enemy. Noak will coerce him, try to force him to support the new supremacy. Failing that, he'll try to destroy him. Me... He may make another attempt on my life. Or not. He can isolate me, turn the rest of the dukes against me, make me irrelevant. I'm not worth more effort than that."

"Forgive me, my lord."

Risch lifted his hand in a vague gesture. "There's nothing to forgive. I'm afraid, though, that I am next to useless to you. I can shelter you. I can offer a bit of gold if you need it. Beyond that..." He shrugged.

Tobias didn't believe this, but neither did he argue.

"If we were to go to Trohsden," Mara said, "do you think Myles would help us? Would he allow us access to his Binder?"

"I don't know. I would advise you against taking that chance. Nothing would enhance his standing with the Sheraighs more than giving you and the princess over to Noak's assassins."

Another glance passed between Tobias and Mara. She had been right. Again. He should have known better than to doubt her.

"Do you know of any other Binders we might approach?" Tobias asked.

"The problem isn't the Binder, of course. It's the noble. Someone on another isle might care less about crossing Noak, but Daerjen remains a power in these seas. Diminished, yes, but formidable nevertheless. Even on other isles, some might think twice about setting themselves against House Sheraigh. You would have to be very careful."

Not the answer Tobias had hoped to hear. "We will be," he said. "For now, we need to get a message to a merchant captain. We require passage to another isle."

"Which?"

He opened his hands. "Any isle. We need to leave here."

"Belvora can track you over open sea as easily as they can on land. And I still believe you're best off remaining in Daerjen. Few would think to look for you here, and any insurgency we mount will have a greater chance of succeeding from within the sovereignty than from outside of it."

Tobias heard truth in this, as well. They had only bad choices before them—how many times had he said this to himself in recent turns?

"I wouldn't know where to go," Tobias said. "Then again, that would be true whether we were on a ship or on foot."

"Remain here for a time," Risch said. "The more I consider the matter, the more I believe we can keep you safe. There are others here who wield magick—we can keep the Belvora from finding you. My castle may be small, but it's not without a few hidden chambers and stairways. The Sheraighs won't find you either."

"And a Binder?" Mara asked.

Risch lifted a shoulder, then grinned. "I've always wanted one in my court. What better time to employ one?"

The duke had his steward settle them in a chamber just off the royal corridor. They supped that night with the duke and duchess

—a simple meal of lamb, greens, and roots, and then wandered the gardens under a bright gibbous moon. Sofya seemed content, more so than Mara felt. She missed their home and feared they would never see it again. She also worried about bringing Belvora to Duvyn Castle. She sensed that this concerned Tobias as well.

Risch and Corinne dismissed their fears.

"You wouldn't be bringing them here," the duchess said. "None of this is your fault."

Mara made herself believe their reassurances, and she thanked the Two for such generous friends. They had been forced to leave Seris Larr's crew, but that didn't mean they had no one.

She went to sleep beside Tobias willing to believe that they might be safe in Duvyn for a short while.

That dream was shattered sometime later when she and Tobias woke to the tolling of castle bells. It was still dark. Sofya cried and called for Tobias from her small pallet beside their bed.

He lifted her, spoke to her in whispers, managed to calm her.

That only lasted until the crackle of musket fire echoed outside their shuttered window.

"We need our weapons," Tobias said.

Mara pulled on breeches and a shirt. "Stay here with Sofya," she said. "I'll get them."

She knew he wouldn't like this idea. She didn't wait for him to agree. She was the better shot. He was stronger, better equipped to fight off intruders and keep Sofya safe. This made sense.

Risch was already in the corridor, a musket in hand, trailed by a pair of soldiers in blue and red. They hurried toward the tower stairway.

"Tobias and I need our weapons," Mara said, falling in step beside the duke. "Your gate guards took them."

"Of course." Risch turned to one of his guards. "You heard?"

"Yes, my lord," the woman said. "Right away." She ran off ahead of them.

"What's happened?" Mara asked.

"Demons."

"Belvora?"

"We think so. They may not be alone."

Mara didn't like the sound of that. She thought back on her encounter with the Tirribin, Aiwi, in the Knot. Were time demons helping these Belvora as well? "I'm sorry. We drew them here."

"On purpose?" Risch asked, regarding her sidelong.

"No, but—"

"Then stop apologizing. Corinne and I meant what we said earlier. None of this is your fault. We're fighting for the same cause, you and I. Those arrayed against us include assassins, armies, and, yes, Belvora. There's nothing to be done but fight them off."

"Yes, my lord."

At the base of the tower stairs, they were met by a company of more than twenty soldiers, all armed with muskets.

"There are at least eight of the demons, my lord. We've spotted them flying above the walls and towers. As of yet, none has landed on the castle grounds. That we know of."

"Keep guards on the ramparts. Spread them out so that they all have a clear shot."

"No, my lord," Mara said.

The duke rounded. His soldier regarded her with disapproval.

"You have another idea?" Risch said. He didn't sound pleased.

Mara didn't allow herself to be cowed. She might not have been a noble or a soldier, but she would have wagered every coin she and Tobias had that she had done battle with Belvora more recently and more often than these men. She had the scars to prove it.

"Cluster your soldiers in groups of two and three," she said. "Have them work together: one shoots and then the other as the Belvora adjust course. They'll have more success that way. It's what we did on the Sea of Wraiths. And again near Herjes."

Risch considered her. "It seems we have an expert in our midst." To the soldier, he added, "Do as she says."

"Yes, my lord."

The man started away. Before he had gone far, the torches at the far end of the courtyard went out.

"What are they doing?" the duke said, more to himself. "Get those torches lit again!"

Even as he shouted this, torches atop the walls at that same southern end of the castle were doused as well. This time, Mara saw what she had missed before. The fires were not extinguished so much as they were pulled away from their source. It almost appeared that the flames fled the castle.

"Did you see that, my lord?"

At the same time, Risch said, "Blood and bone."

"What is it? What's causing that?"

Flames lighting the crenellations atop the west wall vanished next, slipping over the lip of the battlements as might a fugitive attempting escape.

"Get inside," Risch told her. "Get back in the castle!" he cried to his guards. "Lock the entries! Guard the doors with muskets and bows! No swords! No swords!"

Mara lingered, watching, not understanding. The duke grabbed her hand and pulled her after him back into the castle.

"What could be doing—"

"Hanev!" he said. When they were inside, he pulled the door shut and bolted it. "Somehow the Belvora have allied themselves with a Hanev."

Mara frowned. "A Hanev?"

"A shadow demon."

That term was familiar to her.

"Very rare. They feed on light—candles, torches, hearth fires. Any light at all. During the day they're not a danger, but at night... By now, every torch on my palace walls, and every torch in the courtyard, is out. And Belvora can see in the dark."

CHAPTER SEVEN

7th Day of Sipar's Ascent, Year 634

Mara tried to remember all she had heard about shadow demons. The truth was, she knew precious little. A part of her had wondered if they were even real, or merely creatures of myth.

"So the danger from a Hanev is what, exactly?"

Risch dragged a hand over his face. "Just what you saw: their appetite for light. The Belvora are the greater threat. I think. To be honest, I've never dealt with Hanev. Most humans never do. I haven't heard of Hanev hurting people or being vicious in any way. They simply feed, which in this case helps our enemies."

"What would make them work with Belvora?"

"That I don't know. I've never understood the commerce of Ancients."

The click of boots on stone made them both turn. A guard approached, laden with weapons—the muskets, pistols, and blades taken from Mara and Tobias upon their arrival.

"I need to get these to Tobias," she said, taking half the weapons from the guard. "Then we can join your forces when you decide how you want to deploy them."

"Is that wise?"

"We're as good as any marksmen you have. Windhome training and all that. Can Corinne take Nava?"

Risch nodded. "Of course. I'll send word immediately."

Mara hurried back to their chamber, the guard following. She found Tobias pacing in the room, Sofya in his arms. A candle burned atop a small table. Mara wondered if the Hanev would take that flame, too. Seeing the muskets and pistols, the princess began to fuss.

The guard gave Tobias his weapons and left. Mara closed the door.

"I heard shouting," Tobias said. "What's happened?"

"There are Belvora. Eight of them, maybe more. And they have a Hanev with them."

He blinked in the candlelight. "A what?"

"Shadow demon." She explained what she had learned of the creatures from Risch and concluded, "This one appears to be working with the Belvora."

Sofya struggled in Tobias's arms and reached for Mara, who took her. She scowled at the musket slung over Mara's shoulder, faced away from it, and rested her head on Mara's shoulder.

"So we have to fight Belvora in the dark?"

"That seems to be what they want."

A distant bang shook the castle. Tobias eyed Mara. A knock at their door kept either of them from saying anything.

Tobias opened the door, stepped aside, allowing Corinne to enter. The duchess wore a heavy robe and carried a second, identical to her own, but tiny.

"Who would like to try on a royal robe?"

Sofya raised her head and stared at the robe. A smile stole across her face. "Me."

"I have a crown as well. Would you like to see that?"

The princess nodded. She held out her arms, allowing the duchess to take her from Mara.

As Corinne carried Sofya back to the door, she said, "Risch is in the central hall, deploying the guard. He'd like you to join him there."

"Thank you, my lady," Tobias said.

"The Two keep you safe." She left with the princess. Mara saw that two armed guards waited for her in the corridor, which eased her mind a bit.

She and Tobias left the chamber as well, making their way to the hall. Twice more as they navigated the corridors, the castle shuddered as from a blow.

When they reached the hall and opened the door, the chamber was dark. They leveled their weapons and backed away from the entry.

"Come in." Risch's voice. "And close that door."

They traded glances and did as the duke instructed.

"We're acclimating to the darkness," Risch said as they joined him and his soldiers in the middle of the hall. Another impact jarred the walls and floor. "We need to fight them out there before they force their way in. You said you have experience with Belvora?"

"Yes," Mara said, remembered pain lancing her shoulder and making the scar on her cheek itch. "They're strong, deadly, but they're not canny as other Ancients are, and they possess no magick of their own, other than their ability to sense magick in those they prey upon."

"You," the duke said. "Both of you."

Tobias dipped his chin. "That's right. And your Spanner and Crosser as well."

"If we join you on the walls or in the courtyard," Mara said, "they'll be drawn to us first."

"Then you should keep out of sight."

"No, my lord. Use us. Put us on the wall. Doing so will make the Belvora more predictable."

Seris Larr had balked at employing such a tactic. The duke did not. "Yes, all right."

He led them out of the hall through a doorway that opened directly onto the courtyard. Even having stood in the darkness with the duke and his guards, Mara could barely see at first.

Somewhere to the west a crescent moon hung just above the horizon casting faint light across the surrounding fields. The courtyard, however, was steeped in shadow.

Mara glimpsed a shape overhead, dark, winged, blotting out stars as it swept across the sky. But she couldn't tell how high it was, and she doubted she could have aimed and fired in time to kill it. She didn't doubt that the creature sensed her and Tobias, or that it could see them despite the darkness.

"This is madness," Tobias whispered beside her.

She didn't argue.

The guards around them dispersed. Mara and Tobias kept their backs to the stone, their muskets raised to their shoulders. They faced that faint moon glow, hoping for any advantage the meager light might offer.

"We're over here," Tobias called to the duke. "Along your east wall."

"Good! Guard the east wall," he relayed to the soldiers.

Another dark shape swooped by, lower than the first form Mara had seen.

"Did you see that?" Tobias asked, his voice low.

"Yes." Mara tracked the creature with her musket. "I've got it sighted."

"Me, too. You first."

She pulled the trigger. A flash of fire left a trace on her vision, and the weapon blared.

The Belvora shrieked, veered.

Tobias's musket flashed and boomed. The winged shape tumbled to the ground near them, drawing a shout and a curse from more than one guard.

"Remove its head," Tobias called as he knelt to reload his weapon.

Mara loaded hers, too, checking the sky as she did. She and Tobias had been trained to load their weapons in darkness. A skill demanded by Windhome weapons masters in any time.

Two weapons discharged in quick succession on the far side

of the courtyard. Then two more. At least one Belvora wailed in agony. Mara thought she saw a demon fall.

A soldier screamed. Weapons went off—muskets and pistols. Another Belvora screeched and was silenced.

Tobias straightened, fired almost immediately, shouted her name.

Mara snapped her gaze up in time to see a huge, fell form hurtling toward her. She fell back, raised her musket, and fired all in a single desperate motion.

The flame from her musket illuminated the creature, allowing her to see it for a single instant—blood shining high on its chest, talons reaching for her, amber eyes burning, mouth open—whether to wail or feed, she couldn't tell. It crashed into her.

Pain, then darkness.

The demon shifted, grunting. Tobias dropped his musket, drew one of his pistols, and closed the distance to the Belvora with a single stride. Before the creature could strike at Mara, or turn on him, he set the barrel of his pistol against the demon's head and fired.

It spasmed. A splatter of dark, foul blood sprayed across the castle wall. Tobias heaved the creature off of Mara and dropped to his knees beside her.

"Mara!"

No response. He felt for a pulse, rested his head to her chest. She was breathing. Her heart drummed, rapid but steady. He closed his eyes, relief flooding him.

More muskets thundered. He reclaimed and reloaded his musket, stood over her as Belvora blocked the stars above him. He'd lost count of how many demons had been killed, but he could see that at least two lived still.

He called to the duke, who soon joined him. Seeing Mara, he hissed a breath.

"She's all right," Tobias said. "But I need help keeping her safe."

"Of course."

Muskets flared to their right, the reports following closely.

Risch cried a warning and fired. Tobias tracked the shadow as it wheeled and fired in turn. The demon crashed into a wall, fell to the ground.

"Well done!" the duke said, kneeling to reload.

Tobias did the same, then scanned the sky, ready to fire. He saw no more demons. After some time, he lowered his weapon.

"Is that all of them?" Risch asked, pitching his voice to reach his soldiers.

"I believe so, my lord," came a reply.

Risch nodded and moved off.

Tobias drew his sword and hacked off the heads of the demons he'd had a hand in killing. He hurried to Mara's side, examined her more closely. She had an egg-sized knot on the back of her head, and a darkening bruise on her brow. Her breathing sounded clear, and her heartbeat remained strong.

"I've called for my healer," Risch said, emerging from the darkness. "I count eight dead demons."

"And your soldiers?"

The duke gazed back across the courtyard. "A few are hurt. Two are dead."

Tobias let out a breath. "I'm sorry, my lord."

"It could have been worse."

"Yes," Tobias said, gently brushing a strand of Mara's hair off her injured forehead.

A young man stepped into the courtyard through a nearby doorway and paused, seeming unsure of where to go.

"Over here, healer," Risch said.

The man walked in their direction, a hand trailing along the castle wall. Tobias's eyes had long since adjusted to the dark; this man's had not. On the thought, Tobias gazed toward the main gate.

The healer reached Mara and knelt.

"She has a bump on the back of her head," Tobias told the man. "And the bruise you can see."

"Actually, I can't."

"Of course. My apologies. It's on her forehead."

"No blood anywhere?"

"None that I can see."

"My lord," the healer said. "I need to get her inside and tend to her wounds."

"Of course, healer. There are other wounded as well. I'll have all of them carried into the hall."

"Very good, my lord."

The duke called for soldiers. Tobias helped carry Mara inside.

He didn't linger, trusting the healer to take care of her. Instead, he went back outside and crossed the courtyard to the gate. He carried his loaded musket, his pistols, and his blades.

The gate guards eyed him with interest, but let him pass.

He followed the path out of the castle and around to the west side, staying close to the wall, watching for stray Belvora.

Once he had put some distance between himself and the gate, he halted, and said, "I would speak with the Ancient who took light from the castle."

Tobias kept still, listening for movement or breathing or any response to his summons.

"I will not harm you," he said. "I wish only to speak with you."

Nothing.

"The Belvora are dead. As I understand such things, whatever commerce you might have had with them ended with their lives. You risk nothing treating with me."

He waited. A spirecount passed, then another. Perhaps his instincts had misled him. Or maybe the Hanev was more loyal to his fellow Ancients than Tobias had anticipated. Fear pebbled the skin on his neck. He pivoted, intending to head back to the gate, his eyes raking across the star-splattered sky once more.

"You wish to engage in commerce with us?"

The voice stopped him as much as the words. It was oddly muffled, as if the speaker's head were wrapped in cloth, but also sibilant and sharp. And it came from much closer than Tobias had expected. It occurred to him—far, far too late—that calling out to an unknown Ancient might have been breathtakingly stupid.

The words had come from his right, putting him between the Hanev and the castle wall. He faced that way, trying to spot the demon. To no avail.

"I wish to speak with you," he said. "I had in mind no commerce—"

"A summons then," the voice said. "This carries a cost."

Again, Tobias winced at his own foolishness. "Commerce" to an Ancient implied far more than it might to most humans. Certainly a conversation might qualify as commerce if information was exchanged, as he hoped it would be.

"Forgive me. It is commerce I seek."

"You do not know your own mind."

Judging from the sound of the creature's voice, it stood directly in front of Tobias, no more than two or three strides away. Nearer than Tobias would have preferred, especially since he still could not see it.

"In fact I do," he said. "Know my own mind, that is. I forget sometimes that Ancients see commerce in interactions humans see as...more casual."

"True, true," the demon said. "For a species obsessed with material wealth, you are remarkably oblivious to the reach of commerce."

There. Ahead of him. A hulking darkness, a shadow of shadow. It had to stand five hands taller than Tobias, and it was twice as broad as well. He wondered if it had teeth like Arrokad or Tirribin, or talons like the Belvora they had killed this night. He couldn't help inching backward. Too soon, he bumped up against the stone wall.

"You fear us."

"I'm unfamiliar with your kind. You are...formidable."

The demon made an odd rasping sound. It took Tobias a full breath to realize it was laughing.

"We are, yes. What commerce do you wish to pursue, human?"

"I want to know who sent you."

"You seek information."

"That's right."

"And in return?"

"What do you want?"

"What all our kind want. Light. The torches atop this structure were lovely. Warm, amber with hints of blue and orange and red at their base. They were numerous as well, but they merely whet our appetite. We would have more before the moon sets and we are left with only starlight."

"I can ask the duke to light more."

"That would be acceptable."

"First, though—"

"What makes you believe we were sent? Belvora hunt magick, and there are those in this castle who possess it."

"Yes," Tobias said. "I'm one of them." He wasn't sure why he revealed this to the demon. Instinct. He trusted himself.

"Interesting," the Hanev said.

"I've seen Belvora before. I've fought them. What I saw tonight was not simply winged ones on the hunt. This was an attack. You helped them, by taking our light—"

"That is what our kind do."

"How often do your kind hunt with Belvora?"

Silence. Tobias sensed that he had angered the creature. A risk. But they were engaged in commerce. Based on what he knew of Ancients, he didn't think the Hanev could kill him now without disgracing himself. He hoped he was right.

"This is not a matter that concerns humans," the Hanev said at length, ice in the words.

"We were the Belvora's prey. I'd say that concerns us."

"The commerce of prey and predator is separate from our transaction, and separate from all other commerce as well."

As the Hanev spoke, Tobias caught up with their exchange. Ancients would not lie during commerce either. They might seek to mislead, by omitting information or keeping their statements so vague as to lack meaning. A direct lie, he was reasonably certain, would be a violation of customs that dated back thousands of years.

And just now the Hanev had said this was not a matter that involved humans. Tobias had been certain beyond doubt that Orzili and his allies sent the Belvora. Could he have been wrong?

He refused to believe that the attack on Duvyn Castle was a random act. He and Mara had arrived here with the princess this very day, only to be hunted this night by demons that fed on magickal beings. It was too great a coincidence to ignore.

"We were more than prey," he said, ending a long silence. "The Belvora wanted us in particular. Isn't that so?"

After another pause, the Hanev said, "Belvora will feed on any magickal beings, and so, yes, they would have fed on you."

Tobias grinned in the darkness. A mistake.

"Do we amuse you, human?" the demon asked, the rasp in his voice more menacing this time. It reminded Tobias of Droë at her worst.

"I was not laughing at you, Ancient One," he said, sobering. "I was merely struck by the care with which you phrased your answer."

"Is that so?"

"Were you sent to kill us?"

"Our kind do not kill. We came here to take light from this structure, as we would take light from any human structure illuminated by flame."

Another evasion.

"Were the Belvora sent here to kill us?"

"As we have said, the winged ones hunt for magickal beings. Always."

Tobias opened his mouth to try again.

"We tire of this exchange," the Hanev said, perhaps to forestall questions that would be harder to evade. "We have told you the one thing that matters, the one thing that should tell you all you need to know."

"That this is not a matter for humans."

Tobias thought the demon would refuse to say more. The Ancient One surprised him. "Just so."

Commerce among Ancients then. Why would an Ancient send Belvora to kill them? What Ancient had they angered? Aiwi, the Tirribin they bested in the Knot? A Belvora that escaped them, or sought vengeance for the killing of their kind in the Sea of Wraiths or the bay at Vondehm? A third possibility presented itself in his mind, but before he could ponder the matter, the Hanev said, "We would have our light now."

"Of course, Ancient One. I will speak with the duke."

The huge shadow before him shifted, the way a man might alter his stance to put his weight on the other foot.

"That is acceptable."

"With our commerce done," Tobias said, "I would prefer not to have dealings with you again."

"Yes, we imagine so."

Tobias stifled another grin. "Would that be acceptable as well? Will you pledge not to help other Ancients prey upon us?"

The Hanev made a rumbling sound. "We regret that we cannot. You are clever for a human. We would pledge such if it were within our power to do so, but commerce may demand that we undertake another venture like tonight's. We beg your forgiveness."

Ancients rarely offered any sort of apology to humans. The Hanev would expect Tobias to be grateful, and to the extent that he could reconcile himself to possibly being hunted again, Tobias was.

"And you have it, Ancient One. You honor me."

Another rumble greeted this.

"Farewell, Ancient One."

Tobias started away from the shadow, hoping he didn't give offense by doing so. He heard ponderous steps beside him, the occasional snap of a twig or crinkle of dried leaves. The Hanev didn't speak to him again or try to stop him, but Tobias grew uncomfortable with their proximity to each other. When he reached the gate and entered the castle without the Hanev following, he breathed easier.

Risch awaited him in the courtyard.

"My men said you left the castle." His words carried a tinge of accusation.

"I did, my lord. I spoke with the Hanev."

Even with the grounds lit only by stars, Tobias could see that the duke stared at him.

"I cannot decide," Risch said after a fivecount, "if you are the most reckless man I know, or the most courageous."

"Can't I be both?"

The man let out a huff of laughter. "Yes, I suppose you can."

"The Hanev was helpful. I promised him that you would relight the torches once or twice and allow him to take their light."

Risch frowned. "You want me to feed it."

"It's a matter of commerce. With an Ancient."

The duke blew out a breath. "All right." He whirled away, barked orders to the soldiers atop the ramparts.

Tobias entered the duke's hall and found Mara, who lay on a low pallet, a damp cloth on her forehead, her eyes closed. He knelt beside her, whispered her name. No response. Fear rose in his chest.

"She'll be all right."

Tobias looked back. The healer stood behind him, his sleeves rolled to the elbow, sweat shining on his face.

"Has she woken?"

"Yes, briefly. She emptied her stomach when she did—that's not uncommon with head wounds. I gave her a draught to make her sleep, and I reduced the swelling on the back of her head and on her brow. She needs rest, but I expect her to be well in a day or two."

"Thank you." Tobias blinked away tears of relief. "And the others? The duke's soldiers."

"Those who were wounded should recover. I fear one woman might lose an arm. Time will tell."

"You're to be commended, healer."

"You're kind." The man moved on.

Tobias leaned close to Mara, kissed her cheek, the one that bore a scar from another Belvora attack. Theirs had been a fraught path.

"I love you," he whispered, the words stirring her hair. "Rest well. I'll see you come morning."

He left her there, made his way to the quarters of the duchess. Almost the moment he knocked, the door flew open, revealing Corinne, worry sharpening her features. She held a finger to her lips, joined him in the corridor, and closed the door with care.

"Your daughter is asleep," she said. "How fares the duke?"

"He's well, my lady. He came through the fight without injury."

She closed her eyes for a heartbeat, murmured a prayer of thanks. "And the others? Mara?"

"Mara was wounded, but she'll recover. The same can be said for most of the duke's guards."

Her forehead furrowed. "Most?"

"Two were killed."

"And the demons?"

"All the Belvora are dead."

She made no mention of the Hanev, and for now Tobias thought it best to say nothing about the Ancient, lest he renew her fears. Instead, he asked to see Sofya.

She lay on a small pallet that had been set near the hearth. Her eyes fluttered when he kissed her and shifted her blanket, but she remained asleep.

"She can stay here tonight," Corinne said. "There's no need to move her."

This suited his intentions well, but he didn't tell her as much. He merely thanked her and left.

He found Risch again, told him he needed to leave the castle one more time. He didn't explain himself. The duke scowled but didn't try to stop him.

"You're armed?" was all he said.

Tobias was, of course.

He followed a winding lane away from the castle, through the dark streets of Duvyn proper to the waterfront, and finally south along the eastern shoreline leading away from the city. Stands of pine loomed behind him, fragrant, rustling in a light breeze.

As he walked, he continued to reflect upon his exchange with the Hanev. Since coming to this time, he had interacted with a number of Ancients, fighting some, befriending others, engaging in commerce of one sort or another with most of them.

Belvora were hunters. They understood the interplay between predator and prey, even if prey sometimes prevailed. They were unlikely to seek revenge for others of their kind who were killed in a battle.

Aiwi had been humiliated in front of the Arrokad, Ujie, who wrung from her a promise that she would never trouble Tobias and Mara again. He didn't think she would risk the wrath of a Most Ancient One by seeking vengeance.

Droë had no reason to wish them harm. Neither did Ujie. Or Maeli and Teelo.

There was one other Ancient with whom they'd had contact, though at the time this demon had shown little interest in Tobias and Mara, and even less in Sofya.

That said, the other Arrokad, the one who had come aboard the *Sea Dove* with Droë in her adult form, did have cause to wish them ill. They had witnessed his humiliation, had watched as Droë threw off his control and made him subservient to her.

Qiyed. That was the name.

Might he have sent the Hanev and the Belvora?

This is not a matter that concerns humans...

He had taken Orzili all the way to Flynse. Or Droë commanded him to do as much. Who knew what they discussed as they journeyed so far? Even for an Arrokad, such a journey would have taken several bells. What if they had engaged in commerce of their own?

Orzili was dangerous, a foe to be respected, even feared. Having an Arrokad as an enemy would carry perils of an entirely different order.

Tobias walked along the coast, parallel to the roiled tideline of the Firth of Rime. When he was far enough from the city—from any human habitation—he halted, faced the water line, and said, "I would speak with Droë of the Tirribin. I am her friend and a Walker. I am Tobias Doljan."

His words sounded thin, a needle seeking to penetrate the slap of waves, the wind, the night, leagues upon leagues. Nevertheless, he remained there, staring out across the firth, waiting for an answer to his summons.

CHAPTER EIGHT

18th Day of Kheraya's Settling, Year 634

"Ujie."

The rush and retreat of waves swallowed her words. Cool brine lapped at her toes.

Droë shivered, though the night wasn't particularly cold. Summoning the Arrokad might have been a terrible error. At the very least, she would need to reveal difficult truths before she asked anything more of the Most Ancient One.

Her desire for Tobias, twined with the anguish of realizing that he loved another and would never be hers, still seared her heart. Had she angled her body even slightly, adjusted her line of sight only a little, she would have seen the ship on which he and his woman sailed.

It was not too late for her to return to the vessel, kill the woman, and claim him as her own. Except no. That had never been a possibility. Not really. She knew that now. With this matured body and her more nuanced understanding of love came as well an awareness of how foolish her dreams of being with Tobias had been.

She didn't allow herself even to glance at his ship. It might have been within sight, but it had already passed beyond her reach.

She didn't have to wait long for the Arrokad. Droë spotted her as she surfaced, a pale oval face framed by dark hair and inky waters. Ujie dove, emerged again closer to shore, dove a second time.

When next she rose from the bay, she was near enough to stand and slosh through the shallows to where Droë waited.

She was as Droë remembered her: beautiful, remote, austere, her eyes serpentine and as silver as star glow. The Arrokad halted a short distance from her, appraised her with a sweeping gaze.

"Cousin," she said, her voice like swells surging through kelp. "You are...changed."

It seemed Ujie both remembered her and recognized her. She hadn't doubted the former but had feared she would have to explain to the Most Ancient One who she was. That would have been humiliating beyond words.

She kept her chin raised. "I am."

"You found an Arrokad to do this for you."

"I did."

"Against my advice, in spite of my warnings."

"Yes. I wanted this, more than anything. I made a terrible error."

"I am sorry to hear it. But if you have summoned me to undo this thing—"

"I haven't. I know better. I will live in this form, with the consequences of my misplaced desires, for the rest of my existence. However belatedly, I have learned from this." She essayed a smile and gave a quick shake of her head. "No, I summoned you because I wish to be away from this place. The Arrokad who did this will be searching for me. He has reasons to wish me ill, and I have reasons to hope I never see him again. I would ask that you carry me from here across the sea, in whatever direction you wish to go."

"You would ask me to set myself against one of my kind? To interfere in your commerce."

Droë bristled. "I am not simple, Most Ancient One, nor am I a fool. My commerce with the Arrokad is ended. I ended it, with his agreement, reluctant though it was. But he is violent and cruel, and he will feel that I wronged him by speaking of certain things in front of humans. I don't wish to treat with him ever again."

"Do you fear him?"

She weighed the question. "I am stronger than he is, and more clever, despite his vast knowledge of the world, which exceeds my own. I am faster than he, at least on land. I believe if I had to, I could defend myself or escape him. That said, I do not wish for a confrontation with him. I...I do not like the way he makes me feel. And I suspect that any attempt on his part to do me harm would be insidious—difficult to anticipate and perhaps impossible to prevent."

Ujie canted her head. "A subtle response. More than you would have offered some turns ago. You *are* changed," she said again, the words sounding more certain this time.

The statement did not demand a response, so Droë offered none. Rather, she waited.

After a long silence, Ujie smiled, sly and amused. "Very much changed." She lowered herself to the sand, folding her legs beneath her. She gestured for Droë to sit as well.

"You ask a good deal of me—a boon in addition to your summons. What would you offer me as recompense?"

Droë was slow to answer. She had erred from the start in her dealings with Qiyed by bargaining in haste, carelessly, recklessly even. She would not make that mistake again.

"I retain my time sense," she said. "I am more powerful now than I have ever been, and I have wisdom I did not have in my child form."

"Interesting. Your time sense in particular could prove useful. Might you be willing to tell me more about the Arrokad who brought you to maturity?"

Droë pondered this. "Perhaps, yes."

"And now that you are mature in form, are you able to engage in...sport?" Another smile curved her lips.

Droë's cheeks warmed. In her child form, she would have dropped her gaze. She might have called the Arrokad rude and used this as a pretense to end their conversation.

She did none of these things. Meeting Ujie's hungry gaze, she said, "That is a subject we can discuss in the future. It will not be part of any bargain we strike."

Ujie straightened, her smile fading. "You wear your years well, cousin. This is acceptable to me. I propose that we journey together starting tonight—now, if you wish it. You can tell me the tale of your transformation. I would consider that payment for the summons and for this first leg of our journey. Beyond that I make no promises and ask none of you. Is this acceptable?"

Droë sifted through the words, searching for snares, phrases that one might construe in different ways. Her days with Qiyed had left her leery. She sensed no subterfuge in Ujie's offer, but Arrokad were canny negotiators. After a spirecount or more during which she said nothing, she began to feel that she was being rude. Ujie had come to her, was offering a boon for relatively little in return. More to the point, Droë's instincts told her Ujie could be trusted. The very first night she met Qiyed, she was wary of him.

"It is acceptable," she said. "Freely entered and fairly sworn."

Ujie gave a decisive nod. "Freely entered and fairly sworn."

She stood, the movement as liquid and smooth as an ocean swell. "I would bear you if will let me."

Droë rose and followed her into the surf. When Ujie halted and motioned for Droë to climb onto her back, she hesitated. She was close enough now to smell the Arrokad—sea and rain, lightning and foam and wind. She could have remained as she was, breathing in the Most Ancient One, for days on end and she would never have tired of it.

Qiyed had smelled lovely as well, had been beautiful in his own right. Then again, his scent had been more astringent, his beauty harder, more honed.

"You are reluctant?" Ujie asked over her shoulder.

"No, Most Ancient One. I am... You smell of storms and tides. I was... I like it."

The Arrokad favored her with a heart-staggering smile. "Come, Droë. Swim with me."

That night, as Ujie proposed, they spoke of Droë's transformation. Droë told her all that she could remember of each magickal push Qiyed gave her—how each one felt, what the effects were, how they changed her body and her mind.

Occasionally, Ujie prompted her with questions or had her repeat certain phrases. No detail seemed too small to snag her attention, or too private to prevent her from seeking clarification. Maybe Droë should have balked at answering some questions. The old Droë, in her Tirribin form, would surely have objected to some lines of inquiry, would have called the Arrokad rude.

Now she didn't mind, not even when, close to dawn, Ujie steered their discussion to Qiyed's final act of magick: his awakening of her desire.

Ujie's questions about that wondrous, unsettling night were as probing and bold as all her other questions. Droë answered them as honestly as she could, her face aflame the entire time. If the Most Ancient One noticed her discomfort, she had the grace to say nothing about it.

There was but one question the Arrokad never asked, though Droë expected it throughout the night.

Ujie did not ask for Qiyed's name.

In time, with the sky above them still black and filled with stars, Ujie brought them to land in a small village at the southern tip of Vleros. Droë crept into the village to hunt, but found few humans abroad, all of them in a single cluster. Unable to feed, she returned to the shore and spoke Ujie's name. The Arrokad came to her almost instantly.

When Droë told her she hadn't found prey, Ujie carried her

northward to a larger town, where Droë had more success. Soon they were on the sea once more. Having eaten, and having endured much this one night—her confrontation with Qiyed, her encounter with Tobias and Mara, her negotiation with Ujie—Droë could barely keep awake.

"Then do not," Ujie said when Droë told her this. "I do not expect you to go without rest, cousin. And I will not let you drown. You have my word."

Droë smiled at this, surprised by the Most Ancient One's kindness.

Ujie stopped swimming, turned to face her, while keeping her afloat in the gentle currents of the Bone Sea. Her expression had grown grim. "What did he do to you, this Arrokad with whom you traveled?"

This once, Droë found it difficult to look her in the eye. "As I told you," she said, voice low, "he was cruel."

The Arrokad dipped her chin, grim still. Angry, it seemed. "We will speak of this. For now, rest. I will carry you while you sleep."

She turned, held Droë to her back, swam at speed over the sea.

Droë slept, trusting her to keep her word.

They continued their conversation over the next several nights. Their bargain had been explicit about only the one evening, but neither of them mentioned this. Droë was content to stay with the Most Ancient One, and she sensed that Ujie enjoyed her company.

She was keenly interested in the other Arrokad and his treatment of Droë, but she continued to refrain from asking for Qiyed's name. Droë didn't know if she would consider the question a violation of their agreement, or if she simply didn't care. Another possibility occurred to her, but she said nothing. When Ujie wanted to know—if she ever did—she would ask. She had proven herself immune to diffidence.

They circled Oaqamar, threaded through the Sisters and the

Labyrinth, lingered in the quiet waters around Chayde and Flynse. Swimming with Ujie was every bit as exhilarating as it had been with Qiyed. More so, in fact, since she didn't spend each moment of each day on guard for another assault, or plotting her escape from the thrall of a Most Ancient One. Ujie treated her with courtesy, with kindness. At times this made her suspicious. Might the Arrokad seek to unbalance Droë with generosity and then take advantage of her, or even harm her? As much as she wanted to abandon all to trust, she couldn't.

One evening, as they skimmed over whitecaps in Kheraya's Ocean back toward the Sea of the Labyrinth, Ujie said, "Tell me why you are not with the human. He is the one whose love you sought is he not? The reason for your change?"

"He is." She stared past Ujie's shoulder and neck over the roughened sea. "I'm not with him because he doesn't love me. He loves another. As you told me, I believe, when we spoke of this, before my change."

"I was unkind to you that night," Ujie said. Unexpected, yet nothing compared with what she said next. "I would ask you to forgive me for some of the things I said."

"I... There is nothing to forgive, cousin."

"I disagree."

"Then I forgive, and I ask that you give it no more thought."

"A kindness?"

"Repayment for not letting me drown."

Ujie glanced back at her. Droë crooked a smile.

"So he loves another," the Arrokad prompted.

Droë adjusted her hold on the Most Ancient One's neck as spray from a wave dampened her face.

"He does." Admitting this stung less than she expected. "And they have created a family together."

"A pretense. A gambit to keep the child safe."

"Yes, but more than that as well."

Ujie didn't answer.

"I considered killing the woman," she admitted. "I dreamed of taking her years so that she would be gone and he would have no choice but to love me."

"Why did you spare her?"

"Because love doesn't work that way. Once I would have thought it did, but by that night I knew better. He would mourn her and hate me. It would have been petty. An empty vengeance. Years taken and then forgotten, like any human on any lane in any city. It would not have given me what I sought." She faltered. "And it would have made him unhappy, which I also didn't want."

"You learned well, cousin. Despite all Qiyed did to you."

Droë started. Ujie slowed, perhaps only now realizing what she had said.

"How do you know his name?" Droë asked.

Silence for a tencount.

"Ujie?"

"I have had dealings with him. I thought it might be him the first time you mentioned him, but I was not certain. The more you told me, however, the more certain I grew. His name has been in my mind for days now."

"Yet you didn't ask me."

"I expected you would tell me when you were ready."

"And I expected you would ask when you wished to know."

They fell silent for a time. Questions flooded her mind, but she didn't know which were permitted. One did not demand too much of the Most Ancient.

"He *is* cruel," Ujie said after some time. "There is a darkness in him that I have never understood. It was ill-fortune that led you to him. Almost any other Arrokad would have been a better choice."

"I would imagine that any other Arrokad would have refused my request, as you did. It's possible the darkness was not only in Qiyed, but also in me, in what I wanted."

Ujie halted again, turned, put her arms around Droë, holding her afloat, but also... holding. "You blame yourself for the things he did to you?"

She didn't know how to answer. The truth was, she did blame

herself, at least in part. She also knew that this was misguided, a continuation of the torment to which he subjected her.

Ujie touched her lips to Droë's brow, something Droë had seen human mothers do to their children. A gesture of love, of comfort.

"Thank you, Most Ancient One."

Ujie faced forward and swam on. Droë clung to her.

Over the next ha'turn, they continued to journey together. Ujie did not appear to have as much purpose in her wanderings as had Qiyed. He attended gatherings of Ancients, menaced Tirribin and Shonla with whom he'd had dealings in the past, and sought out humans for sexual encounters on nearly every isle.

Ujie, it seemed to Droë, journeyed to explore, to find adventure, for the sheer joy of movement, and for the simple reason that she could go anywhere she chose.

As their time together went on, their conversations ranged. There was just so much Droë could say about her transformation and her interactions with Qiyed. They spoke of the mundane—the foibles of humans and other Ancients, shifts in the weather, Ujie's favorite delicacies. And they spoke as well—mostly Ujie spoke and Droë listened—of things Droë scarcely understood: of history so ancient it had slipped into the realm of myth, of phenomena the Most Ancient One had witnessed over the millennia—earth tremors, meteors, enormous waves that had swept away entire isles.

Sometimes they spoke not at all. They had gone entire days without a word passing between them, not because one was angry with the other, but merely because nothing needed to be said. For Droë, who had spent much of life alone, these were, in many ways, the best days of all. She had never imagined that being with another—human or Ancient—could be so...easy.

Early in Sipar's Stirring, they crossed from the isles of the Knot toward the Inward Sea through a heavy storm. The sea pounded at them with swells that would have towered over both, even if they could stand on the water's surface.

A warm autumn wind—rare in these waters, Ujie said—howled over the waves. Tongues of Lighting tasted the sea on all sides. Thunder rumbled continuously, one clap blending into the next.

The storm posed no danger to them, of course. Ujie dove through the waves with the abandon of a human child, and actually laughed aloud once or twice. Droë clung to her with more urgency than usual, but she enjoyed the rough waters as well. On land she had paid little heed to rain and thunder and wind. She was a creature of the lanes, a predator, and storms drove humans indoors, making hunting more difficult. Other than that, weather meant little to her. Out here, however...

She had never seen anything more beautiful than lightning carving across the sky and igniting clouds from within. She watched the storm, avid, anticipating the next flash, trying to guess where and when it would come. It was fascinating, like the most delicious of riddles.

Thunder roared the first time Ujie spoke the words; Droë didn't hear her, didn't even know she had spoken. The Arrokad stopped swimming and faced Droë. She held her afloat with one hand and pointed with the other. Droë stared off in the direction she indicated, squinting in the rain, trying to see over the swells.

Another glimmer of lightning lit the sea. A flicker, no more. But that was enough. Her eyes might not have been as keen as Ujie's, but she remained a hunter.

"A ship," she said over the gale and the splatter of rain.

"Yes. They are struggling in the storm. I do not believe they can survive this night without our aid. Shall we go to them, or continue on our way and let them perish?"

She asked this the way she might ask if they should go north or west across an expanse of sea.

"You would let them die?"

Ujie lifted a pale shoulder, silver eyes on the vessel. "I have allowed humans to die in the past. And I have saved others. Humans die every day. It is not our responsibility."

"I know." Droë watched the ship as well. Compared to some vessels she had seen, this one was small—a Kant, she guessed. Her sails were down; oars jutted from her hull. She listed heavily to one side and waves pounded her like fists. Droë wondered if her crew were already dead, washed overboard.

"You wish to save them." A statement.

"I'm not certain. I've never faced such a choice. It seems wrong to let them die if we can prevent it. And yet I wouldn't hesitate to take the years of one of them, or even all of them over time." She faced the Arrokad. "What does that make me?"

"I do not believe it makes you one thing or another. We are Ancients. On occasion we confront moments such as these." She motioned Droë onto her back. "Let us help them. That seems to be your preference." She peered back over her shoulder. "They may repay us in some way. Humans can be diverting, for a short while."

Droë wasn't sure what Ujie meant, though she had an inkling, one that unsettled her.

They closed the distance to the ship in little more than a spire-count. Upon reaching it, Droë detached herself from the Most Ancient one and together they climbed onto the deck. The ship rolled and bucked, and too late Droë remembered that she didn't like ships. Experiencing the sea with Ujie didn't bother her at all, but the vessel's motion disoriented her.

Men and women of the crew went still at the sight of them. Most had ropes tied around their waists. A few clung to lines that hung from the ship's rigging. One of the ship's spars had broken and fallen to the deck, where it punctured the wood.

"Who are you?" one of the sailors finally asked. He was white-haired but straight-backed, tall and hale. Droë guessed that he had many good years left. If he survived this night.

"I am Ujie. This is Droë. We would help you, if you wish it."

The humans exchanged glances.

"Where is your captain?" the Arrokad asked.

"Gone," the man said. "Swept away. I was first mate, so I suppose I'm in charge now."

Ujie didn't respond, but watched the man, motionless, perfectly balanced, unaffected by the motion of the ship. In that instant, Droë thought her the most captivating being she had ever seen.

"If you can help us...well, we'd be grateful."

"Very well." Ujie pivoted, as graceful as a heron. "Droë, I would like you to take the helm and steer the ship after me."

"After— I don't understand."

"I will be in the sea ahead of the vessel. Human eyes are weak. They will not be able to see me. You will."

"What will you do?"

"Calm the seas enough to make them navigable. Together we will steer them to an isle. There are a few small ones east of here, near enough, I believe." To the first mate, she said, "Is this acceptable?"

"I think so. You want us to row?"

"Raising sails in this wind would be inadvisable, would it not?"

The old sailor frowned. "I suppose."

"I can smooth the sea, or I can ease the wind. I do not believe I can manage both in a storm of this size. Which would you prefer?"

"The sea," he said without pause.

"Very well. You know what to do?" she asked Droë.

"I think so. I haven't steered a ship before."

"It's not so hard," the man said. "I'll show you."

In short order, Ujie had returned to the waves, Droë had taken hold of the ship's wheel, and the first mate, whose name was Gaven, had taught her to steer. As he promised, this was not difficult.

Ujie swam ahead of the vessel, her form tiny in the vastness of the sea. Somehow, she smoothed the swells directly in their path, allowing the ship's crew to row them, despite the storm raging all around. She guided them for the better part of two bells, through rain and wind and those jagged, brilliant streaks of lightning, until, at last, they came within sight of a cluster of small islands. Some were no larger than oversized rocks, under assault by the sea, white with plumes of foam. Others were larger, with small patches of sandy beach and tight copses of wind-bent trees.

Ujie led them through shoals toward one of these. When the ship could go no farther without coming aground, Gaven had sailors lower the anchor and shuttle crew members to the isle on the ship's small rowboat.

Before long, all were safely on land. Ujie emerged from the water, her steps plodding, her breathing heavy. Droë had never seen her like this, and she hurried to her side, concern squeezing her heart.

"I am all right," the Arrokad said. "That was not easy, even for one like me."

Droë led her to the strand, where Gaven waited with the rest of his crew.

"We're in your debt, Most Ancient One," he said. None too wisely.

"You acknowledge a debt, human?" Ujie said, raising her eyes to his.

He flinched from her gaze, but he seemed to understand that there was no retreating from what he had said. "I do."

"Good." The Arrokad scanned the faces arrayed before her, desire in the look. "We would each choose one of you for sport," she said. "Payment for what we have done."

The sailors, soaked and exhausted, traded glances, most of them fearful, a few appearing eager.

"Do not be afraid," Ujie said. "Whoever we choose shall survive the night, and they will derive much pleasure from it."

Droë's face warmed. Qiyed had imparted desire and passion to her, but since that one night, she had not experienced it again. She wasn't certain she wanted to, at least not with one of these humans.

"Ujie, I'm not—"

The Most Ancient One silenced her with a raised hand. She

strode away. Droë followed. When they were beyond the hearing of the sailors, Ujie halted, faced her.

"This is commerce," she said, her voice level. "It would be better if you did not contradict me in front of them."

"I'm sorry."

Ujie waved the apology away. "I am not angry. Just...remember. For next time."

"Of course."

"You do not wish to couple with one of these humans?"

Her face burned. "I don't... I never have. With anyone."

The Arrokad smiled, tipped her head. "You might enjoy it. As I recall, you wanted to experience love, the emotion and the act. The emotion you have known, albeit not to your satisfaction. The act is not always tied to the emotion. It can be, of course. But it can also simply be the deriving of pleasure from another. Think of this as an opportunity."

Droë started to answer, stopped herself, flustered. "I— I don't know what to do."

"I would guess that whichever human you choose will know."

"Whichever...but how do I choose?"

"Do you prefer a man or a woman?"

Panic crept up her chest. "I don't know!"

"You do not have to do this, Droë. I will not force you, nor will any of the humans."

Droë considered saying that she didn't, that she would sit on the sand and watch the lightning while Ujie amused herself. But the idea of this bothered her. Perhaps she *did* wish to try.

"For the longest time I thought only of loving men," she said. "I would be willing to...to try either."

"Women tend to be more gentle, though not always. And they have a better sense of what will arouse you. Men, with some exceptions, can be quite clumsy in this regard. Especially the younger, prettier ones. On the other hand, some men are quite entertaining."

"Who do you intend to choose?"

Ujie stared past her, back toward the humans. "There is a

woman I noticed. She didn't look afraid as some of the others did. Dark-skinned, bronze hair. From the Labyrinth, I would assume. I believe I shall choose her."

"Will you allow her to refuse?"

"Yes. It is said that some of my kind take whom they please, regardless of what the human wants. I am not one of those."

Droë decided that she would not be either. There was, however, another problem.

"I'm hungry," she said.

"Interesting. I believe the humans would not have asked for our help had they known you would wish to feed on one of them when their ship was safe."

"You think I shouldn't feed here."

"You can if you wish to, of course. I won't stop you, and none of them could. Still, I think it would be better if you were to wait."

"Then I will. And I have made my choice."

A smile. "You're certain?"

Droë straightened. "I have waited long enough."

"Very well."

They walked to where the sailors waited. Ujie pointed at the woman she had mentioned. She was young, pretty, with a round figure and plump cheeks. She glanced self-consciously at her comrades, but she didn't hesitate to step forward and offer her hand to the Arrokad. Ujie led her away to the far end of the strand.

"I would choose you, if you'll have me," Droë said, leveling a finger at Gaven. Her pulse raced, but her hand remained steady.

The man's eyes widened. "Me?"

"Yes. Do you enjoy coupling with women?"

"Well...Yes...I mean...Yes, I do."

"Then you shall couple with me."

"But... Are you sure? I mean...I'm old."

Droë eyed him critically. "You are, but you're also pleasing to look at." A thought came to her. "Are you too old? I have heard that when humans are too old, they don't function as well. Down there, I mean."

Someone behind Gaven snickered. Other sailors smirked.

"No, I'm not too old," he said, a hint of indignation in the words.

"Good. Come with me, then."

She started away, padding through the wet sand to the other end of the strand, away from Ujie. She glanced back once to make certain the man was following her. He was. It occurred to her that he might find her smell—the smell of all Tirribin—unpleasant.

She decided that she would say nothing of this. If he complained, she would let him leave her. She didn't expect that he would.

At the end of the beach, she halted, faced him. After an instant of uncertainty, she pulled off her shift and dropped it to the sand.

He stared at her, blinking in the rain and the flickering light of the storm.

"You might well be the most beautiful woman I've ever seen," he said.

She blushed. "You're kind. I'm not really a woman, though."

"Well, you're not an Arrokad either, are you?"

"No."

"Then what are you?"

She didn't tell him she was Tirribin. That would have scared him. "I'm me," she said. "And I've never been with anyone before."

He opened his mouth, closed it. "Well, all right then. I'll... I won't hurt you."

Droë nodded, solemn, scared, but ready as well. "Thank you."

CHAPTER NINE

9th Day of Sipar's Stirring, Year 634

She enjoyed her time with the human. Gaven was gentle, kind, and also skilled. At least he seemed so to Droë. She had no one to whom she could compare him, of course, but he pleased her. More than once.

After, she was eager to dress and be gone from the isle. And from him, truth be told. She did not wish to converse with him or even look at him after their coupling. Her own response—and his, if she was honest—embarrassed her. Once again, as she had the night Qiyed introduced her to passion, she wondered how humans treated with one another after surrendering all to their most animal needs and sensations. It was a mystery she would need to explore further. But not here, not this night with this man.

Besides, being with him in that way had left her ravenous, and she decided it would be rude to take his years after he pleased her so. She wanted to find Ujie and be on their way, preferably to an isle where she might find a meal and a place to sleep.

Droë thanked him—that struck her as the polite thing to do—and she let him kiss her one last time. She liked kissing. It felt good, without the complete loss of self-control that came with the rest of what they had done.

Gaven returned to his crew. Droë followed the waterline, suspecting she would find Ujie waiting for her at the edge of the sea. She was right.

The Arrokad reclined in the shallow surf, languid as a purring cat, her body glistening with brine and rain.

"I would leave when you are ready," Droë said. "I need to feed, and I agree that it wouldn't be right to take a member of the crew."

"Very well. You had a satisfying encounter?"

Droë reddened to the roots of her hair and stared to the side. "I did."

"Was it what you expected it to be? More? Less?"

"It was fine. All I expected."

Ujie angled her head. "Is there—"

"I wish to go," she said, eyes still averted. "I'm hungry."

"As you wish." The Most Ancient One stood, watching Droë as she did. Droë wouldn't look at her, but she sensed the Arrokad's concern. "Did the human hurt you?"

At that, Droë did meet the argent gaze. "No. He was kind. I...I have no complaints."

Ujie gestured, her hand blurring in a small circle. Acquiescence. They waded into the surf, Ujie allowed Droë to climb onto her back, and she swam away from the isle. Droë clung to her, regretting her behavior, the tone of her answers.

"Forgive me for being rude," she said eventually. "I am...embarrassed."

"At what?"

She considered the question with mounting frustration, not yet knowing how to speak of such things. "Everything," Droë said, the word coming out with both laughter and a sob.

Ujie slowed.

"Please don't," Droë whispered. "It will be easier for me to explain if I don't have to look at you, or know you're looking at me."

They accelerated again.

"How do you face them? After, I mean. I feel the things I do, and for those moments I have no control, no...composure."

"It is lovely, yes?"

"Yes! But also horrifying!"

Laughter shook Ujie's entire form. Droë clenched her jaw, anger and shame silencing her.

"Forgive me, cousin," Ujie said. "I do not mock you. Truly. I am merely amused by your honesty. Certainly, I can see how succumbing to newfound passion can be as mortifying as it is wondrous. We do surrender our composure in the act of love, even our dignity in some small way. This is why humans prefer that the emotion accompany the act. With love comes trust, which makes the act easier. And this is also why violations of a physical nature are so very evil. They betray trust, deny dignity, debase love."

Droë considered this. "You don't love the humans with whom you couple."

"No. I have been intimate with many, many humans—Ancients, too—over a span of thousands of years. I have genuinely loved very few of them. I have grown accustomed to that loss of composure. I look forward to it; I am not at all embarrassed by it. In time, you will feel this way as well."

Droë didn't argue with the Arrokad, but she wondered if this would ever be true for her.

They glided over rough seas, and then calmer ones as they emerged from the storm into a softer rain. Ujie steered them to the isle of Preszir, and a small fishing town along the southwestern shore. She left Droë near the wharves there before striking out on her own along the shoreline. The Arrokad didn't say so, but Droë sensed that she sought another human for "sport." She wondered if her hunger for such things would ever be so voracious.

A puzzle for another time. Right now, she wished to hunt. She scented the air, sensed years not far from where she walked. A woman, not truly young, but not old either. A fine way to begin her meal.

She crept along a shadowed lane that led away from the pier, placing her feet with care, intent on the human ahead of her, abandoning all to the hunt.

Careless.

Magick crashed over her like a breaker in a storm. She crumpled under the weight of it. A cry escaped her, only to die on her lips.

Agony in her chest. She clawed at her heart, tried to draw breath. Couldn't.

Qiyed.

She struggled to push him out, to use the power she had discovered and mastered in their time together.

Panic is the enemy. Hate is the enemy. I need only myself to prevail.

Nothing. If only she had shielded herself earlier, hadn't allowed him in. Now...now all was lost.

"Droënalka."

He stood over her. She hadn't seen him approach. Hadn't heard him. She might have been a predator, but he was Arrokad.

He was as beautiful as ever. Dark, silken hair, silver eyes, flawless chiseled features, a sculpted form that would have been the envy of any human male. He hadn't bothered to scale himself; he appeared to glory in his nakedness.

"I've been searching for you for some time," he said in a tone both light and hard, like a perfectly balanced blade. "I've been waiting for this."

She couldn't speak or scream for help. She tried to stand, found that her legs didn't work as they should. No part of her did.

"I know what you're thinking. We had an agreement, freely entered, fairly sworn. I wasn't to harm you ever again."

Droë managed to shift her eyes, to glare up at him. They did have such an agreement. He had broken it. Despite the threat of Distraint, formal censure by the Guild of Ancients.

"As I remember that agreement, I did not enter it freely. You had threatened me, humiliated me." He raised a hand to forestall a rebuttal. "Yes, I said I would agree. I even acknowledged your invocation of Distraint." He squatted before her. "Fortunately, none heard our exchange. None who matter. There were no other Ancients there that night. Only humans. You could bring a grievance before a gathering of the Guild, but who would believe you over me? Would Arrokad?" His grin exposed razor teeth. "I think not. Tirribin?" He shook his head. "You abandoned your own kind. Being Tirribin was not enough for you. You believe you are better than they are, more complete, wiser, rich with sophistication. They do not know, as I do, that you are none of those things. That you remain simple and foolish and a naïf. They will see the results of your transformation, however—this thing we did together." He motioned with an open graceful hand, encompassing all she was. "And they will know that you are not of their sept anymore. They will not believe or support you.

"Hanev? Belvora? Shonla? None will risk angering one of the Most Ancient by accepting your word against mine. You are alone, Droënalka, as I predicted not so long ago."

She despaired at the truths he spoke. It was possible that Tobias or one of the other humans had heard them forge their agreement that night on the ship, but he was right: no Ancient would care what a human said. Nor would any Ancient believe her over Qiyed or come to her rescue.

Except one.

She couldn't speak the name aloud, but in her mind, she shouted for Ujie. She hoped the Arrokad would hear.

"She is elsewhere," Qiyed said. "Engaged in sport now with a particularly attractive and ardent human male. I expect she will be occupied for some time."

He started to rise, stopped, wrinkled his nose. "You stink of human." His expression changed, brightening, though only after twisting another way first. "You have coupled this night. With a human male. How fascinating."

The weight on her chest had grown almost unbearable. Her vision blurred, spun. Consciousness began to slip away.

"Oh, no," he said. "I have more in mind for you than an easy death. Especially now that you seem to have overcome your...inhibitions."

The pressure eased. She gulped at precious air.

Qiyed seized her shift in his fist and lifted her off the ground, straightening to his full height. And with his free hand he struck her across the face, a bone-rattling blow that left her addled, pinpoints of white light swimming before her eyes.

"You were so strong that night," he said, hitting her a second time, and a third. "And you're so weak now. How did that happen?"

He landed one last punch, released her so that she collapsed again to the filthy street.

Droë tried to speak Ujie's name but couldn't make a sound. She tasted blood. Qiyed loomed over her again, looking down upon her as if she were detritus. He didn't move, but abruptly his hand was at her throat, his iron grip cutting off air again, crushing her.

She cried out, gripped by panic.

Panic is the enemy. Hate is the enemy. I need only myself to prevail.

"You cannot stop me," he said. "Nothing can, except my own will." And he did stop. "I will refrain from hurting you anymore than I have."

She glowered, knowing there was more, sensing that they had come to the crux of whatever he sought.

"I will spare you tonight, and during the days and nights to come. All you need to do is join me again. Journey with me as we journeyed before. Complete our arrangement, an arrangement you ended prematurely, in violation of the agreement we reached, freely and fairly."

She opened her mouth, tried without success to speak. He made the smallest of movements with his hand. The hand that had bruised her.

The clamp on her throat eased.

"I will not submit to you again," she said, her voice scraped thin. Where was her Tirribin rasp when she needed it? Where was her power, her strength?

"You would die instead?"

"Gladly."

"I can do anything to you. You know this. I can torture you, impose a slow death. I can take anything I want." This last he said pointedly.

Droë wished to be brave. Fists and kicks and suffocation she could endure, until they killed her. But to have him touch her in that way? To have him claim her so? From that, she quailed.

"I see your fear. I smell it. You speak bravely enough, but you know what I can do to you, and you are afraid. Was that bluster, the night you left me?"

"You know better. I bested you. And I can again."

He quirked an eyebrow. No more.

The invisible hand slapped her face, closed again around her neck. "You can do nothing to me."

This was intolerable. She closed her eyes, sunk into the memory of their time together, a memory she had shunned since calling for Ujie. She was not this helpless thing. Regret had made her question her decision to take this grown form. It had isolated her, made her other than she once had been. And yes, she missed being purely Tirribin. Now, belatedly, she recalled that there had been more to her change than loss. She was strong. She was clever. Most of all, she was free. That freedom had come at a cost. She had suffered too much as she prepared to throw off Qiyed's thrall. And he wanted her to go back?

"Never." She spoke the word, heard herself say it. Despite his magick at her throat.

Her power hadn't left her. He wasn't any stronger. He had surprised her, caught her unprepared, which, she now understood, she could never be again.

She sensed his magick, followed it from him, the figure menacing her, to the touch of it, that rigid hand holding her down.

And drawing on skills she had honed for days and days, only to forget them when the need for them vanished, she wrapped her own magick around his.

He snarled. A blow snapped her head to the side.

She fought through pain. Opened her eyes. Pushed herself up off gritty cobblestone.

Another blow. This one passed through her. She barely felt it.

He was taller than she, broader. Blood ran from her nose and a cut on her lip. She didn't care.

He attempted another magickal attack. When that brushed past her like a fall breeze, he reared back to hit her with his fist.

She blurred, was beside him when his hand flew through the space she had occupied an instant before. He had time to register shock, to turn his head her way.

Her own punch connected flush on his cheekbone, staggered him.

Qiyed lashed out with a foot. She was behind him before he had completed the kick. She shoved him with both hands. He stumbled, fell forward.

Magick assailed her from all sides. He rained blows upon her with his power. Not one of them connected.

After a tencount of this, the attack ceased. He stood, brushed off his hands with what little dignity he could muster.

"I will not allow you to harm me again."

"No? How do you intend to stop me?"

"As I did that night aboard the Walkers' ship, and as I just have again: by being better than you."

His laugh sounded strained. "You are the one who is bleeding, Droënalka, not I. You have never been better than me."

"Haven't I? Shall we continue this fight? Battle to the death? I'm ready, if you are. We can settle matters between us once and for all. If you prevail, so be it." She took a step toward him. "I think we both know you won't."

She blurred once more, behind him this time. She kicked him in the back of his knee, and he pitched onto the cobbles again. She grabbed a handful of his hair, yanked his head back, and stooped, her mouth at his neck.

"I held you like this once before and threatened to take all your years. I could do so now. I'm hungry. I was hunting when you found me. Shall I sate myself on your years, Most Ancient One?"

Qiyed didn't move. She sensed his terror.

She laughed, as he had a short time before. "You should leave," she said, releasing him.

Again he stood, putting some small distance between them. Not nearly enough to compensate for her speed, but she kept this to herself.

"There is still the matter of our arrangement," he said. "You cannot keep me from addressing the Guild."

"I think the Guild will listen to me, Qiyed. I may not have a sept, but I am not to be ignored. You know this as well as anyone. And if you dare accuse me before other Ancients, I will tell them that you have broken an agreement sworn on pain of Distraint."

"He did what?"

Droë and Qiyed both turned toward Ujie, who stood at the mouth of the lane.

"You're hurt," she said, seeing Droë's face. She growled, a rumble that seemed to emanate from the ground beneath her. Even knowing the Arrokad's wrath wasn't directed at her, Droë flinched at the sound.

Ujie shifted her glare to Qiyed, who had already edged away from her.

"You dare risk Distrait?"

"She lies!"

Ujie shook her head. "No, I do not believe she does. I have never known her to utter a false word, and I will say as much before every Guild gathering between the oceans if I must."

"She broke an arrangement. She has ignored fundamental rules of commerce, and *I* will say as much to the Guild."

"You are known to be false, Qiyed. Your reputation spans the seas." She walked to where Droë stood. "And if you ever touch her again, with your hand, with your magick, I will kill you, even if it means my death as well."

"You do not want me as an enemy, cousin. If you know my reputation, you know this to be true."

Ujie laughed. "You have been an enemy for a thousand years. You walk in darkness. Everything you touch is poisoned, though, as Droë has demonstrated, not fatally." Her smile melted. "Now, go. I do not wish to see you again."

Qiyed darted a glance at Droë, a sneer lifting his lip. She expected him to offer some parting word—a taunt or a threat. He did neither. He strode to the waterfront. He didn't look back, nor did he hurry, but she sensed that he was eager to be away from them. And with reason.

For the first time since she and Ujie began to travel together, it occurred to her that they were a formidable pair, unique in all of Islevale. For too long, she had considered herself the Arrokad's ward, dependent on her, guarded by her. But if she was Qiyed's equal, or more, wasn't she Ujie's equal as well?

The Most Ancient One watched her, concern mingling with something else that Droë couldn't name.

Ujie raised a hand, shifted a finger.

Magick feathered over Droë's face, easing the throb of her wounds. She knew without having to check that she no longer bled.

Perhaps it was too much to say that she was Ujie's equal. Or Qiyed's. She was wise enough to understand that equality in battle was not all, or even close to all.

"You fought him off," Ujie said.

"Eventually. Only after he hurt me. At first, before I remembered what I once learned to do, he could have killed me."

"And yet, you fought him off."

Droë smiled this time. "Yes, I did."

"It is true, about the Distraint?"

She nodded. "His attack on me was violation. It's also true that I ended my arrangement with him before he was ready."

"Because he hurt you."

"Yes."

Ujie waved this away, impatient. "That is not how commerce among Ancients works. The moment he harmed you, he invalidated whatever agreement you and he reached. Unless you gave him permission to hurt you as part of your negotiations."

"I did not."

"Then you are blameless." She stared in the direction he had gone. "I do not know where he will go from here, but we should leave."

"I need to feed. I haven't yet."

"Very well. Quickly. I do not fear him, but neither do I wish to fight him. Not tonight."

"You wouldn't fight him alone."

Ujie's expression softened. "I know that, and so does he. Still, it would be better if we avoided him."

"Of course, Most Ancient One."

Droë turned, intending to prowl the wharf.

"Droë."

She halted, faced the Arrokad again.

"I believe the time has come for you to stop calling me that. To you, I am Ujie. Nothing more."

This drew another smile. "All right."

Their journeying after that night changed in ways both subtle and significant. Ujie still asked occasional questions about the folds of time, and Droë continued to ask her about, well, everything else. The Arrokad had experienced so much, had seen every corner of every sea, had interacted, sometimes intimately, with all manner of human and Ancient. How could Droë not question her?

Their interactions, though, felt...different. They conversed more, expounded less. Droë told Ujie about her travels with the Shonla, Treszlish, only to have the Arrokad admit that she, too, enjoyed songs but had no ability to sing. Droë had missed singing for the Shonla and was happy to sing for Ujie as they sped over swells and troughs.

In time, Droë tired of life on the sea. Not of Ujie herself—that she didn't believe possible—but of waves and brine and constant motion. They agreed that they would separate for a time and resume their journeys at their mutual agreement.

The first place Droë asked Ujie to leave her, a turn and a half after their confrontation with Qiyed, was Hayncalde.

The Arrokad peered back at her, sly amusement in her gaze. "Revenge?"

"Nothing so crass," Droë said. "Though if I can humble the girl just a little...well, where would the harm be in that?"

Ujie's laughter was like the sloshing of the sea in a rocky inlet. "I would enjoy watching this, but of course I will not. Have a care, though," she added. "They are still Tirribin and dangerous as a pair."

"I will."

Later that night, Ujie carried her the length of the Gulf of Daerjen to the torches and lamplights of Hayncalde. She left Droë along the strand south of the city's waterfront, a jumbled expanse of sand and boulders that Droë recalled from her previous visit.

She followed the shoreline toward the city, watchful and tense. For all her talk of taming the Tirribin who had mocked and threatened her when last they met, she knew better than to dismiss Ujie's warnings. She was entering their demesne, putting herself at risk. If any Ancient in Islevale would join with Qiyed in seeking her destruction, it would be Maeli.

As she neared the wharves, she slowed, sensing...something. Time knew no boundaries—it cared nothing for human cities or kingdoms. Yet in this place, on this night, time tasted and smelled sour somehow, like meat left too long in the sun.

She had thought to wander the city and find the Tirribin by happenstance. Now she abandoned that plan.

"I would speak with the Tirribin who inhabit this city," she said, pitching her voice low so as not to attract the notice of humans. She knew her kind would hear.

Within moments, the two Tirribin stood before her, blinking in the light of a low gibbous moon. They remained much as she remembered, exquisite and nearly identical. Black hair, fine features, his eyes ghostly blue, hers palest green. Both of them looked pinched though. If they were human children, she would have said they had gone too long without food.

"What is it?" Maeli asked without her usual derision. "It is familiar somehow and yet..."

"You will not call me 'it,'" Droë said. "You have mocked me before, not so long ago. I am much changed since then and will not tolerate it now."

Teelo, who had been kind to her during their last encounter—or at least kinder—eyed her guardedly. "An interesting riddle, that."

"I would remember you," Maeli said. "You smell like Tirribin, but you're not. You have power—you're an Ancient—but I can't tell what kind. I don't like that. I'm not sure I like you."

Rude, but she was talking *to* Droë, instead of talking about her, which was something.

"I am Tirribin," she said, "despite how I look. When last you saw me, I appeared as you do: small, in child form. I have been transformed."

"Droë?" Teelo said, breathing her name.

She smiled. "Yes."

Maeli's eyes went wide. "How did you do this? And why?"

"I had help from a Most Ancient One, and I entered an agreement to effect this transformation for reasons of my own. I don't wish to be rude, but I will respectfully decline to share them with you."

"Why are you here?" Maeli asked. At a warning glance from Teelo, she added, "If I may be permitted to ask." The words seemed to be wrung from her.

The corners of Droë's mouth twitched. "I came intending to exact a small measure of revenge for the way you treated me last time."

"That's rude."

"No more so than telling me you don't like me."

Maeli's face fell. "Forgive me," she said.

Droë motioned, dismissing the apology. "My vengeance will

have to wait. Time is...wrong here. The city is rank with misfuture."

"We know," the boy said.

"Teelo!"

"She senses it," he said to Maeli. "Wouldn't it be helpful to have another here to help us learn the cause?"

Maeli didn't answer.

"Has it been like this for long?"

"I'm not certain," he said. "I think so. It was subtle at first, so we might not have been aware of when it began. It's getting worse."

Droë sensed the effect it was having on her. She felt queasy, as she might after eating years spoiled by misfuture. She could hardly imagine living with this day and night. In time, it would be like a poison in her blood.

"Is it making you ill?"

Teelo hesitated, then nodded. Maeli nodded, too, surprising her.

"I can help you get away from here. You can go to another isle."

"This is our home," Maeli said. "We don't want to leave."

"Then we should find out what's happening and try to stop it."

"You would help us?"

"If you would let me."

Maeli dropped her gaze, her mouth twisting. "That is...kind of you. More than I deserve, I fear."

"I intruded on your city. You had cause to want me gone."

Before Maeli could answer, Teelo's gaze sharpened. "You were searching for Tobias!" he said. "Did you find him?"

A twinge of remembered pain constricted her heart. "Yes, I did."

"Is he well?"

"When last I saw him, he seemed well enough."

"Did your...meeting with him go as you hoped it would?"

"Our interaction was satisfactory."

An evasion. Both of the Tirribin knew it, she was sure. Neither challenged her.

"Do you believe he may be connected to this haze of misfuture?" she asked them.

"I believe Walkers are," Teelo said. "I haven't sensed Tobias in some time—a very long time for a human."

Maeli stared up at the towers looming over the city. "There is at least one other Walker in the castle," she said.

"And you think that's who is doing this?"

The Tirribin shrugged, appearing to wince at what she sensed from within those walls. "I do. And I don't know how to make them stop."

24th Day of Sipar's Settling, Year 633

He has instructed them to watch the ancient door, knowing they think him mad. Cobwebs drape over the entryway in the back of the dungeon. Bones and rodent droppings and the desiccated corpses of mice and rats block the threshold. No one has used this door in a hundred years. That is what the guards would say if they didn't fear him so. And they would be right.

That doesn't mean the door won't be used later this night. Lenna has told him it will be.

A Walk back through time of a few turns. Likely no farther. She looks much the same when she arrives. Silver streaks in her bronze hair, tiny lines at the corners of her mouth. But he notices an odd, distant look in her lovely eyes that troubles him. Is this a product of her journey through time, or the result of something that will happen to her in a future of which he knows nothing? He shies from both possibilities.

He assumes she and he—the future him; journeys through time are enough to twist even the most agile of minds—have taken every precaution to ensure that she doesn't meet herself in this past.

She comes to him in his bedchamber, which should be enough to prevent such an occurrence. She hasn't set foot in his quarters in some time now. Whatever dreams he once had of loving this Lenna—of convincing her to love him—have long since died. She also has timed her arrival so that she comes to him in the middle of the night, waking him from a sound sleep. She dons his robe, her chronofor clutched in one hand, a lit candle in the other.

"He escapes." The words bald and harsh. No affection, no attempt to cushion these tidings, no hint of all they have shared over decades together.

"Who does?" His thoughts muddled with sleep.

"The boy. The Walker, Tobias. From your dungeon. You need to take precautions. Someone—servants of Sipar, you believe—will use the ancient tunnels under the city to free him from your prison and spirit him to safety. You sent me back to tell you this."

He remembers sitting up, can still see her eyes falling to his naked torso and darting back to meet his gaze.

"How soon?"

"Soon. As early as tonight—the coming night, not this one."

"Yes, all right. Thank you."

"Set guards on the old door at the back of the dungeon. Don't leave the boy unguarded."

"I understand."

"Good. Look the other way. I'm leaving now."

The cold efficiency of an assassin, which they both are, but still...

He does as she asks and only knows she is gone when he peeks over his shoulder to find the robe and candle on the floor near his bed.

He spends the entirety of the day thinking about their exchange, wondering what he can do to prevent Tobias's escape. He goes so far as to contemplate a move against the sanctuary itself, but quickly dismisses the idea. So soon after Mearlan's death, the Sheraighs' hold on Hayncalde remains too tenuous. Angering the city's populace with an occupation of the temple carries grave risks. Better to prevent the escape from within the dungeon. His men are well-trained. Surely, they can fight off a band of sword-wielding clerics. That is what he thinks.

Arrogance. Long has it been one of his great flaws.

In this case it has cost him four good men.

Four more stand behind him, silent, waiting for the eruption they must believe is imminent. He will surprise them. This is no one's fault but his own.

The four dead lie in a tight cluster, like an archipelago in a sea of blood. One has been decapitated, another gutted. His stench fills the dungeon. The last two have been slashed through their hearts.

Those cobwebs over the hidden doorway now hang in tatters,

and the debris on the floor before the entry has been disturbed. He turns away from the carnage, tells his men to clean up the mess, and assures them that they will find the lad again. Tobias can't elude them forever, he says.

He wonders, though. Lenna has Walked back to issue her warning. He has sent her back—her words. Given how stingy he is with her years, doesn't that suggest desperation? Clearly there is more to the Walker than Orzili has assumed.

He draws his sword, retrieves a torch from a nearby sconce, and pushes through the ancient stone door. It gives grudgingly, but makes not a sound as it swings inward. He enters the tunnel, walks perhaps one hundred strides with guards behind him before reaching the first of what he guesses must be a series of locked, iron doors. For which he possesses no key.

"Where does it lead?" one of the men asks, his voice echoing in the narrow passageway.

"These tunnels probably branch, and branch again—I'd wager they lead to every corner of the city. The boy could be anywhere."

But he's in Sipar's sanctuary. I know it.

He leads them back, leaves them to tend to their fallen comrades with the promise of a night off duty when they have finished. In the meantime, he needs to have a conversation with Lenna. Another one, it seems.

24th Day of Sipar's Settling, Year 633

He has lived this day before. Lenna tells him so. It seems she has sent him back once already to prevent Tobias's escape from the Hayncalde dungeon. To no avail.

Something about secret doors and ancient tunnels under the city. Last time—according to Lenna; he, of course, has no memory of any of this—he ordered men to watch the entryway and guard the boy. The night proved fatal for them. She doesn't tell him more than that, and he isn't certain he wants to know.

There are twelve of them this time. Including Orzili himself. If his men have doubted the gravity of this task, his presence here will convince them.

Lenna's visit to his bedchamber in the middle of the night is brief, her explanation terse, her tone icy. He wants to ask whether her Walk back through time was necessary; he doesn't wish to spend any more of her days than they have to. In the end, he swallows the question. She wouldn't have come back—twice now—if the boy hadn't proven elusive. Men have died trying to keep him in the dungeon!

"You told me to tell you not to be an arrogant fool," she says. "The people who won his freedom are willing to kill to get what they want. You should be too. That's what you said."

A fivecount later she is gone, leaving only a half-burned candle and a discarded robe to tell him he hasn't dreamed her.

He and his guards array themselves around the dungeon. He positions two men by the main entrance, and another two by Tobias, not that the Walker will be going anywhere. He can barely stand, much less walk. Or *Walk*.

The rest of the soldiers guard the back of the dungeon and that old door. His men eye the cobwebs and dead rats doubtfully, appearing unconvinced that anyone will use the entry after so many decades.

Lenna, however, is certain. She says *he* is certain.

Someone will be coming for the boy. Tonight. Probably from the sanctuary.

In the meantime, they turn their attention back to the Walker. As long as they must be in this accursed place, they will try again to learn of the princess's whereabouts. It isn't long before the boy's screams reverberate through the dungeon, blotting out all other sounds.

Foolishness and carelessness on his part.

He doesn't hear the initial screams of his own men until four of them are dead. Crossbow bolts to the neck, the temple—one improbable shot takes a man in the eye. The remaining three by the door are overpowered before Orzili even knows they are under attack.

A bolt buries itself in his shoulder, ripping a scream from his chest. He draws his sword with his left hand, excruciating pain pinning his right arm to his body. Swordswomen in white and gray swarm through the dungeon, overwhelming his men. One of the women disarms Orzili in a matter of moments. She slams him across the jaw with the hilt of her sword, knocking him to his knees. Her second blow explodes at the base of his skull, and all goes black.

When he wakes, the invading soldiers are gone. Eight of his men lie dead, blood pooling in low spots throughout the dungeon. Two of the others are unconscious. The third leans against the wall, blood staining his uniform, sweat glazing his face. Orzili fears he won't survive the night.

Tobias is gone, of course. The door to the tunnels is closed again. Tracks of blood lead to it. Orzili pushes himself to his feet, the torches and stones around him pitch and spin, as if he is on a ship in the most violent of storms. He braces himself against the nearest wall and empties his stomach.

He reclaims his sword, staggers to the ancient doorway, and pushes on the opening. The stone gives slowly, revealing a lightless tunnel. He grabs a torch, thrusts it into the passageway. More tracks. Trailing his hand along the rough wall, he follows the tunnel to a locked iron door. One of many, he's sure.

A part of him wants to lead the entire Sheraigh army to the gates of Sipar's sanctuary, the God and his clerics be damned. Another part of him knows the Sheraighs will never agree to such a gambit. They are too new to their power, the city's population too devoted to the God.

Tobias has escaped him. Again, though he doesn't remember the earlier instances. He needs to prevent this and doesn't know how. He can bring more men down into the dungeon, escalate the battle further still.

And next time that bolt in your shoulder might find your heart instead.

He hears the words in Lenna's voice, as if she has walked back from yet another iteration of their future to warn him.

Orzili plods back to the dungeon, closes the door, examines the stone of the entryway, wondering if there might be a way to drive iron into the walls and prevent the door from being opened. It would be easier if the door swung outward, rather than into the tunnel. Still, it might be done. Lenna can go back again—one last time—and instruct him to bar the door before bringing the boy here.

Yes, this is what he should have done sooner. The barb imbedded in his shoulder makes that much clear. He climbs the stairway to the main entrance and calls for help, the night air chilling the sweat on his face. He will need to see a healer first.

Then he will talk to Lenna.

24th Day of Sipar's Settling, Year 633

He is not a man prone to excessive drinking, or rather, he wasn't before this madness with the boy began. Yet here he sits, alone in his chamber, well into a second flask of Miejan red.

The warnings should have been enough to thwart Tobias's rescuers. Finally.

Iron on the door should have prevented any from entering the dungeon through those ancient tunnels. It should have prevented a recurrence of his failures. And in a way it has. Arrogance on his part. Again, it seems, though this, too, he must take on faith, on her knowledge of shifts in time and history and future.

Once the door is barred, he assumes the boy cannot get away. He makes no effort to increase the guard within the dungeon. His men have no desire to reside in that place for longer than their questioning of the Walker might require. And he has no desire to subject them to such unpleasantness.

On such trivial decisions are fates altered.

The boy is gone. Again. The ancient door—secured with iron so as to keep out whoever might free him—has been destroyed. Hammered to rubble.

He can send Lenna back again, of course, but he is reluctant.

She tells him he has done so already. She suspects she has come back several times.

Orzili has no awareness of such things, but he believes her, despite his reluctance to spend her days on futile Walks into an uncertain past. If the boy has escaped them before, if he has eluded them, perhaps even managing to leave Hayncalde, Pemin will have been furious, and Orzili will have been desperate.

She—the future her—also tells him that he returned from his last attempt to prevent Tobias's escape with a crossbow bolt in his shoulder. What perils might lurk in subsequent attempts to bend the past? Do any of them compare with the danger of reporting yet another failure to the autarch?

These are the questions that consume his wine-dulled mind, that have him reaching yet again for this second flask.

He does not wish to send her back even one more time. He doesn't like the vague, unfocused glaze he sees in those gorgeous eyes. And his shoulder aches with the suggestion of pain that he now will never know and does not wish to risk again.

He and Lenna are resourceful, canny. They have associates—he won't go so far as to call them friends—on every isle between the oceans. Tobias cannot elude them forever.

Is this why you let the boy's escape stand when first it happened? Has time proven your confidence naïve and facile? Is this the reason you sent her back again and, perhaps, again?

Uncertainty. Trepidation. He is not a man usually prone to either. Any more than he is a man who drinks to excess.

Orzili decides that he will wait to demand another Walk of her. Tobias is a boy in a man's body, forced to care for an infant. Given time, he is bound to make mistakes. Even Pemin cannot question such reasoning. They will find him eventually. Tobias's good fortune has to spend itself.

What if you've convinced yourself of this before?

He would prefer to have this conversation with Lenna. She might bring insight, relief from the appalling circularity of his own thinking. But she has no more interest in sharing his wine than she does in sharing his bed. No, in this, as in all things now, he is alone.

A laugh escapes him, startling the doves in their cage by the shuttered window. How maudlin he has become. How self-pitying and bitter. Is it any wonder she avoids him?

The hardest question of all. Better to ponder Pemin and the boy than to wander down that particular path.

His musings resume their orbit.

He drains his cup, pours out what remains of the flask, and calls for more.

CHAPTER TEN

8th Day of Kheraya's Stirring, Year 634

The moment she slipped out of Hayncalde Castle wearing the red dress she took from the half-crazed version of herself, Lenna felt as though iron bars had been lifted from her shoulders. She was free, spurred by the promise of a reunion with the Orzili she loved, and had loved since he was Cresten and her last name was Doen instead of Stenci.

Her departure from Hayncalde, and eventually Daerjen as well, proceeded precisely as the other Lenna said it would. Maybe the woman wasn't as crazed as Lenna thought. Orzili—this younger Orzili—would have his hands full with her. The idea of this brought a smile.

She carried an abundance of gold, easily enough to secure her passage to Belsan aboard a well-appointed merchant ship. The better vessels, particularly those flying the gold and blue banners of Aiyanth, reserved space in their hold for passengers, men and women who would eat and sail without the expectation of labor. Lenna had the means to buy herself onto such a ship.

Less than a ha'turn later, she disembarked in Aiyanth's royal city. The sea smelled different here: sweeter, cleaner. The sun burned brighter; the caress of the breeze seemed gentler. She was home.

She surveyed the lanes with care as she left the wharves. Orzili had an agent here: the woman, Gillian Ainfor. She might recognize Lenna. Their interaction had been brief, in a darkened chamber, but it had also been memorable. Lenna's own fault, that. Seeing the woman—likely the same servant of the autarchy whose missive had sent her back in time fourteen years—had unsettled her. Gillian would have noticed, and would recognize her.

Lenna crept through the city, smelled fish roasting on coals, heard gulls laughing overhead, passed the lane on which she and Orzili would live in the future. A future to which she intended to return this very day.

Her heart hovered with excitement, like a hunting falcon. Too long she had been away from him, captive of the younger Orzili, who had trapped her in this past, driven by a cruelty she had never seen in her beloved version of the man.

The guards at the city gate made no effort to stop her. Why would they? A woman of means. Yes, her skin was dark, her hair bronze, but here in the Axle, in the center of all Islevale, Northislers were common.

She followed the familiar road, and then the less-worn path she and Orzili took the night she left him. And found people in the clearing. A couple. Young, flushed with desire and excitement. Seeing her, the girl blushed and adjusted her gown; the boy grinned, buttoned his shirt. She left them and wandered farther along the road. At another time, under different circumstances, she might have found the encounter amusing. Today, impatience stifled her humor. She wished only to Walk, to see him, to be reassured that he still loved her, despite all the years she had lost in the Walk that brought her back to this time, and the one that would carry her forward to where she belonged.

In time, as the sun swung lower in the west, she retraced her steps to the clearing. The young lovers were gone. She sat on a low rock, awaiting dusk, nervousness driving her to her feet several times until, at last, she surrendered and paced.

As darkness crept over the surrounding wood and into the glade, she removed her clothing and piled it neatly under a bush. The day had been warm, but with evening had come chill, damp air. Her skin roughened, and vapor billowed with each breath.

Her purse, which held the remainder of her gold, she left in the middle of the clearing, near where the couple had been. Perhaps they would find it when next they visited this spot.

By the last light of the gloaming, she set her chronofor for the Walk. She had done the arithmetic every night aboard the ship from Daerjen, calculating and recalculating, counting years and turns and days and bells until she knew just how far the Walk back would be. The chronofor would not—could not—carry her past her proper future, but that didn't mean she could be haphazard with her calculations.

She was older than she'd been when she Walked back, and she didn't know how much her body could withstand. She would not attempt to cover all fourteen years in one Walk. She would go halfway and then reach home with her second Walk. Even that might prove too much for her, but how many times could she risk emerging from the between into this clearing? Going so far, she couldn't depend on precision. She might aim for night and arrive at midday, surprising other young lovers, or soldiers, or children. Two Walks then. Seven years each.

She set the chronofor for the first leg of her journey, took several breaths, bracing herself for what she knew would be an ordeal. Allowing herself one more deep breath, she pressed the central stem.

The between snatched her out of the peaceful glade into a storm of raging light, burning sensation, stomach-seizing tastes and odors, ear-battering clamor. She held her last breath for as long as she could, knew it wouldn't be long enough. Too soon, desperate instinct over-mastered logic and years of training: Even knowing she could not breathe in the between, she exhaled, gasped for more. The lack of air was like a fist in her throat, an anvil on her chest. Strange that an absence of something could press upon her so. Noise began to fade, the glare of sun and lamp and candle to darken. Not good. Not at all.

Tears ran from her eyes. Finally free, and fated only to perish.

The stench and the terrible assault on her tongue gentled. A small mercy—a gift at the end.

She awoke on the ground, shivering with cold, damp with rain. In darkness. She tried to move. Could not, save for a twitch of her hand. The back of her fingers brushed the chronofor, which rested beside her. She pawed at it but could not control her muscles enough to reclaim it. Had a thief come upon her at that moment, she would have lost the device. And that would have been the least of her worries.

The cold would kill her if she didn't soon regain control of her body.

You have to do that again.

A paralyzing thought.

She recovered slowly, but recover she did. In time, she struggled to her feet. She walked in tight circles, rubbing her arms, her legs, her hands. The rain fell harder. She wasn't going to get warm, but in time, she felt well enough to set the chronofor for the remaining turns and days. Dreading a second Walk, but eager to complete her journey, she halted in the middle of the glade, whispered a prayer, and pressed the stem a second time.

Lenna didn't remain conscious for the entirety of this second Walk, either. Neither did she die.

Awareness came slowly. Relative warmth. The rustle of wind in leaves. The subtle smell of lilac. The hooting of a nearby owl. She remembered this as a lovely night, bittersweet.

This time, she had managed to maintain her hold on the chronofor. She opened her eyes to dappled moon glow on her skin and the soft grass around her. When she could sit up, she scanned the clearing and spotted what she had known she would find. Her clothes, piled as she had left them. As he had left them as well. An act of love. For all she knew, Orzili—*her* Orzili—had only just left the clearing when she emerged from the between.

She rose on stiff legs, winced at an ache in her back. She started toward the clothes, then stopped, apprehension stealing her breath. A shaft of moonlight angled through the treetops to the grass of the glade. Lenna would have liked to postpone this, but she couldn't. Before she faced Orzili, she needed to know what the Walk had done.

She stepped into the silver light and stared down at her arms, her hands, her body.

Disappointment stabbed through her. She should have known. Time was as immutable as the between itself. She could gasp all she wanted as she Walked, and no air would come to her. In the same way, she could hope, and hope, and hope some more, but fourteen more years was just that.

Her hands were wrinkled and spotted with age. The flesh on her arms, which had been firm and muscled not so very long ago, now hung loose. The rest of her body...

Lenna sighed, walked away from the light to her clothes. Dried leaves lay on them, along with a thin layer of dust. Odd. She shook out the gown and undergarments and started to dress.

She could imagine what her face looked like: the lines in her cheeks, at her mouth and eyes. The white in her hair would have crowded out what was left of the bronze.

Orzili loved her, she told herself as she buttoned the gown. In any time. This Orzili most of all. He was kind, gentle—at least with her. *Come back to me,* he said the night she Walked fourteen years into the past. And so she had.

That was this night, she had to remind herself. For him, a bell or two might have passed. Surely no more. He would be back at their flat, mourning her, knowing the younger woman he loved was gone forever. She would be now the embodiment of his grief, proof of the injustice inflicted on them both by Pemin. Lenna was going back to him, but he would see her arrival as something utterly different. Not a reunion, but the return of someone he wouldn't wish to see. And probably could never love.

This gave her pause. She stood in the middle of the clearing, wondering if she should go elsewhere. Give him time—an irony—to grow accustomed to her absence before appearing before him as...as this old woman.

If she'd had any coin—anything at all that she could use to buy food or lodging, she might have put aside her eagerness to see him and left Belsan. As matters stood, she couldn't.

Or was that merely an excuse?

She forced herself into motion, strode from the clearing, followed the footpath, and then the road, back to the royal city.

The gate guards didn't stop her. They barely acknowledged her. An old woman? What threat could she pose? What enticement could she offer? She might as well have been invisible.

Was this what life held for her from this night forward? For most of her life she had taken for granted that she was beautiful, alluring, not to mention strong, skilled with weapons, and deadly with fists. She had always been someone of consequence, and, as much to the point, no one looking at her would have doubted this.

Now, however... She was certain she could still shoot or throw a blade. The techniques of hand combat remained fresh in her mind, though she didn't know what this aged body could do. She was experienced in the ways of assassination. She understood the nuances of court politics. Her mind had lost none of its sharpness. But there was still more to being an assassin.

How many men and women had she lured to their deaths with the promise of a tryst? How many guards and soldiers, merchants and city officials had revealed secrets to her, disarmed by a low-cut gown, or a flirtatious smile, or the simple act of unbinding and shaking loose her hair?

Those tools were lost to her now. No royal wished to bed a woman of such advanced years. No guards would stare hungrily at the swell of her bodice when they were supposed to look her in the eye. The Walks demanded of her by Pemin had robbed her of her youth. Without it, how would she earn her coin? This was a young person's profession.

For a second time, she balked at the notion of presenting herself to Orzili. For a second time, need drove her on. Need of gold, of a meal, of a place to pass the night. Mostly, need of him.

She hurried through the streets, turned down their lane, halted, swaying at the sight of their flat.

In truth, it hadn't been so long since last she trod these cobbles and saw this place. It felt like decades.

Lenna's legs trembled as she climbed the stairs to their door. Stopping before it, she hesitated, reached for the doorknob, faltered again, raised her fist to knock, lowered it. A breathless laugh escaped her. After enduring Walks that almost killed her, to be stymied by a door... She raised a hand again and rapped on the door before doubt could stop her.

Nothing happened. She heard no one within. Descending the stairway, she checked the window. Shuttered, but she thought she glimpsed candlelight leaking around the edges. She approached the door and knocked again, harder this time. After waiting for a spirecount or two, she pounded on the wood with the base of her fist.

The scrape of a chair. Heavy footsteps. The lock clicked, the door flew open, revealing Orzili. Hers. The one for whom she had pined every moment since leaving this time. His hair was disheveled, his shirt wrinkled. She smelled wine on his breath. A blade glinted in his hand.

His mouth was open, his eyes blazed. He had drawn breath to berate her for interrupting his reverie. Instead, he exhaled and stared at her, his mouth hanging open. His blade hand fell to his side.

At least he recognized her.

"Are you going to let me in?" she asked. Her voice, she was pleased to hear, sounded much the same.

"Yes, of course."

Still he stared. He didn't back away from the door—not immediately. He finally tore his gaze from her face, but only to look her over, head to toe.

"How long ago—"

"Tonight. I probably arrived back in the clearing only moments after you left it."

"No, I meant..." He shook his head, backed away from the door. "Come in. I'm sorry. I should have... You must be exhausted." *Because you look ancient.*

She stepped in, closed and locked the door behind her. It occurred to her as she did that this would not be the Orzili she had left behind. Not really. Foolish of her to think so. She had considered this Orzili as a man completely distinct from the one who had been so cruel to her in the past. He wasn't. Nor was he the same man who had left her in the clearing—within the past bell by his reckoning, turns ago by hers. All that had happened between her and the "other" Orzili was now part of this man's life. He would remember it all. He was changed. He had to be.

Eyeing him more closely, she saw that this was so. He had more silver in his hair than she remembered. Not just at his temples, but streaked throughout. He also wore his hair longer. He seemed wary of her. Not merely put off by her appearance, but mistrustful. It made sense. He would recall a version of her beating him senseless on the strand near Hayncalde. He might even suspect by now that the Lenna who remained with him in the castle after that day was not her, but rather the addled version of her he had pursued through the city's lanes.

She surveyed the flat, thinking that she would never have allowed it to become so cluttered. How long *had* she been gone?

"Wine?" he asked, already bearing a second cup.

"Yes, please."

He poured it for her, set the cup on a table before retreating to their larder.

"Bread? Cheese?"

"That would be lovely." She picked up the cup, sipped. Miejan red. Some things were immune to change.

A pause, and then, "Before, when I asked how long, I meant how long did you Walk today. To come back."

Lenna needed to tread carefully. Had he not yet learned of the deception she and the other Lenna perpetrated, she didn't wish to alert him now. Fortunately, this was easily avoided.

"I'm not sure I should tell you that. A long way. Years. Beyond that..."

"I understand."

She circled the room, pausing at the doorway at the far end to peer into their bedroom. It, too, was messier than she would have allowed, the bed unmade, clothes on the floor. His clothes. She didn't linger there, but she saw none of her own possessions. She couldn't recall precisely how she had left the chamber that last day. This day.

Lenna shook her head and heaved a breath. Navigating time could confound even the most skilled Walker.

She heard a footfall behind her, turned and sipped her wine again. Orzili set a small platter of food on the table where they always ate. He had to move a few items—an empty scabbard, a doublet, a rolled piece of parchment that might have been a missive from one court or another—from her usual seat.

"Come and sit. Have some supper."

She joined him at the table, thanked him. The bread was fresh, the cheese, a soft Daerjen blue, pungent and smooth. She savored a bite and then another, her gaze traveling the room until it settled on him.

"How long have I been gone?"

Orzili thinned a smile. "Ought I to answer? Don't the dangers of time and misfuture cut both ways?"

More mistrust even than she had anticipated.

"I suppose they can. Tell me this, then: As I recall this future, I left here this very night, only a bell or two ago. Yet, from what I can see of the flat, it seems you've been alone for far longer."

"I have."

"Days? Turns? Longer than that?"

"Somewhere between days and 'longer than that.'"

"And what terms were we on when we parted?"

He shrugged, gaze sliding away. "The usual, I suppose."

Lenna's heart clenched. For as long as she remembered, their life together had been filled with passion and love, adventure and laughter. Hardly "usual" in any way.

"I see."

"You remember it differently?"

She heard bitterness in the question, but longing as well.

"I remember loving you with a ferocity that I sense would be alien to you in this future."

She didn't shy from the look he gave her. In time, he shifted his eyes from hers, though only to study her: her face and hair and what he could see of her form. She refused to shrink from his scrutiny. Their love, she gathered, had long since been lost. That made it easier somehow. To see the man she loved, who was supposed to love her, appraise her so, would have been humiliating. It would have scored her heart.

This man... She hardly recognized him. Yes, he was beautiful, as she remembered. He was also diminished in ways she couldn't quite explain to herself. The Orzili she loved had been strong, confident to the point of arrogance, indomitable. Aside from Pemin, whom everyone in Islevale feared, he had been frightened of nothing, of no one.

The Orzili before her had lost much. Until this moment, she had never understood fully how much her own love contributed to the man she adored. Without it, she now realized, he was a shadow.

"I would have enjoyed being loved like that," he said after some time.

"But not by one as old as me."

He started to reply, stopped himself.

"It's all right. You are changed, Orzili. I recognize your face, but little else."

"Changed for the worse, I take it."

"You've lost something, yes."

"Lost what?"

"Us, I think. Being loved in that way...it strengthens a person, makes him, or her, more than he might otherwise be."

"I can't love you, Lenna."

"I'm not asking you to. I can't love you either. Not like this." She took another bite of cheese and bread, washed it down with the balance of her wine, but her appetite had fled. She set down the cup more loudly than she had intended. "I need a place to sleep tonight, and in the morning, I'll need coin and a blade."

"You can have the bed. I'll sleep out here. And I have plenty of blades. Coin... How much would you need?"

A plan had already begun to take shape in her mind. Purpose—vague for now, but insistent. A life beyond this place and without this man.

"As much as you can spare."

"I can give you a round or two, and some treys and quads. Beyond that—"

"That will do. Thank you."

He nodded. "If you don't mind," he said, speaking slowly, "I would like to see your chronofor."

Lenna frowned. He was no Walker. What did he know of devices like hers? Still, it was a small enough request. She pulled it from the pocket of her robe, held it in her palm, and extended her hand to him. He leaned closer, peered at it, but made no attempt to take it from her.

"Thank you."

"Why—"

At a shake of his head, she swallowed the rest of her question.

"It's nothing."

She thought otherwise and nearly said so. Thinking back on all that had happened in the past she had lived, she kept silent.

"There are others of you here, in this time," he said. "One at the very least. Maybe more. I know the danger of meeting yourself. You should be careful."

"Here, in Belsan?"

"To be perfectly honest, I don't know."

Interesting. "Yes, all right. My thanks for the warning."

He stood, reclaimed the platter, and carried it back to the larder. She stood, stretched. This body did not yet feel right. She wondered if she would ever grow accustomed to being old. Her mind was, at this point, after so many Walks long and short, close to thirty years younger than her body. How did one ever grow accustomed to that?

Orzili fetched fresh water for the basin in the bedchamber—a kindness—and also found her an extra blanket, remarking, correctly, that she was often colder than he at night. He then stepped into the main room, leaving her alone in the back of the flat.

Lenna undressed and climbed into bed, weary beyond words. Within her, sadness warred with determination. She could not help but be disappointed with what she had found in this future. Then again, she should have been devastated. Her dreams of a reunion with the Orzili she loved had come to nothing. Maybe "disappointed" was as good as she could hope for.

She fell into a deep, dreamless slumber and slept through to morning, when she was roused by noises from the street below, and the heat of sunlight beating on the shuttered window.

After washing herself and pulling clean clothes from the wardrobe on her side of the chamber, she stepped into the main room. Orzili was gone. She should have anticipated that.

He had left her coin—two rounds and a handful of silvers and quads—as well as a narrow blade and leather sheath. A search of her wardrobe revealed a second knife, more substantial than this one. She took both. Let whatever other Lenna might return here find a new blade for herself. She had come a long way, and she couldn't yet afford to buy a weapon of her own.

Orzili had placed an apple beside the money. She ate it, as well as more bread and cheese. With a final glance around this place, which once had been her heart's home, she let herself out of the flat and descended the stairs to the street.

She wished fervently that she had been able to carry her coin purse from the past. She needed gold to get where she was going; she was too old to work in exchange for passage aboard a ship.

She might sell one of the knives, but she preferred always to have two.

Then again, the coin Orzili had given her only had to get her across the Aiyanthan Sea, to Qaifin. To the one man in all of Islevale who might have use for her, who might celebrate her arrival.

Pemin, Autarch of Oaqamar.

CHAPTER ELEVEN

7th day of Sipar's Ascent, Year 619

Lenna stumbled through her escape from Vondehm in a haze of pain and grief and fear. Had Cresten—had Orzili—not been by her side for every moment of it, she surely would have collapsed or surrendered or made some fatal error. He stayed with her, guiding her, protecting her, encouraging her with kind words and a strong, gentle hand.

The changes wrought by all he apparently experienced in their time apart served them both now. The sheer force of his confidence calmed her and seemed to serve as a credential everywhere they went.

He secured passage aboard a ship that first night—also headed to Milnos, though obviously not with the minister and his soldiers. Lenna didn't believe the minister would be pleased to learn that they had followed him, nor would Cresten's king. Cresten claimed not to care.

"We need to leave this place," he told her in a voice both soothing and authoritative. "And we need to reach a healer quickly. It's either the Bow or the Shield, and of the two, I know the Shield far better. Trust me in this."

And she did, completely.

She had brought her purse, her blades, and her chronofor. That was all. After so many turns in Jispar's court, she had enough coin to pay their way onto a ship, but he didn't allow it. "I have gold," was all he said.

That was just as well. She really was in quite a lot of pain. He tried to offer her food and water, but the thought of trying to swallow anything made her stomach crawl. She hoped for placid waters on their passage across the Herjean Sea.

Losing the child was...complicated. At first, she had resented the pregnancy, seen it as yet another manifestation of Jispar's control over her. Later, it had occurred to her that having someone to love might have made the court bearable. Now that it was gone, she mourned the loss of that promise. Giving birth to the babe in some other land would have been one final declaration of her freedom, a way to salvage something bright from these turns of darkness. Cresten's words echoed in her head. *He or she would have been strong and smart and beautiful, like you...* She allowed herself to believe he might have been right, which only deepened her grief.

He escorted her below, helped her onto a pallet, tore strips of cloth from his finery so that he could soak them and lay them across her brow. She dozed. Sometime later, she woke to the mild rise and fall of the ship. Calm seas. Cresten was still beside her.

"How long was I asleep?"

"Not long. We've leagues to go. Sleep."

And as if his words were magick, she did.

Each time she awakened, he was there. She didn't say a word to him, nor he to her. It was enough for her to know he hadn't left, and, she sensed, enough for him to know that she was alive, able to open her eyes.

At some point, during the course of that night, she fell in love with him. She couldn't have said when. She knew only that when morning finally came, bringing sunlight and a freshening wind, she had decided that she would never willingly leave him. No one had ever cared so much about her. Not in her memory. Perhaps her parents had, but they had eventually sent her to the palace in Windhome, so how much could they really have loved her?

She didn't tell him, of course. She wouldn't have known how. Later, she would wonder if he figured it out for himself. It seemed he missed nothing.

He accompanied her onto the deck, stood with her at the ship's prow, prodded her to eat. At last she could. His relief was palpable. And her love for him grew.

She soon tired and allowed him to take her below again. He didn't have to stay with her, she said to him. He knew that, and remained anyway.

They reached Milnos the following morning, docking in Caszuvaar not far from where the minister's ship was moored. Lenna again questioned the wisdom of this, but Cresten assured her that all would be well. He practically carried her to the home of a healer he knew, an old man who did no more than look her up and down before asking, "How far along were you when you lost the child?"

This brought fresh tears, but relief as well. This man would know how to care for her. As Cresten had said.

He gave her a sleeping draught. Foul to smell, worse to taste. But she slept, and when she awoke—after nearly two days, Cresten told her, taking her hand—she felt better. The pain in her gut had abated. She was famished, weak but eager to be up and about.

As she sat up, Cresten presented her with a gown of blue linen, simple yet lovely.

"I thought you should have something to wear other than soldier's garb."

She stared at it, and then at him. "You mean you left me in order to wander the city in search of clothes?"

He gaped, speechless, his newfound composure abandoning him for the first time since their reunion.

She couldn't keep her laughter at bay for long. He appeared relieved and chagrined in equal measure.

"It's perfect," she said. "Thank you, Cresten."

He stiffened.

"Quinnel. Forgive me. For the past several days I've been..." She glanced around the room they were in. When she continued, it was in a whisper. "You're still Cresten to me."

"I understand. But to the rest of the world—"

"I know. I'll be more careful."

"I'd be grateful." He stood. "I'll leave you so you can dress."

He crossed to the door. Before he could open it, she spoke his name. His new name.

Orzili halted, looked back at her, the movements elegant, fluid.

"You should know that I've fallen in love with you. I just...I thought I should tell you."

An odd little smile touched his lips. "I'm glad," he said. "It would have been lonely had I been the only one."

That was all. He stepped out of the room. She joined him a short time later. After paying the healer, they left the man's home and started in the direction of the Milnosian royal castle, an angular, graceful structure of red stone, perched on a rise above the city. They entered an inn near the castle gate and took a table in the back of the great room. Orzili claimed a chair that offered a view of the main entrance. Lenna was too hungry to care where she sat.

As she attacked a small loaf of bread and a platter of roasted quail, he sipped a cup of Brenthian white and watched the door.

After about a quarter bell, he murmured, "Ah, at last."

Lenna twisted to look back, her eyes going wide at the person she saw.

Wink. Fesha Wenikai. She remembered Wink as the most feared novitiate in Windhome Palace. Now she wore ministerial robes of blue and green, embroidered with silver.

She approached the table but didn't sit.

"You have a lot of nerve coming here," she said to Orzili. "Kraetas told me what you did. He told the king as well."

"I assumed he would."

"And yet you came. Did you think Arlis would reward you?

Your actions might well precipitate a war! Did you honestly believe—"

"Sit down, Spanner."

He didn't raise his voice, or even hint at anger. Yet his words stopped her. How far they had come from Windhome, where he had been a lowly fingerling, and she had been as royalty among them. She sat opposite him, next to Lenna, whom she had yet to acknowledge. Lenna wondered if, in her indignation, Wink had even recognized her.

"You shouldn't have come here," she said, speaking more softly now. "None of us can help you. You can't serve in this court anymore."

Orzili drank a bit of wine. "I didn't come here for help, or for a job. I came here because it was the closest isle to Herjes, and Lenna needed a healer."

At this, finally, Wink looked her way. "I'm glad you're feeling better," she said. "Kraetas told me what happened, what...what Jispar did to you. I'm sorry."

Lenna hesitated, nodded.

"And," Orzili said, commanding their attention again, "I came here to thank you, and to apologize. I'd be grateful to you if you conveyed my gratitude and my regret to His Majesty as well."

Wink sat back and considered him. "You wanted to thank me?"

"You've always been a good friend, and you welcomed me to your court when you could have seen me as a rival. I'll never forget that."

She looked away, a grin forcing its way onto her lips. "I had to take pity on you. You being nothing more than a shit-beetle and all."

"A shit-beetle?" Lenna asked.

"He hasn't told you about that?"

"No, I haven't. I'd no intention of telling her."

Lenna and Orzili shared a smile.

"He will now," she said.

"I searched your quarters," Wink told him, sobering. "I thought you might need your money, your weapons."

"I have them all with me."

"So I learned. You knew what would happen in Herjes before you sailed."

"No," he said. "Truly I didn't. I did think it possible that I wouldn't be coming back. I went for Lenna. Nothing else mattered to me."

Again the realization came: never had anyone loved her so much. It scared her and thrilled her and spurred her pulse to a gallop.

Wink regarded them both, her expression betraying something unexpected: envy. "Well, I should return to the castle. Don't remain in the city for too long. Someone is bound to recognize you." She paused. "May the Two keep you safe. Always." To Lenna, she said, "Take care of him. Keep him out of trouble."

Lenna smiled. "If I can."

The Spanner left them there, Orzili gazing after her. When she was gone, he shifted his hazel eyes to hers. "So, where shall we go?"

"I don't know."

"We're outlaws now. Jispar's Seer will tell everyone in the world that you're an assassin and I'm your accomplice. Most places won't be safe for us."

"Most places," she repeated, sensing that he already knew the answer to his own question. "Why don't you tell me where you wish to go and stop playing games?" She smiled to soften this, though she really was curious.

"I'll do better than that. Finish your food."

When Lenna had eaten her fill, they left the inn and walked back to Caszuvaar's wharves, following a roundabout path along narrow, deserted lanes. However confident Orzili might have been, he had taken Wink's cautions to heart.

It didn't take Lenna long to understand that he wished to book passage on another ship. She was less eager. Sea travel unnerved her. It was a measure of how much she had come to trust him over these past few days that she didn't give voice to her objections. Not even when he told her where he wished to go.

In many ports—most, truth be told—finding a ship bound for Qaifin, or any other city in Oaqamar, would have been difficult. The autarchy was hated and feared on nearly every isle, in almost every sea.

Not in Milnos. As Lenna had learned while still a novitiate in Windhome, the two lands had been allies for centuries. Milnos depended on the autarchy for ships, for arms, for protection against Vleros and her allies among the Ring Isles. The autarchy needed Milnos for...well, nothing really. Oaqamar had few rivals, either military or commercial. The fleet of Daerjen, in the Ring, might have been a match for hers, and Aiyanth might have been as wealthy. No other realms came close. Milnos offered some strategic value, largely as a buffer between the autarchy and the pirate-infested waters of the western seas. Mostly, though, trade between the isles provided Oaqamar's new autarch with his favored foods, wines, and teas.

Lenna and Orzili had little trouble finding a ship that would bear them to the seat of the autarchy. The price was high, but, Lenna was beginning to understand, Orzili did not want for coin. Once they had been accepted as passengers, he joined the crew in oaring the vessel away from the port, and later in working the lines and scrambling up into the rigging. He seemed at ease aboard the ship—one more surprise among so many. Was there anything this man who had been Cresten couldn't do?

At night, he slept among the crew, leaving her to the privacy of a pallet in the forward hold. She guessed that he did not wish to compromise her virtue in the eyes of the captain and sailors. She wondered if he regretted his choice as much as she did.

Their voyage was slowed by strong westerly winds and rough seas. She had feared such conditions but found to her surprise that the ship's motion barely bothered her. She was more suited to a life of journey and adventure than she had thought.

Almost the moment their ship entered the Gulf of Qaifin, Oaqamaran marauders—enormous warships, each bearing thirty guns—converged on them. Soldiers boarded and searched the vessel, taking an immediate interest in Orzili and Lenna. They even demanded to examine Orzili's sextant and Lenna's chronofor. It wasn't often that a Spanner and Walker, both with Bound devices, voyaged together. They did not confiscate the devices, as Lenna feared they might. Much to the captain's displeasure, though, the commander of one of the marauders announced that his ship would escort them to port. Lenna didn't know if Orzili had anticipated this. If it disturbed him, he hid his concerns well.

With the marauder trailing them, they sailed through the gulf, past other vessels that might have been forced to wait for an open berth at the Qaifin docks. Lenna would have imagined this would please their captain, but it only darkened his mood. Orzili, speaking lightly but in a whisper, suggested to her that the ship might be carrying contraband goods that the captain would have preferred to unload elsewhere, before they reached the wharves.

"He's a smuggler?"

"Most merchant captains are, to one degree or another."

She recalled Orzili telling her that he had treated with smugglers while in Windhome, after leaving the castle, and later when he left Trevynisle and worked at sea.

"Did you know he was smuggling when we boarded the ship?"

"I assumed," he said. "Fewer surprises that way." He glanced her way. "You disapprove?"

She plumbed her thoughts, decided that she didn't. She merely wished she had known from the start, and she said as much.

"All right," he said, eyes on hers. "Next time, you'll know whatever I know. My promise."

Just having him look at her that way was enough to warm her cheeks and neck. She faced forward again, didn't object when he took her hand.

As they neared the wharf, the captain ordered the ship onto

sweeps, his every word crackling with rage. Orzili went below to help the crew row.

"The least I can do," he said as he left her side, "given that we seem to have cost the captain some gold."

Lenna watched him go, then looked past him to the captain, who stared daggers at them both.

By the time they had docked in Qaifin and were ready to disembark, the cool breezes of morning had given way to a hazed sky and overly warm winds. Qaifin's harbormaster, an officious man in black and gold, boarded the ship and strode to the stairway leading into the cargo hold. The captain followed, nervous and pale.

Soldiers from the marauder came on board next and, while courteous and barely able to speak the tongue of the Ring Isles, made clear that Orzili and Lenna were to follow them off the ship. The two of them gathered their belongings and did as they were told. Again, the soldiers took note of their devices, but made no attempt to take them. Still, a creeping fear made her wary. Her hand strayed repeatedly to her bodice, where she kept a blade.

"I don't think they mean us harm," Orzili said. "We're Travelers. They won't know if we come from Windhome or another court, so they won't want to give offense. They'll watch over us, maybe interrogate us. They won't hurt us."

She nodded, still eyeing the soldiers.

"At least I don't think they will."

Lenna fired a glare his way, drawing a rakish grin.

The autarch's guards escorted Lenna and Orzili through the massive city gate onto broad lanes that wound past shops and homes and up toward a formidable castle flying banners of black, brown, and gold. In most cities Lenna had seen, the lower streets adjacent to the waterfronts tended to be seedy, rundown. The quality of home and storefront improved with proximity to royal castles and the sanctuaries erected in honor of the God or Goddess, or as on her own isle in the Sisters, both deities.

As she and Orzili crossed through Qaifin, she saw no such progression. Every street was clean, every home and shop well-maintained. From all Lenna knew of the autarchy, she didn't believe this to be a sign of shared prosperity. Rather, she thought it likely that even the poorest denizens of Qaifin didn't dare allow their poverty to show, for fear of punishment.

Yet, despite her willingness to believe the worst of the autarch and those who served him, she also could not deny that she had never seen a lovelier city. The temple of Kheraya dominated Qaifin's center, its soaring spires delicate and carved from pale stone. The royal castle stood to the west, atop a rise. This structure she would not have called beautiful or graceful. Its battlements of pale red stone were broad and blunt, its towers—six on the outer walls, eight more within—might even have been called ponderous. But she could not help but be impressed by the sheer size of the structure, its implacability, its might. It was, she realized the perfect complement to the sanctuary. The one promised nourishment of the spirit, the other protection of the body. She had seen more refined palaces, but none that appeared less vulnerable.

Soldiers led Lenna and Orzili to the outer gate, relieved them of their weapons—her knives, his sword, pistol, and dagger—and made them wait there. None of the soldiers had said a word to them as they navigated the city streets, and none of the gate guards spoke to them now. The uniformed men and women around them stood at attention, gripping muskets mounted with bayonets. Swords and pistols hung from their belts. They didn't threaten in any way, but the longer she and Orzili waited, the more nervous she grew.

At last, a guard she hadn't seen before entered the gated archway, bowed to them, and gestured for them to follow. They emerged from the gate into an enormous courtyard where they were presented by the guard to a man in ministerial robes of brown and gold. He was tall, powerfully built, his hair wheaten, his trim beard tinged with red. Beyond him, Lenna saw fountains, a tiled plaza, gardens of riotous color. There was beauty here after all.

"Greetings, and welcome to Hastwek Castle," the man said in

the language of the Ring Isles, the words accented but clear. "I am Roen Shimijan, Minister of Protocol to His Excellency, Pemin of Hastwek, Autarch of Oaqamar."

"I'm Quinnel Orzili."

He didn't presume in introduce her, which Lenna appreciated.

"And my name is Lenna... Stenci."

She sensed a subtle shift in Orzili as she used the name, which had long been in her family, on her mother's side. He didn't look her way, though, and the minister didn't seem to notice his reaction or her small hesitation.

"I am pleased to meet you both," he went on. "I am, however, curious as to what brings you to Qaifin." He began to walk, motioning for them to follow. "A Spanner and a Walker voyaging together, bearing Bound devices no less. Surely you can see that this might draw notice." He led them to a pair of low benches in the shade of a sprawling tree with copper leaves and smooth, silver bark. He sat, indicated that they should do the same.

"I wonder, were you sent from Windhome? An offering from the chancellor there to the autarch? Are you emissaries from a court? Perhaps word of your intent to seek an audience failed to reach us? Such things have been known to happen. Though neither of you is a minister, and I take it you have come alone."

"That's right," Orzili said.

"Most curious. And so we wonder—a darker thought this—whether you might be spies, or even assassins." He studied them both, dark eyes narrowing. "You are young for such professions, both of you. And yet Oaqamar has many enemies, some of them clever to the point of deviousness." He opened his hands. "So you see our dilemma." The minister looked from one of them to the other, expectant.

Lenna, too, sent a quick glance Orzili's way. They were here by his choice. She would allow him to speak for them. For now.

"We understand perfectly, minister. This is...unusual, to say the least. We are not here as emissaries of any court, nor were we sent from Windhome, though both of us are Windhome-trained."

"I see. That leaves us with the darker possibilities I mentioned."

"We haven't come to spy on the autarch, nor are we foolish enough to attempt to harm anyone in this castle. We are..." Orzili paused, appearing to search for the correct word. After a moment, his expression brightened. "We are independent of any court or palace or any other entity. And we have come here, of our own volition, to offer our services to the autarch."

The minister sat straighter, unable to conceal his surprise. "You belong to no court?"

"That's right."

Surprise in the man's gaze gave way to suspicion. "You say you are Windhome-trained. Did you fail to complete your study in the palace? Were you deemed unworthy of a court summons?"

"Both of us have served in courts," Orzili said, neatly skirting the issue of his own dismissal from the Travelers' Palace. "You have my word on that. We don't serve those courts anymore, and we wish to serve here."

"Why? I will be blunt, Mister Orzili. The chancellors of Windhome have long been leery of the Autarchy, as have many of the courts to which they send Travelers."

"True. But only a fool can ignore the obvious: that Oaqamar is the most powerful and most prosperous isle between the oceans. And I assure you, Lenna and I are not fools."

"What drove you from the courts you served?"

Orzili shook his head. "Forgive me, minister, but some matters we will discuss only with the autarch."

The minister's smile could have frozen every fountain in the courtyard. "You are young, so I will forgive your presumption. The autarch has sent me to speak with you. You will not see him except with my sanction. And so you will answer my questions, or you will leave."

Orzili glanced Lenna's way, as if seeking permission to reveal something of her recent past. Lenna used his look a different way.

"You know it's too bad," she said, surveying the courtyard. "This is such a beautiful place. I would have liked to serve here."

She stood, held out a hand to Orzili. "Come, Quinnel. There are other courts."

He didn't falter for an instant but stood as well and took her hand. "Our thanks, minister. We regret that you've chosen to refuse our offer of service. I'm sure the autarch will understand. Walkers with their own chronofors, particularly ones who don't cost piles of gold, are so very easy to find."

They started away, back toward the gate.

"Do you think they'll actually let us leave?" Lenna whispered through tight lips.

"I'm hoping we won't need to find out."

They were nearly to the gate when the minister relented.

He called to them by name. They halted, turned. He strode in their direction and stopped before them, amusement in his faint smile.

"Children you are not," he said. "I'll give you that. Fortunately for you, the autarch values cleverness and resolve in those who serve him. And I can report to him with confidence that the two of you possess both in abundance."

A tencount passed without either of them offering a word. He chuckled and shook his head. "Very well. Please follow me." He signaled to two guards, who joined them, and followed as the minister led them across the courtyard, past those magnificent fountains and the brilliant gardens. They walked through a second, smaller square that might have been more beautiful than the first and entered the palace through a soaring carved entryway. Spacious corridors led to broad, winding stairways, which opened onto additional corridors. On the top level of the palace, they followed a pink marble hallway to twin doors inlaid with woods that formed the image of a striped lion. Its eyes were amber gems, its claws narrow strips of gold. Another wonder, in a castle filled with them.

Two more soldiers, also in brown and black, also well-armed, flanked the doorway.

Minister Shimijan had them wait with the soldiers outside the doors while he let himself into the chamber beyond.

The minister remained in the chamber for another quarter bell and more—long enough to deepen Lenna's fears.

Pemin of Hastwek had ruled in Qaifin for but three years, and already he possessed a reputation as fearsome as his father's, the late Pravin of Hastwek. He was said to be brilliant, quick-tempered, extravagantly generous with those he favored and brutally cruel to his enemies. Perhaps she and Orzili had been too quick to challenge the man's chosen representative. They had come here seeking to serve the autarchy, assuming he would admire their audacity. What if instead he found it impertinent? This was not a man to whom she wished to give offense.

The door opened, startling her. The minister appeared to notice, and to take some satisfaction in this.

Orzili had taken a seat on a low stone bench while she paced. He stood now and joined her, placing a steadying hand at the small of her back.

Shimijan closed the door and approached them.

"You are to address him as 'Your Excellency' and will offer obeisance upon entering the chamber. A deep bow. He will offer his hand to each of you, and you will touch your brow to the back of it, and then remain as you are until he bids you rise. Do you understand?"

"Yes," Orzili said. "Thank you."

The minister faced her, a question in his gaze.

"I understand," she said. Her heart beat very fast.

Shimijan opened the doors, stood aside, and motioned them within.

They entered the chamber. Three strides and then they bowed in unison. Someone walked to where they waited. Black breeches and matching leather boots, well-worn, but not scuffed or dirty. She didn't dare look to see more. A hand hovered before her. She took it gently, pressed her forehead to it, waited as the man shifted leftward and allowed Orzili to do the same.

"Please, be welcome." A smooth baritone.

She straightened, and beheld for the first time the most powerful human between the oceans.

He was trim, muscular, handsome, younger than she had expected—not too much older than she. Feathery brown hair swooped over a steep, smooth brow, shading eyes that were gray and cold and piercing. He scrutinized her boldly, then did the same to Orzili.

"My minister of protocol tells me you wish to serve in my castle, but that you have been less than forthcoming about how it is you are free to do so. I should tell you that I do not like secrets, except for my own."

The words carried no accent. Surely he was born and raised in Oaqamar, yet he spoke the language of the Ring Isles like a native.

"Our apologies, Your Excellency," Orzili said. "We are—"

Pemin stopped him with a mere twitch of his hand and indicated Lenna with a lift of his strong chin.

"I would hear from the Walker. Forgive me for saying so, but Spanners are"—another gesture, dismissive—"common. Walkers, on the other hand, are coveted in every court in Islevale. How is it no one has claimed you?"

She chanced a look at Orzili, unsure of how much to say.

"Don't look at him!" Pemin snapped. "I asked the question. In this chamber, in this city, my word is life and law. You will address your response to me."

Lenna couldn't keep the scowl from her face. She'd had too much experience with kings who thought they could control her. She didn't care if this man had her beheaded or hanged or thrown off the castle's highest tower, she would not be treated that way again.

"I was claimed, Your Excellency. By Jispar IV in Herjes. He claimed me as his Walker, and then again, against my will, as his concubine. He raped me almost every night for the first several turns I was there, until finally he got me with child. Then he stopped."

Pemin stared, clearly unprepared for her outburst. It might have been funny if not for the rekindling of her rage and shame.

"You escaped him?"

"In a manner of speaking. He's dead."

The autarch blinked, his mouth opening, then closing again. "I hadn't heard," he said, his voice low. "I am..." His smile was unexpected. "I won't lie to you and say that this displeases me. He was a pig, but a dangerous pig." He eyed her. "How did he die?"

Already she knew Pemin was not a man with whom she could dissemble, particularly on a question regarding the murder of a royal.

"I killed him," she said.

Orzili whispered her name, drawing a sharp glance from the autarch.

"You did," Pemin said to her. A statement.

"Yes. I went back in time so there would be two of me—an easy alibi—and I threw a knife into his eye. Though not before he beat me and caused me to lose the child he had given me."

The autarch regarded her for a moment longer, then flicked another look at Orzili. "You will sup with me," he said. "Both of you. I would hear more before I offer you employment."

CHAPTER TWELVE

7th day of Sipar's Ascent, Year 619

Pemin allowed them to accompany him to his private dining hall, on the ground level of the castle. There, he treated them to a feast of roasted barbed lobster, blue conch, and chilled, raw red oysters. While in the Travelers' Palace, she had tasted lobster and conch in stews, but never had she been given a lobster of her very own, nor such large, succulent slices of conch.

He offered them fresh greens as well, and rounds of bread still warm from baking, and a Fairisle white wine that might have been the best she had tasted anywhere.

Her appetite had returned and she gorged herself, until she realized that the autarch was watching her, entertained by the sheer volume of what she ate.

"Do you always eat so, or only when the food is free?"

"Only when it's this wonderful, Your Excellency," she said, and meant it. "And...and I have been unwell. Only recently have I been able to eat again. Forgive me if—"

He waved off her apology, his smile melting. "The loss of the child?"

She nodded.

Lenna expected more questions, but Pemin faced Orzili. "What role did you play in Jispar's death?"

Orzili had just cracked a claw in half. He set it on the platter before him, keeping his attention on the autarch. "I knew what she had in mind to do, but that's all, really. I was with the other Lenna, so I suppose you could say I was part of her alibi."

"He was more than that. If not for Quinnel, I wouldn't have escaped the castle."

"Interesting. How did you get her out?"

Orzili told him of the negotiations between Milnos and Herjes, and explained the intricacies of the escape. Pemin, though, was more interested in his service to the court in Caszuvaar.

"You have left Arlis?" he asked. "After he paid Windhome for your service?"

"He didn't pay Windhome, Your Excellency. I approached him as I have you—as a Spanner without allegiance to any court."

"You were not deemed worthy by your masters on Trevynisle?"

"Not quite. I was asked to leave the palace before my worthiness could be determined. A boy died. I was deemed responsible."

"Unfairly," Lenna added.

Pemin frowned at her, seeming to resent the interruption. "So the sextant you carry," he said to Orzili, "it is an affectation? Something you carry to make others think you're more accomplished than you really are?"

Lenna bristled. Orzili merely smiled.

"Hardly, Your Excellency. I *am* a Spanner. Self-taught, and as skilled as any Windhome-trained Spanner you're likely to find."

"Self-taught," Pemin repeated. "I should have asked this earlier: How old are you? Both of you."

For the first time, Orzili appeared discomfited. "Almost fifteen, Your Excellency."

"Almost sixteen," Lenna said.

"Children."

Lenna shook her head. "Products of Windhome. We're all of a

similar age when we leave the palace. Did you dismiss your other Travelers as children when you paid for them?"

"Cleverly argued."

"It's more than cleverness, Your Excellency. I've killed a king. Quinnel was abandoned to the streets of Windhome when he was only twelve. He fended for himself, treated with smugglers, killed when he had to. I doubt many of your travelers have done as much at twice our age."

Pemin answered with a vague nod, a thoughtful distance in his pale eyes. "Yes, well, as it happens, I have a Walker, whom I trust, and more Spanners than I can use."

Orzili's mouth twitched.

"That said, I may have something for you to do, something that would be most useful, and well-suited to your talents and your cleverness."

They shared a glance.

"I need to think on this more. In the meantime, I can shelter you for a time. We have guest quarters in the east wing. Two chambers?"

"One, Your Excellency. Thank you."

She spoke with surety, but her pulse had quickened again. She sensed Orzili's gaze on her, chose for the moment to ignore him.

Pemin regarded them both, then shrugged. "Very well."

He had a steward and two guards conduct them from the dining hall to yet another broad, tastefully decorated corridor on the east side of the castle. The steward led them to a chamber, generously appointed with two wardrobes, a pair of standing desks, two night tables bearing basins of warm water. And one large bed.

When they were alone, Orzili crossed to the single window and opened the shutters. Warm, fragrant air flooded the chamber. Even from near the bed, Lenna could see that the room overlooked one of the many gardens in one of the many courtyards. Orzili braced his hands on the windowsill and gazed out at the shrubs and flowers below. Neither of them had said a word since leaving Pemin.

"Would you have preferred your own chamber?" Lenna asked, unsure of whether she wanted him to answer.

He tensed, but kept his back to her. "No. I just... I've never been with anyone, Lenna."

"You're not going to be with me, either. Not yet."

Orzili turned, puzzlement and—dare she think it?—relief on his square face.

"Jispar..." She broke off, cursing the tear that slipped from one eye. "He ruined the act of love for me. I'm not ready to be with anyone in the way you mean. I hope I will be in time. And then I'll be with you or no one at all. But we don't have to make love. We can be together in other ways." She walked to him, kissed his lips lightly. "More to the point, Pemin already thinks us children. He sought to treat us like children by giving us separate chambers. I wasn't going to let him do that."

"I hadn't considered that."

"I would have thought you presumptuous if you had."

He grinned.

"So are you willing to share a room with me—and a bed—under those conditions?"

"I am," he said, earnest, young, so beautiful.

She kissed him again, more deeply this time. "Good."

They were summoned to Pemin's royal chamber again on the morning of their third day in Qaifin. They had spent the previous days in the castle enjoying the beauty of the courtyards and the largess of Pemin's kitchen. They spent the nights reveling in each other. As Lenna promised, they did not lie together in the truest sense. They did kiss and touch, with the light of the moon angling into their chamber through the open window. The nights were cool in Qaifin. Lenna didn't notice.

By that third morning, she was hopelessly in love with him. Quinnel. Cresten. Orzili, which is what she called him. She didn't care who he claimed to be. He was hers, and she his. After all she had been through, she considered their love a miracle.

The minister of protocol met them at the autarch's quarters along with a man he introduced as the castle Binder, and a woman who wore a commander's uniform. Over the next two bells, she and Orzili were tested, separately. Lenna went first with the commander, who drilled her in sword work, marksmanship, archery, and hand combat. In all, Lenna felt that she acquitted herself well. Sweating and weary, she returned to Pemin's quarters accompanied by the commander. The woman then took Orzili, no doubt to test him in the same manner.

Lenna remained with the Binder, who took her to another chamber and had her Walk back a single bell. He awaited her there in that past, told her to repeat a phrase when she Traveled to her own time, and sent her on her way. Neither Walk proved difficult for her. Once she delivered her message to the Binder in the present, he explained, somewhat unnecessarily, that they needed to be certain she and Orzili were precisely what they claimed to be.

"Your friend is an accomplished Spanner," the Binder said. "I find it hard to believe that he taught himself."

Lenna smiled. "That's because you don't know him."

Once Lenna and Orzili had proven themselves, they were presented to Pemin, who greeted them expansively, inquiring after their comfort, their satisfaction with their quarters and the food they had been given.

When they were settled in chairs before his dormant hearth, he asked, "What is your opinion of Windhome?"

Lenna and Orzili looked at each other, faced the autarch again.

"I don't follow, Your Excellency," Orzili said.

"It's a simple question. You told me that first morning that you were forced to leave the palace. Did this anger you?"

Orzili glanced at her again. "It did, yes. They blamed me for something that wasn't my fault and would have sent me away empty-handed had I not forced them to give me coin, a weapon, and a sextant."

This Lenna hadn't known. She had assumed that much of the self-assurance she saw in him now developed during his time in the streets, after his dismissal from the palace. Only now did it occur to her that there might have been more to him when he was still a novitiate than she had credited.

"Forced them how?" Pemin asked.

"By threatening to reveal more of what happened than they wished to be known."

The autarch watched him, waiting for more.

"Forgive me, Your Excellency, but I can't say more. I made a promise to the chancellor. Whatever I might think of him, I did give my word."

Lenna wondered if this would anger the autarch. He'd said when last they spoke that he didn't like secrets other than his own.

He surprised her.

"That is well said, Spanner." To Lenna he said, "And what about you? What is your opinion of Windhome?"

She weighed the question. "They sent me to a brute," she said after a pause. "They took his gold and delivered me to him. I might as well have been chattel. Is that what you wanted me to say, Your Excellency?"

"I didn't want you to say anything in particular. But I had a similar thought."

"What is this about, if I may ask?"

Pemin sat back, his fingers steepled. "Has either of you ever heard of Sholiss?"

Orzili briefly shifted his gaze in her direction. "It's a city on the southern coast of Oaqamar."

"It's much more than that. It is home to a...well, to a palace of my own. In time, it will be a rival to Windhome."

"You have your own Travelers' Palace?" Orzili asked.

"Essentially, yes. And I would like the two of you to go there, to help train my Travelers and make Sholiss worthy of the comparison to Windhome."

Lenna wasn't sure how to respond. She had never envisioned herself as an instructor, or as someone who would have any role in training other Walkers. The confusion and doubt she saw in Orzili's face mirrored her own emotions.

"I'm not certain we're the right people for this, Your Excellency," he said. "The day we arrived, you called us children, and while we don't think of ourselves as such, we're too young for a task like this."

"I don't believe you are. I need people with intimate and immediate knowledge of Windhome and its practices. Who better than the two of you?"

Orzili started to reply, but Pemin stopped him with a raised hand.

"Windhome has long considered Oaqamar an enemy. My father managed to bring Spanners and a Walker to the isle, but only at great cost. His later requests for Travelers were ignored for years. Some were never honored. I said before that I have Travelers already, and that's true. What I neglected to say is that most of them are old. My initiative in Sholiss is more than a lark. It is a matter of survival for the autarchy. If I cannot find my own source for your kind, I will, before long, find myself at a distinct disadvantage in my struggles with Daerjen, Aiyanth, and other isles." He regarded them in turn. "I would pay you generously for your work in Sholiss, and, in time, I would bring you back here, where you would enjoy all the benefits of living in Islevale's most prosperous court."

Seeing that they still hesitated, he said, "You must understand that I intend to keep Oaqamar the most powerful isle between the oceans. I intend to build on my father's legacy. One day, Sholiss will be more renowned than Windhome. I'm offering you the opportunity to change the course of history for all Travelers, and to strike a blow against the palace at the same time. Surely that idea must appeal to you."

Lenna found that it did.

She sensed that he had piqued Orzili's interest as well.

The autarch met their silence with a conspiratorial smile. "I see that I have intrigued you both. Splendid. Allow me to make my offer irresistible. You will go there for a year to start, and I will pay each of you ten gold rounds per turn for that first year."

Ten rounds. Per turn! Lenna had never even dreamt of making so much money. To do so would have been to engage in the most foolish sort of fantasy.

"At the end of the year, we will decide together what the following year will bring. If you insist upon leaving Sholiss at that time, I will honor your wishes, and allow you to serve here in my court at the wage currently enjoyed by my other Travelers. If you agree to remain in Sholiss for another year, your pay will increase to twelve rounds per turn each."

Orzili looked stunned. Lenna felt the same. Perhaps they shouldn't have been surprised by the amount Pemin was offering. He had decided to create a rival to Windhome itself. Windhome, which had been training Walkers, Spanners, and Crossers for the royal courts of Islevale for nearly six centuries. Seeking to displace the Travelers' Palace was akin to seeking to transform Chayde or Flynse into rivals to Oaqamar for pre-eminence between the oceans. What would twenty rounds of gold per turn matter to this man?

Pemin dismissed them a short time later, telling them to ponder his offer and to request an audience when they had an answer for him.

"I'll expect to have your response, one way or another, within three days," he said. "I'm willing to be patient, but I will not wait forever."

That his patience ran out after three days told them much about the man. As it happened, Lenna didn't believe they would need more than a single day.

"It's a lot of gold," she said when they were alone.

"Ten rounds is a lot of gold," Orzili said. "It's more than I was paid for all my turns of service in Milnos. What Pemin is offering..." His slow head shake was eloquent. "After one year, we would never have to work again. After two, if we stayed that long, we could live anywhere, do anything."

She stared, unable to keep from smiling.

"What?" he said.

"You keep on speaking of us, of if *we* stayed and what *we* would have."

He walked to her, took her hands. "That's how I think," he said. "I never want to leave you. I know we're young, barely more than children, but I want to spend the rest of my life with you, Lenna."

Her heart was like the wings of a swift.

"Then we should go to Sholiss," she said, speaking with great care, her hands shaking in his. "Together. And we should make our fortune and plan the rest of our lives."

He kissed her, brushed a strand of hair from her brow with a finger as gentle as a spring breeze, and kissed her again.

"I'd follow you anywhere," he whispered.

CHAPTER THIRTEEN

2nd day of Sipar's Ascent, Year 634

The between dropped her onto cold stone. Her legs gave, and she fell onto her side. She lay there like a landed fish, sucking at air, skin pebbled, eyes adjusting to the darkness of the chamber, chronofor trapped in aching fingers. Another walk. Too many now. For someone who had initially resisted spending her years, Orzili had grown all too willing to send her back.

"It hasn't changed." His voice, unwelcoming and unwelcome. "My memories might be different—I can't be certain. But we don't have the boy or the princess. He still escapes the dungeon. He still eludes me that night on the strand. I remember it all."

"I need a blanket." Her voice sounded thin, rough.

Lenna heard footsteps. A soft blanket landed on her legs. She sat up, shook it out, and wrapped it around herself. She stood, walked to the table near his hearth, and poured herself a cup of wine. Miejan red. Always the finest in whatever court Orzili served. In certain ways, he and Pemin were so alike. She swirled the wine in her cup and moved closer to the fire, its warmth a balm.

"And how do you expect me to change this?" she asked, after

drinking half the cup. "I've walked back for you too many times already. It doesn't appear to do much good."

She faced him. Seeing this version of him so soon after leaving the one she had gone back to warn, she realized that he looked worn, tired. Old. An irony, since she was the one spending turns at a time with each Walk.

"The warnings. They need to be more specific. If I'd known they would batter that ancient door..." He trailed off, scowling at her as she shook her head.

"I know this isn't the first time I've given you warnings. I don't remember how many times I've gone back—it's not within my power to know. I would guess I've done it too often. I feel the years in my bones. There is no warning I can give you, Orzili. Sometimes the past can't be altered. He's fated to escape the dungeon. He's fated to wound you on that strand and evade you. You might be fated to capture him in the future. We can't know. But I will not go back again. I'm done."

"What if Pemin says otherwise?"

"Then Pemin can Walk back himself."

They glared at each other, the light of the fire and a single candle shifting, flickering, casting dark shadows all around them. Orzili looked away before she did.

It had been like this for some time now. She couldn't have said when exactly it began to change—around the time she realized that he no longer loved her. She had never loved him, not really. He couldn't know that, of course. He thought she was his Lenna—older, to be sure. A refugee from a lost future.

He had not yet figured out the truth: that she was the other Lenna, the one who came back from yet another lost future, the Lenna he once dismissed as mad. The one who had bested him in hand combat by the shore several turns earlier and sent Tirribin to claim his years.

Recollections of that confrontation had to make the distance between them all the more difficult for him to accept. For so long, they had been lovers, life-long partners. Only recently had he given up on the memory of that love. When he did, he began to fear her. Lenna thought she understood why.

This was not the first time he had used the threat of Pemin's wrath against her. She believed he might follow through on the threat. Better the autarch should direct his ire at her than at him. That would be what he thought.

Once he stopped loving her, everything changed. He could imagine sending her back through time as often as necessary in order to tease from history the outcome he wanted. He could imagine spending all of her years the way he might use up a handful of bullets or a pouch of Aiyanthan powder. He could imagine killing her if he had to. And because he could now imagine all of these things, he understood that she could as well.

Because she stopped loving him before he stopped loving her. He knew this. And because ever since their fight on the strand, he had also known she could defeat him if she had to. He might not have understood that she was that same Lenna, but if one of her could best him, all of them could. That would frighten him, give him pause every time they found themselves at odds, which happened now with some frequency.

This younger Orzili and the older Lenna she replaced were never lovers. They were partners briefly, but those threads soon frayed. All that had remained was common purpose and shared fear of Pemin. At this point, even that much was gone.

"We have to find him, Lenna."

"*You* have to find him. *You* let him escape. Every time."

He winced at this, and she almost felt sorry for him. Almost.

"You kept me here too long," she said. "You made me a prisoner. You have no one to blame but yourself."

This she said for the other Lenna, the one who had Walked to her own time fourteen years from now. That Lenna's memories were part of her, the pain caused by his treatment of her accessible if only she reached for it.

She had different grievances, and a different solution in mind.

"This again?" he asked. "You want to leave, to go back? You wish to be old?"

A cruelty, a barb that might have struck true had he been speaking to that other Lenna. It passed through her like a Crosser through a wall. She felt nothing.

"I wish to leave, yes," was all she said.

"Well, I can't stop you. You've spoken of leaving me for a long time now. I don't believe you'll do it."

She regarded him in silence until he shifted his gaze again.

"Where do you think he is?" he asked after some time. A familiar question.

"I don't know any more than you do. He might be anywhere. If he wishes to put the girl on the throne and restore the Hayncalde Supremacy, he won't be far from here. On the other hand, if he's driven more by fear of you, he could be back in the Sisters or the Labyrinth."

He nodded, still not looking at her. An old exchange. Ground they had covered several times before. This was where he took their conversations when he didn't know what else to say.

She had learned the correct response, how to deflect his questions. He wished to engage her in this mystery, to interest her in the hunt. She wouldn't allow it.

She wasn't crazed anymore. Not even a little. She wasn't Lenna, either. Not really. Not in any way he would have recognized if he could read her thoughts. She was Lenna-in-red. That was what the other Lenna had called her.

She was...herself. She went by Lenna because he couldn't know the truth, not for a little while longer. Whoever she was, she knew she was sane. Her thinking was as clear as his, as clear as that of any she encountered in Hayncalde Castle. The other Lenna had confined herself to her chamber, choosing a cloistered existence for as long as he kept her here, as if by making herself cope with loneliness and boredom, she might punish him, or force him to take pity on her and let her go.

Lenna had followed this example for a time. Eventually she grew tired of isolation. Why should the feud between this man she disliked, and the woman who had left her behind circumscribe her life so? She spent more time walking the grounds. She allowed soldiers to escort her to the shoreline. She passed bell after bell in the library of the old sovereign, the one the Sheraighs killed. A volume she had borrowed from the collection—with permission, of course; the old keeper of the volumes had taken a liking to her—rested on her bed back in her chamber. She was almost finished with it and longed to read those last few pages.

"I intend to Span to Qaifin in the morning," he said after a long pause. "Pemin will want to know what's happened."

"He'll be angry?"

"Probably."

"Will he punish you?"

"He might. Do you care?"

She considered this for a breath. "No."

Another scowl. "I expect he'll order me to send you back again, to try to prevent Tobias's escape from the dungeon. Or maybe the strand this time."

"You've come close to dying in both places."

"So you've told me. Pemin won't let that sway him. He's no more concerned with my well-being than you are."

"Who knew we had so much in common?"

"Blood and bone! What's happened to you? We're supposed to love each other!"

"We haven't in a long time. Surely you know that."

No answer. She drank her wine.

He stepped to the door, opened it for her, though she had made no move to leave him. "You should sleep," he said. "You might have another busy day tomorrow."

Not in the way you mean.

"Shouldn't I dress first?" she asked. "You might have need of the blanket."

"Keep it. I'll get another."

Lenna gave a thin smile and crossed to her piled clothes. Gathering them in her arms, her chronofor still clutched tight in her hand, she joined him at the door.

Halting beside him, she glanced up into his eyes. "Have a care with Pemin tomorrow. Yes, he'll be angry, but the greater danger is your defensiveness. You provoke him when you feel you've failed him. You can't do that this time."

"One moment you hate me, and the next you express concern. I don't understand you anymore."

You never have.

For the other Lenna, she said, "I'll always care about you. You know that. Just because I don't love you doesn't mean I want to see you killed."

The muscles in his jaw tensed, but he dropped his chin and mumbled a thank you.

At Orzili's order, a guard walked with her back to her chamber. She wasn't certain whether Orzili did this for her safety or his peace of mind.

Once in her chamber, she pulled on a nightgown and robe and settled into the chair beside her own hearth. She felt she had been gone for ages though she knew that in this time it had been less than a bell. She poured herself more wine, picked up the volume from the library—a colorful history of the First Bone Sea War and the Oaqamaran Revolution—and resumed her reading. She was determined to finish the book this night. And determined as well to leave in the morning, while Orzili Spanned to the court of the autarch in Oaqamar.

She continued to hold her chronofor; even while she dressed, she hadn't put it down. Odd that she should feel such attachment to the device on this of all nights. Or maybe not so odd. It had defined her through many iterations of her life. It was nearly as much a part of her as her arm, her leg. She rubbed her thumb across the etchings on its golden back, took comfort in the familiarity of those edges and whorls.

She finished reading the final pages and climbed into bed, setting the chronofor beside her on the night table. After only a tencount, she reclaimed the device, cradling it in her hand, the gold still warm from having been held for so long. She slipped that hand under her pillow and fell asleep that way.

She slept well past dawn, knowing there was no point in waking early. Orzili had said he would Span to Pemin's castle this day, but he might come by before he left. He had done this before, on those occasions when he thought he might not survive his audience with the autarch. She dressed, took her breakfast tea in her chamber beside the open window.

By mid-morning bells, Lenna assumed he was gone. She packed a few of her most prized belongings in a small carry sack. Most of the gowns Orzili ordered made for her she left behind. She had no need for so many. She didn't want them with her. She took two, along with a change of shoes and both of her blades. The volume from the library she left on her desk.

She had yet to relinquish the chronofor.

Orzili had left his chamber unlocked but guarded. She hoped the men wouldn't stop her. They were accustomed to her coming and going from his chamber, just as they were used to Orzili visiting her in her room. No doubt they believed the two of them remained in love. Orzili might have had reasons for wishing to perpetuate the deception. Today, it worked to her advantage.

"Good morning," she said, approaching the men.

They nodded, murmured responses.

"I need something from within his chamber," she said. "Is he here, or has he already Spanned to Qaifin?"

This would be more information than they had, would indicate to them that she had more intimate knowledge of their lord and his affairs than they did.

The guards shared a glance. The taller one shrugged. "He's not here, m'lady," he said. "We don't know where he's gone."

"No matter." She indicated the door with a graceful turn of her hand. Her off hand. The one without the chronofor. "May I?"

Another look passed between them.

"I won't be long," she said. "I have business in the city." She repositioned her carry sack, drawing attention to it. "Something Lord Orzili has asked of me. I need one item before I can go. I don't wish to wait until his return. You know how long his discussions with the autarch can take." Of course they didn't. She favored them both with smiles to soften her request.

"One of us would have to... I mean, we probably shouldn't allow..." The man sent a silent plea his companion's way.

Lenna allowed her smile to fade, narrowed her eyes. "Are you trying to say that you don't trust me to be in his chamber? Do you have any idea how long Lord Orzili and I have known each other? Do you understand that we were at Windhome together when we were children, that we have lived together, loved together?"

The guard colored to the tips of his ears.

"Forgive me, my lady. But he did tell us that no one was to enter, and he didn't—"

"Very well," she said, as haughtily as she could. "When he arrives, you can explain to him why I was not able to complete my task in the city today." She pivoted, started away, hoping her gambit would work.

"My lady, wait."

Her lips curved while she had her back to them. Schooling her features, she faced them, waited.

"You can enter, of course. He would—" The man adjusted his stance. "He would welcome you. We know that."

"Thank you." She kept her tone chilly enough to keep him intimidated.

The soldier opened the door for her, stood back as she swept past him. Once inside, she closed the door smartly. Let them think twice about disturbing her.

She and Orzili hadn't loved each other in a long time. They hadn't really trusted each other for several turns. She was what she was, though. Little escaped her notice. She knew which drawer on the desk she needed to open, and, when she found it locked, she knew where to search for the key.

She worked quickly; she had told the guards this was a simple matter. And it was.

Lenna took five gold rounds and a number of treys and quads, filling her purse, and hiding a few of the rounds in a small pocket within her bodice.

She then took one of the kerchiefs from her sack, intending to wrap it around her chronofor. Here, though, she faltered. The device... It was lovely, the most beautiful thing she had ever called her own. And she was a Walker. That would never change.

Had it not been for the other Lennas—the one who had left her, returning to their rightful time fourteen years in the future, and the other, the young one who wasn't even aware of her, who lived in Fanquir, alone right now, likely unaware that her chronofor couldn't work so long as this one existed—she would have returned the kerchief to her bag, clutched the chronofor ever more tightly in her fingers.

But no, she and Lenna-in-blue had an arrangement, one she would honor now.

There is one way, they had said in unison that last night. This was that way.

Her eyes brimmed.

Taking a breath, she set the cloth on a table, placed the chronofor in the middle of it, and carefully folded the kerchief over it.

Long ago, she had decided what she would use: Orzili kept on his desk a small stone figure, a carving of Sipar, his arms held wide in supplication, or perhaps benediction.

It wasn't his, she knew. Both of them had been raised as worshippers of the Two, to the extent that they worshipped anything. The Hayncaldes were Siparites, as were most of those who lived in the city. The figure must have belonged to the previous occupant of this chamber. She assumed that person was dead now.

The statue had a heavy, round base, flat on the bottom. Lenna hefted the figure, carried it and the cloth-wrapped chronofor to the corner of the room farthest from the door. She knelt, tears streaming now, and placed the device on the stone floor. She lifted the stone figure, and with a quick, wary glance toward the door, hammered its base down on the chronofor.

The cloth muffled the crunch of glass and metal but could not blot it out entirely. She knew she didn't have to hit it a second time. She did anyway, to be certain. It was possible a part or two would be salvaged. The gold might be melted down for a ring or some other bauble, but this particular chronofor would never be repaired.

Lenna stood, dried her tears with the edge of her sleeve.

She carried the chronofor to Orzili's desk, unfolded the cloth to assess the damage: tiny shards of glass; dented, flattened gold; time hands bent beyond hope of redemption. One of the stems had come loose.

It was enough.

She left it like that, so that he would see. She wanted him to know what she had done, how they—how both Lennas—had deceived him.

Reclaiming her carry sack, heavier now with the coins she had taken, she crossed back to the door.

A knock, and then, "My lady? Is everything all right in there?"

She opened the door, surprising the guards. Both took a step back from the door.

"Everything is fine," she said, keeping her voice bright. "I found what I was looking for." She joined them in the corridor and closed the door behind her. "Thank you both for your kindness."

Lenna didn't give them time to answer. She walked away, took the nearest stairway to the courtyard, and followed a stone path to the castle's east gate.

She had feared that the soldiers there might keep her from leaving. They did stop her, to ask where she was going. She told them the same story she had told the men in the corridor: dealings in the city, tasks Lord Orzili expected her to complete. They wouldn't dare risk angering him. They let her go.

From there, she could go anywhere she wanted. The wharf to find passage aboard a ship? The countryside beyond the city walls? The Notch?

Orzili would never see her again. Not until she wished it.

The Span to Pemin's castle was no more or less harrowing than usual. He fell out of the gap in the castle's west courtyard, naked and tender, his skin abused by the gap wind, the edges of his sextant digging into his fingers.

Soldiers surrounded him, muskets leveled, bayonets gleaming dully with hazed sunshine. He gave his name with as much dignity as he could muster, told them he had come to speak with the autarch, asked for clothes or some sort of covering.

"Is the autarch expecting you?"

A more difficult question than the man could know.

"No, he's not. But he'll want to see me."

The same guard gave orders in a low, even voice. Guards hurried off in different directions.

"I don't suppose you're carrying any weapons."

A laugh escaped him, the humor unexpected.

"No, not this time."

The soldier helped him to his feet. Another emerged from the guard house with a blanket and handed it to him. Orzili covered himself.

Soon, yet another soldier approached the gate from deeper within the castle and nodded to the man who had stayed with Orzili.

"He'll see you," the man said. "Let's get you dressed first."

"Ministerial robes," Orzili told him. "That's what I usually wear."

"Very good, my lord."

Within half a bell, they had found him robes—brown, black, and gold—and escorted him through the gardens to an open expanse of green lawn. The autarch and his wife—his new wife—stood at the near end of the clearing, both holding bows. Targets had been set some twenty paces away.

As if Orzili needed for the man to be armed.

"Orzili," Pemin said, a grin splitting his face. "An unexpected pleasure. You have met my wife, Queen Deya."

"Of course." Orzili bowed. "A very great pleasure to see you again, Your Majesty."

"And you, Lord Orzili."

He had met the woman once before, shortly after she and Pemin were married, in a ceremony that made the coronation of most kings seem modest. She was stunning: skin the color of dark honey, emerald eyes, satiny black hair. Clearly she hailed from the Sisters, or maybe the Labyrinth. Orzili wondered if she was a magi or had Traveler blood in her family. She was almost as tall as he, and of a similar height to her husband. She wore brown breeches, leather boots, and a white silk blouse, looking every bit the warrior.

Pemin's first wife had been his contemporary, but theirs, most agreed, had been a marriage of convenience. She died giving birth to their only child, who also died. Pemin didn't grieve for long, and with this second marriage had found a love-match. Deya had to be ten years his junior, but that didn't appear to matter to either of them.

Orzili could tell that the queen knew how to hold a bow. Already she had an arrow nocked. Looking past her, he saw that her target bristled with arrows, many of them clustered in the red center. Her target was very nearly a match for Pemin's.

"Come, love," she said, "it's your turn. Three more each—I'm eager to see who's won. I think I might have you this time."

Another grin greeted this: pride, though whether in her or in his own skill Orzili couldn't tell. The autarch toed his line, aimed, drew his bowstring, his form perfect, the muscles in his back and shoulders tightening beneath his own silk shirt.

He released the string with a concussive twang, watched as his arrow arced and buried itself in the red circle of his target. Two arrows around this newest one trembled with the impact.

The queen frowned. "Now that wasn't very nice." She eyed Orzili. "Do you shoot, Lord Orzili?"

He hesitated, eyes finding Pemin's. The autarch stared back at him, a small smile tugging at his lips.

"I have been known to, Your Majesty."

"He's Windhome-trained, my love. Of course he can shoot."

"Then I would cede my last three arrows to him." She arched

an eyebrow at her husband. "I fear that is my only chance at victory."

"Nonsense. You can beat me still. Though I do like the idea of allowing Orzili to join us." Pemin motioned to his attendants.

A flurry of activity followed. Within a few spirecounts, a new target had been set next to the others, and a bow and fresh quiver of arrows had been placed with those of the autarch and his queen.

Deya was next to loose an arrow. Her form was as good as Pemin's, and so was the result, though her barb had to arc higher to fly as far.

She smiled, peered at her husband over her shoulder. Teasing, loving, alluring. There had been a time, not so long ago, when Lenna looked at Orzili that way. The ache in his chest was dull, as if he had overtaxed a muscle long neglected.

"A fine effort, Your Majesty," he said.

"You next, Lord Orzili. I am not familiar with Windhome training. I should like to see it in action."

He couldn't tell if this was mockery, and of course he didn't dare respond with anything more than a sketched bow.

He pulled an arrow from his quiver, stepped to the line, checked the trees around them for the wind's direction. It was light; what little he noticed was helping and from the left. He drew the bowstring to his ear, his left arm locked and steady, his first finger above the butt of the arrow, his middle and ring fingers below, all of them gentle on the sinew.

The flight of his arrow resembled that of Pemin's—low, straight, and swift. He found the center of that red spot.

"Well done, Orzili," Pemin said. "Good to see some of your skills remain polished."

Another barb finding its mark. He would have some idea of why Orzili had come. Good tidings could be sent by bird. Bad news was delivered in person.

The queen gave no indication of having noticed the tone of Pemin's remark. She had reached for her next arrow and she instructed the autarch to do the same.

The two of them loosed their remaining arrows in quick succession, hers finding red and then the yellow ring just around the center, his doing the same. Orzili thought Pemin might have missed with his last arrow intentionally, but a quick glance at the autarch disabused him of this notion. His expression had tightened, and he eyed the trees around them with genuine anger. Had he felt a sudden gust of wind? Orzili hadn't.

The autarch and queen walked to their targets, tallied their points.

Orzili noted Deya's pout from where he remained, bow in hand. Pemin hugged his wife, kissed her lips. They returned to the edge of the clearing. Orzili bowed to the queen and she bid him farewell. Once she and her attendants were gone, Pemin sent away the others, leaving Orzili and him alone save for two guards who lingered at some distance, both armed with muskets.

Pemin regarded him, set himself, and loosed an arrow with a resonant thrum. Red.

"You are here, Orzili," he said, squinting at the target, "which tells me you have failed in some way. And you are wearing ministerial robes you would have been given by my men, which tells me that you came by sextant. On your own. Am I to assume that you have lost another set of tri-sextants?" A pause and then, "Your shot."

CHAPTER FOURTEEN

3rd day of Sipar's Ascent, Year 634

Orzili pulled another barb from his quiver. His hands were steady, but sweat tickled his temple. He aimed and released. Tracking the arrow, he knew this was not as good an effort, the arc too high, the flight less certain. He did find red again, but only barely.

He glanced at the autarch. Pemin watched him, expectant, awaiting an answer to his question.

"Yes," he said, spending a breath on the word. "The boy has eluded me again, and yes, I'm afraid the tri-sextants are lost. I found Tobias, and the princess. A source in Belsan located them first, and I managed to confirm where they were, who they were with. I even lured them to Herjes, which was the perfect place to take them. I had my men with me, the tri-sextants worked just as they should. The boy and I fought. I had him. *I had him!*"

"It would seem you didn't," Pemin said, voice cold.

"Ancients intervened." He wouldn't mention Droë specifically if he didn't have to, nor his exchange with Qiyed. Though the latter might prove useful before long. "Tobias and his allies summoned a Shonla hoping his mists would confound the Belvora. And when the Shonla was shot, its cries drew two more

Ancients, including an Arrokad. They put a stop to the fighting, and, as punishment for one of my men killing the Shonla, they helped the boy, the princess, and those with them get away."

"More excuses."

"No, Your Excellency. Not excuses. Facts."

These might have been the bravest words he had ever spoken. Pemin glowered, nostrils flaring.

"I understand your anger," he added quickly, "and I intend to do all I can to repair the damage resulting from this setback. But this is no excuse, and dealing with Ancients is no trifle. Have you ever treated with an Ancient, Your Excellency?"

Not the wisest of questions, that last. For an instant, Orzili thought the autarch might grab an arrow and bury it in his heart. He didn't. After a pause, Pemin shook his head. He did pluck another arrow from his quiver, but only to nock it to his bowstring.

"In truth, I haven't. In certain respects, mine has been a cloistered life." An unexpected admission, and a more generous reply than Orzili had anticipated. Yet the autarch wasn't done surprising him. "That took some courage, Orzili. I have wondered about you in recent turns. It seems you have lost your way a little. I find your... *passion* reassuring."

"You're kind, Your Excellency."

Pemin took his stance, aimed, and let the arrow fly all in one smooth motion. Another barb in the red. "Tell me about the trisextants."

Carefully. "It seems the Ancients were familiar with the boy, and even had some sort of commerce with him. Commerce is everything to Ancients and these two—"

"Do not speak to me like I'm a naïf. I said I had never treated with Ancients. I did not say I was ignorant in their ways. And my forbearance only goes so far."

Orzili's mouth went dry. "Forgive me, Your Excellency. The boy owes one of them a boon, so they were inclined to help him and punish me for trying to kill the lad. They...they took the trisextants from us and gave them to the boy."

The expression in those gray eyes hardened again. "Not the first time he has walked away with your devices. The tri- devices were an innovation I had hoped to keep as my own. There seems little chance of that now." He waved a hand at Orzili's arrows.

Orzili readied himself and let fly. Center.

"Tell me about the woman."

The woman. He did this intentionally. He controlled them both, was master of their lives. And he liked to remind them of this whenever possible.

"She is...well."

Pemin had drawn back his bowstring to fire again, but now he lowered the bow, let the tension drain from sinew and yew. "Well?" he repeated. "Hardly reassuring."

Orzili cursed himself. He could never allow himself an unguarded moment with this man. He knew this, and yet he had just done so.

"She's fine, Your Excellency."

Pemin didn't look away or retake his stance.

"She grows restive," he admitted. "This Lenna. She wishes to return to her own time, fourteen years in the future. And this has...has taken a toll on our marriage."

"Maybe you should let her go. The other Lenna—the one you should be with—she waits for you in your home, yes?"

"In Fanquir, yes."

"Might she be more useful to us?"

It was a fair question. For too long, Orzili had allowed his fascination with the older Lenna to overmaster his judgement. He knew she wished to leave, but he was in love with her—more than he had ever been with the younger woman in Kantaad. He didn't love her now, and hadn't for some time. He clung to her because their contest of wills had taken on its own exigencies, had become more important to him than their marriage, than Tobias, than Pemin's wishes. He kept her here, in this time, not because he loved her or wanted her, but because he wished to win, to show her that he could be as resolute as she. Foolishness.

"She might be, Your Excellency. It is...a question worth considering."

"You love her."

"Of course."

"I mean the older one."

"I love her in any incarnation. But yes, I have allowed myself to fall in love with this other Lenna. A mistake."

"I know what it is to love, Orzili. I cannot imagine how I would choose between two Deyas if I had that opportunity. That curse."

The man was full of surprises today.

"Your Excellency is too kind."

"You've said that twice now this morning. We both know it's not true."

Orzili considered the bow he held before leaning it against his quiver. "I should Span back to Hayncalde, Your Excellency."

"Our contest isn't done."

"I concede. You're the better bowman."

Pemin grinned. "I find it's easy to win such contests when everyone fears that besting me will cost them their lives."

Orzili laughed. "Yes, Your Excellency." He sobered. "The boy and the princess—thoughts of them consume me day and night. I want you to know this, so that you'll believe me when I say that I will find them. I will make right all that's gone wrong. Or I'll die in the attempt. I swear it to you."

He expected the autarch would respond with some warning of what another failure might mean for him. This had been an unusual conversation, however, and it remained so.

"I believe you, and I trust you'll find them in time. I look forward to receiving word of your progress."

Orzili approached the autarch, bowed low, pressed his brow to the man's extended hand. He started away, intending to return to the castle, and Span back to Daerjen. As he reached the edge of the clearing, Pemin spoke his name, stopping him.

"The woman. The older Lenna. Let her go. I'm sure I'll find use for her in our shared future. I don't know as much about

Walking as she does and you might, but I understand that with her here there is...a loss of balance. Send her back. Perhaps your fortunes will improve after you do."

His throat tightened. He didn't wish to let go of her, because he was still drawn to her, and because he didn't like to lose any more than Pemin did. This was a command, however. Obligating. And also wise.

"Very well, Your Excellency," he said, and left the man.

The Span back to Daerjen proved more difficult than usual, as if the gap wind not only abraded his body, but also slowed him. Upon reaching the battlements of Hayncalde Castle, he crumpled to his knees, fell against the harsh stone of the crenelated wall. The sun still burned high overhead, searing his tender skin. He remembered the last time he Spanned back from Qaifin. He arrived at nightfall. Lenna greeted him with a blanket and kind words. It seemed another lifetime.

Orzili forced himself to his feet, shuffled like an old man to his piled clothes, and dressed. He needed food and a generous cup of wine. He also needed to speak with Lenna.

He beckoned to the nearest soldiers walking the wall, ordered them to summon Lady Stenci to his quarters. With each step he took toward his room, he felt a bit more himself. He needed to Span more often. When he fell out of practice, the gap affected him too much.

Upon entering his chamber, he crossed directly to the table on which he had left a half-full carafe of wine. He poured himself a cup, downed it, poured another. Crossing back to the door, he ordered one of the guards in the corridor to have food brought to the chamber.

Before he closed the door, the guards from the wall-walk approached, swords and armor jangling with each step.

"Lady Stenci hasn't returned from the city, my lord. Shall we have her sent to you when she does?"

Orzili stared. "She went to the city?"

"Yes, my lord." This from one of the soldiers guarding his door.

"You saw her? Spoke to her?"

The man eyed his companion. "Yes, my lord. She came here and told us she was going."

Orzili resisted the impulse to brace himself against the door frame. Something was wrong. This was...different. Why would Lenna go to the city? Why would she tell his guards where she was going? Recently, she had taken to leaving her chamber with some frequency, but rarely did she explain herself to anyone. She went on her walks, took soldiers with her to the shore, spent bells alone in the castle library. The city though... And this announcement of her intentions...

"Did she say why she was going?"

Another exchange of glances, both men clearly unnerved. "She said you sent her, my lord. She was going for you. A task she was to complete."

It was, he decided, very important that he hide from them the panic rising like a tide in his chest. He couldn't say why. Fear of Pemin, fear of her, fear of the sheer embarrassment that might result if they knew she had escaped him in this way. "She said that," he repeated, false brightness in his tone.

"Aye, my lord."

"And she came here to tell you this, to inform you of her intentions?"

"No, my lord. She needed something from your chamber. We assumed that you wouldn't—"

He broke off as Orzili whirled away to stride back through his chamber. He started toward the far end of the room, but before he reached the chamber's center, he veered toward his desk. Even in this, she would avoid his bed.

Three steps from the desk, he slowed. He recognized the kerchief as one of hers, couldn't quite make out what rested on top of it. It glinted like gold.

Another step and he knew.

"Get out," he said, voice low.

"My lord, is she—"

"Get out!"

He heard them scramble away from his door. One of them had the good sense to close it.

Orzili could do no more than gawk. His first thought was to fear for her. Had he driven her mad by keeping her here against her will? Had he driven her to take her own life, to leave her shattered chronofor as an accusation, one last golden barb aimed at his heart, in this day filled with barbs?

No. Had she meant to do the unspeakable, she might have destroyed her device in this way, but she also would have taken her life right here and left her bloodied corpse on his floor. A memento more damning by far than the chronofor.

She lived still. He was certain of it. So why would she leave without any means to Walk? Why would she destroy the device? And why would she leave it like this, as some sort of signal to him? Not a signal—a declaration. But of what?

It struck him like a thunderclap, sending tremors through his chest. He staggered, fell forward another step, so that he could have reached out and taken hold of the broken chronofor, bloodied his hand on those shards of glass.

For days and days after their encounter with the crazed Lenna he had asked her if her chronofor worked yet. It hadn't, and wouldn't, she had assured him, until the mad woman returned to her own time. Only one chronofor could work in any given place.

At some point, as his worry about the mad Lenna faded, and his obsession with finding Tobias and the princess reasserted itself, he stopped asking, forgot to care. And so did she, this woman who had lied to him day after day after day. Eventually, she did Walk again, *could* Walk again. The change went unremarked. It had fled his mind, and perhaps hers, too. Her mind wouldn't be what it was, even after all this time.

He was certain, though. It explained so much: the growing distance between them, her sudden indifference to him, her casual cruelty.

The Lenna he loved had long since Traveled to her own time fourteen years in the future. In all likelihood, she left him that very night, mere bells after the madwoman in red first entered their lives. And for all the time since, he had been sparring with that second, crazed Lenna. The one who bested him on the strand and sent Tirribin to feed on his years. Not so crazed after all. More clever than he in any future or past.

"Oh, Lenna," he whispered. He reached a hand toward the chronofor, stopped himself before he touched it.

In a way, it made no difference. Pemin had told him to send her back. What did it matter if the Lenna who'd come from so far in the future left him today, or a turn ago?

And knowing that the Lenna who had been so cold toward him in recent days was actually the mad Lenna, the one he'd fought on the strand, made the distance between them easier to accept. He hadn't been at odds with the Lenna he'd loved, but rather with a shadow of that woman, an accident of time and history.

None of this comforted him.

Yes, Pemin had told him to send the real Lenna back, but he didn't have that opportunity. She'd left him. She had felt compelled to sneak away, like one escaping a prison. Forever she would think of him—this version of him—as her jailer, as the man who had refused to grant her the dearest wish of her heart. Had she waited, he would have been able to send her back himself. To be sure, the command came from Pemin, but she wouldn't have needed to know that.

He scowled at the workings of his own mind. What had he become that he could think so, that he could wish to delay her happiness in order to lie to her and thus make himself appear more kind and generous than he really was?

The question led him to his second thought. The crazed Lenna had destroyed her chronofor and left it here as a message. She wanted him to know that she remained in this time. Why? Did she mean this as a threat? An invitation to pursue her?

In his mind, she was the crazed Lenna. Now he knew better. If she could deceive him for this long, match wits with him day after day without ever revealing who she was and what the other Lenna had done, her mind was clear enough. As he learned when they fought, she retained all the skills and experiences of the Lenna he loved. She was Windhome-trained, hardened by years as an assassin. She didn't love him and hadn't since that day she entered their lives as an addled version of the true Lenna, but she knew him intimately, as the other Lenna did. She would be a formidable foe if she chose to pit herself against him.

One had left him to return to her true time. Another had chosen to flee the castle rather than continue their partnership.

In destroying her chronofor, though, this second one had created a third possibility. He could almost hear the older Lenna speak of her.

There's another Lenna, remember? Young? Pretty? Alive and well in Fanquir?

And now, with this chronofor broken, likely beyond repair, hers would work again.

He needed an ally. Against Tobias, possibly against this Lenna who had left him today. What better ally than Lenna herself? Younger, stronger, her years not yet spent on Walks. She might even be glad to see him. Though, he realized now, he had neglected her for a long time. Too long. He hadn't even bothered to send a bird, much less a longer missive by ship.

That couldn't be helped. He was alone now. He had need of a Walker. And maybe he could repair with this Lenna what he had broken so utterly with the other two.

He retrieved his sextant from the table that held his wine and left the chamber. Mere moments ago, he had remarked to himself that he needed to Span more, to reacquaint himself with the gap. So be it.

She was in a foul mood as she followed the cart back into the city, the welts on her hands throbbing still. One of them had begun to itch. Her hair stank of the smoke she used to control the hives. It had barely worked today. The bees always grew more aggressive as the warmer turns gave way to autumn. But six stings in a single day. She couldn't remember the last time she had fared so poorly with her hives.

Yes, she had three jars filled with honey to show for her efforts, but the swelling in her hand bothered her. Her reactions to stings were getting worse.

If she'd had help as in past years, someone to watch the hives and apply smoke while she harvested...

She pushed that particular thought away, unwilling to tread what had become a well-worn path through grief and anger.

The honey would bring a bit of coin, not that she wanted for much. Mostly, she welcomed the excuse to visit the marketplace.

After entering the city, she followed the twists of Fanquir's streets to the narrow lane on which they—she—lived. Skav's mallet beat an inconstant rhythm, rattling the worn stairway as she climbed to the flat. Cradling the three jars in the crook of one arm, she managed to open the door.

She spotted him immediately. How could she not? He sat at their dining table, an insipid grin on his face. He remained beautiful, but his hair was longer, his face leaner. Looking more closely, she realized that the grin was less certain than she'd assumed. It couldn't quite mask his uncertainty, the uncharacteristic diffidence in his bright hazel eyes.

Lenna took a breath, stepped into the flat, and set the jars on the table directly in front of him. Then she turned, closed the door, locked it as an afterthought. She untied her shawl and hung it on one of the hooks by the door. Next to an overshirt of his that she had refused to move for all this time.

Her every motion was deliberate, controlled. She feared doing anything that might unleash the emotions churning beneath her outward calm. If he was smart enough to notice, he would fear this as well.

At last, when she could delay no longer, she approached the table and halted beside his chair.

He stood, eyes fixed on hers. He smelled like sweat and leather and the sea, just as she remembered. She had to resist the urge to close her eyes and breathe him in.

Instead, she balled her fist, reared back, and punched him in the face as hard as she could.

He fell back, tumbled over his chair, and sprawled on the rough wooden floor.

Lenna shook out her hand, cursing at the pain. First the damned bees and now this.

Orzili sat up, dabbed at a cut high on his cheek.

"I deserved that," he said.

"You're damn right you did, you shit! Where have you been? Eight turns, Orzili. Eight bloody turns I've been waiting! For you, for a message, for word of any kind. And I've gotten nothing. Nothing!"

"I know. I'm sorry. I've...I've meant to. Truly."

"Meant to what, you bastard? Meant to come back? Meant to tell me what you've been doing, and why you decided you could do it without me?"

"I haven't done it without you. I've been..." He pressed his lips thin, his gaze sliding away.

"You've been what?"

When he didn't answer, she stalked around the overturned chair and stood over him. "You've been what, Orzili? Tell me now, or get out and don't ever come back."

Staring down at him, she noticed things she had missed before. His sextant rested on her table. He wore ill-fitting clothes —stained breeches that were too loose and cinched tightly with a piece of hemp rope, and a threadbare linen shirt, its sleeves barely reaching his wrists. He had Spanned to Kantaad and found clothes here. For her? Had he gone so quickly from not needing her at all, to being desperate for her?

"There was a second you—she followed another Walker from fourteen years in the future. We were to kill him, and with him, Mearlan IV's infant daughter."

Lenna glowered through narrowed eyes. "Mearlan was killed, and his entire family with him."

"That's not quite true, though it is what Pemin and the Sheraighs want people to believe. The princess lives."

"And you've been hunting her with this other me?"

"That's right."

Jealousy flared in her chest. "And what else have you been doing with this older Lenna? Is she better than I am? More skilled, more experienced?"

"I wouldn't know."

Something in the way he said this...

"Your choice or hers? Mine?"

"Lenna—"

"Answer my question!"

He wouldn't look at her.

"You tried to seduce her, didn't you?"

"I didn't think of her... She's you! And yes, I am helpless before you, in any incarnation, in any time or place."

She had to admit, that was neatly done.

"Nothing happened between us," he went on. "You have my word on that."

"And where is this other woman now?"

"In her own time, where and when she belongs." He climbed to his feet, and touched a finger to that cut again, smearing the trickle of blood. "Our work isn't done. This other Walker lives still, and he has Mearlan's daughter with him. There's also a woman who has joined him—a Walker as well. And they've been helped by Ancients."

"It's your work, not ours. Why haven't these Walkers gone back to save Mearlan's life?"

This smile appeared genuine. "Their one weakness. They have no chronofors. His was broken the night Mearlan died. The woman's was taken from her by agents of Sheraigh. They're trapped in this time."

"Then why aren't they dead? You and me, working together—a different me, but still—they shouldn't have eluded you."

"I told you they had help. From Ancients, from servants of the God, from sheer dumb luck. I've come close to killing them any number of times."

"And she did as well?"

Again, his glance wandered. There was more to this tale than he wished to tell her. Lenna crossed her arms.

"I think you should go," she said, her heart breaking on the words. "You wear your secrets poorly, Orzili, and you're not the man you were when you left me."

Orzili winced. He looked to be on the verge of tears. "No, I'm not. I still love you, though. I need you more than I ever have. I work for Pemin, as you do, and also for the school at Sholiss—the school we both built."

"You left me!" she said, voice rising. "You took on this task without telling me anything! You just vanished!"

"I had to!" A plea as much as a defense. "You couldn't meet her, not without risking your sanity! And she insisted that we tell no one, not even you. Especially not you. The dangers of telling you about your own future, particularly a Walk of such length. So yes, I kept secrets from you, not because I wanted to, but because I had to."

She thought this plausible—all of it. And yet, to her great surprise, she didn't trust him. They had known each other for decades, had loved each other for nearly as long. But this man before her struck her as unfamiliar and, more, untrustworthy.

"I don't believe you," she said.

"It's true! I swear—"

"I can accept that you worried for my sanity, and that the other me wanted to limit the damage she did. That all makes sense. I'm saying that I don't believe you—I don't believe *in* you. You're too different, and I sense that there's much you're not telling me."

He nodded. "There's another you," he said. "A third. She showed up one day, having Walked back a qua'turn with a message for the other Lenna and me. They met and she...she lost her mind. She lives still, in this time, but without a chronofor. She and I didn't get along very well."

A third Lenna. She felt sick. "Why not?"

She had some difficulty following his explanation, but she gathered that he feared so much for the sanity of the woman who had come back fourteen years that he was willing to consider any remedy, regardless of what they might mean for this third Lenna. No wonder the woman didn't trust him.

No wonder she didn't.

"What else?" she said when he had finished. "I want to know everything. You wish to have my help? First you'll confess all, explain all. No secrets. That's how we've lived for all these years."

To his credit, Orzili agreed to this. She sat at the table. He paced their flat. And he told her of the tri-sextants he'd been using—an advance from their shared future. He described Mearlan's assassination, his own pursuit of this Walker and the princess, his torture of the boy, their confrontations, all of which had ended with the boy's escape and Orzili's humiliation.

The sky outside their flat darkened, and still he spoke, until Lenna started to believe that perhaps they had come to the end of his secrets.

She didn't like all that she heard. He had treated the older Lenna poorly. He admitted as much. And his treatment of the boy... Yes, they were both assassins. She had made peace with their profession long ago.

Torture was another matter. She couldn't have done it.

At some point, as dusk gave way to night and she rose to light candles, Lenna realized that she no longer loved him, and would not ever again. This both saddened her and came as a relief. She missed the man who left her so many turns ago. For some time now she had mourned what they once shared. It would be easier, though, to help this Orzili if she didn't also have to learn to love him again.

She said as much when he finished his tale.

He stared at her in silence for a long time before finally saying, incredulous, "I'm your husband."

"You are. You left me anyway."

"I've explained—"

"Yes, you have. And I'm grateful. That doesn't mean I have to love you again. Love doesn't work like that."

"It's also not something you can simply snuff out, like a candle flame. You might come to love me again, if only you remain willing to try."

"I don't want to try. Losing you this time was... I don't want to go through that again."

"You won't!"

"I don't believe you." She stood, stretched. "I'm going to bed now. You can sleep out here. As far as the world is concerned, we'll remain husband and wife. I have no interest in anyone else, and I know that presenting ourselves as married will make everything easier. But I don't love you anymore. I won't love you again. And I don't want you in my bed."

She didn't wait for his reply but walked into the bedroom that had been theirs and shut the door behind her. Only when she was in bed, her face pressed to her pillow, which smelled of him to this day, did she allow herself to cry.

CHAPTER FIFTEEN

4th Day of Sipar's Ascent, Year 634

After her exchange with the Tirribin, Maeli and Teelo, Droë approached Hayncalde Castle and circled its walls, walking at normal speed, trying to sense the Walker or Walkers within. And failing.

The miasma of misfuture enveloped the entire city and had, she guessed, spread into the land beyond. But she thought that whoever had caused it must have left Hayncalde. Tirribin were as attuned to Walkers as Arrokad were to storms at sea, or Shonla were to light and fear. If the Walker remained, Droë would have known, even through this cloud of altered time.

It struck her as odd that Maeli and Teelo could not tell, but maybe they had been immersed in this misfuture for too long.

As she passed the castle's main gate for the second time, several of the soldiers eyed her. One pointed, and another said, "If you're lookin' for company, you'll have to wait. I'm off in another two bells."

The others laughed.

"You're rude," she said. "I'd sooner seek company with a horse."

The man glared, but his companions laughed even harder. Droë moved on, pleased with herself.

She returned to the waterfront, found the young Tirribin again.

"Did you sense the Walker?" Maeli asked.

"I didn't. I'm sorry. I believe he or she has left the castle, which means that this cloud of misfuture shouldn't grow any worse."

"It's bad enough as it is," Teelo said. "Even if the humans don't alter time any more than they already have, the damage is done." He glanced at his sister. "I think we need to leave."

"No. This is our city. It's been our home..." She made a small gesture that seemed to encompass all of memory. "I can't remember any other place. I won't leave. Tell him," she said to Droë.

"It's not my place to tell either of you anything. In this case, though, I have to agree with Teelo. None of us should remain here. Both of you should have sensed that the Walker is gone. Neither of you could because of what living here has done to you. You'll be yourselves again once you get away from this place. Ujie can help you leave, carry you somewhere else. Or there's a Shonla I know. He can—"

"I won't leave!" Maeli scowled at Droë and then at her brother before blurring away at Tirribin speed.

Teelo stared after her. "She'll be back. She always comes back." He turned to her. "You've seen Ujie?"

"She and I have journeyed together."

"Is she the one who...who changed you?"

"That's rude."

"Is it?" he asked. "I thought I was merely expressing curiosity."

Droë frowned. "I think it's more than that." After a pause, she said, "No, she's not."

"Then why has she befriended you?"

Droë raised an eyebrow.

"Forgive me," he said, staring at his feet. "That might have been rude."

"It's a long tale. What matters is the Most Ancient One and I are friends. And I consider the two of you friends as well. She'll help you if I ask her to."

"Why would you consider us your friends? Maeli has been quite rude to you. And I...well, I've allowed her to be."

"The first time we met, you had cause. I came to your city uninvited and did not ask permission to hunt until I was forced to. I handled matters poorly. And this time...I would have questions about me, too."

"You're more generous than I would be."

"Or me."

They wheeled. Maeli stood behind them.

"You've been listening?" Teelo asked.

"Yes. If I'd been hunting, you both would have given years." She sauntered forward, ghostly eyes fixed on Droë. "I won't claim to understand this transformation of yours, but you have grown, become more than you were, and more than I am. I'm jealous, to be honest. I admire what you are. And I won't deny that you're quite beautiful. More than any human I've ever seen. More even than any Tirribin."

Droë wasn't sure how to respond. She had spent little time with the girl, but she had some inkling of how difficult such an admission would be for her.

"Thank you," she said, sketching a small bow. "You honor me."

Maeli wrinkled her nose. "No, I don't. I just said something nice, which is odd, I know."

Teelo's eyes widened. "Did you make a joke about yourself?"

"Careful, brother," she said. Droë couldn't tell whether she spoke in jest or in earnest. The Tirribin glanced around. "I'm hungry. Is either of you hungry?"

They were, and they set off in different directions to hunt.

As she stalked her evening meal, Droë pondered again the problem of the city's misfutures. Why would anyone bend history so many times? Walkers paid a dear price for each journey back through time, and yet the very air in this city was so confused with altered timelines that she thought it likely the castle's Walker had braved the between again and again and again.

Droë had yet to eat, and she was close behind a young sailor who would have made a fine meal, but she halted at the mouth of a narrow alley and gazed back at the towers and battlements of Hayncalde Castle. Tobias had come here. He told her as much that night on the ship in Herjes. Cresten—Orzili—had come here, too. He had tortured Tobias in the dungeon of Hayncalde Castle. He had pursued the Walker and the dead sovereign's infant daughter.

To no avail, as far as she knew. She herself had thwarted him, stopped a battle he might well have won, ordered Qiyed to carry him to far-off Flynse. She didn't believe these setbacks would keep him from trying again, and as often as was necessary, to achieve what he sought. If he had access to a Walker, he would not scruple to change history repeatedly until he achieved his desired ends.

Was he—or a Walker working for him—responsible for these misfutures?

She continued her hunt. The sailor was safe on his ship, but she contented herself with an older man, fed well.

After, she walked to the edge of the sea and called for Ujie. She didn't raise her voice, but the Most Ancient One's name rang across the shoreline like a plucked note on a lute. Within a spire-count, the Arrokad surfaced before her, her pale, tapered face framed by sleek black hair. She emerged from the waves, strode toward her, naked in the dim glow of a sickle moon.

"Well met, cousin. You are ready to leave this place?"

Droë shook her head. "I'm not. This city is troubled. Teelo and Maeli need our help."

Ujie did not conceal her surprise. "You came to humble them—the girl in particular—now you wish to give them aid?"

"They're Tirribin, Ancients, like you and me."

Drops of water wound twisting courses over Ujie's face, down her chin and neck, over her body. "This is true. What sort of trouble?"

"A question of time. It is confused here. Misfuture piled upon misfuture. I believe humans have sought to bend history to their purposes. One particular human, actually. A man I know from some years ago. He is..." She felt her expression curdle. "He has changed since I knew him. Once I declared him a friend, but I've come to regret this."

"You know I care little for the affairs of humans," Ujie said, distaste flattening her tone.

"He pursues the human you know. Tobias—he who owes you a boon."

"Does he pursue the Walker or the child the Walker shelters?"

"Both."

The circling of the Arrokad's hand betrayed impatience. "Politics, vengeance, bloody squabbles over power and gold and matters that are too trivial to warrant our attention. Humans grow tiresome."

"Yes," Droë said, knowing she needed to proceed with care. "And yet there remains the matter of your boon."

Ujie grinned, bearing her fearsome teeth. "You are clever, and you have come to know me far too well."

Droë smiled, her cheeks warming.

"Do you love him still?"

Her smile fled as quickly as it had come. "I care for him. I expect I will until he dies. I don't believe I love him anymore. I would certainly never think to interfere in the commerce between the two of you. But neither will I allow this other human I know to kill him. Or the child."

"And so you summoned me..."

"For guidance. I wish to know how I might gain entry to the castle. I wish to speak with the other human."

"To what end?"

"I don't know yet. To confirm my suspicions. To warn him of my continued loyalty to..." She trailed off.

Ujie was shaking her head. "This is a mistake, I think."

"My mistake to make," Droë said, knowing that she risked angering the Arrokad.

"Yes. You are free to do as you please." Ujie's voice remained level. "I will not try to stop you. I choose not to help you either."

Disappointed though she was, Droë could not fault the Arrokad. "Very well, cousin. Thank you. If there is a price to pay for my summons..."

She broke off at another shake of the Arrokad's head. Ujie's mien softened, and she canted her head. "We are beyond such things, Droë. Surely you sense that by now. We are kin, friends, companions. There is no cost to you in any summons, nor is there even the commerce of boon and promise, at least not for my part."

"You honor me," she said for the second time that night. She meant it even more in this instance.

"I honor what we share." She shifted, appearing eager to be in the surf once more. "When you are ready to leave this place, you will call for me again?"

"Of course, cousin."

Ujie nodded, sloshed back into the waves, dove. When Droë could no longer see her, she started toward the city. An idea had come to her, startling in its simplicity.

Impatient to see it through, she blurred into Hayncalde and through the lanes to the castle gate.

The guards there, the same ones she had seen earlier in the night, gawked as she slowed to human speed. To them, it would seem she had simply winked into view.

The man who had called to her was the first to regain his voice.

"Couldn't bear to be away from me, eh, doll?"

She entered the gate, walked to where the soldiers waited. "I've come to speak with Orzili. Is he within the castle?"

They regarded one another.

"Who are you?" another guard asked. He had more years than the others. Their commander perhaps.

"I am an Ancient," she said. "He knows me as Droë."

"You're an Ancient?" The lustful one. "I'm not sure I believe that." Rude still.

She eyed him, blurred. An instant later, she stood behind him. She grabbed him with both hands, lifted him off his feet, and shoved him against the nearest wall. His cheek pressed to the stone, she could hardly make out his words when he said, "All right, all right! I believe you!"

Droë set him back on the ground and faced the commander. "As I said, I would speak with Orzili. Is he here?"

"He's not, Ancient One. He's...he's gone away for a time. I don't know where, or when he'll return."

She hadn't reckoned on this. After a pause, she said, "What about your Walker? You have one of those, don't you?"

The soldiers exchanged another set of furtive glances. "We did, yes. She's gone, too."

Most interesting.

Orzili refused to sleep on chairs in his own common room. Even this Lenna—the one from his own time, the one whose love he had taken for granted—didn't want him anymore. Fine. As she said, they would go on as husband and wife. As far as the rest of the world was concerned, they would remain as they had long been.

For his part, though, he would not live in his home as an exile. Better to Span back and forth between Fanquir and Hayncalde each day. He told Lenna as much in a hastily scrawled missive that he left on their dining table. His wording might have been harsher than was wise under the circumstances. He didn't care. If she didn't like what he had to say, she could tell him as much when next they spoke.

He climbed the rickety staircase to the roof of their building, stripped off his clothes, aimed, and activated his sextant. This once, he welcomed the abuse of the wind. Let it scour away his anger, his hurt, his loss.

So it was that he reached the inner courtyard of Hayncalde Castle in time to see that blond, dark-skinned beauty blur to one of Sheraigh's fine soldiers and hoist the guard off his feet as she would a sack of flour.

Orzili hurried toward the gate, saw Droë pivot away from the soldiers.

"Don't let her go!" he called.

"Who—"

"This is Orzili. Give me a moment. Keep her there."

He entered the castle and made his way to his chamber. He dressed in a pair of black breeches and a silk shirt he was still buttoning when he emerged from the stairway back into the courtyard.

Only then did he realize he was weaponless. He hesitated, walked on. From what he had seen in Herjes, he gathered that she was an Ancient, a Tirribin and much more. If she wished to kill him, a sword wouldn't save him. Neither would a flintlock. So be it.

Reaching the gate, he stepped into the torchlight, nodded to the commander, addressed Droë.

"Thank you for waiting for me."

"You've been Spanning."

"Your kind can sense this?"

She shook her head. "Your hair is wild, your face is red from the gap wind, and you appeared quite suddenly in the courtyard."

"You were always observant." He opened a hand, a welcoming gesture, he hoped. "Would you care to speak in my chamber?"

"Your gardens, I believe," she said. "My kind do not like to enter human habitations."

"The gardens then." He took a step in that direction, eyes on her. She followed, as did two of the guards.

"No," Orzili said. "We'll be fine."

The guards frowned—all of them. Fear of Ancients ran deep.

"You will guarantee my safety?" Orzili asked Droë.

"So long as you make no attempt to harm me, no harm will come to you. You have my word."

The soldiers didn't look satisfied, but Orzili walked on, Droë with him.

He regarded her sidelong as they walked. Moon glow and the occasional torch illuminated her features. Most of the time when he thought of her, he imagined her as she was long ago. A normal Tirribin, childlike in stature and behavior. In those odd moments when he remembered that she was now grown, he envisioned her as menacing, more demon than person. He had forgotten how exquisite she was, how desirable.

"I did not come here to lie with you," she said.

He missed a step and nearly sprawled on the stone path they followed. "I didn't think you had."

"No? I've seen how men look at women when they think they won't be noticed. I saw how you were looking at me."

"I was... Yes, I was staring. Forgive me."

"That's more polite of you than I expected. Last time we met you were very rude."

"Last time we met, you denied me something that would have made my life much easier."

"Tobias's death."

"And that of the princess, yes."

Droë shook her head, faced forward again. "I haven't come here to speak of them. Not really."

That was disappointing. "Why have you come?"

She didn't answer immediately. A faint crease roughened her forehead. "Perhaps I *have* come to speak of them. You have been using a Walker. Repeatedly. In doing so, you have spawned misfuture upon misfuture until this city is steeped in them. My kind live here, and you're hurting them."

He sensed an opportunity, knew there were risks to pursuing it.

They reached one of the gardens and he slowed, indicated a stone bench on which they might sit. Droë remained standing and crossed her arms over her chest.

"It wasn't my intent to hurt any Ancient," he told her. "That said, I can't concern myself with such things. I have a task to complete, one that will have great implications for the future of every human in this city. I can't worry about a couple of Tirribin."

She bristled, as he had known she would.

"You dare to dismiss Ancients in that way."

He remembered that rasp in her voice from their earlier interactions and feared he had miscalculated.

"I'm merely telling you what you would tell me if our positions were reversed. If I were to inform you that commerce among Ancients was doing harm to humans, I think you would tell me that your affairs were not our concern. What I'm saying is no different."

The furrows in her forehead deepened, but she didn't argue.

"You had your chance to help me, on that ship near Vondehm. You chose instead to offer your aid to Tobias and the woman with him. Now, you see that you made an error. I seem to remember that whatever bound you to the two of them was no more significant than the friendship we once shared. And of the three of us, I am by far the most influential, the one best able to negotiate not only with humans but also with Ancients. I have access to power and wealth. At a word from me, the Walks from this castle that are harming your friends will cease. But I need something in return, namely your help in finding Tobias and Hayncalde's princess. My Walker goes back to prevent their escape, and each time, Tobias and the woman elude me anyway. Which means I have to try again, and again. As I said, I intend no harm to anyone but my enemies, but what can I do?"

He didn't mention, of course, that his Walker was gone, that there would be no further Walks from this castle. He didn't have to.

"Your Walker has left you," she said. "Your guards told me so."

"A temporary absence." He said it too quickly. Not for most humans, but Pemin would have noticed. He expected Droë would too.

Her thoughts took her in a different direction. "They said 'she' when they spoke of the Walker. Is it your friend from Windhome? The one you loved? Lenna. That was her name."

His cheeks heated. Again, not enough for a human to notice.

Droë though was an Ancient, a predator. Gauging such reactions was in her very nature.

She smiled, baring teeth that made him want to back away. "It *is* her. I can tell."

"Yes. We're...we married long ago."

"I'm glad for you," she said in a voice devoid of irony. "I recall that you missed her very much. It's good that you found each other again."

He remembered this about her as well. She could be cold and shrewd one moment, caring and innocent the next, and terrifying the one after that. They had spoken of Lenna a good deal when he was a boy, newly exiled from the Travelers' Palace, living in the lanes of Windhome. It wasn't a conversation he wished to have now.

"She may come back here," he said. "Though our home is elsewhere. So I might have to find a different Walker. One way or another, I'll have to send someone back. I have to find the boy."

"Tobias isn't a boy. As I recall from that night, he nearly bested you. And clearly he has managed to defeat you repeatedly."

Shrewd was certainly the right word.

"He was fortunate that night. Your arrival saved him. He may be Windhome-trained, and I'll grant that he's both clever and brave, but in the end, he *will* die. Since we knew each other I've become far more than I was. I'm a man other men fear, and for good reason."

"You're a braggart."

"I'm an assassin."

She considered him, unimpressed. "Lenna is, too?"

"Yes."

She shook her head. "It won't matter. He loves the woman and the child too much. And the woman loves him. You can't beat them."

"Lenna and I love each other." The words rang hollow.

She said nothing. No doubt she would have thought it rude to argue the point.

"You have to choose, Droë," he said, forcing himself past the dull ache in his chest. "Do you care about Tobias more than you do about your fellow Tirribin? You can help him or them. You can't save them all."

"I could if I took all your years."

It seemed that ice water dribbled over him, prickling the skin on his scalp, his neck, his chest and arms and hands.

"You swore that you wouldn't harm me." He silently cursed the flutter in his voice.

"And I won't this night, in this garden to which you invited me. I swore no oaths beyond that."

She blurred, as she had in the gate when he first spotted her this night. In less than a heartbeat she was so close to him that her breath warmed his neck. He caught the elusive scent of decay that clung to all her kind.

He tried to pull away, but she grabbed hold of his arm, her grip like iron, and put her lips to his throat.

"You presume to dictate to me what I must choose and when I must do so?" she whispered. The words tickled and chilled. "That is beyond rude. It is a mortal affront. You claim friendship, but you seek to twist me to your purposes. You still think of me as a child. I'm not. Truly, I never was. I am older than you by centuries. I'm smarter than you, stronger and faster than you, far more deadly than you ever will be, no matter how many times you kill."

Orzili thought he might die then. He had watched her take years, had seen in more than a few nightmares the shifting, oily glow that emanated from her when she fed.

Instead of killing him, she stepped away and laughed, not kindly.

"You will not send Lenna or any other Walker back from this castle again. If you do, I will consider it an assault on all Ancients, and I will respond accordingly."

He drew breath to respond.

"Do not think to challenge me, Cresten. Or next time I *will* feed." She started away, back toward the gate.

First Lenna and now this. "My name is Orzili," he said, mustering what little pride he had left.

"Not to me," she said over her shoulder. "To me, you will always be Cresten."

She blurred again, and he lost sight of her. His legs, already shaky, gave way, and he lowered himself to that stone bench.

CHAPTER SIXTEEN

4th Day of Sipar's Ascent, Year 634

When Orzili could stand again, he left the castle by way of the west gate. Fewer guards there, fewer questions about where he was headed.

Droë thought she had defeated him, but she couldn't have known all that transpired between the Arrokad and him that night on the bay in Herjes.

He strode through empty lanes to a lonely stretch of shoreline and spoke a name to the wind and the rush and retreat of the surf. Soon, he spotted a pale form slipping through waves like a porpoise, approaching the strand at speed.

The Arrokad emerged from the brine scaled from his waist down, moonlight gleaming on his wet shoulders and broad chest. Watching him walk out of the gulf, Orzili tried to control his breathing. He hated treating with Ancients, this night a stark reminder of why.

"Human," Qiyed said by way of greeting. Silver, serpentine eyes scanned the coastline before settling on Orzili.

"Good evening, Most Ancient One."

"You summoned me."

Carefully. He did not wish to owe anything to this creature. "I did as you instructed."

The Arrokad's gaze sharpened. "You have seen her?"

"Just now. She's here, in Hayncalde."

Qiyed glanced around again, lifted his chin as if sniffing the air. "I sense...something. Tirribin. More than one."

"She said there are Tirribin in this city. She's concerned for their well-being. I have been using a Walker, and she told me that the misfutures we've created have been harmful to them."

"That could be useful. Thank you."

"Have you seen Tobias?"

The creature stilled and for a second time that night, Orzili feared for his life. "Did I not tell you that if I did I would inform you?"

"Yes, but—"

"That is what I will do."

"You have much that occupies your time, Most Ancient One. I merely thought—"

"I know what you thought. You believe I am likely to disregard your wishes, to take all I can from you and offer little in return. You believe I bargained in bad faith. You are correct about all but that last. I do not care about human squabbles. But commerce is all to an Ancient. If I find the Walker, you will know of it."

He wasn't certain he believed the Arrokad, but he could only say, "Of course, Most Ancient One."

Qiyed flashed a cold smile—Orzili wasn't fooling him—and began to wade back into the surf. "You have done well. I will remember that you have done me a service."

"Thank you," Orzili called after him. Already the Arrokad had slipped under the water's surface.

Orzili stood on the strand for some time, too weary and dispirited to walk back to the castle. Not so long ago, he had been a man others respected, even feared. He had love, he had gold, he had whatever future he might choose for himself. Or so it seemed.

Now Lenna was gone, Ancients treated him with contempt,

and Tobias remained a threat to all his ambitions. It was infuriating.

Eventually he left the shore and trudged back to the castle, his boots as heavy as stone. He would Span in the morning. To Lenna. Perhaps to Belsan as well. He had seen to it that the Walkers would not easily find a chronofor. So long as they were trapped in this time, there was only so much they could do to reestablish the Hayncalde Supremacy. And after all that had gone wrong these past few turns, he had to believe his fortunes were due to change.

Droë moved at Tirribin speed through the castle grounds and then along lanes leading to the waterfront. Before long, she found Maeli and Teelo and told them of her encounter with Cresten. She couldn't assure them that he wouldn't send a Walker back again, but she told them that if he did, she would take his years.

"I made this clear to him," she said. "And I won't hesitate to punish him if he defies me. I give you my word."

Both Tirribin thanked her. Maeli seemed truly grateful. They invited her to remain in their city for as long as she liked, for which she thanked them. In truth, she had no desire to spend more time than was necessary in Hayncalde. She had come here to make peace with the Tirribin, and that she had done. Tomorrow evening she and Ujie would leave this place for...for wherever they might choose to go. She longed to journey again. Odd. For so much of her life she had lived in Windhome, content to speak with novitiates at the palace and hunt that city's lanes. Only in the past few months had she started to explore other isles. Now she couldn't stand to remain in any one place for too long. She thought Tresz would find this amusing.

She hunted again with the Tirribin, found a place to sleep, looked forward to leaving.

Upon waking the next evening, all of that changed.

The stench assaulted her the moment she stirred. Within a fivecount she was fully awake, alert, even alarmed.

She left the place where she had slept and called for the two Tirribin. Their names had barely crossed her lips when they blurred into view, halting before her, wringing their hands.

"You smell them?" Teelo asked, his voice higher than usual.

"How could I not? Have you seen them?"

They shook their heads.

"We haven't had Belvora here in a very long time," Maeli told her. "I hate them. I don't want them here now. And I sense there are a good many of them."

Droë agreed. Five at least. Maybe more. They would be hunting for magickal creatures. Travelers probably. Perhaps Magi and Binders as well. Only when she heard the harsh shriek of a winged one overhead did it occur her to wonder if they might be hunting her and her friends.

A second Belvora trumpeted in reply, also close, difficult to spot against the dark sky.

A third screeched from farther off.

The Tirribin and Droë searched the sky for them. Maeli was the first to spot one.

"There!" She pointed.

Teelo pointed at another one. As Droë's eyes adjusted to the gloom and the contrast of membranous wings against it, she spotted two more. The Belvora certainly appeared to be converging on the three of them.

"I brought you playmates, Droë!"

She went cold at the sound of that voice. Not panic this time. Yes, she feared for herself and for the Tirribin, but mostly she felt fury: icy, controlled, a blend of rage and hatred she had never experienced before.

She rounded on him slowly. He stood some distance from her, though not so much that she couldn't blur to him in the span of a heartbeat. He had scaled himself, swept his hair back from his face. He was as beautiful as ever.

Maeli and Teelo pivoted as well, stared at the Arrokad and then at her.

"I find it fascinating that in this one instance—with respect to fighting the winged ones—humans have been more successful than our kind. What would you give now for a musket or two?"

"You have allied yourself with Belvora? You've brought them here to fight your battle? Are you so afraid of me, Qiyed?"

He aimed a rigid finger at her. "Last time we met, you had the other Arrokad with you! Do not dare speak to me of being afraid!"

"Shall we fight now, you and me? Send the Belvora away. My Tirribin friends will do nothing. It will be just the two of us. Will you fight, Most Ancient One?" She infused as much sarcasm as possible into the honorific. "Shall I issue a formal challenge, under rules of the Guild?"

"She's dead, you know. Your friend, the Arrokad. I've seen to her end as well."

At that, terror did grip her. Not for herself, but for the one closest friend she had in this world.

"You lie!"

His smug grin returned. "You would wish it so, but I assure you I do not. You are alone again, Droënalka. As I promised you would be."

She wanted to weep, but she didn't dare. Not now, not in front of this creature, with winged hunters wheeling overhead.

"She's not alone," Maeli said, taking a step in Qiyed's direction. "She has us."

"He's not an enemy you want," Droë said softly.

Teelo looked up at her. "He summons Belvora to attack a fellow Ancient? He's not a friend we want either. We'll stand with you."

A different sort of tear stung her eyes. "Thank you, friends," she whispered. "Have you fought Belvora before?"

Both of them shook their heads.

"Take their years as you would any creature. It can be done.

I've done it, long, long ago. Beware their claws and teeth. Be ready to drop a long way after you have killed."

The Tirribin nodded, flanking her, putting distance between them so they would have room to fight.

Qiyed laughed, then shouted a command. And it began.

A storm of wings and talons and teeth raged around them, souring the air. Droë counted six Belvora, but she could have been wrong. They were swift, agile. They soared in and out of sight like wraiths. She had spoken true: She had once killed a Belvora by taking its years. But never had she battled so many. And that one had been on the ground when she scrambled up its back and latched herself to its neck. She doubted these creatures would accommodate her so.

Two swooped low, speeding toward her from opposite sides. She dove to ground. The Tirribin were forced to do the same.

These Belvora had no sooner swept upward and away than another pair stooped at them. At this rate, they would have no chance even to fight back. Droë refused to allow that. She leapt to her feet, drawing warning cries from Maeli and Teelo. She ignored them, eyed the nearer of the two winged Ancients. The Belvora reached for her, talons extended, teeth bared.

Droë leapt again. The Belvora twisted its wings, trying to change course. Failing that, it attempted to flip over in mid-flight. Too late. Droë caught hold of the creature around its neck, crooked her arm to maintain her grip. The Belvora screamed, reached for her with its claws, buffeted her with its wings.

Droë held fast. Girl-Droë would have put her mouth to its neck and taken its years, riding the Ancient as it swooped and dove and bucked. Now, she didn't need to. She wrapped her other arm around its throat and with a quick, violent jerk, snapped its neck.

The Belvora went slack and its wingbeats ceased. It started to spiral downward. Droë jumped clear, shifted as she fell, and landed lightly on her toes and hands.

The Tirribin weren't where she'd left them. It took her a moment to spot them. Both rode Belvora, the oily colors of their feeding glow making them easy to follow. The winged ones tried in vain to throw them off.

Two more Belvora came for her, attacking in tandem. She ran at one, jumped at it, and managed to throw a punch that caught the Ancient square in the face. It veered up and away. As Droë dropped, she tried to spin to face the other.

The Belvora was on her faster than she had anticipated. Talons raked across her neck and face. She gritted her teeth against white-hot pain. Blood stained her shift.

Two more Belvora crashed to the cobbles. The Tirribin landed near her, as graceful as cats.

Droë searched quickly for Qiyed but didn't see him.

Blood and bone.

The three remaining Belvora glided toward them again. Better odds now. Smarter creatures might have fled, seeing what had happened to the others. The winged ones, though skilled hunters, were dull-witted.

Teelo vaulted onto one of the Belvora, avoiding its flailing arms, and attached himself to its neck.

Maeli jumped as well. Her Belvora might have been smarter than the other, or more observant. Or maybe it was just fortunate. It altered its flight with perfect timing, caught Maeli in its talons.

The Tirribin yowled, and the Belvora cried out in triumph.

The last Belvora had almost reached Droë, its claws stretching toward her. She grabbed the creature's wrists and allowed its speed to carry her into a tight, violent pivot. She spun once, twice —the Belvora fought to free itself. On the third orbit, she released it. The winged one whirled out of control, slammed into the wall of a nearby shop. It collapsed to the cobbles but started to stand.

Droë closed on it with Tirribin speed and, before it could right itself, gave its neck a vicious twist, as she had the first.

She straightened, wheeled, in time to see the other Belvora hurl Maeli toward the ground. Droë raced to catch her, but even at speed, she knew she couldn't get there in time. Maeli contorted herself, but she fell too fast. She didn't have a chance.

The Tirribin hit the stone lane with a stomach-turning thud and lay still, her body and limbs at impossible angles.

The Belvora dove after her and stepped out of its landing to loom over the Tirribin. Droë collided with the winged one while still in her blur, knocking the creature off its feet. In her rage and her grief, she grabbed the Ancient's hideous head with both hands and ripped it off the body. Dark, foul blood stained her hands and shift. She didn't care. She threw the head away and rushed back to Maeli.

The last Belvora shrieked above her. Teelo landed an instant later. He made not a sound. Didn't move toward his sister. He simply stared. Droë watched the Belvora he had been fighting fly out of sight on labored wingbeats.

Magick lashed at Droë, but this she had expected. It bounced off her defenses, harmless, impotent.

Tracing this attack to its origin, she spotted Qiyed. He stood in shadow, not so smug now.

"I challenge you, Qiyed," she said, her rasp distorting the words. "A combat of Ancients, by the customary rules, with promise of Distraint for he or she who violates those rules or refuses a rightful challenge."

He stepped forward, gaze jumping from Droë to Teelo. She knew what he was thinking. If he could kill them both, he might avoid a fair test of combat.

"I have heard this challenge, and I will swear as much before the Guild."

All of them turned.

Joy bloomed in Droë's chest.

Ujie stood at the mouth of a nearby lane, her body scored with bloody gashes, her face a mask of blood and bruises. She came forward limping, her right arm stiff and held close to her torso.

"He said you were dead."

Ujie kept her eyes fixed on Qiyed. "I should be. Twelve Belvora he sent for me."

Qiyed appeared unperturbed. "I sent no one."

"You lie. One of them confessed before I killed her. Their

bodies lie on a strand at the south end of Fairisle. Beheaded all. I was aided by a Shonla before all was done, and he heard this confession. Your crimes are known, Qiyed. You were to be called before the Guild for sanction and execution. Droë issued her challenge before I could tell you so. You should consider yourself fortunate. Now you have a chance, faint though it may be."

He regarded them both, calculation in the silver eyes, his lips pressed thin.

"Very well," he said. "By custom, I have the first right to choose time or place. I choose the strand near the Notch, to the south of here."

Predictable. He would seek to lure her into the sea, and he would hope to use the boulders on the shoreline to mitigate her speed.

"Fine," she said. "Tomorrow night, three bells past the moon's rise."

His mouth twitched. He would have hoped that rage would embolden her, make her rash. He wanted to fight her now.

"Tomorrow," he repeated. "Three bells past moon's rise."

"On penalty of Distraint."

He sneered. "On penalty of Distraint." He didn't wait for her to say more, but left them there and strode off in the direction of the sea.

Droë pulled her attention back to Maeli. The Tirribin hadn't moved, but Droë sensed that she lived still, if only barely.

"Can you heal her?" Teelo asked, his voice breaking on the question.

Ujie hobbled closer, knelt on Maeli's other side, every motion seeming to pain her.

She held a hand over the Tirribin's broken form and closed her eyes. After a tencount she opened them again, sorrow lining her lovely face. Droë knew what she would say before she spoke the words.

"I am sorry, cousin. The damage is too great. She is...shattered."

"I'm sorry, Teelo. Qiyed hates me, and I did something last night that alerted him to my presence here. If not for me—"

He cut her off with a small, sharp gesture. "We're friends. Even Maeli accepted this before..." His chin quivered. After some time, he went on. "We chose to fight beside you, and I would again."

Ujie eyed her, gave an almost imperceptible shake of her head.

Droë said, "Thank you." Nothing more.

He lowered himself to the sand near Maeli's body but didn't once look at his sister.

"Where will you go now, cousin?" Ujie asked him, her voice as gentle as early morning waves.

"Why would I go anywhere?"

"Because this place holds nothing for you but sadness and dark memories."

"And," Droë added, "because misfutures still poison the air here."

"Maeli didn't want to leave. This was our city. That's what she said. So, I should stay. That's what she would want."

Ujie caught Droë's eye as she had before and again shook her head.

"Very well," she said. "How can we serve you?"

Surprise penetrated his grief. "You honor me, Most Ancient One. I require no service beyond the obvious: I would see the other Arrokad dead."

"We want that as well," Droë told him. "I've challenged him—you heard me do so. If possible, I'll kill him tomorrow night. But you should know that both Ujie and I have our doubts as to whether he'll honor his acceptance of my challenge."

"Then you'll have to hunt him down. You apologized to me, and I told you that wasn't necessary. But I want him dead, Droë. I want you to promise me that you'll do it."

"Teelo—"

"Forgive me, Most Ancient One, but this is between Droë and me. It's...it's commerce."

Normally, Droë would have expected Ujie to bristle at the

interruption and the words. In this instance, she didn't. Leaving it to Droë to confront the raw anguish in Teelo's expression.

"I'll make every effort to avenge her. I give you my word. I can promise no more than that."

He dropped his chin, wiped at his eyes, and turned his gaze back to the sea.

The following night, Ancients gathered on the strand. Several Arrokad and Shonla, an alarming number of Belvora, a pair of Tirribin from Ysendyr, south of Hayncalde, and even a Hanev, who drew stares from many of the other Ancients.

Ujie had summoned some and had requested that the Shonla inform others.

"The more who come, the better. We want as many Ancients as possible to know of his treachery and to understand that congress with him will make them outcasts among those in the Guild."

Droë didn't believe it would be so easy to turn others against Qiyed. He was charming, brilliant, cunning. She kept her doubts to herself, though, and she stood alone by the shoreline, watching the sea for any sign of the Arrokad. More than once, the arrival of others launched her heartbeat into a sputtering frenzy.

She knew she could defeat him, but she also knew how dangerous he was, and she didn't wish to die this night.

Teelo stood alone as well, apart from the other Ancients, apart from her. He eyed the Belvora with unmasked hatred and even glowered at all the Arrokad except Ujie. Droë thought he looked paler and younger than usual. She wanted to go to him, but she had no idea what to say, and she sensed that he would have fled had she tried to speak with him.

The appointed time came and went without any sign of Qiyed. Still they waited. What was another bell to Ancients?

At last, Ujie stepped away from the others and faced them, moonlight gleaming on black hair and bare shoulders.

"Qiyed of the Arrokad has refused a challenge that he swore, on pain of Distraint, he would accept. I witnessed the challenge and his acceptance of it."

"I issued the challenge," Droë said. "I witnessed his acceptance of it."

"I witnessed the challenge and his acceptance of it," Teelo said, his voice as thin as mist.

Ujie spread her arms. "Three of us, Ancients all. I thereby declare that from this night on, Qiyed of the Arrokad is subject to Distraint. None shall engage with him in commerce of any sort. None shall offer him boons of any sort. Any who have been tied to him by commerce in the past shall now be free of any and all obligations, even those assumed freely and fairly. Those who hear my words are bound by Ancient law to impart these tidings to others who are not here this night. And should one or more of you choose to take Qiyed's life for offenses given, or commerce conducted in bad faith, you shall do so without threat of sanction."

Droë thought of a Shonla named Mivszel who would delight in this. She would have to get word of the Distraint to the isle of Djaiste in Sipar's Labyrinth.

A Belvora stepped forward. "Before we agree to this," the winged one said, in a deep harsh voice, "I would know what that is, and how it came to be so." He aimed a taloned finger at Droë.

Ujie had warned her that this might happen. Still, the words stung. It was one thing for a fellow Tirribin to refer to her as "it," as Maeli had done, and Strie and Kreeva, the Tirribin on Rencyr, before her.

But to be called "that" and "it" before a gathering of the Guild, and by a Belvora... She struggled to keep her chin raised.

"I am Tirribin," she said. "I sense misfuture, feed on years, walk at speed as Tirribin do."

"How did you come to look like that?" asked one of her kind from Ysendyr.

"Arrokad magick. I entered into commerce with Qiyed. He

transformed me, as I requested, in exchange for services I offered to him."

"Why did you want this?"

"I had my reasons," she said. "Qiyed and I first met when I called for an Arrokad for this purpose, so one might say that our arrangement lies at the root of tonight's challenge. That said, it is not the cause of our dispute. Thus I choose to keep my intentions private."

"It is unusual for any Ancient to change so utterly the essence of what she is," an Arrokad said. He was tall, his form as chiseled as Qiyed's. They could have been brothers. "To do so is to defy nature itself. You may consider your reasons a private matter, but I find myself questioning whether you are to be trusted. An Ancient who would do this might do anything."

So be it. "Very well. I did it because I have long been fascinated by love—the act and the emotion. I wished to experience it for myself, and given the nature of Tirribin, and the nature of desire, I could only do so in adult form."

"And did you lie with Qiyed?"

"That's rude!" the Ysendyr Tirribin said, rounding on the Most Ancient One.

"It's all right, cousin." Droë faced the Arrokad. "I did not. And, in fairness, Qiyed did not ask me to."

The Arrokad raised an eyebrow. "Very well." He looked to Ujie, nodded once.

By now, murmured conversations had rippled through the gathered Ancients, but no one else addressed questions to her. At Ujie's raised hand, they quieted.

"We were about to declare Qiyed of the Arrokad under Distraint. Do others wish to speak before we do?"

Silence.

"Very well. I so declare."

"We so declare," the others intoned.

Ujie glanced Droë's way, dipped her chin in satisfaction. Droë remained unsure that any of this would make the least difference.

Orzili could have sworn that the knock came not from his door, but from his shuttered window. He remained seated by his fire, watching the shutters, listening for the sound to repeat. It did moments later.

He stood, loaded and cocked a flintlock, and crossed to the window. Probably he would have been wise to bring in the guards outside his door, but they were Sheraigh men, not his own. He didn't trust them.

He drew his sword and used the tip of the weapon to unlatch the shutters and push them outward. As they swung open, he let the sword clatter to the floor and braced his pistol hand.

Seeing what climbed into his chamber, he stepped back, considered shouting for the soldiers, regardless of what uniform they wore.

A Belvora.

He shouldn't have been surprised. Droë had come to him two nights earlier. Just after dawn this very morning had come word from patrolling soldiers that a lane near the waterfront was littered with dead Belvora, all of them headless. And late this day he had been informed of additional winged demons spotted over the city, of Arrokad seen in the shallows south of the wharves. For reasons he longed to understand better, Ancients had taken a sudden interest in Hayncalde.

This Belvora hopped down from the window to the stone floor, unfolded itself to its full height. Its mane of silver hair framed a face he recognized. This demon had sparred with him—and taunted him—when last he visited the Sana Mountains on Pemin's behalf.

The creature appeared even more huge and threatening in the closed space of the chamber. But her face was lined now, her shoulders stooped. Or was that a trick of the shifting light?

Amber eyes flicked around the chamber, coming to rest on Orzili's pistol. It held up both hands, a gesture of peace.

"I bear tidings," she said, her voice like the scrape of metal on stone. "That is why I have come. I intend you no harm. You are Orzili?"

"I am. And you and I have met before."

"Yes, in the highlands. I remember."

"You wanted to make a meal of me, I think."

The demon crooked a smile, huge teeth gleaming. Orzili took a steadying breath. "You are a Spanner, and so are prey. My hunger was not an expression of animus."

"Well, that's...good to know. Your tidings?"

The demon's smile sharpened. "From Qiyed of the Arrokad," she said. "You are not to call to him by name again. He is under Distraint, and other Arrokad may be listening for such summonings."

Orzili frowned. How was he supposed to ask the demon for help in finding Tobias if he couldn't summon him?

"He told me to tell you that he wants the Walker dead more than ever. He has commanded me to help you. I am allied with other Ancients who will defy the Guild in this way as well."

"Very well. How do I call for you?"

"I am called..." The name she gave was something between a screech and a growl. He couldn't hope to pronounce it.

The Belvora bared her teeth again—less mirth, more bitterness. "You may call me Glimik."

"Thank you." Orzili said this absently, abruptly consumed by a thought that should have come to him two days ago.

Droë was here. Other Ancients were here. Qiyed was here. Drawn by his summons, but still... Why hadn't he considered this sooner? If Tobias and the woman wished to restore the Hayncalde Supremacy, they would have to bring the princess to Daerjen eventually. So why not do it now? They would surmise—correctly—that this was the last place Orzili would search for them.

The Belvora watched him, a grimace distorting the blunt features. At last, it turned to go.

"Wait," Orzili said. "Please."

The winged demon peered back at him.

"We're still searching for the Walkers, as we were when you and I last spoke. It's possible that they're somewhere on this isle."

"You know this?"

"I'm guessing, but I'm right."

She canted her maned head. "Very well. We will begin our search tonight."

The demon climbed out the window, leapt from the sill. The last Orzili saw of her, she was banking up and away from the torchlight and castle walls on outstretched wings.

He closed the shutters and poured himself a cup of wine, his mood lighter than it had been in several turns.

CHAPTER SEVENTEEN

7th Day of Sipar's Ascent, Year 634

Tobias waited by the shore of the Firth of Rime, watching for Droë, unsure of why he expected her to arrive by sea. Changed though she was, she remained Tirribin.

Nevertheless, he repeated his summons and continued to scan the surface of the firth. A half bell passed. More.

He thought about calling for her a third time but dismissed the idea. She would think his persistence rude. He smiled at memories of Windhome.

He had made up his mind to leave when he saw something disturb the water's surface far from the coastline. It skimmed over the swells, heading directly toward him, moving at speed. Far too fast to be a swimming Tirribin. He had taken a risk in coming here, in calling for her. Had he drawn Qiyed's notice instead of hers?

Backing away from the strand, he drew his pistol, made certain it was full-cocked and ready to fire.

As that swimming form neared and took form in the darkness, he realized it was two beings rather than one. Upon reaching the shallows, they slowed, separated, stood. Fair-haired and dark, clothed and naked, both of a similar height, both more beautiful than words could convey. Both with a claim on him.

Droë and the Arrokad, Ujie.

They walked to him, halted so close that he could smell the brine and sweet scent of seaweed coming from Ujie, the faint hint of decay emanating from Droë.

"Tobias," Droë said. "You summoned me."

"I did. Forgive me."

She shrugged, seeming to find it difficult to hold his gaze. "It isn't a matter of forgiveness..."

"There's a cost," he said.

"Yes."

To Ujie, he said, "And for you, too, Most Ancient One?"

She shook her head. "You and I have a boon to settle, and we shall before long. This is commerce between you and Droë. You summoned her. She answered. That I carried her here is a matter between us, not you."

"Very well. You both may be interested in what I have to tell you. Mara, the princess, and I were chased from our home by Belvora. We came to Duvyn, seeking shelter in the castle of the duke, but the castle was attacked. Eight Belvora, and a Hanev."

Droë and the Arrokad shared a look.

It was Ujie who said, "Ancients sometimes cooperate with others of a different sept. Belvora see well in the dark. They would find a Hanev a valuable ally against humans. You are limited at night. The theft of light—that would serve the winged ones."

"I understand. But I spoke to the Hanev."

This drew stares from both Ancients.

"You conversed with it?" Ujie asked.

"With him, yes. I *think* it was a him."

"To what end?"

"I thought it odd that he would work with Belvora. I wanted to know why he had done it. I wondered if he and the winged ones had been acting in partnership with a human who wants us dead."

"Cresten," Droë said. "Orzili."

"That's right."

"What did the Hanev tell you?"

"Something odd. He said that their reason for attacking the castle was 'not a matter that concerns humans.' I tried to learn more, but the Ancient was evasive."

"Ancients do not appreciate being questioned by humans," Ujie said, a chill in her tone. "Our commerce is not something we wish to discuss with your kind."

"I understand. In this case, though, I believe there was more to the Hanev's partnership with the Belvora. When I expressed my belief that the Belvora had come for Mara and me in particular, he didn't deny it. He didn't confirm it either—he talked around it, said Belvora hunt all magickal beings. A direct denial would have been easier, but as I understand it, once an Ancient begins to negotiate commerce, even with humans, he can't resort to falsehood. Is that right?"

"It is," Droë said.

"I had the sense that he couldn't answer my question—probably a matter of previous commerce. And I believe that commerce was with the Arrokad, Qiyed. The one who—"

"We know who he is," Ujie said. The words were abrupt, but her tone had softened. "Qiyed is under Distraint."

"He should be thrice over," Droë said, scowling. "If this is true, he is working with Orzili, which I prohibited, also under threat of Distraint."

"That's why I summoned you. I heard enough of your exchange aboard the ship to know this would bother you."

She eyed him. "You're doing me a service?"

"No. I'm trying to help myself."

"And the child. And Mara."

"Yes."

"You could have lied, offered this information as payment for summoning me."

Tobias grinned. "Isn't this valuable information—suitable payment—even if sharing it helps me too?"

She didn't smile, and he wondered if he had erred, given offense in some way.

After a fivecount, Droë said, "Ujie, would you leave us for a time?"

The Arrokad regarded her, then walked back into the water. After a few steps, she slipped under, vanished from view.

Droë hadn't watched her go, but had kept her gaze on Tobias, intense, hungry even. He thought he understood. He would have preferred her rage to this.

"I have lain with a man," she said.

He opened his mouth, closed it again. What was the correct response?

"I tell you this so that you will know I am no naïf, no child in a woman's body."

"Droë—"

"I didn't tell you the last time we met, because I didn't know how." She took a breath and gestured at herself. "I did this for you. The promise of you, really, since we hadn't met, not in my reckoning."

"I'm...I'm honored."

She gazed to the side, her face in profile, moonlight making a halo of her golden hair. "You told me last time that you thought I was beautiful. Do you still?"

She had steered them into dangerous waters.

"Of course I do."

Droë faced him. "Then I would lie with you. Here, now. Where no one else would see or know. If...if you would like that."

"I can't."

"Why not?" An edge to the question.

"Because I love Mara. Because in all ways that matter, she's my wife. It would be a betrayal of her, of what she and I share."

"She wouldn't know."

"I'd know, and it's not any less of a betrayal if she doesn't find out."

She nodded, looked away again. "I thought of killing her."

His heart froze in his chest. He couldn't draw breath. Terror for Mara, of what Droë might still wish to do to her.

"I thought of taking all her years. And then I thought of taking only most of them and leaving her old and bent and hideous to you."

"Please don't," he whispered, trembling in the cool air.

Annoyance flickered in the wraithlike eyes. "I said I had thought of it, not that I'm still considering it."

"What stopped you?"

"I knew that if I hurt her, or killed her, you would hate me. I didn't want that. And she *is* my friend." Her gaze found his again. "I could make you lie with me, as the price of your summons. Would that not make it less of a betrayal?"

"I would prefer that we found some other way for me to repay you."

"Why?" she asked, the question wrung from her. "Are you so repulsed by me?"

"Of course not!"

"Then why are you so unwilling?"

"Because I'm still just a boy!" His turn to look away. "I'm young, Droë. I look like a grown man, but I'm a Walker, and you know what that means better than most. I came back fourteen years. Which means I'm still... I'm a boy," he said again. "It took several turns before I was ready to lie with Mara, despite how much I love her. I needed to feel...comfortable with her. And I do now. But only with her. I don't want to be with anyone else in that way."

"That seems unusual," she said. "For human males especially."

"It might be." He smiled at a memory. "Maybe this will make you feel better: The reason I owe a boon to Ujie is that I wouldn't lie with her, either."

Her eyes widened. "You refused to lie with an Arrokad?"

Tobias nodded. "So you see, it's not that I'm repulsed by you. Far from it. I'm just... I love Mara."

"You refused Ujie." A statement this time, tinged with amazement.

"Don't tell her I told you. Please."

"No, I think it would be best if I kept this to myself." A small smile curved her lips. "Thank you for sharing that with me. Between that and what you've told me of the Hanev, your debt to me is paid."

"I'm grateful to you." He paused. "What will you do about Qiyed?"

She sobered. "I have issued a challenge of combat to Qiyed. The next time he and I meet, we will fight. And he will die."

Another chill went through him.

"You should know," she said, "that he sent Belvora to kill me. I was not alone when I fought them, and we prevailed, but a Tirribin you know was lost. Maeli."

Tobias gawked. "Maeli's dead?"

She nodded.

"And Teelo?"

"He survived."

"He must be... They were inseparable."

"They were. He grieves. His life will be lonely without her."

He shook his head, disbelief warring with sorrow.

"You cared for her?" Droë asked.

"I—" A dry laugh escaped him. "I wouldn't have thought so. She was..."

"She could be difficult."

"Yes. And she wanted desperately to take Sofya's years. We argued about it all the time. And yet she helped me—us. Both of them did."

"Another reason I look forward to killing Qiyed."

"What about Orzili?"

"I have spoken with Cresten. He and I are no longer friends. He pursues you still. He and a woman named Lenna. A Walker. They are assassins."

That last was valuable information—more than he had known.

"He and Qiyed are working together."

She shook her head. "That is an exaggeration. Qiyed is

Arrokad. He does not 'work together' with humans. I would guess that he helps Cresten because he believes your death will hurt me."

It was odd to hear someone—anyone—speak of his death with such equanimity.

"We may need help against them," he said. "It's vital that we keep the princess alive."

"Forgive me, but it is only vital to humans. To Ancients..." She made a small dismissive gesture. "The politics of your courts matter little to my kind. If Qiyed attempts to harm you in any way, you may summon me without cost. Cresten is a different matter. You're my friend—I have declared Mara a friend as well. But a summons to intervene in a human conflict—that would be an invitation to commerce. It would carry a price."

This disappointed him, but it didn't surprise. "I understand. Thank you." He glanced at the moon, gauging its position. "I should return to Duvyn. Mara was wounded tonight. She'll be all right, but I should check on her. And on Sofya."

Droë crossed her arms, lifted her chin. "I'm glad you called for me. I found our conversation...illuminating."

He bowed to her. "I'm grateful for your friendship, Droë. May the Two keep you safe."

He started away from her, back toward the city and the castle beyond. As he walked from the strand, he heard her utter Ujie's name.

Tobias's walk back to Risch's fortress took the better part of a bell. Along the way, he came to a decision.

Guards stopped him at the gate and were reluctant to let him pass even after he identified himself. One of the wall guards recognized him, however, and they allowed him into the castle.

He went first to the Duke's hall and found Mara much as he had left her: sleeping on a pallet among the other wounded from the night's battle. Tempted though he was to check on the princess, he thought better of waking Corinne and Risch. Instead, he made his way to his quarters and managed to sleep until sometime after daybreak.

Tolling bells in the courtyard roused him with the fear that they were under attack again. But the peals soon ended; likely they marked mid-morning. He rose, washed, and dressed, then went in search of Sofya.

He found her in the garden with the duchess. When the princess spotted him, she squealed with delight and ran to him. She wore the royal robe and tiny crown Corinne had brought to her the night before. He wondered if she had slept in them. He doubted he and Mara would ever convince her to give them back.

"I'm a queen, Papa! I'm a queen!"

A shiver jounced through him, head to toe. "Yes, you are, love."

He cast a look at the duchess, who gave a small, reassuring shake of her head.

"Don't worry about it," she said under her breath. "Put a crown on any boy or girl and they pronounce themselves royals. No one will think anything of it."

He knew she was right.

Reassured that she was well and safe, he went next to the hall. Mara remained abed and unconscious. The healer hovered near her, as did the duke, who looked weary, like he'd barely slept. Tobias's stomach clenched.

"How is she?" he asked, approaching them.

The healer shook his head. "Not as well as I would like. I had thought that the swelling would go down more and that she'd be awake by now. I attended to her again just a short while ago, and I'm hopeful that she'll be better by late in the day." A catch in his voice filled Tobias with dread.

"But?"

The young man replied with a helpless shrug. "My first ministrations should have worked. I don't know why they didn't. And with head wounds, the longer she remains unconscious, the more uncertain her prognosis."

Tobias stared down at her. He felt ill. "I shouldn't have left last night."

Risch laid a hand on his shoulder. "She'll be all right."

Empty words, albeit well-intended.

"I need to check on the others," the healer said, appearing reluctant to leave Mara's side. "I'll be back before long. The duke is right: I expect her to recover. Stay with her, speak to her, hold her hand. And pray. The God will heal what I cannot."

Tobias nodded, numb, unable to say more.

"Thank you, Tarrod," the duke said as the healer walked away.

A guard brought two chairs and set them beside Mara's pallet. Tobias sat. He took Mara's hand, as the healer had suggested. He kissed her fingers, whispered to her to let her know he was there.

Risch remained standing beside him. "Where did you go last night?" he asked after some time.

Tobias told the duke of his conversation with Droë, though he left out any mention of her affection for him. Without this bit of information, Risch didn't understand why an Ancient would want him and Mara dead, and Tobias wasn't sure how to explain, except to say that it was a matter of Ancient commerce.

"You have dangerous enemies."

Tobias didn't take his eyes off Mara. Aside from the bandage on her brow, she looked as she always did: lovely, strong. "We do. And we need to balance them with powerful friends."

Risch shifted beside him. "Whom do you have in mind?"

Tobias glanced up at him, saying nothing.

"You want to go to Trohsden, don't you? You intend to speak with Myles."

"There's no one else. All the other dukes have pledged themselves to Noak."

"Myles might have as well."

"Not openly. Not yet. He and Mearlan were close. It may be that Noak is pursuing an alliance. He might even be near to securing one, but Myles can't be happy about any of this."

"As I've told you, he can't risk defying the Sheraighs. They need Trohsden too much. They would sooner attack him and place a puppet in his place than allow him to oppose them."

"Right. I understand. So what if he doesn't openly oppose them?"

Risch narrowed his eyes. "You think you can convince him to support the Sheraighs in word while working to restore Mearlan's line in deed?"

"Why not?"

"Tobias, the risks—"

"I know. Think about it, though: I would be offering him a way to get everything he wants—the security of falling in line behind the new supremacy, and the satisfaction of avenging his friend's death."

Risch weighed this for some time. "When would you go?"

"I had wanted to ride today, but I won't leave until I'm sure that Mara is all right."

The duke nodded, looked down at Mara. "She'll be all right," he said again. "Tarrod is young, but he's very good. I have no doubt that he'll have her well and on her feet again before long." He hesitated. "I don't think you should ride alone."

"A lone rider won't attract much notice."

"A lone rider will attract exactly the wrong kind of notice—road thieves, Sheraigh guards looking for Hayncalde-sympathizing rabble. Not to mention the sort of notice you'll draw with Belvora soaring above you." When Tobias didn't answer right away, he added, "Even if you manage to switch mounts along the way, it will take you a ha'turn at the very least to traverse the length of Daerjen. You'll have rivers to ford, highlands to cross, plus the other dangers I've mentioned. Aboard one of my ships we can be there in half the time."

"My lord, journeying with a duke and his guard would make me far more conspicuous. Besides, I thought you hated this idea."

"You won't be conspicuous if you're part of my guard. And I do hate the idea, but I also see some value in it. We can make it seem that I'm going to Trohsden to beg him to withhold his support from House Sheraigh. It would be a ruse that helps all of us. It conceals your mission. It makes me appear even weaker and more isolated than I am, and therefore less of a threat to Noak. And it makes it seem that Myles is on the verge of supporting the Sheraigh Supremacy, which could help him withstand for a while longer whatever pressure Noak is putting on him."

"You said that Myles has no choice but to throw his support to Noak. You made it sound as though he might have already."

Risch lifted a shoulder. "Yes. In which case both of us might be handing ourselves over to the enemy. But your trust in him is...contagious. Since Mearlan's death, I've seen enemies everywhere. Corinne fears that I've become too mistrustful. And so I find myself wanting to trust that Myles won't betray us. He is a good man, and he and Mearlan were very close. And our friendship—his and mine—spans the length of our lives. I've no doubt that he's under enormous pressure to capitulate to the Sheraighs. But I owe it to him to trust that he hasn't gone over to their side yet."

"Of course, my lord."

"So you'll sail with us?"

"There is still the matter of Belvora."

"I'll bring my Crosser," Risch said. "That should make it harder for any Belvora to sense you on the ship."

This was true. "What if we're boarded?"

"Trade among the houses of Daerjen is as common as commerce among Ancients, even now. We had a ship arrive from Sheraigh two days ago. From Sheraigh, of all places. Selling silks, buying wool and hemp."

"Still, with you aboard—"

"With me aboard, they'll be less inclined to do anything foolish. If Noak wants me dead, he'll send an army to my castle. He'll want to make a show of it, make me an example for others who seek to defy him. No, on this voyage, we should be fine. If you'll allow my soldiers and me to accompany you, that is."

This was one of the many things Tobias loved about this duke. The man could have ordered him aboard his ship, or could have refused to lend him a horse for the journey north. That wasn't his way.

The truth was, Tobias much preferred the duke's idea to his own. He had little experience with horses. A ha'turn? It would take him twice that long to reach Myles's castle, and another turn to ride back. That was too long to be away from Mara and Sofya. Covering the distance by ship appealed to him. He missed life at sea and knew enough about ships to be of use to the duke during the voyage.

"I would be honored to sail with you, my lord. And I'm grateful for your offer of company and protection."

Risch grinned. "Good. I'll inform Corinne."

"Where are you going?"

Tobias twisted around so quickly he nearly overbalanced his chair. Mara's eyes were open, though only barely.

"Sipar be praised," Risch said. "I'll get Tarrod." He strode away.

Tobias leaned closer to her, kissed her fingers again. "How are you feeling?"

She closed her eyes, opened them slowly. "Terrible," she said. "My head hurts and everything is blurred."

He didn't know if this was normal, so he merely nodded. "You've had us worried."

Before either of them could say more, Risch returned with the healer, who also asked how she felt and received the same response. Mara's words came slowly, and she struggled to keep her eyes open.

"I'd expect your head to hurt for some time, but I'd hope your vision would clear within the next day or so. Are you hungry?"

"Not at all."

"What do you remember from the battle?"

"There was a battle?"

Tobias and the healer shared a glance. Tobias saw his concern mirrored in the young man's face.

"I'm kidding," Mara said. "I remember all of it."

Risch laughed; the healer scowled. Tobias was so relieved he could hardly see through brimming tears.

"I remember there was a Hanev," she said, "and eight Belvora. I remember standing with Tobias and killing at least one demon. And then that last one— I was loading my musket when it came for me. I saw it, tried to fire, but it rammed into me."

"You've been unconscious ever since," Tarrod told her. "More than half a day. But I think you'll be all right now. I'll fix you a tonic for the pain."

"My thanks, healer."

Tarrod left them, as did Risch.

"Where are you going?" Mara asked again.

He kissed her brow. "Aren't I allowed a moment to enjoy having you back?"

"No," she said, but she smiled. "Tell me, Tobias."

"We're sailing north, to Trohsden. I spoke with the Hanev last night, and then with Droë and Ujie."

Her eyes widened. "You've been busy."

"When Droë stopped our battle with Orzili, she was with an Arrokad."

"I remember."

"Based on what I learned from the Hanev, and then from Droë, I think he was the one who sent the demons for us last night."

"Not Orzili?"

"I don't believe so."

She pondered this. Every breath seemed to bring her back to herself a bit more. "All right, what does this have to do with you going to Trohsden?"

He opened his hands. "We've been at war with Orzili. Now we're at war with an Arrokad as well, and all the demons he might control. We need a Binder. We need support from more than just House Duvyn. And I don't think we can risk taking Sofya north. For now, she's safest here. You are, too."

Mara bristled. "My safety—"

"As long as you're still healing, your safety means everything. Besides, who else would I trust to guard Sofya?"

He saw the logic of this seep through her resentment.

"I'm jealous," she said at length, her voice dropping. "You get to go on a ship."

"I know. I'm sorry."

"When will you leave?"

"Tonight perhaps, tomorrow at the latest. Going by sea, it shouldn't take too long."

Her eyes closed again. "Yes, all right."

"I have your blessing then?"

Mara regarded him, a puzzled smile creasing her bandaged brow. "My blessing?"

"I won't go if you tell me not to."

"We both know that's not our choice," she said, her expression grim. She touched her bandage. "This was close. The Hanev? The Belvora? I'm afraid we're running out of time. So you should go, and do what you have to do, and come back to us so we can go on being a family."

Tobias smiled, kissed her. "Yes, ma'am."

She remained grave. "Take the musket and both pistols. And take one of the tri-sextants as well. Orzili and his friends shouldn't be the only ones who have them."

It was a fine idea, one that hadn't occurred to him, one that might give Myles another reason to help them.

CHAPTER EIGHTEEN

8th Day of Sipar's Ascent, Year 634

Tobias, the duke, a trio of merchants, Risch's Crosser, and eleven of his soldiers set sail from Duvyn the following morning. Bidding Mara farewell was difficult. Saying goodbye to Sofya left Tobias heartbroken and wishing he had simply asked Mara to explain his departure to the princess. Sofya wailed and begged him to take her with him. He tried to explain that the voyage would be too dangerous for her, but that only made her cry more and plead with him to stay in Duvyn. He had no choice but to leave her sobbing with her "mother."

They rowed away from the wharf under clear skies and raised the ship's sails into a brisk westerly breeze. She was a fine vessel, about the size of Seris Larr's *Gray Skate* and armed with twelve guns. Two banners flew atop her center mast: one white and red for Daerjen, the other blue and red and marked with the bear sigil of Duvyn.

Tobias wore a uniform and carried himself as would any man of the duke's guard. The merchants thought him as much, and the soldiers themselves—eleven of Risch's finest—treated him as they would a comrade. He ate with the soldiers, slept among them, was subject to all of their commands and duties, and enjoyed his tasks and their companionship.

To any who saw the ship, or interacted with its crew, he would be notable only because of his appearance. He was, along with Ejino Kerrijor, the duke's Crosser, one of only two Northislers on the ship. The two of them stood out like cormorants among gulls. No one could help but notice their dark brown skin and bronze hair. Tobias, of course, also bore ugly raised scars from his time in Hayncalde's dungeon, when he was at the mercy of Orzili and his men. These made him that much more obvious.

Unknown to anyone else aboard the vessel, he also differed from the others in the things he carried. The carry sack he stowed in a remote corner of the hold carried his weapons, one of the tri-sextants he and Mara had taken from Orzili, and, wrapped in a white cloth, the pieces of his broken chronofor. He hoped that by the time they left Trohsden for the voyage home, he would again possess a working device.

That first day, the ship, the *Bear's Tooth*, emerged from the Firth of Rime into open water and carved westward, to follow Daerjen's western shore. The wind stiffened as they entered the Inward Sea, but the weather held, and they made good progress. They stopped at Ysendyr on their second day so that the merchants could trade for food and wine, some of which they shared with the crew. As a precaution, Tobias remained below while they were in port, only returning to deck once they were away from the city and under sail.

Their voyage slowed in the days that followed as the winds slackened and cold rain and mist enveloped the isle and its surrounding waters.

Over this time, Tobias developed a friendship with Risch's Crosser. Ejino was slight, narrow-shouldered, with a dark complexion, deep brown eyes, and neat, short bronze hair. He was slow to laugh but always wore a faint, inscrutable smile. He spoke in a soft tenor and struck Tobias as friendly, intelligent, and easy going. That impression lasted less than two bells.

The man was keenly intelligent and armed with a razor-sharp wit. He soon proved himself willing to say anything and argue with anyone, including his duke. He freely offered his opinions on the shortcomings and foibles of the nobles he had met, and several he had not.

"Don't they teach diplomacy at the Windhome Palace?" Risch asked Tobias on their third day, after Ejino had spent some time telling them both what an ass he considered the Duke of Ysendyr.

Tobias noticed that the duke didn't argue with Ejino's assessment of the man.

"And protocol, my lord," Ejino said before Tobias could answer. "I know all the rules of court, and I know how to conduct diplomacy, in case you're ever so foolish as to send me somewhere as your emissary. But while they taught me diplomacy, they never convinced me of the value of being diplomatic. There *is* a difference you know." This last he said with a wink for Tobias.

Risch laughed. "Serves me right for asking."

Later that evening, when Tobias had completed his duties on deck, he and Ejino drank from a flask of Miejan red and shared stories about their experiences in Windhome. Tobias guessed that the Crosser was no older than Tobias himself appeared, which meant the man was about ten years older than Tobias's actual age.

At a pause in their conversation, Ejino regarded Tobias's face, his head canted. "How did you get those scars?"

Tobias flinched at the directness of the question. "Another demonstration of your diplomatic skill."

"Forgive me. Truly I...sometimes I'm just a fool. I am curious, though."

"I can't tell you much. I have information a man wants. He captured and tortured me, hoping to extract it. He didn't."

"They don't look so bad."

A laugh escaped him. "You're kind."

"You're a Walker, yes?"

"That's right."

"So those stories you told about Windhome—stories of which

I have no memory, stories no one mentioned during my time there..."

"They take place years from now. At least they would have. They're probably lost now."

Ejino nodded, eyed him again. "I won't ask you why you've come on this journey, but I sense that you're the reason all of us are here. And I also—I'm guessing now—I also think maybe we're here because of the woman and child you left back in Duvyn."

Tobias tensed.

"I'm your friend," Ejino said, holding up a hand. "And contrary to what you've seen thus far, I can be discreet when there's need. You have nothing to fear from me. None of you do." He smiled. "That said, I'm hoping that your marriage to the woman is a ruse, and that perhaps you're open to a deepening of our friendship."

Some of Tobias's apprehension abated. "I'm flattered."

"Ah, not a ruse after all."

"A ruse in part, but the love is real."

"Then I'm happy for you," Ejino said, the sentiment seeming genuine. "Although I claim the rest of this flask as my own. Consolation for tonight's disappointment." They both laughed, but Ejino quickly turned serious again. "I meant what I said. You're my friend. Your secrets are safe with me. And I will help you in any way I can."

It took the *Bear's Tooth* two more days to sail around the Hook, and three more after that to reach Cobleman's Firth and come within sight of Trohsden. They encountered no Belvora, but upon entering the firth, Ancients became the least of their worries.

As they neared the port, two warships converged on the *Bear's Tooth*. Both were larger than Risch's ship, though neither was as formidable as the Sea Eagles of the royal fleet. They flew Daerjen colors and the gray and purple of Trohsden. The captain of the lead ship ordered the *Tooth* to lower its sails and informed the duke that the vessel would be boarded and searched.

Tobias slipped below and hid his carry sack in an empty wine barrel.

The search of their vessel revealed nothing incriminating, but Trohsden's captain made clear to Risch that they would be escorted to the port and held there until soldiers from the castle came for them and took them to see Trohsden's duke.

"Am I to assume then that we're being taken into your custody?" Risch asked, voice rising.

"You are being guarded for your own safety," the woman answered, unruffled.

When she wasn't looking, Risch sent a despairing glance Tobias's way. Tobias feared he had led the duke into peril.

A pair of Trohsden guards in gray uniforms hovered near him, watching him with obvious suspicion. Risch wasn't the only one in danger.

Trohsden's captain had the duke order his ship onto sweeps, and they rowed through the firth to the city's wharves.

Trohsden was larger than Duvyn, but a good deal less impressive than Hayncalde. Its shops and homes were built of wood and roofed with dark gray slate. The cobbled streets Tobias could see from the port were clean enough, but drab. The wall surrounding the city was ponderous and gray, as was the massive castle overlooking the firth. Only the sanctuary, with its finely wrought spires, offered relief from the tedium of the place.

They were forced to wait at the wharf for more than a bell. During that time, Tobias and Risch retreated to the hold and added Tobias's carry sack to the duke's personal possessions. A soldier would never be permitted to carry his belongings into the castle of a rival duke.

In time, a company of uniformed soldiers arrived at the dock and told the duke that he was to accompany them back to the castle. When Risch signaled for his men to leave the ship, the commander of Trohsden's soldiers balked and informed the duke that he could bring his Crosser but not any of his soldiers. The merchants were free to enter the city as far as the market, but those in uniform would remain on the vessel.

Risch refused, and for several moments, it seemed that they might be at an impasse, and a risky one at that. Risch refused to leave his ship without at least some of his guards. Trohsden's men seemed equally adamant in their refusal to let any of Duvyn's soldiers leave the ship. And Tobias wasn't at all certain that they would allow the *Bear's Tooth* to put to sea if no compromise could be reached.

"Commander," Risch finally said, "I am going to ask you a question, and if you can answer it honestly in the affirmative, I will go with you alone."

Trohsden's man hesitated before agreeing to this.

"If your duke were to come to Duvyn, would you consent to remain with his ship while he marched unprotected into my city?"

To his credit, the soldier didn't attempt to lie.

"No, my lord, I would not."

The duke opened his hands, saying not a word.

"Four guards, my lord. And the Crosser. That's all I can allow. The rest will remain here. They will be safe—I give you my word."

"Myles has ordered this?"

The man shook his head, glanced at the soldiers under his command, and then toward the city. "No, my lord," he said, his voice dropping. "My duke would have welcomed you and all your soldiers. Duvyn and Trohsden have long been on good terms. There is a woman here, an emissary from Sheraigh. These are her orders."

Risch cast another quick look Tobias's way, color draining from his cheeks. Even Ejino appeared unnerved.

Risky indeed.

They had planned originally to include Tobias in whatever company of soldiers Risch was able to bring with him into Trohsden Castle. That would have been ideal.

With an emissary from Sheraigh in the castle, however, Tobias needed to keep out of sight. This woman might know Orzili. She might be looking for a Northisler with scars on his face. They couldn't risk letting her see him.

Tobias, though, had information he needed to convey to Trohsden's duke. Risch didn't know all of it, and they hadn't time for Tobias to tell him. Moreover, this was Tobias's tale to relate. Myles would have questions, would demand proof. Tobias had to gain access to the castle. But how?

As it happened, Ejino had an idea.

Ejino's lord duke and the Walker agreed that for now Tobias should remain aboard the ship. The Walker chafed at being left behind. A young man's reaction. Younger than his apparent years.

Crossers like him were considered the least valuable of Travelers. Ejino understood that. They were the Travelers minor nobles like Risch brought to their courts for status because they couldn't afford Walkers and Spanners. That was all right. He liked his duke. He liked Duvyn. And right now, he was determined to get Tobias into Trohsden Castle, where he needed to be.

His scheme was simple, and it counted on the indifference—some would say contempt—with which pale Ring Islers regarded his kind.

He accompanied Risch into the city and up to the castle. Duvyn's four guards flanked them, two a stride ahead, two behind. They, in turn, were guarded by the soldiers of Trohsden in their smoke-gray uniforms.

Ejino sensed Risch's tension, knew that others would as well, which could be dangerous.

"My lord," he said, "didn't you say you wished to stop in the marketplace and find a bauble for the duchess? She'll be cross with you if you don't."

Risch looked his way. Ejino held his gaze, quirked an eyebrow just enough to make his point.

"Yes, of course," the duke said, forcing a smile. "Thank you, Crosser. I would have forgotten." To Myles's commander he said, "You don't mind, do you?"

Clearly the man did mind, but what could he say to a visiting noble?

They veered off the main thoroughfare toward a broad, colorful marketplace. There they remained for maybe half a bell, while, ostensibly, the duke searched for a suitable gift.

When Ejino and Risch had put some small distance between themselves and Trohsden's soldiers, the duke asked, "Why are we here? What are we looking for?"

"We're here so that you can gather yourself, my lord. You look and act like a man who's committed a crime. You can't appear so in front of this Sheraigh emissary."

Risch stared at him briefly, then gave a wan grin. "You're right, of course. My thanks."

The soldiers caught up with them. Risch perused the wares of a few peddlers until he found a golden ring for the duchess. Then they resumed their approach to the castle. Their foray into the market had the desired effect: Risch seemed far calmer as they ascended a steep slope to the castle gate.

Ejino was out of breath and sweating as they entered the fortress. He barely took note of the lower courtyard or the gardens beyond; he saw enough to know that Trohsden Castle was as unremarkable within as it had appeared from the wharf.

The guards led them through an entryway, down a corridor lit by narrow translucent windows, and into a hall that was far grander than even the largest such room in Duvyn Castle.

Guards stood at intervals around the chamber, their backs to the stone walls, their faces impassive. Perhaps half a dozen wore Trohsden gray. The rest—no fewer than twelve—wore uniforms of pale blue. Sheraigh blue. Ministers, some in blue, some in gray, stood apart from the table, watching Risch and Ejino, but saying nothing.

A man and a woman stood beside chairs at a long table. The man at the head of the table was tall, lean, strikingly handsome. He had black hair, eyes the same shade as the Sheraigh uniforms, a square jaw, and a straight, aristocratic nose. Ejino had never seen Myles, Duke of Trohsden, but he had heard others speak of his good looks and subtle mind. This, he thought, was a man others would follow to war, or, as the case might be, rebellion.

The woman was handsome as well. She might have been ten years older than the duke. Her hair was auburn, streaked with white. She was nearly as tall as Myles, and willowy. She wore a ministerial gown—blue and black, trimmed in silver. Her eyes, warm brown and widely spaced, skipped over Ejino as if he were nothing, and settled on the duke of Duvyn. She didn't smile, or offer a word of welcome, but merely stared.

Myles, on the other hand, stepped away from the table and came forward to meet Risch before Duvyn's duke reached the table.

They embraced as brothers, though Myles remained grave. Ejino saw Trohsden's duke whisper something before the men separated. He couldn't hear what was said.

"It's good to see you, Risch," he said, his voice deep and a bit rough.

"And you, Myles."

"I wish you had informed me you were on your way. We could have prepared a more fitting reception."

"Not necessary."

The woman cleared her throat.

Myles offered a strained smile and pivoted in her direction. "Of course, forgive me. Risch, Duke of Duvyn, I am honored to present you to Her Highness, Emella of Sheraigh."

Risch's face tightened. Ejino felt a small hitch in his own pulse. This was no simple emissary. This was Noak Sheraigh's sister, next in the line of succession for rule of the Sheraigh Supremacy.

The duke bowed low. Ejino did the same.

"It is a privilege to make your acquaintance, Your Highness."

"My lord duke," she said, her tone as tight as a garrote, "I have heard a great deal about you."

Ejino could imagine: The southern duke who remained loyal to Mearlan, who had refused to pledge his loyalty to Daerjen's new sovereign, who, in the past, had made clear his antipathy for

House Sheraigh. If the delegation from Duvyn left Trohsden alive, it would be a miracle.

"We were about to sup," Myles said returning to his place at the table. "Won't you join us, Risch?"

The duke had little choice but to accept, though Ejino thought that if the sovereign princess offered him the chance to leave the castle in that moment, he would have without pause.

Risch sat across from the princess. Ejino emulated the other ministers and remained standing some short distance from the table.

"What news do you bring?" Myles asked, after a brief, uncomfortable silence.

"Yes," Emella said. "Surely you come with tidings from the southern reaches of our isle. What other cause would bring you so far?"

"No tidings." Risch kept his tone light. "I came with merchants. It's been too long since last I saw you, Myles. I have been eager to discuss recent events."

The princess sat with her hands flat on the table. "And by events you mean..."

"Do you really need to ask, Your Highness? Surely these past several turns have been as momentous as any in our lifetimes. Am I not permitted to speak of such matters with an old friend?"

It was bravely said. Perhaps foolishly so. Risch, for all his talk of diplomacy, had never been a man to mince words. One of the reasons Ejino admired him so.

"Is it an old friend you seek?" Emella asked coldly. "Or a partner in conspiracy?"

Myles rapped his knuckles on the table, forestalling Risch's response. "Forgive me, Your Highness," said Trohsden's duke, "but before we go on, I believe I need to set my old friend straight on a few things." To Risch, he said, "I am a loyal son of Daerjen, and I have sworn fealty to every sovereign who has ruled in my lifetime. This sovereign is no different. If you came here for any hidden purpose, Risch, you should leave now. I will harbor no ill feelings for you, and I am certain Her Highness will allow your departure. You came in peace and will leave that same way. Isn't that so, Your Highness?"

She looked like she had just kissed a lemon, but she tipped her head, fixed a smile on her lips, and said, "Of course it is. We seek no conflict here."

"Nor do I," Risch said. "As I told you, I came to speak with a friend. That's all."

Ejino wasn't sure he believed any of them.

Fortunately, before another word could be uttered, stewards arrived with wine and food. For a long time, the three nobles ate without speaking. In time, Myles muttered something about Westisle pirates, and the three of them launched into an empty discussion of what they all agreed was a scourge on trade.

Later, as they sipped a sweet Fairisle white, Myles asked if Risch intended to stay the night.

"If I may. I can sleep on my ship, of course, but your castle would be more comfortable."

"Of course it would. You have no objection, do you, Your Highness?"

She thinned another unconvincing smile. "It is your castle, my lord duke. I am merely a guest."

"Might you and I speak in private tomorrow, Your Highness?" Risch asked. "Our houses have been at odds for too long."

"Hardly the fault of House Sheraigh. But I can see why, with the recent change in our relative fortunes, you would now seek accommodation."

"I wish only to—"

"You wish to save your neck, Duvyn. That's clear. You have set your house against mine for years. For a time you did this with the blessing and protection of the former sovereign. You no longer have that luxury. You fear for yourself, your family, your castle and lands. And you should."

Risch set his cup on the table and pushed back. "As I was going to say, I wish only to seek a lessening of tensions between our houses. I see now that this is not possible. I should leave."

"Nonsense," Myles said. "You're my guest, and I say you are

welcome. Surely our new sovereign would not presume to tell his dukes whom they can and cannot welcome into their homes." He cast an expectant look at the princess.

She drank a bit of wine, placed her cup on the table as well, and stood. "You are free to host whomever you please, Lord Trohsden, but do not expect me to suffer the company of men who have insulted my family. Until tomorrow." Her gaze flicked toward Risch. "Duvyn."

She swept from the hall, trailed by her ministers and guards. When she was gone, Myles faced Risch and shook his head. "You should have sent a message first. I could have told you not to waste a voyage."

"I had to come."

At a questioning look, Risch shook his head. "Later," he mouthed.

"Well, let's find you a chamber for the evening."

"Thank you, my friend." Risch stood and turned to Ejino. "Crosser, would you be so kind as to gather my belongings from our vessel? It seems I will be a guest in the castle tonight."

"Of course, my lord."

They had counted on this, had assumed Myles would find a way to make it possible. If he hadn't, they would have attempted to sail from Trohsden that night. As it was, they were ready for the next phase of Ejino's plan.

Ejino returned to the ship late in the day. Tobias saw him coming and met him at the rails, a hundred questions on his tongue.

At a cautioning look from the Crosser, though, he swallowed them all and resumed swabbing the ship's deck, which he had been doing before the man's arrival.

Ejino went below, only to emerge some time later wearing a plain shirt and breeches. He perched himself on the rails near where Tobias worked, but he didn't say anything or invite Tobias to join him. Instead, he stared out over the water, and, every so often, scanned the wharf below. Tobias kept his attention on his work but eased toward the Crosser.

"I was followed from the castle," Ejino said, his voice low, his lips barely moving, his gaze always fixed elsewhere. "I don't see anyone now, but I'm not certain they're gone."

"Can you tell me what happened?"

"Well, it wasn't just any emissary." Over the next several spire-counts, speaking in short bursts separated by longer silences, Ejino explained who was at the castle and what had happened in Myles's hall. Alarmed as Tobias was by the presence of Noak's sister in Trohsden, he was more interested in what Myles might do.

In this regard, however, Ejino had less information to offer. "Some of what he said might have been for the benefit of the princess," the Crosser told him. "Not all of it, though. I believe he was genuinely dismayed that my duke came here unannounced. I'm afraid he's not in a position to help us."

"He has to," Tobias said without thinking.

"Why?"

Their eyes met. Tobias angled away from him, continuing his work.

"None of the others are listening to us," Ejino said. "No one on the wharves is close enough to hear."

"I need a chronofor—actually, I have one, but I need a Binder to fix it."

"Myles's Binder."

"That's my hope."

"And why do you need it?"

Tobias faltered, kept his eyes trained on the deck.

For a long time neither of them spoke, until at last Tobias chanced a look at Ejino. The Crosser watched him, cool appraisal in the dark eyes.

"If Myles won't help you, we'll find another Binder. I'm sure of it." Ejino surveyed the sky, which had begun to darken. "We should get you ready."

"What about the people who followed you?"

"I haven't seen them. For all I know, I imagined it."

"Is that what you think?"

He shook his head. "No, I was followed. But you need a Binder, and my duke really does need his belongings, so you should prepare anyway."

Tobias had long since swabbed the entire deck—parts of it twice. He dumped out his bucket, set his mop in a corner to dry, and followed the Crosser below.

As he pulled off his uniform shirt, he heard Ejino suck in a sharp breath.

"Blood and bone. What did they do to you?"

Tobias didn't turn. "Nothing that couldn't be healed."

"Sheraighs did that?"

"Mearlan's assassin. Windhome-trained. A Northisler, like us. He works with the Sheraighs, but I don't think he works for them."

"Then who?"

"Oaqamar."

Ejino handed him the robe he had worn to Trohsden Castle earlier in the day. "This won't fit well, but it's loose enough on me that you should be able to wear it."

Tobias pulled on the robe, which was far too snug in the shoulders, and too short as well. He thought he must look ridiculous. He faced Ejino, held out his arms.

The Crosser tried with little success to hide his grin.

"This isn't going to fool anyone," Tobias said.

"You'll be carrying the duke's belongings. Chances are no one will notice."

Tobias wasn't so sure.

"To be honest, Walker, guards are more likely to take note of your scars."

He couldn't argue. Ejino stepped to him and adjusted the robe a bit. He frowned, adjusted it again, frowned more.

"Walk quickly," he said.

Tobias had to laugh.

He added his own carry sack to the items he would be bearing to the castle. He concealed a blade in a sheath at his calf and loaded his pistols, which he concealed again within the sack. When he was ready, they climbed to the deck. There, they waited until darkness fell and the tolling of the castle bells cascaded down through the city lanes. Ejino believed this marked the end of the day watch at Trohsden's gates and the arrival of the night watch guards.

"With any luck, the soldiers who saw me today are gone, and the ones who have taken their place won't know you aren't Duvyn's Crosser."

"With any luck..." Tobias repeated.

"The Two keep you safe."

Tobias nodded once, left the ship, and started along the cobbled road leading from the wharves to the city gate.

Predictably, Trohsden's gate soldiers stopped him and asked questions. Where was he going? Why was his duke not with him? What was in the satchels he carried? Why did his robe fit him so poorly?

These last two were the most difficult and dangerous. The guards spoke of searching the bags, which, of course, would reveal the tri-sextants and his broken chronofor.

"You may accompany me to the castle," Tobias said, speaking with all the arrogance he could muster, "and explain to my duke why you wish to look through his belongings. For that matter, you can explain to your own duke why you have cast suspicion on a noble whom he names a guest and a friend. But you will not do any of this without my duke's permission."

This gave the men pause.

About his robe, he said, "I'm new in the castle. My predecessor was smaller than I am, and the duke's seamster has not yet made robes for me."

In the end, they let him pass. By now Tobias was sweating, and he still had some distance to walk and a hill to climb.

He followed the cobbled lane from the gate through the heart of the city, which was quiet now, the streets largely empty.

So it was that as he turned a corner and paused to shift part of his burden, he heard steps behind him. They halted an instant later. Tobias walked on, then paused abruptly. Again, a footstep followed by silence.

Ejino hadn't imagined it. He was followed. And now whoever had dogged his steps was stalking Tobias.

CHAPTER NINETEEN

18th Day of Sipar's Ascent, Year 634

Whoever tracked him would know he wasn't the Crosser. He—or she—had followed both of them, probably had observed them on the ship. Everything Tobias hoped to accomplish in Trohsden was at risk.

Yet, what could he do?

Had he not been laden with Risch's belongings, and his own, he might have doubled back and confronted his pursuer. He trusted himself to prevail in a fight if it came to that.

But with his arms full, he had no choice but to walk on and allow himself to be followed. It made no sense to flee—the person behind him knew where he was going.

The guards at the castle gate questioned him much as had those at the city gate. In the end, though, they let him enter the castle. Two soldiers accompanied him into the fortress and to Risch's quarters.

Duvyn's guards flanked the door. The duke was alone within.

Once Trohsden's soldiers had withdrawn, Tobias dug into his carry sack and pulled out his broken chronofor.

"You took longer than I expected," Risch said, standing over him.

"I'm sorry, my lord. Ejino had me wait until nightfall and the evening bells." He straightened. "He was followed, and so was I. We might not have much time."

"Damn," the duke said. "All right." He strode to the door.

As an afterthought, Tobias retrieved the sack holding Orzili's tri-sextant as well.

"What is that?" Risch asked.

Tobias pulled the tri-sextant from the sack and held it up to allow the duke a closer look. Candlelight gleamed on the three arcs, casting bright reflections on the walls. "It's called a tri-sextant. It's a Bound device that allows Spanners to ply their talent in groups, armed, clothed."

"You Span as well?"

He shook his head. "Mara does. I'm just a Walker. We took this from Mearlan's assassin. Most Binders have never seen such a thing, and we thought it was time our side began to use this advance as well. I intend to offer it to Myles and his Binder as payment for repairing my chronofor."

"Clever."

Tobias returned the device to the carry sack. They left Risch's quarters and, with Duvyn's guards arrayed around them, followed the corridors to a chamber on the second level of the castle.

Soldiers stood outside Myles's door, of course. Upon their arrival, one of the guards entered the chamber. He soon emerged again and allowed Risch and Tobias to enter.

The chamber reminded Tobias of Mearlan's chamber in Hayncalde, though it wasn't quite so large. An oil lamp burned on a standing desk, and pigeons cooed in a small cage beside the shuttered windows. Tapestries depicting rolling farmland, forests, and mountains hung along the walls. Candles burned in sconces mounted between them. A round rug woven in shades of red and yellow covered much of the stone floor.

The man sitting by the hearth, his face lit by a low fire, was younger than Tobias had expected. He rose as they entered the chamber, welcomed Risch with a quick smile, and turned the weight of his keen gaze on Tobias.

"Who is this?" he asked, more wariness than welcome in the tone.

"My name is Tobias Doljan, my lord."

"You've sent me messages."

"I have, my lord. I wish to work with you, to find some way to...to undo some of the damage done to our isle in the past several turns."

"*Our* isle," the duke repeated. "Forgive me, Mister Doljan, but you don't look like a man of Daerjen."

"Myles!"

"It's all right, my lord," Tobias said to Risch. To the duke of Trohsden, he said, "I was born on Onyi, in the Sisters. A town called Redcove. I trained in Windhome, my home for much of my childhood. And I served in Hayncalde. Mearlan was my sovereign."

"I never heard him speak of you. How long were you in his court?"

"A few days."

"Days!" Myles glanced at Risch, seeming to gauge his response. Duvyn's duke kept his face impassive.

"That is not a true measure of what I've given to House Hayncalde, nor does it convey my devotion to Mearlan's line."

"This is foolishness, Risch," the duke said to his friend. "What can a Spanner—"

"I'm not a Spanner," Tobias said.

At the same time, Risch said, "Hear him out, Myles."

Trohsden's duke looked from one to the other. After hesitating, he sat again, indicated that the two of them should do the same. He offered them wine. Both refused. Myles pushed his own cup to the center of the table by his chair.

"I'm not a Spanner," Tobias said again, whispering now. "I'm a Walker. I began serving Mearlan nearly fourteen years from now, in a future that's been lost because of subsequent events."

"Fourteen years? You've Walked back that far?"

"I have, my lord."

"Then you're just a boy."

He said this with such sympathy that Tobias's throat constricted. So few people understood.

"That's beside the point, my lord."

Myles considered him, his expression pained, but he motioned for him to continue.

"The very day I Walked back, Mearlan was assassinated, and I was trapped in this time. In part by a broken chronofor, but in part as well by...by circumstance."

"Meaning?"

Tobias paused. They had come to the crux of all. Did he trust this man enough to answer his simple question? Did he dare risk Sofya's life and the last hope of Mearlan's line?

Before he could make his choice, Risch said, "He can't tell you that yet, Myles. Not until you answer a few questions."

Myles narrowed his eyes but acquiesced with a flick of his hand.

"We need to know if we can trust you. You haven't responded to any of our messages."

"I'm being watched," the duke said. "Emella is here. The Sheraighs intercept our ships, stop our riders. Any message I might send you they would read. That's why I haven't answered."

"So you haven't decided to throw your support to Noak?"

Myles stared at Risch for a fivecount, then stood and stepped closer to the hearth.

"You have, haven't you?"

"I've decided nothing, but the pressure from Sheraigh... I want to resist, truly I do. But what's the point? They have Mearlan's ships. They've defeated his army. Those they could press into service now wear Sheraigh blue. Many of those they couldn't are dead." He paused at this, his eyes finding Risch's. "Your life is in danger, my friend. You know this, but I wish to emphasize it. You shouldn't have come. I believe they would prefer to keep me alive. I can help them consolidate power. But if I hold out for too long, they'll kill me, and my sons, and they'll give my lands to Quilyn or even Faendor." He fisted a hand, opened it again. "I can't resist them forever."

"And you shouldn't," Tobias said. "You should order us gone tomorrow and tell the princess that you've made up your mind to support the new sovereign. And all of that should be a lie."

Myles considered Tobias before shifting his gaze back to Risch. "I don't want to help them. I swear I don't. How long have we been friends? I can't remember a time when we weren't. And I loved Mearlan like a brother. If I had any reason to believe that we could fight the Sheraighs, I'd do it. But it strikes me as an empty gesture, a rebellion born of spite and vengeance and nothing more."

Risch's eyes found Tobias, and the two of them smiled.

"What?" Myles asked.

Tobias joined him by the hearth. "There is something more, my lord. I was there the night Mearlan died. I survived, and so did one other. Sofya." He breathed the name. It was so quiet, Myles leaned toward him, even as hope broke across his face like the dawn. Widened eyes, a disbelieving smile.

"If this is a ruse..."

"It's not. I swear it on my life."

"She's in Duvyn now, Myles," Risch said. "Corinne is with her, as is Tobias's wife. Tobias and Mara have been posing as her parents."

Myles looked at Risch and then at Tobias. Tobias sensed that the duke wasn't suspicious so much as he was afraid to hope.

"She looks like Keeda," he told the duke. "Except her eyes are blue. I also met the princess when she was a young woman—she was the image of her mother then, too."

"When you speak of her, you sound like a father."

"I've never had my own child—as you say, I'm young. Even so, I can't imagine loving any son or daughter more than I do the princess." He traced a finger along one of the scars on his face, and then another. "I got these in Hayncalde's dungeon after Mearlan was killed. They wanted me to give her up so they could kill her. I refused."

"You escaped?"

"In time, yes. With help from servants of Sipar."

A click from a far corner of the chamber made all of them whirl. A second door, one Tobias hadn't noticed earlier, swung open.

"I think I've heard enough," said Emella Sheraigh, stepping into the chamber. Four soldiers followed her. She held up a cup for Tobias and the dukes to see. "Thanks to this, I heard most of what you said. A trick I learned from my father. I imagine some time with my brother's interrogators will reveal the rest."

Risch took a step in her direction. "Your Highness, please. We were simply discussing—"

"Don't," she said, steel in the word. "You were conspiring against my house. I'm reasonably certain that one"—she pointed at Tobias—"has been harboring the daughter of Hayncalde's lost duke. And I believe I heard you say that she is currently a guest of your duchess back in Duvyn. That alone should be grounds for execution."

Tobias could barely stand. Despair and terror weighed on him like stone. Mara and Sofya would die. So would he, and the friends he had brought here. Mearlan's line would never be redeemed.

And yet what he felt most was fury. At the ill-fortune of arriving when Emella was here. At the duplicity of the woman. At the sheer audacity of any Sheraigh accusing others of treason! He refused to surrender to her.

True she was Noak's sister, and she had her men with her. But there were soldiers from both Trohsden and Duvyn in the corridor. At a word from Myles...

He looked back at Trohsden's duke, hoping to see his own rage reflected in the man's features. What he saw instead made him want to weep.

The duke's face might as well have been carved from granite, his glower was directed not at Emella, but at Risch.

"Myles," the princess said, "you have done well. The sovereign will be most pleased."

Risch glared back at the man. "I'm certain she's right. Your sovereign will honor you. Your God, though—he will have the final word."

Myles flinched, shifted his gaze to Emella. "They will be placed for now in my dungeon," he said. "They will not be tortured here, nor will they be denied any basic comforts. They will have food, water, blankets. Those are my conditions."

Her smile chilled the room. "I'm not certain it's your place to dictate conditions to me, but in this I will defer to your wishes. Whatever comfort they enjoy here will be temporary."

"Yes," Risch said. "I believe the sole value of such a gesture will be as a salve for your conscience."

Myles pounded his hand on the table, nearly upsetting his cup of wine. "Don't push me in this, Risch! Think of the boy, and your soldiers. I can just as easily begin your torment here."

"Do you honestly believe it matters? Do you think your betrayal of me, and of Mearlan, is any less egregious because you give us an extra blanket? You're a greater fool than I ever imagined. She's a child, Myles. Barely more than an infant. And you've sentenced her to death."

The duke of Trohsden eyed him for another fivecount. "Guards!" he shouted, making Tobias jump.

His door opened. Two soldiers in gray entered the chamber.

"Take the Duke of Duvyn and this other man to the dungeon." He hesitated. "Separate cells. Make certain they have blankets, food, and water."

"Yes, my lord."

They called for two more soldiers from the hallway and approached Risch and Tobias. The guards, all of them bearing muskets fixed with bayonets, disarmed them, took the sack holding Orzili's tri-sextant, and led them toward the door. A guard walked on either side of Tobias, steering him, their grip on his arms firm, though not abusive. They hadn't found his broken chronofor, not that it would do him any good.

He had lost everything that mattered and would soon be back in the one place to which he had vowed never to return: Hayncalde's dungeon, at the mercy of Orzili and his torturers.

Ejino watched Tobias leave the ship wearing his robe, weighed down with Risch's things and the Walker's own carry sack. He had done what he could for the man—the boy. Now it fell to Tobias and Risch to win Myles's support.

As he stared after the lad, though, he saw a shadow detach itself from one of the warehouses near the wharf and steal after him. Likely the same person who had followed Ejino back to the ship from the castle.

He spat a curse and drew breath to shout a warning to Tobias. After a moment's consideration, he kept silent, unsure of whether alerting Tobias would create more trouble for them. The shadow followed the Walker at a distance, appearing content to mark his progress rather than accost him.

The problem was, this person knew Tobias was not Risch's Crosser.

Ejino watched the figure for a breath longer, then ran below, grabbed his golden Bound aperture, and left the ship. He followed the follower, moving with stealth, keeping to shadows. Rather than pass through the gate, he cut away from the path and followed the contour of the city wall until he was alone. He scanned this part of the wall, saw no soldiers on the wall walk. Satisfied that none could see him, he pulled off his clothes, wrapped them around a large stone, and tied the bundle tight with the sleeves of his shirt. He checked the top of the wall a second time, scanned his surroundings. Seeing no one, he heaved the bundle with all his might, watched it soar over the wall. He listened for the thud of its landing on the far side, but heard nothing.

Hoping it had cleared the battlement, he threw his shoes over as well. Next, he spread his aperture so that the hinged blades opened, creating a ring wide enough to accommodate him. Then he pressed the device to the city wall.

The gold melded to the rough texture of the stone like wet

plaster. The metal began to vibrate, like strings under a bow. And a gap formed in the wall. Ejino took a deep breath and launched himself into the shaft he had created.

Darkness took him. Stone pressed on him from all sides, squeezing his chest, scraping his skin, threatening to choke him off from the night, the air, the world he knew.

Apertures worked on stone and wood. Not on forged metal. Some nobles, he knew, set spikes within the walls of their castles as proof against Crossers. Once a Cross began, once one of his kind entered the press, there was no going back. A well-placed spike could kill.

Always at the beginning of a press, Ejino wondered if this was the one that would end his life.

It wasn't.

The wall was thick. The press seemed to last a long time. There was little air here, no light or sound, no room for extraneous movement. Just creeping progress, like the flow of honey.

In time, he emerged from the press, as if birthed into the city. He tumbled from the stone, the aperture clutched in his sore hands, his body raw from the journey. He was in a small garden plot, surrounded by dry wisps of grass and shrub. A dog barked from an adjacent yard. His balled-up clothes and shoes lay a short distance ahead of him. He crawled to the bundle, untied it, and pulled on his clothes, sucking air through his teeth as the shirt sleeves and the legs of his breeches rubbed his tender flesh.

Once dressed, he hurried on to the castle. Finding a lonely stretch of wall here proved more difficult, and he didn't dare throw his clothes into the castle courtyard beyond the ramparts. He undressed in an empty alley, left his folded clothes and shoes in a neat bundle, tucked by a wooden shed, and crossed the lane to the wall.

Working quickly, he spread the aperture again, and entered the press a second time. As before, he held his breath, fearing a steel spike or rod. He managed to pass through this wall unscathed as well.

Now, though, he was naked within the castle. No one had

spotted him yet. Keeping to shadows, flattening himself against walls when necessary to avoid being seen, he crept through the grounds, into the castle, and along various corridors, managing to avoid detection. It was a large fortress, at least compared with Duvyn Castle, but he had been in other castles, and this one was structured like most.

Before long, he heard voices ahead, saw torch fire flickering at the intersection of two corridors. He slowed, eased to the corner, peered into the next passageway. It was choked with soldiers, four wearing Duvyn colors, a similar number dressed in gray, most in Sheraigh blue. The guards from Duvyn had been disarmed.

Not good.

"Guards!" Even from within the chamber, the voice rang in the corridor. Two of the Trohsden guards entered the room. Moments later, the other two joined them, and not long after that, they returned to the hallway holding Risch and Tobias between them. Several of the Sheraigh guards took hold of the four soldiers from Duvyn and fell in step behind these others. Ejino had no doubt that they were all being taken to Trohsden's dungeon.

Worse, all of them were headed in his direction. He ducked back around the corner and ran, the slap of his bare feet covered by the approaching steps of the soldiers and prisoners. He tried the first door he saw, but it was locked. The second opened, and he slipped into a dark room, only to freeze when he heard soft snoring nearby.

If he was found now, naked, in a stranger's bedchamber, his duke in the castle dungeon, they would kill him on sight. He thought about searching the room he was in for a pair of breeches, but didn't dare. He listened at the door as the guards marched by. When they had passed, and he could no longer hear their footsteps, he let himself out of the chamber, crept down the corridor again, and peeked around the corner. To his dismay, two Sheraigh guards stood by Myles's door.

Fortunately, they didn't remain there long. After a few spirecounts, the chamber door opened, and Emella Sheraigh stepped into the hallway, followed by two more of her men. She closed the door, and with the soldiers arrayed around her, she walked away, in the opposite direction. Ejino walked on his toes to the door, but before he reached it, he heard the lock turn.

He assumed Myles was alone in the chamber. And he assumed as well, since he remained free while Risch and Tobias had been taken, that he had cast his lot with the Sheraighs.

Ejino sensed his options dwindling. He could flee to the ship, order the soldiers there to sail from these waters, and abandon Risch and Tobias to their fates, which he refused to do. He could bring the soldiers back here, and the seven of them could raid the castle and win the duke's freedom. Or, knowing that he would never get six Duvyn soldiers through Trohsden's castle gate, he could free the duke and the Walker himself.

No one who knew Ejino would have called him brave, but neither was he a coward. He had come to love his duke. The man was honest, generous, he cared about the people in his duchy, and he would have given his life for Daerjen. Chances were, he would in the next few days. He had earned Ejino's devotion and whatever sacrifices circumstance demanded of him.

Myles's door had iron bands across it. Who knew what metal might lurk within the wood? Better then to Cross through the stone wall.

He walked a few strides back toward the other corridor, expanded his aperture, set it against the stone, and, when the shaft opened, he slipped into the press.

It didn't last nearly as long as had his other two Crossings. Within a few tencounts, he toppled out of the press onto the floor of Myles's chamber.

"Who's there?" The duke was on his feet, squinting into shadows, a sword in hand. "Show yourself."

Ejino stood, stepped forward into the light of the lamp and fire.

The duke peered at him. "Crosser? Is that you?"

"It is, my lord."

Myles lowered his sword and slid it into its sheath. "For pity's sake, put on some clothes."

"I have none. They're outside the walls of your castle." He held up his aperture by way of explanation.

The duke heaved a breath, crossed to another door, and left the chamber briefly. When he returned, he carried a pair of breeches and a shirt.

"These won't fit, but you'll be decent."

He tossed them onto a chair, tended to his hearth.

Ejino crossed to the chair and pulled on the clothes. They were huge, but they warmed him. "You can turn around."

Myles eyed him, the handsome face resolving into a scowl. He drank the rest of whatever was in his cup and poured himself more. "Miejan red. Would you like some?"

"Thank you, my lord. I would."

Myles filled a second cup, set it on the table beside his own, and sat, indicating with a brusque flip of his hand that Ejino should do the same.

"You came to beg for his life?" Myles asked as Ejino took the chair beside him.

"Yes, my lord. I suppose I did. And the life of the Walker."

"A waste of time. One that will likely prove fatal."

He didn't sound angry or menacing. Just weary. And a good ways gone with drink.

"You shouldn't have come. Any of you. I said as much today. You heard me. I told Risch it was a mistake. I hoped he would take that as a warning, return to his vessel, and sail from these waters. I think he might have gotten away at that point." He shook his head, gulped more wine. "But no. He had to request a chamber for the night. And then he had to bring that damned Walker to me."

"The Walker is no more than a boy," Ejino said.

Myles rounded on him, making his chair shift with the scrape of wood on stone. "The Walker is the reason Risch has to die!" His voice rose enough that Ejino had to keep himself from hushing the man.

"He gave offense?"

Myles stared, his anger sluicing away. "You don't know, do you?"

"I know that Risch is your friend."

"You should go. You have a chance to get away, and you should take it. I'll...I'll let you leave the castle, and I'll have my fleet allow the vessel to sail from the firth. I don't want your blood on my hands, too."

"What did the Walker do?"

Myles set down his cup and pointed at the door. "Go. Now."

"First tell me."

"If I tell you, you'll have to die."

That gave Ejino pause, though not for long. He had figured when he entered the chamber that his life was forfeit.

"So be it."

Myles deflated, gazed into the fire. "It doesn't matter."

"Clearly it does, my lord. You don't want to tell me." He pondered this. What could Tobias have told him that would ensure their deaths?

"There's a way to defeat them, isn't there? The Sheraighs, I mean. Tobias knows how to best this new supremacy."

"If you don't know, why are you here? Why come all this way?"

The kernel of a strategy took form in his mind. "I came because the duke needed me as a distraction for Belvora."

A frown flickered across the duke's face. "What?"

"Tobias has been hunted by Belvora, and other Ancients as well. The winged ones are drawn to Traveler magick. By bringing me along, my duke hoped to keep the demons from knowing Tobias was with him."

"And you agreed to this?"

He raised his chin. "I serve my house. And my isle."

Myles looked away again. "You believe I deserve to be shamed. This is more complicated than you know."

"It's not complicated at all, my lord. If you defy the Sheraighs, you risk your life, your lands, your family. You might even risk a civil war that would plunge the isle into blood and darkness. It's easier and safer by far to acquiesce. And if Tobias and Risch have to die... Well, that's a reasonable cost, isn't it?"

Myles kept silent.

"I like men. Did you know that?"

The duke eyed him sidelong, shook his head.

"I tell you this because while men and woman like me are accepted now, we weren't a century or two ago. We were burned alive for loving within our same sex. That changed, not because we hid in shadows, but because a few declared and showed their love openly and were punished for it. And their punishment so horrified the Sanctuaries, and some in royal courts, that the laws were amended."

"I know this," Myles said. "I'm not ignorant."

"Perhaps not, but you're ignoring history."

Ejino thought of his duke, of the patience and reason with which he had convinced Trohsden's soldier earlier that very day.

"Allow me to ask two questions, and if you can answer them truthfully to my satisfaction, I will leave your castle and your city and never trouble you again."

Myles hesitated, nodded, much as his man had done at the wharf.

"Do you value this new supremacy more than you do your friendship with my duke and your memory of Mearlan?"

At first the duke offered no response, and when at last he did speak, it was only to ask, "What's your second question?"

"If love and friendship aren't worth dying for, what in the Two's world is?"

CHAPTER TWENTY

18th Day of Sipar's Ascent, Year 634

Tobias clung to the bars of his cell. Sweat ran down his face, and he gritted his teeth against wave after wave of sickness.

Maybe all dungeons smelled of piss and vomit and rot, of blood and fear. Maybe they all were cold, dank, oppressive. Maybe the flicker of torch fire on ancient stone looked the same in all of them.

He couldn't be sure. He knew only that upon entering this dungeon and being locked in this cell, memories of Hayncalde's dungeon flooded his mind. His joints began to ache. His scars burned with the remembered agony of smoking hot blades and handfuls of lye.

Risch spoke to him in low tones. Trying to reassure, or, failing that, to distract. None of his words penetrated Tobias's terror. He would be tortured again before he died. Not because Orzili needed anything more from him—the Sheraighs knew where Mara and Sofya were hidden, and Tobias could do nothing to warn them—but because Tobias had wounded him and bested him more than once. The assassin would have his revenge before he allowed Tobias to die.

Death didn't frighten him. Not really. Torture though... He would take his own life before he submitted to more torment.

The door scraped open at the top of the stone stairway, and footsteps echoed on the stone treads. Tobias heard voices—someone speaking to the Sheraigh guards outside the dungeon door. An instant later a breath of clean, cool air brushed against his face. He closed his eyes, savoring the sensation.

Myles stepped through the archway at the base of the stairs. Followed by Ejino, who wore clothes that were laughably large. The duke halted in the confined space before the cells, his lips pressed into a whitening gash, his glower aimed at Risch.

"Did you do this on purpose?" he asked.

Risch answered with a glare of his own. "Do what?"

"Force me into this demon's choice."

"No, Myles. This wasn't my intention. Never in a thousand years would I have imagined that you'd find it so difficult to honor a lifetime of friendship."

Myles closed the distance to Risch's cell in one lunging stride. "They will take everything from me!" he said in a rasp. "They will kill my boys! They'll kill Surla!"

"And what do you suppose they intend to do to me?"

Myles straightened. He pivoted, walked to Tobias.

"Is it true? Is she really alive?"

"For now," Tobias said with all the ice he could muster. "I'd imagine Emella is drafting a missive to her brother as we speak. If she sends it by bird, the child and my wife will be dead within a day."

"What did you hope I would do for you?"

"I need a Binder, someone who can repair a broken chronofor," Tobias said. "Risch tells me you have one in your employ."

"I do. What else?"

"I don't know, my lord. I'm not a duke. It may be that pretending to support Noak—for a time at least—would help our cause. Eventually, though, we need to place Sofya on the throne. And we'll need a regent. Before we came here, I thought you would be a good choice."

Myles dropped his gaze. "I would be," he said. "I swear it."

He produced a key from within his robe and unlocked the door to Tobias's cell. He did the same for Risch but stood before the opening so that his friend couldn't yet leave the cell.

"I'm sorry. I was... I'm afraid. I would be grateful if you gave me a chance to redeem myself."

"Of course I will. And so you know, I'm afraid, too, and I have far less to lose than you do."

"I'm not sure I believe that."

The men gripped each other's shoulders. Then they separated, and Myles freed Risch's soldiers.

"You owe your lives to Ejino," Myles said, indicating the Crosser. "If not for him, I'd be drunk in my chamber and you would still be in those cells."

Risch took the Crosser's hand in both of his and gave it a vigorous shake. Tobias thanked Ejino as well.

The Crosser fell in step beside him as they climbed the stairs to the dungeon door.

"Mearlan's daughter is alive?" he whispered.

Tobias shot him a look.

"Thanks to you?"

"How did you—"

"I didn't know for certain until this moment, listening to Myles. I did what I did to save my duke, but I'm thinking now that saving you was the greater service to Daerjen."

Two dozen Trohsden soldiers awaited them in the courtyard outside the door to the castle's prison. Four men in Sheraigh blue stood with them, disarmed, gazes darting from the dukes to Tobias to the soldiers guarding them. Tobias and the others who had been imprisoned had their weapons and belongings returned to them. Myles then led Risch, Tobias, Ejino, and the soldiers from both Duvyn and Trohsden toward the main towers. None of Trohsden's soldiers spoke. Tobias sensed that Myles had demanded stealth of them. The rest kept quiet as well.

"I have more soldiers waiting inside," the duke told Risch, his voice low. "They're guarding the corridors adjacent to where Emella is quartered, in case she tries to leave."

"Already?" Risch asked.

The corners of Myles's mouth twitched. "I assumed you were going to forgive me."

"Bold. Where are her soldiers?" Risch asked.

"There are perhaps eight guarding her chamber. The rest were billeted with my own. They've been disarmed and placed under guard."

"That's more than bold. It's..."

"Folly?"

Reaching one of the entryways, Myles split his company of soldiers, keeping half with them and sending the rest across the courtyard to enter on the other side, where they were to join with the soldiers he had positioned there before. When all were ready, the dukes, the soldiers, Tobias, and Ejino entered the castle. They climbed a flight of stairs and upon reaching the second level made their way toward Emella's chamber.

Before reaching her stretch of corridor, Myles signaled for them to halt. He and a half dozen of his soldiers continued around the corner. Tobias heard him call a greeting to the princess's men. A moment later, sounds of a scuffle reached them, and a tencount after that, Myles called to Risch.

"Come along," Risch said, motioning to Tobias, Ejino, and his soldiers.

They turned the corner, joined Myles at Emella's door, and followed as he opened the door and entered her chamber.

The princess stood at her desk, the quill in her hand poised over a tiny strip of parchment. Seeing them in her doorway, she darted a glance toward the messenger doves.

"Stop her!" Tobias said.

He didn't wait for a reply but ran toward her. Four Sheraigh soldiers converged on him from opposite sides of the chamber. Tobias wouldn't reach Emella before they reached him. He veered toward a standing desk and grabbed the first thing at hand. An oil lamp.

Tobias whirled. The dukes had engaged two of the soldiers. Two others still bore down on him. He flung the lamp at the chest of the nearer man.

The soldier—tall, burly, young—had no time to dodge the lamp. He swung his musket at it, shattering the reservoir so that he was soaked with oil. He yowled, clawed at his eyes with one hand, allowing the barrel of his musket to swing down and away.

Tobias charged him. The man's companion shouted a warning. The soldier aimed the musket again, but his eyes remained half shut. Tobias twisted away, dropped to the floor. The soldier pulled the trigger, the report deafening in that small space. The barrel belched fire. And the oil flared, engulfing the soldier in flame. He shrieked, dropped his weapon, which also burned. He flailed.

The other soldier rushed to his comrade, threw down his musket, and beat at the flames with both hands. Tobias lunged for the musket just as the second soldier realized his error. He dove for it as well. They struggled. This soldier was as broad and strong as Tobias. No doubt he was well-trained.

Tobias, though, had fought Orzili more than once. And he was fighting for the lives of the two people he loved most in the world. The man didn't have a chance.

While holding fast to the musket, Tobias thrust his elbow into the soldier's chin. The man grunted. Tobias rolled so that he was on top of the soldier. He let go of the weapon with one hand, reared back, and pounded his fist into the soldier's face once, and again.

The soldier's grip on the musket slackened. Tobias yanked it away from him, hammered the butt into his jaw, rendering him unconscious.

He stood. The chamber stank of burned hair and cloth. Risch had thrown a blanket over the burning soldier and extinguished the fire, but the man was badly burned. He was certainly no threat to them. Soldiers from Duvyn and Trohsden stood over the other two men.

Myles stood with Emella, his sword drawn and leveled at the princess.

"You have assured your own death, Trohsden," she said, her voice level.

"You stopped her in time?" Tobias asked.

The duke of Trohsden nodded. "The parchment bearing her message is still here, as are all the birds she had as of this morning."

"This means nothing," Emella said. "A delay of the inevitable. My brother will hear of this. You and your family will be put to death, your lands divided among other nobles. Trohsden itself will cease to—"

"Do shut up!" Myles said.

She glared, cheeks blazing.

"What do we do with them?" Risch asked.

"Yes," Emella said. "What will you do with us?"

Myles didn't hesitate. "Kill you, I think. That would be the simplest solution."

The princess blinked, said nothing. Tobias didn't know if Trohsden's duke was serious, but his words certainly silenced her.

"Put her soldiers in the dungeon," he said to his guards. "Don't mistreat them in any way. See to it that the wounded are cared for." He spared Emella a glance. "The princess will remain here. Take the birds from the chamber."

The soldiers of Trohsden carried out the duke's orders with alacrity. Within a few spirecounts, the princess, Tobias, Ejino, the two dukes, and a pair of gray uniformed soldiers were the only ones left in the chamber.

"Wait in the corridor," Myles told his guards.

They left the room, closed the door behind them.

"It's not too late, you know," Emella said.

"I was about to tell you the same thing."

She paled. "Meaning what?"

"You can save your life and the lives of your soldiers if you abandon your brother and tell us all you know about his plans for

Trohsden, for Duvyn, for Hayncalde. We would need to know how he has assigned his army and his fleet."

"And," Tobias broke in, "we would have to know as well what his arrangement is with the autarchy."

"We have no arrangement with the autarch."

"You're lying." He pointed to his scars. "Mearlan's assassin did this to me. I know the man, and I know that he is no Sheraigh. He works for Pemin. Without Oaqamar's help, you never would have destroyed the old supremacy."

"You will tell us all you know about your brother's arrangements with Oaqamar as well," Myles said, reasserting control over the conversation.

"I will tell you nothing."

"You'd rather die?"

She answered with a knife-edge smile. "I don't believe you'll kill me. You know what the consequences would be."

Myles considered her, nodded. "Yes, I do." He crossed to the door and summoned two soldiers. "I've changed my mind. Please place the princess in the dungeon, as far from her soldiers as possible. As with them, she's not to be mistreated in any way. She is also not to be allowed to converse with her men, or anyone else. Do you understand?"

"Yes, my lord."

As the soldiers approached her, Emella took a step back, bumping into the stand that had held her bird cage.

"No, wait. I'll...I'll do as you ask. I'll tell you everything you want to know."

"No, you won't. You'll lie to us. You come from a house of liars, of traitors, of cowards. You'll tell us what you think we want to hear, and you'll do all you can to conceal the truth of what Noak has in mind."

The soldiers took hold of her arms and led her toward the door.

"No!" She fought them, to no avail. She screamed again and again, trying to plant her feet to keep the soldiers from moving her. The two men lifted her off the floor and carried her from the chamber. Her cries still echoed in the corridor as Myles closed the door.

"Will you really have her killed?" Ejino asked.

Myles poured himself a cup of wine from a flask on a table near the hearth. "I haven't ruled it out. Then again, she might be of use to us as a hostage. If Noak attacks us, and I expect he will, we could use her, trade her freedom for safe passage for my family."

"She knows about Sofya," Tobias said. "So do some of her soldiers, which means all of them might know."

Myles slanted a glance his way. "You argue for her execution?"

"I'm merely pointing out that she holds the future of House Hayncalde in her hands. If she's allowed to live, she can't be freed until Noak's hold on power is broken. I'm afraid you can't use her as leverage in your bargaining."

Myles's expression hardened. "You would dictate to me in this matter, *Walker*?"

"I would, my lord. I may be young and a mere court Traveler, but I'm also the guardian of Mearlan's daughter. I'm speaking to you not as a Walker, but as a father. And I'm telling you, you can't risk the child's life. Not for anything."

The duke considered him. "Tell me how you would restore the supremacy."

Tobias faltered. He couldn't explain everything to the man, because his deepest hope was that he wouldn't have to restore the supremacy at all. Rather, he wished to Walk back and attempt to prevent Mearlan's assassination from ever happening. To his mind, that was the only way to defeat Orzili and the autarchy, the only way to prevent the fall of Hayncalde.

He wasn't certain, though, that this was even possible anymore. So much had happened since Mearlan's death. How did one remake history after all this time?

Tobias couldn't say any of this to Myles. Given what he was asking of the man—of both dukes, really—he couldn't let on that, in his mind, this was no more than a contingency, a plan to pursue if the misfuture couldn't be repaired.

"We would need for you to gain the trust and support of the other dukes, my lord. Whomever among them you think you can sway. Sheraigh has the support of Oaqamar. We would need to counter that with help from the Axle and the other Ring Isles. None of Daerjen's neighbors wants to see our isle allied with the autarchy. Fear of Pemin should help you."

"I'm one duke. You honestly believe I can do all of this?"

"We're two dukes," Risch said.

"Duvyn is isolated."

"Not if Trohsden embraces her."

Myles frowned. "Earlier today, you suggested I could pretend to support Noak and work against him in secret."

"I think you ruined that plan when you put Emella in your dungeon."

Trohsden's duke tipped his head, conceding the point. "So we would stand against him, try to rally other dukes to our cause. But you want to keep secret the fact that Mearlan's daughter lives. Without her, I'm not sure any would join us."

Tobias wanted to argue. He recoiled from the idea of sharing this secret with anyone, even as he recognized the wisdom of doing so. He had kept her hidden for so many turns, had built his very life around the secret he and Mara shared. They had protected her from assassins, demons, the army of the sovereign. Revealing that Sofya lived struck him as a betrayal of everything he had done since that bloody night in Hayncalde. And yet...

Miles appeared to read his thoughts, and he smiled with sympathy. "What you have done in keeping her alive is nothing short of miraculous. But those who want her dead know that she lives. Yours is a secret without value. On the other hand, if we share this knowledge with those who loved her father, those who would be heartened to know that she survived Mearlan's assassination, we might indeed win them to our cause."

"Do you believe the other dukes would rally to her?"

"The other dukes hate the Sheraighs. They fear them, but they hate them. Mearlan was the only person strong enough to protect the other houses—with him gone, the Sheraighs stand largely unopposed. None of them love Noak the way Mearlan was loved. Except maybe Ysendyr, but he's a fool and a coward. If the rest oppose Noak, and if it seems we can stand against him, Ysendyr will fall in line."

Tobias stared at the embers of Emella's fire, his thoughts churning. His fears remained, of course. One conversation couldn't overmaster turn upon turn of worry, of pursuit and escape. Nevertheless, Myles had opened his mind to the possibility of a different future, perilous, to be sure, but filled with possibility.

"I'll consider this, my lord. I give you my word. I need to speak of these things with my wife, as well. I hope you understand."

"Of course."

"In the meantime, you will hold Emella here?"

"Yes. I'll keep her in the dungeon for a night or two, just to tame her a bit. Eventually, I'll give her a room in my highest tower—a chamber that will give her no cause for complaint, but whence she can't escape."

Tobias couldn't demand more than that of the duke. "Very well, my lord. All that remains then is for me to speak with your Binder, if you'll allow it."

"I will. First thing in the morning."

"Thank you, my lord."

A plan, the possibility of a repaired chronofor, and allies in his ongoing battle with Orzili. Tobias couldn't ask for more. And yet, more was offered to him.

Risch and Ejino accompanied him as he left the chamber.

"I'm not at all sleepy," Ejino said as they walked the corridors. "Are you, my lord?"

Duvyn's duke grinned at the question. "What do you have in mind, Ejino?"

"The *Apple and Pear*, my lord. What else?"

The Apple and Pear was a tavern in the city, not far from the castle, that served an excellent ale from Kisira and hosted a diverting game of dice, played with rules Tobias had not encountered before. He mastered the game quickly, won a good deal of silver from several players, including Risch, and then lost it all and a bit more.

It was that rarest of things in the life he had led since leaving Windhome so long ago, so long in the future: an evening without danger or fear or responsibility. It also was a very late night.

Risch, Ejino, and Tobias returned to Myles's chamber the next morning. There they met Trohsden's Binder, Lorayenne Thriss. She was white-haired, willowy, of medium height with eyes warm brown and clear.

Tobias began by handing her his wrecked chronofor, which he had carried in pockets and carry sacks for so long that its dented face and shards of glass were mixed with small wisps of lint. The Binder frowned as he placed it in her lined palm. Tobias expected her to tell him that the device was beyond repair.

"What did you do to it?" she asked, a chill in the question, her voice gravelly.

"I've been carrying it for a long time, waiting to find—"

"Never mind that. I'm asking how you broke it."

Anger displaced embarrassment. "In battle," he said, his tone matching hers.

"These are precious devices! They're to be treated with care!"

"Binder," Myles said quietly.

"Well, the next time I see Mearlan's assassins, I'll let them know that you're displeased with their treatment of my chronofor!"

That made her look up.

"Perhaps," her duke said, "it would be more constructive to speak of what can be done to mend the device."

"Yes, my lord," she said after a pause.

"Can you fix it?" Tobias asked.

"I believe I can. It's been some time since last I worked on a chronofor. I hope I remember how." A smile crossed her lips and vanished. "I have the parts," she went on. "I've kept them here all these years hoping I would have cause to use them."

"Do you have enough spare pieces to repair mine and also build a second?"

"A second?" Myles repeated. "You said nothing about this before now. Do you know how dear the materials for a chronofor can be?"

"I do, my lord. Which is why I have this to offer by way of payment." Tobias opened the cloth sack he'd brought with him and pulled out Orzili's tri-sextant.

No one spoke. Ejino eased forward between his duke and Risch, attempting to get a better look. Tobias turned the device one way and then the other, allowing all of them to see it from different angles. At last, the Binder reached for it, stopped herself.

"May I?" she asked.

Tobias let her take it from him.

"It's a sextant, obviously," she said. "But modified extensively. Can you tell me what it does?"

"It allows Spanners to travel in groups, to take people—soldiers, assassins, anyone—with them even if these others can't Span, and it allows them to do all of this fully clothed and armed."

Lorayenne's eyes widened. "Sipar be praised."

"Or cursed," Ejino said, drawing frowns from both dukes.

Tobias caught his eye and nodded.

"Where did you get this?" the Binder asked.

"From Mearlan's assassin. We bested him in a fight and took this from one of his men." He didn't mention that they had taken more than one of the devices. He didn't yet know if he and Mara would need the other tri-sextants in other negotiations. "You should know that these devices were originally created in the future. At least ten years from now, I would guess." To Ejino, he said, "There are tri-apertures, as well."

"Used the same way, to the same effect?"

"Yes."

"These are normal sextant arcs," the Binder said, sounding lost in her examination of the device. "The indices are the same as well, except there are three of each. The release is the same, as is the sighting mechanism. The only part that's unique appears to be this bridge linking the three arcs. That's not something I've seen before. And the index arms have been modified. Otherwise..."

"So you could recreate it?" Tobias asked.

"I believe so. I'd like to see it work first."

"You can't," Tobias said. "It takes three devices, wielded by three Spanners to Travel this way. The three stand in formation—a triangle, of course—and activate their devices simultaneously. Everyone and everything within the triangle they form will be carried into the gap."

"Ingenious!" Lorayenne said.

Ejino rounded on her. "No! Not ingenious! Diabolical! Don't you see the danger? Don't you understand what this new kind of device does? It turns Spanners and Crossers into warriors and killers. It makes us agents of war rather than diplomacy and commerce. This is terrible." He eyed Tobias. "You understand. I can see that you do. So why would you bring this here? Are you that desperate for your chronofors?"

"Yes, I am. But it's more than that. Our enemies have these. They're already using them precisely the way you describe. So we can choose to ignore this advance and be destroyed by those who have embraced it. Or we can fight back, on equal footing."

"Are there tri-chronofors as well?" Risch asked.

"Not yet."

Myles joined his Binder in scrutinizing the device. "You're offering this as payment for the second chronofor?"

"That's right, my lord. You'll need tri-sextants to defeat the Sheraighs."

"Very well. Lorayenne will begin work immediately on the repairs to your chronofor."

"Thank you."

Risch turned to Tobias and Ejino. "The duke and I need to discuss plans for what comes next. Even if we wait until you've spoken with Mara before we approach other dukes, we need to have a strategy in place. There's not much for the two of you to do right now except give us some time." He gave the slightest of nods—a dismissal.

"Yes, my lord," Ejino said. He touched Tobias's arm, steering him toward the door.

Even after stepping into the corridor, Tobias and Ejino didn't speak until they were beyond the hearing of Myles's soldiers.

"Trohsden can be trusted," Ejino finally said. "I promise you."

Tobias cast a dark glance his way. "So he says. I placed my faith in him and wound up in a dungeon. I'm grateful that he changed his mind, but I fear what might happen if he gets a better offer."

"I don't blame you, but you have to understand: All this talk of rebellion and opposing the Sheraighs has him scared."

"And that's just what we can't afford," Tobias said. "Every other duke in the land will be looking to Myles for courage and wisdom and guidance. I'm not convinced he can offer any of that."

Ejino eyed him but said nothing.

CHAPTER TWENTY-ONE

14th Day of Kheraya's Descent, Year 647

It took Lenna nearly a full turn to make her way from Belsan to Qaifin, the royal city of Oaqamar. As easy as had been her journey from Hayncalde to Belsan in the past she'd left behind, that was how difficult this voyage—or set of voyages—proved.

The difference? Gold, of course. That and years.

She left Hayncalde as a woman of means, able to buy her way onto any ship. And she sailed in that past as a beauty, beyond the bloom of youth, but still young and lovely enough to charm men and women who possessed the means to help her.

In this new future, she had neither wealth nor looks. She was poor and old. At best, she could hope that pity would sway some to offer aid. She secured passage on the first ship out of Belsan for six treys. It carried her only as far as Xharef in Sipar's Labyrinth. She slept on a filthy blanket on the floor of the vessel's hold, surrounded by sailors and other desperate passengers. She didn't have to work for her passage, but neither was she given much to eat or drink. Well-watered wine—red swill from Qyrshen—stale bread, and sour hard cheese.

Her arrival in Xharef actually left her farther from Qaifin than she had been in Belsan. Such was the nature of travel for the indigent, and for those trying to reach the autarchy. Aiyanth and Oaqamar fought a war in this future. No ship from Belsan would have taken her to Qaifin or any other Oaqamaran city.

From Xharef, she bought her way onto another ship—barely seaworthy—that was headed west through the Labyrinth, and perhaps into the Sisters. The ship's captain, a taciturn dark-skinned woman, was circumspect about her ultimate destination. Passage was cheap, though, and on this vessel, if it remained afloat, she would sleep on a small pallet.

If Lenna could have sold her chronofor or one of her blades, she would have. She needed her chronofor, however. Without it, she was of no use to Pemin. And she needed her blades as well, lest some unscrupulous sailor or wharf break-law think her easy prey and attempt to steal what little she possessed.

She didn't worry about unwanted advances from captains or crew. At her apparent age, she might as well have been invisible to most. Men and women who would have ogled her before her last Walk through time, now stared through her. She both welcomed and lamented the change. Only after days of this, however, did it occur to her that she might profit from it.

One night in a fishing village in the western reaches of the Labyrinth—she didn't know the name of the isle—she wandered the lanes until she encountered a younger man, well dressed, with a kindly face and too much faith in the good will of others.

She made herself walk with a limp, thought of Orzili until her eyes watered. The poor man approached her, brow bunched with concern, a kind word on his lips. Old as she was, she retained the skills she had honed in her work for Pemin. The man never saw her first punch coming. A kick to the gut and a second blow rendered him unconscious. She emptied his purse, pulled a golden ring from his finger, and hurried back to the wharf and her ship. A bell later, the captain had put to sea again.

At their next stop, Lenna sold the ring in a small marketplace and found a ship that was headed to Bellisi, in the Sisters, and then to Qaifin. She had a pallet for this vessel as well, and the captain, a silver-haired man with a large belly and brilliant blue eyes, doted on her. It seemed that to some, she remained a beauty.

She enjoyed his attention and even ate a meal with him in his quarters. She refused his advances, politely but firmly, and he respected her wishes, though he looked as forlorn as a puppy forced to sleep in the cold.

That night, alone under her blanket, Lenna thought of the young man she had beaten, of the old captain's desire, of Orzili's indifference toward her upon her return to this time. She had, she realized, spent too much of her life judging herself—measuring her beauty, her allure, her strength and skill and wit—by the reactions she drew from men. Sometimes from women, but mostly men. She had used Orzili and Pemin and so many of her victims, as mirrors. She had found in their admiration or praise or attraction or fear reflections of herself, gauges of her worth. What a waste.

She was not some pampered daughter of a court. She was an assassin. Not for her the soft life of luxurious clothes and staid royal courtships. She had lived and traveled and Traveled and loved and killed. She was a different sort of woman, one most people could not understand. Yet, she had been slave to the judgements of the men around her. How had that happened?

And why did she still grieve so for her lost love?

She tossed on her pallet and pulled her blanket tighter, impatient with the thoughts keeping her awake. She was too young in actual years to feel so wistful, to find herself looking back with regret on a life she had barely had time to live.

Resentment stirred within her, like a bear rousing itself from a winter's sleep. She had spent her life on men, on Orzili and Pemin in particular. She had spent her years in service to their ambitions and rivalries. And she had been happy to do it. She needed to remember that as well. Any rage she directed at them needed to be matched, and then some, by anger at herself. She allowed them to take those years, to send her on those Walks.

In fairness, she also needed to remember that whatever else Orzili did to her, however he might have used her in those turns they spent together in the past, he had tried to guard her years. When they understood how far back Pemin would ask her to go, he had spoken of leaving Belsan and hiding from the autarch. *We can run. Leave this place now and make our way north, or out to the Knot...*

He would have done it, heedless of the consequences. *She* was the one who chose to spend those years. There was a time, a line of history, when he loved her as much as she loved him. Even now, steeped in these dark musings, that brought some comfort.

Pemin, on the other hand, had always seen her as nothing more or less than a weapon to be wielded. He spent her years as if they were his, with no regard for the cost she bore. The autarch deserved her rage, her bitterness. Had he even earned her retribution?

Dangerous thoughts given that she was on her way to his castle. She turned over again, began to count in doubles—one, two, four, eight, sixteen... A trick she had learned in her youth while studying arithmetic in Windhome. Before she reached six digits, she was asleep.

Three days later, they reached the wharves of Qaifin. The captain tried to convince her to remain with him, but Lenna told him she had a brother in Qaifin who was dying and needed her by his side. She left the ship under his gaze. He still stared after her as she entered the city and climbed the broad lane to Pemin's castle.

It had been years since last she trod these lanes, yet memories of her first visit to the city swarmed through her mind. She had been so young—she and Orzili both—so easily awed. Yes, Qaifin remained impressive, though no more so than Hayncalde and Belsan and a few others. She recalled her excitement and her trepidation. She felt no excitement this time, but she was frightened. Pemin would think her too old, as Orzili had. And what would she do then?

The guards at the castle gate stopped her, as she had known

they would. She answered their questions in Oaqamaran, which she still spoke fluently after so many years.

No, the autarch was not expecting her. Yes, she had come here before. He would know her name—Lenna Stenci. She produced her chronofor from within her tired gown, held it up for them to see, told them she was a Walker and an assassin. Pemin's assassin.

Two soldiers entered the castle to inform the autarch of her arrival. The others watched her, demanded that she surrender her weapons, which she did. None of them appeared to think her a threat to their safety or Pemin's. Too old.

It occurred to her that an old assassin might enjoy certain advantages. All of her victims would be as unsuspecting as the man she had robbed in the Labyrinth. The two soldiers returned within a quarter bell and asked her to follow them. They led her through gardens and courtyards—the castle had changed little over the years—and finally through broad corridors to the autarch's door with its inlaid likeness of the striped lion.

The men knocked. A voice from within called for them to enter. One soldier pushed open the door and motioned Lenna inside.

She inhaled, exhaled, walked into the chamber. The door closed behind her. Pemin stood at his window, seemingly untouched by the years. There might have been a bit more gray in his hair, a few additional lines on the tapered, handsome face. Nothing compared to the changes she had endured.

Resentment knifed through her. She weighed again all that she had sacrificed to feed the scheming of this man.

Lenna had always thought him attractive in a remote way. Like the moon, or a ridge of distant mountains. As a younger woman, she had been devoted to Orzili, but Pemin's beauty had made him that much more compelling as an employer. Now, too late, she wondered if he had ever seen in her something more than a Walker to be commanded. He had long been said to love his queen, Deya, with uncommon passion. But even a smitten man might stray. Would he have allowed her to seduce him if she had made the attempt? Why did she care? She was old, in body if not mind. Concerns of this sort were behind her, and still she sought to see some reflection of herself in her interactions with this man. Did all women do this to themselves? Or was it just her?

Halfway between his window and the door, she remembered to bow. She halted, bent low, remained that way as he approached her. When he held out his hand, she pressed her brow to the back of it.

"Lenna?" he said. "Is it really you?"

She straightened, winced at a twinge in the small of her back. Damn the years she had lost.

"Am I so changed, Your Excellency? Do you not recognize me at all?"

"You are changed. How old are you, Lenna. How old really?"

"I've lost count, Your Excellency. What year is this?"

He looked pained. "It doesn't matter. Forget I asked."

"Forty-two I think. This is 647, yes?" Seeing him nod, she nodded as well. "Then forty-two. How old do I seem?"

Pemin pivoted, walked to a broad table near his expansive windows. "I was about to eat. Will you join me?"

"Thank you."

"Wine?"

"Of course. You always have the best."

He faltered and glanced back at her. He filled a cup and handed it to her as she joined him by the table.

"Why are you here?"

"Why do you think?"

"I'm honestly not sure. You rarely come to Qaifin. Usually Orzili speaks to me on your behalf."

"Not anymore."

"And why is that?"

"Forgive me, Your Excellency, but that's not your concern. Orzili and I no longer work together. You don't need to know more than that."

While Pemin studied her, she tasted her wine, her hand steady. A Brenthian white. As she'd said, always the best.

"Is Orzili still alive?" he asked after a tencount.

Lenna stared, then laughed. The autarch's stare hardened. He wouldn't appreciate being mocked. She didn't care.

"You think I killed him?"

"The thought entered my mind. It's also occurred to me that you might have come here to kill me."

"An act of vengeance, for all the years you've stolen from me."

"So it is something you've considered."

She shook her head. "Not until just now. You put the idea in my head."

He scowled. Lenna sensed the tension in his frame. He was ready should she attack him, but she didn't sense any fear on his part.

"I didn't come here to kill you, Your Excellency. I give you my word."

"Then why have you come? No more games. No more jests. I want an answer."

Perhaps he was a little afraid.

"I need gold," she said. "And so, I've come to offer my services."

"As a Walker? As an assassin?"

"Both."

He considered her again, his appraisal frank, his gaze sparing no part of her body. Lenna suffered his examination, and understood the implications of doing so. She was submitting herself to his will once again, consenting to having her years spent, her life endangered, all for the sake of his appetites —land, gold, power. It felt different this time. Maybe because she was doing it herself, without Orzili. Maybe because she had made up her mind to finish her life doing the one thing at which she was most skilled, even if that meant working for this man.

"Do you think you can still serve me in those capacities?" he asked after some time. "Let's be honest, you can't Walk back far. Not anymore."

"Whose fault is that?" She said it with more asperity than was wise. As before, she didn't much care.

"Beware your tone, Walker."

"Or what?" She laughed again. "You'll kill me? As you've pointed out yourself, I haven't much life left to lose."

"That isn't my fault."

She sobered. "No, it's mine, for allowing you and Orzili to control me as you have."

"You were paid quite well for all that you did on my behalf."

"I was, for the most part. Where's my gold for this last Walk? Fourteen years. And fourteen more to come back. Mearlan is dead, your war with Daerjen is won. Where is my gold?"

His expression shifted in odd ways, settling at last on something akin to annoyance. "I paid some to Orzili."

She shook her head. "I didn't get more than crumbs."

"That is...unfortunate. And something I can rectify. As to the rest..." He shrugged. "Yours is a young person's profession. I can't imagine what sort of assignment I might give you."

"With all respect, Your Excellency, that shows a lack of imagination. As I've learned in recent days, a woman as old as I appear can go unnoticed in places where a man like Orzili would draw attention."

His eyebrows rose. "Interesting. Perhaps as a spy, then. But as an assassin? I remain unconvinced. And, I'm sorry to say, I don't lack for spies."

He stepped to his desk, pulled from a drawer a leather purse. He poured the contents into his hand—gold rounds, a good many of them—counted them and slid them back into the purse. "Take this," he said, holding it out to her. "Fourteen rounds. That should allow you to go anywhere you wish."

She took the purse and slipped it into a pocket within her gown. She needed the coin, of course, but, she realized, she *wanted* the work. However ancient she looked, she wasn't ready to *be* old.

"You're making a mistake," she told him.

He shrugged. "It wouldn't be the first." He crossed to his door, opened it. Their conversation was at an end. "May the Goddess keep you safe, Lenna, and bless the rest of your days."

She walked to him, bowed, pressed his hand to her brow. Straightening, she said, "And yours, Your Excellency."

"Miss Stenci is to be allowed to enjoy the castle grounds for a bell or two if she wishes," he told one of the guards outside his door. "When she chooses to leave, no one should stop her. She is, and will always be, a friend of this court."

"Thank you," Lenna said.

The autarch merely smiled.

She left the chamber, peered back as Pemin closed the door. One of the guards walked with her to an entryway. Once outside again, she did linger briefly. She had always admired the autarch's gardens and fountains. Mostly, she was confused, disappointed. Her encounter with Pemin hadn't gone as she expected. She had gone in believing that he would leap at the chance to use her again. His dismissal had been abrupt, his gift of gold too quickly bestowed.

On the thought, she glanced around, noticed men watching her, some in uniforms of brown and black, others dressed entirely in black. Too late, it occurred to her that Pemin would never willingly let her go. She knew too much about things he would prefer no one knew. Which made her wonder why he had allowed her to leave his chamber at all. It would have been easier to have her taken to his prison and left there to die.

She smiled at one of the men, gazed at the fountain for another fivecount, then started toward the castle gate, keeping her bearing casual. No doubt she was allowing fear and suspicion to twist her perceptions. If Pemin wanted her dead, he *wouldn't* have sent her from his chamber.

Except that two of the men in black now followed her from this section of the garden. To make certain that she went directly to the gate?

For the moment, they kept their distance. But they had positioned themselves the way she and Orzili would have had they been stalking someone for assassination.

Her weapons were with the gate guards. She had no way to fight off these men should they attack. And they were closer now, still gaining on her. She sensed that they were herding her toward an archway that loomed ahead. Did more men await her there?

Best then to fight these two. If they killed her, so be it.

Lenna halted, faced them. They were young, vaguely handsome, muscular without being bulky. She had no doubt that they knew how to fight. Likely they were experienced killers, though not as experienced as she.

"Shall we do this here, gentlemen?"

They slowed, exchanged glances, continued to advance on her. Both men had knives in hand. She hadn't noticed the blades before. She cast a quick look at the area around her feet, desperate for any sort of weapon. Sand and fine gravel. Nothing more. She stooped, swept up a handful. It would have to do until she managed to disarm one of them.

She edged closer to the larger of the two men. He was probably stronger than his companion, but she guessed that he would be slower as well. At her "age," she valued speed over strength.

The other man altered course, closing on her faster. Still, the big man would reach her first. She spied a stone on the ground—nearly the size of her fist. She seized it with her free hand.

The big man grinned.

"Smile all you like," she said. "I've killed more men than you have. It's not even close."

The two assassins shared a second glance. Lenna took the opportunity to dart around the nearer man. It was midday, and the sun was high, but to the extent that it angled at all, she had it at her back. She also now had the big man between her and the second assassin. Another advantage.

The big man slowed, waiting for his companion. Lenna couldn't allow that.

She strode toward him, covering the distance in three paces. He raised his blade hand, lashed out with his other fist. She ducked, almost stumbled, orbited to the side. Already she was breathing hard.

She lunged at him, hoping to lure him into an error, willing to endure the bite of his blade if she could knock the weapon from his hand. He swiped at her, she dodged the attack, tried to slam the stone into his blade hand. Missed, losing her footing again.

Blood and bone!

She couldn't trust this body to respond as she wanted. She knew what to do but doubted she could actually do it.

He launched himself at her, his knife carving at her, a silver blur in the sun. She tried again to evade him. A burning pain in her side. She'd failed. Still, she hammered the stone into his blade hand as it swept past her. He snarled, dropped the knife. Lenna threw the sand in his face.

He cursed, twisted away. Lenna pounced. She pounded the stone into his face. Blood spurted from his nose. As he clutched at it, blood running between his fingers, she kicked him, once in the gut, a second time in the groin. He doubled over, dropped to his knees. She smashed the stone into the back of his skull. He sprawled onto the ground and didn't move again.

Lenna grabbed his knife, turned in time to meet the attack of the second man. He slashed at her. She dove, rolled, was on her feet again as he spun to face her. No stumble this time. The more she fought in this body, the more at ease she felt.

They circled. She kept herself beyond his reach and outside his blade hand, forcing him to match her movements. He shifted his blade to his other hand. She did the same, as good with her left as she was with her right. Surprise widened his eyes. Lenna laughed.

She bled from the wound the other man had dealt her but could tell it wasn't a deep cut. This man's life was hers.

She leapt at him. He jumped to the side. As she had known he would. While still in motion, as he still moved as well, she threw the stone at his head.

The man flinched away. Lenna shifted, perhaps not as quickly as she would have before this last Walk, but fast enough. The man saw her blade hand swing his way. His eyes went wide. He opened his mouth to cry out...something.

She buried her knife in his chest. He lashed out, too. His knife sliced into her arm before dropping from his fingers. Another shallow cut. Carelessness, age, lack of recent practice. It didn't matter.

Lenna pulled her blade free. The man fell to the ground, not far from where his companion still lay.

"Impressive."

She spun, bloodied knife held before her.

Pemin stood some distance from her. Close enough to have seen all. Close enough that he didn't have to raise his voice for her to hear. Far enough that she didn't pose a threat.

Two men stood with him, both with full-cocked pistols in hand and aimed at her.

"If you wanted me dead, why did you let me leave your chamber?"

"Lenna, my dear, if I wanted you dead, you would be dead."

She stared back at him, confused. "These aren't your men?"

"They are. Were. Are both dead?"

"Only this one." She pointed at the second man. "Why would you—" Again she stared, understanding breaking over her like a wave. "You were testing me."

"You want to be my assassin, my Walker. I needed to know if you still possess the skills I saw in you so many years ago." His gaze dropped to her arm, her side. "You're wounded."

"Yes. Nothing serious."

"And yet..."

"Working as your assassin, I wouldn't be unarmed, fighting two trained killers."

"You can't really be certain of that, can you? That sort of work is hardly predictable. You might find yourself in all sorts of peril."

Enough. She no longer feared him; a part of her hated him. She had enough gold to leave. Yes, she wanted to keep working—for him, for somebody—but she was willing to endure only so much.

"Then don't use me, Pemin." She took some satisfaction in the way his jaw tightened at her use of his name. "Let me go, or tell your men to shoot. But stop wasting my time with games."

"The problem is, I can't simply let you go. You know a great deal about things I've done. I don't want you as a living enemy."

She lifted a shoulder. "Then kill me and be done with it."

"I'm intrigued by what you said before, about how you are noticed less now. There are certain assignments for which you might be ideal."

They held each other's gazes. Lenna tried to keep from smiling. Eventually she failed.

"Come back to my chamber," the autarch said. "Have a bit more wine. I'll summon my healer, and he can see to your wounds. And we can speak of ways you might continue to serve my autarchy."

She let her knife hand fall to her side, then tossed the blade to the ground beside the man she had killed. Pemin's guards lowered their pistols.

Lenna walked to where the autarch waited, her smile lingering as he studied her again.

"You are to call me 'Your Excellency.' Always."

They started back toward his chamber.

"I'm your elder, now. If I have to call you 'Your Excellency,' you should have to call me 'Miss Stenci.' Or 'ma'am.'"

He was still chuckling as they entered the castle.

CHAPTER TWENTY-TWO

21st day of Sipar's Ascent, Year 634

With gold in her purse, a knife hidden in her bodice and another in the sheath at her calf, she left Hayncalde on foot. For many years, years she shared in memory with the other Lenna, who had gone forward in time to where she belonged, she had journeyed by ship and by chronofor. Her device was gone, smashed by her own hand. And ships—there were plenty at Hayncalde's wharf, and perhaps in time she would board one. She found them confining, though. As much as she loved the open sea, she saw little difference between staring out at swells and troughs from a deck, and gazing down upon gardens and courts from a castle window.

For the first time in her life, she was free to do as she pleased, to go anywhere she desired, by any means she chose. She went north, and she did so on foot. Because she could.

Lenna spent that first night in a nearby village but thought it too small for a lengthier stay. She left the next morning and by evening had come to a larger fishing town—Sleeton—nestled in a small cove along the shore of the Gulf of Daerjen. There she took a room at the town's lone inn, enjoyed a fine, simple meal of roasted bullfish, and went to sleep contented and at peace.

Her comfort in this new home lasted no more than a ha'turn.

One night around the middle of the God's Ascent, after supping again at the inn, Lenna walked down to the shoreline. She often walked the strands at night. In a village as small as this one, she had little to fear. And she remained confident in her ability to protect herself.

As she watched a gibbous moon rise from the gulf, blood red and full, like spring buds, she heard a footfall behind her, light and tentative. She tensed, reached for the knife within her gown.

"I know you." A child's voice, flat, emotionless.

She turned. Before her stood one of the Tirribin she had met in Hayncalde the first night of her existence, when she was still addled from her encounter with herself. He was dark-haired, fine-featured, with milky blue eyes.

"Yes," she said. "I remember. I've forgotten your name."

"Teelo."

"I'm Lenna. Where is your sister?"

She remembered the other Tirribin being nasty, menacing. She had sensed then, though, that the two demons rarely strayed from each other.

Still, she wasn't prepared for his answer.

"She's dead."

Several moments passed before she could respond. "I'm so sorry. I... I'm not sure what to say. I didn't think... Forgive me for asking, but it's uncommon for one of your kind to die, isn't it?"

"It is."

She wanted to ask how the girl died but knew better—he would think the question rude. Instead, she asked, "Is there anything I can do for you?"

He regarded her with surprise. "It's kind of you to ask. Walk with me. Please."

He set off along the strand, away from the village. Lenna fell in beside him.

"I didn't want to leave Hayncalde," he said. "I wasn't going to. Maeli wouldn't have wanted us to be anywhere else. But a friend... Someone told me that staying would be difficult. She was right." After a fivecount, he peered her way. "Why are you here?"

"A long tale. I needed to get away from a man in the castle."

His expression turned stony. "The one who is after Tobias?"

Another surprise. "Yes, that's right. Do you know him?"

A bitter smile touched his lips and fled. "I believe you once sent us to feed on his years. He distracted us with a riddle, which seemed at the time like a fair trade. I know better now. If we'd taken his years then, Maeli would still be alive."

"What did he—"

Teelo shook his head. "It's too much to explain. He was helped by an Ancient, or was helping the Ancient. Commerce I don't understand. Because of him, Belvora were summoned." He gave a second shake of his head. "I don't want to think about it."

An instant later he faltered, halted, looked up at her with pleading eyes. "Unless... You're a Walker. You can change it all. You can go back and keep him from calling for the Belvora. Something." Tears ran from over his cheeks. "Please."

Lenna's eyes stung as well. "I'm sorry. I have no chronofor. I can't go back."

He sagged, nodded, resumed walking. "I see. All right then."

"If I could—"

"It's all right. To be honest, I don't know if my kind can be saved in that way. We sense the folds of time, are aware of misfutures. That might make us immune to corrections in history as well."

His voice sounded normal, but his tears continued to flow. Lenna didn't know what to do for him.

He stopped again to face the village. "I should probably hunt now."

"I'd like to help you. Truly I would."

"The Ancient who summoned those Belvora—my friend intends to kill him. This man deserves to die as well. If I could take his years, I would. Can you get close to him?"

Lenna was taken aback by the baldness of the question. "You want me to kill him?"

"You said you wanted to help. More than once, now. You can't Walk for me, but you can do this."

"I do want to help, but this... I'm not sure I can. I loved him once."

"Before you sent us to take his years?"

She should have known better than to try to match wits with an Ancient, even one who looked like a child. "Yes, before then."

His lips twitched. "I'm going to hunt now. I would speak with you again, if you're willing."

She smiled, nodded, and watched him blur away. When she couldn't see him anymore, she started back toward the inn.

Lenna didn't sleep that night. Her thoughts were roiled like a stormy sea. She didn't love Orzili. A part of her hated him, though, out of consideration for the other Lenna, she had kept that feeling in check, refusing to act on it.

She didn't care about the young Walker Orzili hunted. Not really. But she had come to respect him. She didn't know how often she had Walked back in time to give Orzili another chance to capture the boy or prevent his escape. Many, she believed, and each time he bested them. How could she not admire that?

Maeli meant little to her.

Teelo's grief moved her, but he was Tirribin, and he had been only slightly kinder to her than his sister when first she met them. She had just won her freedom from Orzili. She didn't wish to go back to Hayncalde so soon, not for any purpose.

Killing him was out of the question.

Helping the Walker, on the other hand, was not, if only she could figure out a way to do this. He needed a chronofor. If not for his lack of one, he would have gone back long ago searching for some way to prevent Mearlan's assassination. Her device was gone, of course, but if she could find another, surely that would help the boy.

Impossible. She didn't know where to look for a device, nor did she know where to find the boy.

Another idea came to her. Orzili could only do so much with his sextant. Ultimately, if he were to attack and defeat the boy, he would need his tri- devices. He had lost two sets already, and currently had a Binder in Hayncalde constructing more for him. What if she prevented this?

The boy would never know she had done it. Orzili might not either. None of that mattered. *She* would know, and she could tell Teelo as much. He might point out that this wasn't quite what he had asked of her. To which she could reply with what she knew to be true: If Orzili continued to fail in his pursuit, Pemin's patience would wane. In time, Orzili would pay the price. Vengeance came in many forms.

Pleased with this idea, she finally slept. Upon waking, she considered her plan anew. It still struck her as sound. She dressed, gathered her belongings, and settled her account with the innkeeper. By midmorning, she was on the road, clear of the town's boundary and headed back to Hayncalde. What she had in mind carried some risk. This pleased her, made her that much more eager. She loved her freedom, but she was still an assassin at heart. She loved adventure even more.

The summons was delivered by a Spanner, which was enough to convince Gillian Ainfor of its urgency. Lord Orzili's previous missives had arrived by ship and had been delivered by local boys or girls who ran the letters to her home for a trey or two.

This time it was a man, young, handsome, his clothes ill-fitting, his face reddened, and his hair tousled by the gap wind.

All of Orzili's messages were terse; this one was no different. "Return to Hayncalde at once. – Q.O."

She couldn't Span, of course. "At once" might still mean a ha'turn or more. Gillian didn't delay. She wasn't certain whether she should keep her flat in Belsan. In the end, she decided to give it up. She sensed a certain finality in Orzili's message. She wouldn't be coming back here, at least not at his expense. A shame. She had come to like the city—the air, the food, the people. Someday, perhaps, she would find the means to come back, build a new life here, or recommence this one. For now, she gathered her belongings, including a small pistol she had purchased not long after her arrival in the city, and went to speak with the flat's owner. Lies came easily to her—they always had—and this day's was no different. Her mother was gravely ill, her father too infirm to care for his beloved wife. She had no choice but to leave. Of course, he could keep the balance of what she had paid for this turn.

After hearing that she expected no refund, the landlord grew solicitous. He would miss her. He would pray for her mother.

He would have the flat rented again in a day and would enjoy nearly a full turn of double rent.

With autumn's chill in the air and winter storms likely forming already far to the west of Vleros and Westisle, merchant ships raced with increased frequency between Aiyanth and the Sisters, Aiyanth and the Labyrinth, Aiyanth and the Knot, the autarchy, the Ring Isles, and, yes, Daerjen. Gillian had no trouble finding a ship that would carry her. Two bells before dusk, she set sail from Belsan with a captain who promised to have her in Hayncalde within eight days.

It didn't occur to her until they had cleared the harbor and unfurled their sails, to wonder if Bexler—her husband!—still lived in Hayncalde. Did he still occupy their flat there? She hadn't spared him a thought in some time. She could think of no greater measure of how completely she had embraced life in Belsan.

She wondered if he thought of her. Did he pine for her? Would he welcome her, or would he greet her with rage, accusations of betrayal, maybe even physical abuse?

She could avoid him. No one would make her go to the flat. If she told Orzili that she wanted nothing to do with Bexler, he would shelter her within the castle. She was certain of that. The question was, what did she want? In this one regard, she didn't know her own mind. She didn't love him, and wasn't sure she ever had. She hadn't missed him. Then again, she hadn't fallen in love while living on the Axle. She hadn't even lain with a man, though she'd had opportunities. Did that mean she was still devoted to the Binder? The idea of this both amused and intrigued.

The question of what to do about Bexler vexed her throughout her voyage back to Hayncalde. The closer the ship drew to the city, the greater her ambivalence. Their last turns together had felt interminable; her last days with him had been excruciating. Whatever romance there had once been in their marriage died long ago. She had become ever more reliant on *his* influence, *his* gold, even though her mind was more nimble than his, her nerve more steady. By the time she left, her dependence on him had galled her.

Memories of those last bitter days grew more vivid as the ship neared Daerjen, hardening her resolve on the one decision that mattered above all others: She no longer wished to be married to him. Living alone all these turns had been exhilarating. She didn't need him, or any man for that matter. She could care for herself, earn for herself. She could spy. She was good at it.

And yet, she regretted how she had left him. She had snuck away, without a goodbye, or an explanation, or—and this surprised her—a word of thanks for their years together. For all his flaws—and they were numerous—he had loved her in his way. He had been kind, if moody. He never hurt her, or even berated her, as her own father had done often to her lovely mother. His emotional weapon of choice had been an overgrown boy's sulkiness that rankled, and often bent her to his will—anything to make him stop.

That tendency to sulk was revealing. He was, in too many ways, a child in a man's body. Early on, it had made him a fun companion. Later, it was simply sad.

Now it was cause for guilt. Her unexplained departure would have confused and devastated him. She owed him an apology and a chance to tell her how angry and sad she had made him. She would go first to the castle. Her duty to Orzili was paramount. After that, she would seek out Bexler one last time.

The ship's captain proved true to her word. Seven days out from Belsan, they entered the Gulf of Daerjen. On the eighth morning, the crew lowered their sails and oared them to the city wharf.

As soon as they had docked, Gillian left the ship. Guards at the city and castle gates let her pass without question, though the castle soldiers did take her blade and pistol.

Before long, she was in the corridor outside the man's chamber, waiting to be admitted.

She remembered Orzili as beautiful, intimidating, somewhat condescending. She was nervous to meet with him. When his guard opened the door and stepped aside so that she could enter, she took a long breath, exhaled, walked into the chamber.

He stood at his desk, as he had the last time she saw him, and turned as she entered. He remained trim, and he wore ministerial robes. In other ways, however, he was much changed. His face, lean and chiseled before, appeared sunken now. His cheekbones were too sharp, his chin too tapered. She wondered if he had been eating. The warm brown of his skin had given way to something more sallow, like an old bruise. His hair was long, unkempt. Once, that might have been a good look for him. Not now.

"Minister," he said, the smooth baritone unchanged.

"Lord Orzili."

"You got here quickly. I appreciate that."

"Of course, my lord."

He crossed to a chair near his hearth, sat, indicated she should do the same.

"I don't believe I ever thanked you for your idea of luring the Walker to the Sea of Gales," he said, once they were both seated. "That was well done."

"Of course, my lord. Did you find him?"

He answered with something between a grin and a grimace. "I did find him. I didn't capture him."

"I'm sorry."

"It wasn't your fault, nor was it mine. It's simply what happened."

She thought better of pursuing the matter.

For a fivecount he said nothing. He brooded, eyes on the fire. Without looking away, he said, "I summoned you because I believe Tobias and the child are somewhere in Daerjen. I have...allies searching for them—"

"Other Travelers?" she asked, knowing she was taking a risk.

"Some," he said, guarded.

"I ask, because the first time I came to the castle, there was a woman—"

"She's not your concern."

"Forgive me, my lord."

He stood, added a log to the blaze in his hearth, though Gillian didn't think it needed one. "The woman you saw is a Walker," he said, speaking low. "She's...she's not here anymore." He sat once more, faced her. "As I was saying, we're searching for Tobias and the child. In the meantime, I would like you to visit the other courts. Not Sheraigh, of course, but the duchies. You would have some knowledge of the dukes, yes? From your time as Mearlan's minister of protocol?"

"Yes, my lord."

"Good. If all goes as we intend, we'll find Tobias, eliminate this last threat from House Hayncalde, and move to stabilize the new supremacy. As you've noted, however, Tobias has proven elusive. I need you to make inquiries, with discretion and subtlety. Most think all of Mearlan's family is gone. I want to maintain that deception. Tobias and those working with him have kept the girl a secret thus far. That could change. She would be a powerful symbol, a way of sparking an uprising. We mean to prevent that, a harder task than many in House Sheraigh would like to admit." This time he managed a smile. "It won't surprise you to learn that Noak is not well-liked in the lesser courts. The dukes need to be convinced that, personal animus aside, it is in their best interests to remain loyal to the new supremacy."

"I understand."

"You'll have gold, of course. I'll send uniformed guards with you as well. You travel now as an emissary of House Sheraigh."

"I'll need robes, then, my lord."

"Indeed you will. From here, you'll go to the castle seamster. He should be able to provide you with all you need within a day or two." He paused, slanted a look at her. "Will you need sleeping quarters here at the castle?"

She colored but kept her gaze steady. "Please, my lord."

"He's late with my tri-sextants."

She sat forward. "You *still* haven't gotten them?" He had been building tri-sextants for Orzili when she left, half a year ago. She had done more damage to Bexler than she ever would have imagined.

Or so she thought.

Orzili shook his head. "Forgive me. I wasn't thinking. He delivered one set. They were taken from my men and me by Ancients. He is building yet another set. *These* are late. A matter of days, not turns."

That eased her mind.

"I grow impatient," Lord Orzili went on, "but I'm not yet desperate."

"He can be slow, my lord. But he does fine work."

"Spoken like his wife."

Gillian bit back the first response that came to mind. "Is that all, my lord?"

He levered himself out of his chair. "It is."

She stood as well. "I assume I'm free to come and go from the castle as I please."

"You are."

With a nod, she turned on her heel and stepped to his door.

"Forgive me," he said as she reached for the handle. "That last was...rude of me. I have..." He stopped, shook his head. "I have no excuse."

She thought he had intended to say something else. Still, she knew that a man like Orzili didn't offer apologies lightly.

"Thank you, my lord."

He joined her at the door, told one of his guards to arrange a room for her and escort her to the seamster.

Gillian thanked him a second time and left with the soldier, glad to be away from the man. She wouldn't have believed that possible before this day. The truth was, for a long time after she left Hayncalde for Belsan, she had been infatuated with him, with the memory of him. Not anymore. He was...smaller than she recalled, and not nearly so compelling.

She left her belongings in a small, nondescript room and made her way to the chamber of the seamster—a new one, not the man she remembered from Mearlan's castle. After she was measured for robes, she visited the kitchen for a small meal.

After that, she could delay no more. She left the castle, reclaiming her weapons as she passed through the gate, and followed the city lanes to the flat she had shared with Bexler after Mearlan's death.

She hadn't lived there for long, but her memory of the place, of the buildings she passed on her way there, slowed her steps, weighing on her physically.

You don't love him. You never did.

Too facile that. She decided that attachment and lack of love, of passion, could exist side by side. Whatever she had felt, they were together for a long time. Those years meant something. How could they not?

Reaching the steps to the flat, she paused, tried to gather herself. She considered postponing this conversation until the next day. He wouldn't know the difference.

As she stood with one foot on that bottom stair, though, she heard voices from above. His, and then that of a woman. Both raised.

A lover? A business associate? An enemy?

Doubts forgotten, Gillian charged up the stairs, her pistol in hand, prepared to break open the door if she had to.

Lenna's walk back to Hayncalde took much of the next day. She reached the city's west gate only a bell or two before sunset, found a room in a small, run-down inn, and took immediately to the lanes. The marketplace had already emptied by the time she reached it. She walked to the waterfront and called for Teelo, but the Tirribin didn't come to her. Perhaps he was still in the town she'd left. Perhaps he was too stricken with his grief to treat with anyone.

She had resolved to return to her room when another idea stopped her.

"I would speak with an Ancient," she said, facing the waters of the gulf. "Any Ancient, but in particular, a friend of Teelo, the Tirribin."

Lenna waited, heart beating faster. This might have been an error.

When she received no response, she started away from the strand rather than repeat her summons. She was fortunate that no demon had taken notice of her.

"Hold, human."

Damn.

She was still on sand. Her pivot made not a sound.

Two women stood at the water's edge, both of them so unnaturally beautiful it was almost funny. Almost.

One was naked. Water ran from her black hair, pooled at her feet. The other was yellow-haired, dark skinned. She wore a tattered shift. They were of similar heights and both had oddly pale eyes.

"You summoned us," the naked one said. "There is a cost for this."

Lenna walked back to them, seeing as she drew near what she had missed before. The naked one had silver eyes that put Lenna in mind of a snake. An Arrokad then. The eyes of the other, palest gray, could have belonged to a Tirribin.

"What cost?"

"A question of commerce," said the Arrokad. "What is it you want? Why did you speak of Teelo?"

"I know him. He told me last night what happened to Maeli. I want to help him."

The Ancients regarded each other.

"Help him how?" the other asked.

"There is a man, a human. Teelo seeks vengeance."

The yellow-haired Ancient gave a slow nod. "Yes, I would imagine. That is my fault. I spoke to him of the human. I shouldn't have."

"Did you promise to kill an Ancient for him?"

Another glance passed between the two.

"You wish to help him by hurting this human," the Arrokad said.

"In a way. He's formidable. Hard to reach, and harder to hurt."

The other woman leaned toward her. "You know him?"

"For many years."

The Ancient considered her and appeared to sniff the air around them. "You're a Walker."

Lenna didn't mask her surprise. "You're Tirribin?"

"I am."

A dozen questions leapt to mind. She had never seen a Tirribin in adult form. She could almost hear Maeli telling her that to remark on this would be rude.

They continued to eye each other, until the Tirribin let out a small gasp and held a hand to her mouth. "You're Lenna! And yet you're not."

"How do you—"

Recognition came to her the force of a blow. "Droë," she said in a faint whisper. "Is that really you?"

"Something about you," Droë said as if she hadn't heard. "You're the Lenna I know, but I sense that we've never met. Your time is..." She made a small, uncertain circular gesture.

Lenna couldn't help the sigh that escaped her. How many times would Tirribin remind her that she didn't belong in this world?

"I know. There are more than one of me in this time—a result of an ill-fated Walk. You're right: You and I have never met. But I carry Lenna's memories, and, in most ways, I am her."

"And you wish to hurt Cresten."

"Orzili."

Droë frowned. "By either name he's the same man."

"I'm not sure that's true. Cresten was kind, a friend. Orzili and I loved each other, killed together. Not anymore. He's changed."

"To be honest, I've sensed this as well." She narrowed her gaze. "You would kill him?"

"No. I would keep a Binder from delivering tools he needs to pursue the Walker."

"Tobias."

Yet another surprise. "You know him, too."

Droë's expression wavered like a flame guttering in a sudden gust of wind. Then she was composed again. "Yes, he is a friend, as is the woman with him."

"I have no patience for this," the Arrokad broke in. "The politics of human courts, the barbarity of their feuds—she summoned us. There is commerce to be completed. The rest matters not."

"It matters to me," Droë said, her tone as gentle as a spring rain.

The Arrokad didn't argue more but made a circular motion of her own. Impatience, acquiescence, more. Every motion the demon made was as liquid and eloquent as stream flow.

To Lenna, Droë said, "The debt of your summons is paid by your desire to comfort Teelo." She glanced at the Arrokad, who nodded her agreement. "What would you do to this Binder?"

"I don't know yet. Keep him from delivering the...the devices Orzili needs. If Orzili fails again to find the Walker and kill the child with him, others will be displeased. Orzili will suffer."

"Very well," Droë said. She sounded puzzled. Understandable, since she wouldn't know the details of what Lenna had in mind. "What did you hope we could do for you?"

"I thought you could help me find the Binder."

"Foolish," the Arrokad said before Droë could reply. "Do you think we walk the streets of this city, making note of street names and marking the presence of every human?"

"Ujie—"

"She wastes our time."

"She does so for Teelo. For Maeli."

"I don't expect you to know where all humans live," Lenna said, speaking to Ujie and forcing them to face her again. "But this is a Binder I seek. A user of magick. Is it so foolish to think that an Arrokad might be aware of such a person?"

Silence.

After more than a fivecount, Ujie lifted her chin. "No, it is not foolish. That is the sort of thing I might sense. As it happens, I have not, but neither have I made the attempt. Given how rude I have been to you, I believe I should. And so I would propose that we meet here again tomorrow night. If that is agreeable to you."

Even Lenna, who had not treated with Arrokad before, understood how rare it was for Ancients—the Most Ancient in particular—to give such consideration to humans.

She bowed. "Thank you, Most Ancient One."

Ujie turned and strode back into the surf. Droë remained with Lenna.

"I do not understand your feelings for Orzili. You say that you loved him, but you seek to hurt him. And you also claim that there are others of you in this time, that you share a common past with them."

"It's...very complicated. What matters is that I am Lenna, but I'm also separate from her. That distance—it's everything. As you say, I remember loving Orzili, because it is part of who I was before the Walk I undertook, the one that created me, for lack of a better term. Since I came to be myself, though, I have not loved him. I couldn't. He is..."

"Grim," Droë said. "Dark. Hardened in a way."

"Yes."

"Tobias is not."

"Him I don't know," Lenna said. "For some time now, I've helped Orzili in his pursuit of the boy. No more."

Droë nodded. The more Lenna looked at her, the more she saw of the child she remembered—the perfect, delicate features, the expressive smile—knowing one moment, guileless the next.

"That is well." She glanced over her shoulder toward the water. The Arrokad floated in the low waves some distance from the strand. "Ujie waits for me. I must go. I'm pleased to see you again, Lenna. In any form."

Lenna watched the grown Tirribin wade out to her friend. Then she returned to her inn to await tomorrow night's encounter.

CHAPTER TWENTY-THREE

22nd day of Sipar's Ascent, Year 634

Lenna hunted down the Binder's name the following day in the marketplace. With her dark skin and bronze hair, it didn't take her long to convince those she approached that she was exactly what she seemed: a Traveler in search of a Binder. She never said she needed a device; she didn't have to. The people she spoke to simply assumed, and she said nothing to correct them.

Several people confirmed that a Binder came often to the marketplace seeking material for his devices. None of them knew where he lived, but they were happy to share rumors about his past. He had been Mearlan's Binder, they said, and left the castle after his assassination.

"The Sheraighs like him well enough," said one woman. "Otherwise he would have had to run much farther than just to the city, wouldn' he? Prob'bly workin' for them, traitorous bastard. Him and that woman of his."

Lenna's knees weakened. Until then, she hadn't made the connection, though of course she should have. The Binder's wife. Gillian Ainfor. The woman had been in Orzili's chamber the very night Lenna Walked back. She had also penned the missive fourteen years in the future that sent Lenna back to this time. If not for Gillian Ainfor, Lenna realized, she would not exist. A startling thought.

She could picture the minister in her mind—odd, since she herself hadn't met her. Another shared memory. A square, handsome face, bright blue eyes, short hair. Orzili had made her one of his spies and sent her to Belsan, but she might as well have been right there beside Lenna, a hand at her throat.

The old woman in the marketplace spoke still, railing at the Sheraighs and Hayncalde traitors. Lenna interrupted her to say thanks, walked away without awaiting a reply.

It made her task easier in a way. That was what she told herself. These people were not her allies, and they were not innocents. They'd had a hand in a rebellion and an assassination. So had she—she would not lie to herself about that, but neither would she scruple about harming the Binder or striking at Orzili.

Several in the market had pointed her to one peddler in particular, an obese, grizzled man with a gruff manner and expensive wares. She gathered herself and crossed the market to his stand. He ogled her as she approached, greeted her in a rough Vleran accent.

When she told him she was searching for a Binder, he laughed.

"Yes, I know. Everyone in the marketplace knows. You have not been subtle."

"Should I have been?"

"That depends. What do you want with him really?"

"A sextant."

He shook his head. "Court Spanners are provided with their devices. As are court Walkers and court Crossers."

"Who says I belong to a court?"

His eyebrows arched upward. "Interesting."

"Do you know his name?"

"I do."

She made herself laugh. "Will you tell it to me?"

"In exchange for what?"

"My eternal gratitude."

His smile was a blade edge. "I can't sell gratitude. I can't eat it or buy wares with it."

"If I hire him to build me a new sextant, he will buy the material from you. We both gain."

"Logical, but not terribly compelling."

"What do you want?" Lenna asked.

"More information."

She didn't like this man, and she didn't trust him. She would find the Binder with Ujie's help. Having his name would be useful, but it wasn't necessary.

"I have none to give," she said, and turned to leave.

"You have nothing?" he called after her.

"My need is not so great."

She continued away, stopped at a few more tables. Not to ask questions—the Vleran peddler was right: she had been too obvious—but merely to be seen so that people wouldn't think her too single-minded in her pursuit of the Binder. At one point, she glanced back in the heavy man's direction. He was watching her. At her look, he waggled his fingers, urging her to return. Reluctantly, she did.

"You are truly a Spanner?" he asked as she halted before him.

"Why do you ask?"

"I might tell you what you want to know for the promise of a future Span or two on my behalf."

"A short time ago, you didn't want to help me at all. Why the change of heart?"

He shrugged, his chair creaking. "Because you're pretty, and business is slow. And because having access to a Spanner could be quite profitable."

"It would be a fair exchange," she said, choosing her words with care. She had yet to lie to him. She was going to the Binder for a sextant—a tri-sextant, to be precise. Everything else had been evasions and deflections. "You would agree to these terms?"

"I would, if you will."

"Done."

He leaned forward, glanced past and around the market. "His

name is Bexler Filt. He lives not too far from here, on a lane off the main street leading to the castle's east gate." He bent forward a bit more. "They say his wife—"

"I know who his wife is."

The peddler straightened. "All right."

"Thank you."

"Remember our bargain," he said.

"I will."

Bexler Filt. And Gillian Ainfor. With the vague directions the man had given, their names would be enough for her to locate their home without the help of the Ancients. She followed the thoroughfare that approached the castle, searching every byway between the market and Hayncalde's fortress.

The process proved more time-consuming than she had expected. At last, though, as she entered yet another lane, she passed an elderly woman sitting in a doorway, smoking a fragrant leaf from an ivory pipe. Lenna asked her if she knew of a Binder living nearby. The woman bobbed her head and pointed with her pipe at the next building.

"Up there," she said. "Sometimes at night I see his room all glowy. Works a lot, that one."

Lenna thanked her, hurried to the stairs, and climbed them to a worn oaken door. She drew the knife from her bodice, held it concealed in her off hand. The woman below gazed up at her, but there wasn't much to be done about that. Lenna rapped on the door.

At first, nothing. Then lumbering steps shook the building. The door opened, revealing a bear-like man, soft around the middle. He had dark eyes, which regarded her with impatience. His chin was thick, doubled by the loose flesh of his neck. His nose was straight, his lips full. He might have been handsome in a plain way, if only he were to smile. Somehow Lenna sensed that he rarely did.

"Yes?" he demanded in a voice higher than she had expected.

"Binder Filt?"

The eyes narrowed. "That's right."

"I am a...a Traveler. I'm not affiliated with a court right now, and I need a new device." With her other hand, the one not hiding her weapon, she held up her purse and shook it. Coins rang within. He didn't need to know how few of them were golden.

"I'm quite busy right now."

"Too busy to earn gold? I envy you."

His expression soured. After a pause, he stepped aside, motioned her into the flat.

Lenna walked in, didn't turn when he shut the door. She didn't see any tri-sextants, but that didn't surprise her. They were precious, virtually unknown in this time. He wouldn't have come to the door without hiding them first.

"You didn't say what sort of Traveler you are," he said from behind her, his steps rattling the building again.

"No, I didn't."

As he attempted to walk past her, she pounded her elbow into his gut. He grunted a breath, folded in on himself, his arms wrapped around his middle. She whirled, pounded the heel of her hand into his nose. Bone snapped, blood spurted. He fell onto his back, hands now clutched to his face.

Lenna sat on his chest, straddling him. She laid the edge of her knife to his throat. He froze, eyes going wide.

"I'll kill you," she said. "Everything I want, I can get with you dead. Do you understand?"

He gave the smallest of nods.

"Where are they?"

"Where are what?"

"The tri-sextants, of course. What else would I want with you?"

He faltered. She could tell that he was searching for a lie that might convince her they weren't here. She wondered how much Orzili had promised him for delivery of the devices.

Lenna leaned back and jabbed her blade into his thigh. The Binder screamed, bucked, nearly throwing her off. She set the knife against his neck, and he stiffened again. Tears leaked from his eyes.

"Where?"

"Behind the workbench. A cloth sack."

She started to stand, stopped herself. "I *will* kill you if you try to stand or flee or hurt me in any way. Lie still, and no harm will come to you."

"Y-yes, all right."

Lenna stood, backed to the workbench. She peered over the back edge, searching for a cloth bag. Seeing none, she stalked toward him again. He had already started to climb to his feet. Seeing her come at him, he scrabbled away, clawing desperately at a table drawer. Lenna pounced, drove her blade into the back of his other leg, just above the knee. He howled, whipped a fisted hand at her. She dodged the blow. Punched him in the throat.

The Binder collapsed. Lenna grabbed a handful of his hair and set the point of her knife at the corner of his eye.

"Lie to me a second time and you will never see again, never Bind again."

Sobs shook him. He snaked out an arm and pointed toward the small kitchen. Lenna dragged him away from that table, kicked him in the gut, and left him curled in a ball on the floor.

This time, she found what she sought. A cloth sack, as he had said. Brown, stained. It could easily have been mistaken for a bag of roots or smoked meat. Lenna opened it, looked inside.

Gold winked at her. Three tri-sextants, two of them complete. The third had only one arc rather than three. A second arc lay at the bottom of the bag, waiting to be attached. Other parts rested beside it.

"How long until this last tri-sextant is complete?"

He groaned a response. Lenna hoisted the bag and crossed to where he lay. "How long?" she repeated, raising her voice.

"I don't know." His voice sounded strained.

"Of course you do. You're a Binder. You've been doing this for years. Now tell me!"

"Nothing is certain! It could be a bell, or it could be a ha'turn! I won't know until I try to find that last arc. If it comes from far off or if it needs adjustment—"

"But if it doesn't, how long?"

Before he could answer, the door burst open, revealing a figure in silhouette. For an instant, Lenna thought it was a soldier, or one of Orzili's men. Then the person entered the flat, leaving the door open. Light touched the face and form.

"Blood and bone! Bexler! What is this?"

Gillian Ainfor, exactly as she appeared in the other Lenna's memory. The woman held a pistol, small, but full-cocked. Lenna wondered if she had learned to shoot.

The minister's sharp gaze found Lenna. "Who are you to—" She fell silent, gaped. "You're Orzili's..." She didn't finish the sentence, perhaps unsure of the nature of their relationship. Lenna had time to think the statement apt as it stood.

"What are you doing here?" Gillian asked. "Why have you hurt him? Is this because the sextants are late?"

As good an answer as any. "Yes. He should have delivered them some time ago."

"I think she's lying," the Binder said. "She said nothing about them being late until now. She means to take them."

The woman shook her head. "He said he wasn't desperate for the sextants. Not yet."

Lenna tensed. "You've spoken to him?"

"He also said you were gone," the minister continued, ignoring her. "Why would he say that if you're not?"

"He wouldn't tell you everything," Lenna said.

"The way he would you, you mean."

"That's right."

"Very well, why am I here, in Hayncalde?"

Clever. Lenna should have had an answer for this, but she didn't know. It had been a ha'turn since she had left the castle, and a good deal longer than that since she had been in Orzili's confidence. "He uses you as a spy," she said, grasping at anything she could think of. "He wants you to search for the Walker, lure him into the open."

"She's lying," Gillian said to the Binder, though she kept her eyes on Lenna.

She had miscalculated, and now she needed to get away from here, quickly. She still held her knife in one hand, and in the other, the bag containing the tri-sextants; that was what she came for. The rest didn't matter. The Binder would recover, would build new tri-sextants. All she had done was delay Orzili's victory, but that would have to be enough.

"I'm leaving now," she said, starting toward the door.

Gillian placed herself in Lenna's way. She still held her pistol, and she raised it now with a shaking hand. "I think he would want you to remain here. He'd want to know the real reason you've come." The minister's voice sounded steady enough.

Lenna didn't bother to hide her amusement. "You're a protocol minister, not a killer. I know, because I do kill. For gold. I've done it for a long time." She tempered her expression. "Now get out of my way!"

The minister flinched at the lash of Lenna's voice, but she remained where she was. Lenna stalked toward her, knife held before her. The woman held her ground.

"Stop. I'll fire. I swear I will."

Lenna didn't pause until she stood directly in front of her, the barrel of the small flintlock only a hand's width from her chest. She let her blade hand fall to her side, confident she had nothing to fear from the minister.

"No, you won't." She pushed the pistol to the side so that it no longer menaced her. Gillian let her, her face paling. Lenna stepped around her, glanced down at the Binder, who quailed at the touch of her gaze.

Before she reached the door, something crashed into her from behind. Someone. Gillian.

Lenna stumbled, dropped the sack, wheeled, slashing with the knife. Her blade sliced through the skin on Gillian's arm. The minister cried out. At the same time, she tried to raise the pistol. Lenna threw a punch that landed high on the minister's cheek. Gillian's knees buckled, and she started to fall.

But she grabbed Lenna's gown, kept her feet.

Lenna tried to pull away. She didn't want to kill the woman, but she had to leave. She drew back her arm to stab at Gillian. Her shoulder, or her side. A wound that would stop her without killing her. That was her intent.

Gillian tried to seize her blade arm, and managed to briefly. Lenna was stronger. She ripped her arm out of the minister's grasp, slashed at her again. Gillian shoved her with both hands. Lenna's blade bit a second time. Gillian's collar this time.

The minister wailed, but the sound was lost beneath the blare of her pistol.

Flame. Smoke. A burning in Lenna's chest. She looked down, thinking her gown had caught fire.

The cloth did smoke, but there was no blaze. Only blood. So much blood. She coughed. Blood flew from her lips, staining Gillian's gown and face and neck.

The minister stared open-mouthed, glanced at the pistol in her hand, and then at Lenna again. At her middle. A haze of smoke hung between them.

Somehow Lenna found herself on her knees. The burning in her breast tipped over into agony. She huffed a breath, wrapped herself in her arms, cradling her wounded heart. Blood soaked her gown, her sleeves. She raised her gaze to Gillian's, her vision darkening, blurring. Breathing was hard. Her hearing was muffled. She thought Gillian said something. Or maybe the Binder. She couldn't tell. A moment later, she toppled to her side. Darkness settled around her.

Her arm hurt. So did the cut at her clavicle. Smoke stung her nostrils and eyes, and her ears rang. And none of that mattered. She edged closer to the woman. To her body. She was reasonably sure the woman was dead. Reaching her, she knelt in a spreading puddle of blood and held her fingers to the woman's neck. Feeling nothing, she tried the wrist. No pulse. No rise and fall of the chest.

She should have been unnerved, distraught, sick to her stomach. She was none of those things.

Can you kill? Orzili had asked her once, long ago.

When she said that she didn't know, he said, *Then you probably can't.*

He'd been wrong.

"Gillian, are you all right?"

Bexler. She rose, crossed to him, set the pistol on a table, the drawer of which held another pistol. His. She knelt beside him.

"You came back to me."

"I came back," she said.

She scrutinized his wounds. She didn't know much of such things, but she guessed he would live. She didn't think his injuries would keep him from completing the tri-sextants.

Footsteps on the stairway. They looked toward the door. A soldier in Sheraigh blue entered the flat, eyed them, stared briefly at Lenna's body, turned back their way.

"You both are hurt," the man said.

"We're all right. Please inform Lord Orzili in the castle that there has been...an incident. A woman is dead. A woman he knows. He should come right away."

Orzili would be upset, perhaps enraged. He might blame her. But the soldier was here. He had seen. There was nothing to be done except the right thing.

"Yes, all right."

"Bring a healer as well. Please."

The man cast another look at Lenna and left.

"Who is she?" Bexler asked, dark eyes returning to the corpse.

"A Traveler. She served Orzili, who serves the Sheraighs and, I believe, the autarch of Oaqamar. She and Orzili might have been lovers. Certainly they worked together. If he does work for the autarchy, chances are she did as well."

"And who are you?"

She turned at that, found him watching her, his expression grave. He looked much the same as he had when she left, despite the pain etched around his eyes and mouth. She did still care about him. But she was more certain now than ever: She didn't love him and wouldn't ever again.

"A spy, I suppose," she said. "An agent of the supremacy."

"Where have you been all this time?"

"Belsan, searching for a Walker who has eluded the Sheraighs."

"Were you alone?"

A brave question. She knew he feared her answer. "I was," she said. "And to be honest, I quite liked it."

He nodded, still grave, but clearly relieved. Men were odd. She guessed that Bexler would prefer she choose to be alone rather than with another man, even if either option left him without her.

"How have you been, Bexler?"

"Lonely. Confused. I've made a lot of tri-sextants." A smile flickered.

Gillian answered with a dry chuckle. She surveyed the home they had shared, her gaze coming to rest on the dead woman. She sobered, stood, winced at the pain in her arm. With some effort, she helped Bexler off the floor and to a nearby chair. Both legs of his breeches were glazed with blood. She knew better than to move anything else. The soldier had seen, and nothing she might hide or alter would change the essential truth: She had killed a woman Orzili probably loved.

In the end, she shifted a second chair so that it rested next to Bexler's and she sat as well. They didn't have to wait as long as she had thought they might.

Footsteps on the stairs made the building tremble, and men swarmed into the flat. Four of them, all in Sheraigh uniforms, and Orzili, in his robes. He regarded Gillian and Bexler wordlessly, stepped to the middle of the flat, and halted over the woman.

Gillian watched him, wary and afraid. Emotions played across the handsome face. Shock, grief, anger, anguish. He squatted beside the corpse, ran fingers over her bronze hair. He heaved a sigh and stood again, rounding on Gillian and the Binder.

"What happened?" His voice was tight, not particularly loud, utterly compelling.

"She came to my door claiming to need a Bound device,"

Bexler said, though Orzili had asked the question of Gillian. "I had never seen her before, but given her appearance, I had no reason to doubt her. Once she was in the flat, she attacked me and demanded to know where the tri-sextants were. She would have taken them, but Gillian arrived and recognized her. They fought, and in the struggle, Gillian's pistol went off." As he said this, he pointed to the flintlock resting on the table.

Orzili crossed to it, picked up the weapon, and sniffed at the barrel before setting it back down.

"You say she wanted the tri-sextants?" At Bexler's nod, he asked, "Did she say why?"

"She said you had sent her, because they're late. I...I didn't believe that."

Orzili walked to the dead woman again and stood over her. "No, I don't imagine."

To Gillian, he said, "Did she recognize you?"

"Yes, my lord."

"And you recognized her."

"Almost immediately."

He nodded. For a long time, he regarded the woman's corpse, pain carved in his features. At last, he spun away and walked to the door. He halted there, light from outside warming his face. "You were right to send for me. Thank you. This changes nothing. Our arrangements remain. I need those tri-sextants, Binder. Soon. I'm tired of waiting. And minister, you're to leave here in the morning."

"Yes, my lord," she said, speaking for them both.

"A healer is coming," he told them. He lingered for another fivecount. Gillian thought he would say more. He didn't. His footsteps scraped the stairs, and he was gone.

"Where are you going now?" Bexler asked.

"Away," she said. "Orzili has forbidden me from saying more." A convenient lie.

Two of his soldiers remained at the flat. The other two followed him back to the castle. Both were smart enough to keep their mouths shut.

This Lenna had long since declared herself his enemy. Even before he knew who she really was, she had tried to feed him to Tirribin. She had avoided him, mocked him, fled from him. Her death shouldn't have bothered him.

Foolishness. Of course it would bother him. How could it not? The sight of Lenna—any Lenna—bloodied and still was like a sword through his heart.

One had returned to her future. One had banished him from their home in Fanquir. One lay dead in a flat in Hayncalde. He had lost them all.

What bothered him most, though, was that this Lenna had chosen to pit herself against him. There was no other explanation for what the Binder said of their encounter. What use would a Walker have for tri-sextants? He supposed she could sell the devices to someone. If nothing else, the gold had value. But she had stolen coin from his purse before she left Hayncalde. She wouldn't need more.

No, this had been an act of defiance, an attempt to thwart his plans and help Tobias. Did she hate him so much?

The answer was obvious.

"Fine," he said.

The soldiers behind him had been whispering to each other. Now they fell silent. He didn't look back at them, but said, "I want a watch set on the Binder's flat. Not so that he'll know, and only until he delivers to me the devices he owes. I don't want him being attacked again, and I don't want the devices lost."

"Yes, my lord," said one of the men.

He glanced back in time to see them turn and head back to the Binder's lane.

Orzili walked on. He needed a cup of wine. Several. The image of Lenna on that blood-stained floor would remain with him for some time. He'd be fortunate if he slept at all this night.

Pemin would tell him that he had been lucky. He had lost a

woman who was already lost to him. The tri-sextants remained his. This day could have been a disaster. Instead, it was merely a tragedy. Lucky indeed.

Droë and Ujie arrived at the strand south of Hayncalde's waterfront shortly after sunset, expecting to find Lenna—this Lenna—waiting for them. Ujie had sensed the Binder's magick early in the day, but not later. Still, it was enough that she knew approximately where the man could be found.

They waited on the shore for some time, Ujie standing like a statue, only her eyes moving as they scanned the coast. Droë sat, then paced. After nearly a bell, she left the Arrokad and walked the lanes near the wharves, thinking that perhaps Lenna had thought to meet them there. She didn't find the woman. When at last she returned to the strand, she found Ujie exactly as she had left her.

It made no sense. Lenna had summoned them. She had seemed quite eager to help Teelo and to deny Orzili his Bound devices. Had she changed her mind? Or had she located the Binder on her own?

As the moon climbed higher in the night sky, its glow muted by high haze, she and Ujie decided this last was most likely. It was much like a human to cast aside an arrangement that no longer suited her. She should have come to the strand anyway. That would have been the polite thing to do.

Eventually, she and Ujie swam away. Ujie was annoyed. Droë glanced back repeatedly toward the city. Something troubled her. The Lenna she knew had never been rude. Then again, all creatures could change. Who knew that better than she?

CHAPTER TWENTY-FOUR

9th Day of Sipar's Ascent, Year 634

By the time Tobias, Risch, and the others sailed from Duvyn for Trohsden, two days after the battle with the Belvora and Hanev, Mara had started to feel better. Her vision was clear, her speech didn't sound so sluggish, the throbbing of her head had eased. Which was not to say that she had recovered completely.

A dull, persistent ache had settled deep in her skull. She guessed it would linger for a few more days. If she stood too quickly, she grew dizzy, though not for long. And bright light hurt her eyes.

She mentioned these things to the young healer, who told her they were normal after an injury like hers.

"Rest," he said. "That's the best cure for what you're feeling. Don't exert yourself, don't do any more than you have to."

An easier remedy to prescribe than to embrace. She had a child to care for and arrangements of her own to make. Tobias placed a great deal of faith in the willingness of Trohsden's duke to help them. She hoped that faith would be rewarded, but she knew better than to count on any one man. During the night, even before Tobias left, she had made up her mind to get a message to Seris Larr aboard the *Gray Skate*.

It felt like an aeon had passed since she Spanned through the rain from their home in the highlands to speak with the captain on her ship, but in truth, it had been only days. She might not even have reached Tirayre yet. If Mara could dispatch a message this day—this morning—Larr might receive it before she had gone too much farther toward Herjes.

But that meant leaving the castle and walking or riding the short distance to the Duvyn waterfront. The healer would not approve. So she wouldn't let him know until after she returned.

They had moved her from the hall to the chamber she and Tobias briefly shared, making her escape easier.

She thought.

Mara rose, carefully dabbed water on her face with a cloth, and ran wet fingers through her hair. Then she dressed and eased out of the chamber. The corridors were clear, and she didn't believe the gate guards would trouble her about leaving the castle, despite the bandage she still bore on her brow.

As she emerged into the courtyard, however, she heard a familiar voice cry out, "Mama!"

Joy overmastered chagrin. She scooped the charging princess into her arms. Pain made her squeeze her eyes shut. The strain of lifting Sofya, the stab of sunlight.

"How awe you feewing?"

"I'm fine, love. Are you having fun?"

Sofya nodded, her eyes as wide as her smile. "We'we hunting!"

"Hunting? Hunting what?"

The princess's smile slipped. She twisted in Mara's arms to look back at Corinne, who walked toward them. "What awe we hunting?"

"Sweet violet," the duchess said. To Mara, she added, "The chef requires some for a dessert he's preparing."

Mara kissed Sofya's cheek and set her back on the ground, weathering another twinge as she straightened. "You're very kind to spend so much time with her."

"It's my pleasure. With her mother wounded, whom else would I trust to care for her?"

Mara's cheeks warmed.

"Of course, her mother is supposed to be recuperating, which, according to my healer, means resting in bed and not taxing her strength in any way."

Mara sensed no hint of mirth in Corinne's face or tone. This was as close to angry as she had ever seen the duchess.

"What are you doing?" Corinne demanded.

"I have to go to the waterfront. Not for long, but—"

She broke off. Corinne was shaking her head.

"That's too far for you to walk. As I understand it, the other end of this courtyard is too far."

Corinne stood taller than she, and right now her eyes had a flinty look to them. Mara met her gaze as best she could.

"I'm grateful for your concern, my lady, as well as for your hospitality and your kindness toward Nava."

The duchess waved away the niceties. "Get to it."

"I have to do this. We need a second option, in case Tobias and Risch fail. I have to get a message to someone, and—forgive me—but I can't entrust this to anyone else. We're using couriers known only to us and those I'm contacting."

"I can offer you a mount."

"I don't ride, and in my present condition, a fall would be far worse than the walk. So would a Span, for that matter."

"A carriage then?"

She shook her head. "It would draw attention. Please, I'll be all right. And I won't be gone long."

Disapproval continued to crease Corinne's brow, but she made a small gesture of surrender.

Mara glanced at Sofya, who circled the small plots of flowers.

"She'll be fine. And if you leave while she's 'hunting,' she won't even know you've gone."

Mara thanked her and started toward the gate, glancing back every few steps to make certain Sofya hadn't noticed her leaving. Corinne kept the princess occupied until she was beyond the castle walls on the cobbled lanes leading down to the firth.

She kept her pace leisurely, for appearances and for her own well-being. Upon reaching the wharves, she searched for a fishing vessel, a Kant, that Seris Larr had described for her some time ago. *A little worn, with several patched sections of hull and a sail marked with the image of a soaring bird. The* Sand Hawk.

Her captain's name was Lanton. Mara didn't know if this was a given name or a surname. She gathered that it didn't matter. She didn't find the ship on her first pass along the wharves, and before she undertook a second search, she needed to sit. The sun blazed overhead, not overly hot, but bright enough to bring on a steady, throbbing headache.

As she rested, she scanned the firth. Before long, a ship caught her eye. Small, the hull mottled at this distance, the billowing sail bearing the outline of a hawk. The vessel carved toward the docks. Mara was glad to have to do no more than wait.

It took a half bell for the ship to furl its sail, go to sweeps, and glide to the wharf, and then a bit more time for the ship's crew to offload their catch, which was ample.

In time, as the comings and goings of sailors slowed, Mara stood and approached the vessel. She felt better.

"Ahoy, the *Sand Hawk*!"

"Ahoy," came an immediate reply. A woman stepped to the rails. She was tall and lean like Seris Larr, with white hair and a tanned, oval face. "Who are you?" Her tone was far less abrupt than the question.

"Are you Captain Lanton?"

"Possibly. I'd have your name."

"I once sailed aboard the *Sea Dove*," Mara said, as Larr had instructed. "I wish a word."

The woman surveyed the wharf and waved Mara toward the plank leading to the ship's deck. Mara boarded and gripped the captain's proffered hand.

"Mara Lijar," she said.

"She's mentioned you. I'm Lanton. Seris was here not long ago."

"I know. We spoke, but much has happened since then."

The captain's eyes flicked to Mara's bandage. "What do you need?"

"I have to get a message to her. We need for her to return here as soon as she can and then await word from Tobias or me. We might have to flee this place at a moment's notice. The last I heard the *Skate* was sailing—"

"I know where she's gone. I should be able to get word to her within a qua'turn. Sooner, with any luck."

"My thanks." Mara faltered. "Do I need to... I mean, I have some silver..."

The woman shook her head and grinned. Her teeth were yellow and crooked, but the smile softened her features, revealed her beauty. "There's no fee for this. Will Seris know where to find you?"

"Please tell her we're in Duvyn, at the castle."

"Very well."

"I need to be going," Mara said. "I can't thank you enough."

"From what I hear, it's us who ought to be thanking you." She walked Mara back to the plank. We'll send word as soon—" She broke off, muttered a curse.

Mara followed the direction of her gaze and swore as well.

A cluster of soldiers, all in Sheraigh blue, stood at the head of the wharf. They were speaking to sailors and laborers, stopping everyone who left the pier or stepped onto it.

"Were you followed?"

"I'm sure I wasn't."

"Bad luck, then. You know your way around a ship?" At Mara's nod, she said, "Then make yourself useful. With any luck they'll move on before long."

Mara moved away, found a mop, and set to work cleaning the deck. Swabbing had been her least favorite task while on the *Sea Dove*, but it allowed her to remain above decks, where she could mark the soldiers' progress along the wharf. Too soon, the men ventured farther along the pier in the direction of the *Sand Hawk*.

She eased away from the rails but remained on deck. If the

men chose to search the ship, she couldn't appear to be hiding from them.

When the soldiers reached the ship, Lanton greeted them coolly, but with courtesy. She invited them aboard, and two came up the plank. As soon as they boarded the vessel, they spotted Mara. She pretended not to notice.

"Who is that?" she heard one of them ask.

"A member of my crew. Cajess, come here."

Mara leaned the mop against the rail and joined the captain and the soldiers.

"These men wish to speak with you."

"Yes, all right," she said, adopting the accent of the Sisters that she had heard so often during her time in Windhome Palace.

The soldiers proceeded to pepper her with questions. Where was she from? How long had she served on the ship? What did she do onboard? They even asked her to tie a running knot and a half hitch. Mara silently thanked Old Yadreg from the *Sea Dove*, who had taught her a variety of knots during her time on the ship.

Satisfied that she belonged on the vessel, the men searched the rest of the vessel and left. Mara remained aboard as they completed their search of this wharf and the two on either side of it. Eventually, they withdrew to the lane fronting the shore and marched back toward the city.

When they were no longer in sight, Mara leaned against the nearest rail and shut her eyes. Her head pounded. A fine sheen of sweat covered her face and neck and darkened her shirt.

"That was well done," Lanton said, joining her. "I especially liked the accent."

Mara managed a smile.

The captain frowned. "You don't look well."

"I don't feel well. I should be in bed. A head wound from two nights ago. I need to get back to the castle, but I fear meeting up with those men."

"I can help with that."

Lanton sent another member of her crew into the city. Within a quarter bell, the man returned with a peddler in tow. The woman was a fishmonger. At Lanton's request, she agreed to drive her cart to the castle, with Mara as a passenger. Lanton made clear that they needed to keep their distance from any soldiers they might see, but she said no more than that. The fishmonger appeared to find nothing unusual about Lanton's request.

"Maybe the duke will buy some fish," she said with a toothless grin.

With transport arranged, Mara thanked the captain, bade her farewell, and followed the woman into the city and to her cart.

The fishmonger talked the entire time, not just as they walked, but once they were on the road as well. She asked Mara no questions, but spoke at length of the fish trade, of the weather, and of her hatred for the Sheraighs. Mara didn't have to say a word, which suited her well. Her headache persisted, and the smell of old fish emanating from the ancient cart soured her stomach.

They avoided the soldiers and reached the castle before dark. Mara had the woman wait at the gate and searched out Corinne. At Mara's urging, the duchess bought up most of the fish the woman carried. The peddler went away happy. Mara repaired to her chamber, with Sofya at her side telling her story after story about her day.

By the time Corinne joined them, she was in bed, with Sofya lying beside her, still talking about their hunt through the garden.

Eventually, Sofya began to sing a song she had learned that morning and lost herself in play.

"You were gone a long time," Corinne said, voice low.

Mara told her of her encounter with the uniformed men.

"You think they were looking for you?"

"I'm sure of it. The moment they saw me, they wanted to know where I was from, what I was doing there. I think they were told to search for Northislers."

The duchess nodded, grim-faced. "Well, I hope whatever you went to do was worth the risk."

"It was."

"How are you feeling?"

"A little better." The truth.

"Good, because we have a lot of fish to eat."

Over the next two days, Mara followed the healer's instructions and rested in her chamber. He was furious to learn of her foray into the city, and after feeling so poorly upon her return, she couldn't blame him. By the third day, she felt well enough to leave her bed and join Sofya in the gardens, and in the days that followed, she strolled and rested, giving her body time to recuperate.

Always Mara kept watch on the castle gate. She knew it was far too soon to expect word from Captain Larr, but that didn't keep her from growing impatient. She imagined Sheraigh soldiers combing the countryside, surrounding the castle. Everyone in Daerjen knew that Risch had set himself against the new supremacy. If the Sheraighs and Orzili believed that Tobias, Mara, and Sofya were hiding on the isle, their search would bring them here sooner or later. Likely sooner, and in numbers.

Duvyn spies in the city reported an increased presence of Sheraigh soldiers. They were said to be harassing ship captains and merchants, all in the pursuit of "Northisle instigators." Mara wondered if they were doing this in all cities, or only here. Corinne believed they must be conducting searches throughout Daerjen. Mara was less sure. First the attack by the demons, and now the arrival of Sheraigh soldiers. Orzili knew where they were.

On the sixth evening after her visit to the city—too soon for Captain Larr to have sent back a message or sailed to Duvyn—her worst fears were confirmed.

She had already returned to their chamber and put Sofya to bed, when an urgent knock at her door quickened her pulse. She opened it, found Corinne in the corridor with several of Duvyn's soldiers, all of them holding torches and muskets. She stepped out of the room and closed the door silently.

"Soldiers are on their way," Corinne said in a whisper, her demeanor reassuringly calm. "According to the warning we received, there are at least three dozen of them, perhaps more."

"From Sheraigh?"

"Yes."

"How soon will they be here?"

"Within a quarter bell. I can have the gate guards and those on the walls delay them a bit, but there is only so much I can do. They'll be in the castle soon."

Mara took a steadying breath. She wished Tobias was there, just to have him with her. "I'll wake Nava."

"Good. I have an idea of where to hide you."

Mara had not yet changed into her sleeping gown. She entered the room once more, retrieved her blades and her pistol, and then knelt beside Sofya's pallet and lifted the princess into her arms.

Sofya stirred, wrapped her arms around Mara's neck, and was soon asleep again, snoring softly against her chest.

Corinne left guards in Mara and Tobias's chamber to hide their belongings and Sofya's small pallet, and led Mara and Sofya to a tower stairway that climbed to a narrow corridor Mara hadn't seen before. The passageways were unlit. Only the torches carried by the duchess and guards allowed them to see. The stone walls were unadorned, the ceiling low and angled. Mara guessed that it conformed to the roofline of the castle itself.

The hallway ended at a low wooden door, locked. Corinne removed a key from her robe and opened the door. The room within was small, but it contained a pallet, small stores of food, and what Mara took to be fresh water, and candles, which one of the guards lit. The space smelled of old stone and dust, the air stale, but clean enough.

"What is this?" Mara asked.

"It's exactly what it seems: A hiding place. When the guards and I leave here, we will set a wooden board in place at the top of the stairs. It will appear that the corridor is blocked off and cannot be accessed, and that will be the case. Eventually, when the Sheraighs have gone, we'll call for you and you can remove the board. Only you can. Once we block it off, we can't open it from below."

"And the food—"

"Risch's idea. He had the room stocked before he left with Tobias. He thought this might happen." She pointed into the chamber past the area illuminated by the candle. "There's a privy back there. It's safe to use. No one will find you that way."

Frightened though she was, Mara couldn't help but think again how fortunate she and Tobias were to have been claimed as friends by this duke and duchess. "I haven't the words to thank you," she said.

Corinne actually smiled. "That's all right. I haven't time to hear them." She signaled to the guards, who started back toward the stairway. "No one will see the candles, because there are no windows up here. And with this door shut, no one should be able to hear you, even if they're standing on the top stair. From the corridor below this one, they can't hear at all, regardless of the door." She gave Mara's shoulder a gentle squeeze. "You'll be safe here."

The woman's gaze shifted, and she winked. Mara looked down and saw that Sofya was awake. Corinne waved and walked away. The princess waved after her.

When Corinne and her soldiers were gone, Mara set Sofya on the pallet.

"Whewe awe we, Mama?"

"We're in a room high in the castle, love."

"Why? I liked our room." *I wiked ouw woom.*

"I know, but some men have come and they're looking for us. We need to hide here for a time."

Sofya responded with a solemn nod. It broke Mara's heart that she didn't ask why again, that she didn't question this at all. She was too accustomed to hiding, to running, to living her life in danger, her parents in a constant state of vigilance.

The girl looked around, candlelight in her deep blue eyes. "It's small."

"Yes, it is."

Mara kissed Sofya's cheek and lay down beside her, doubting she would be able to sleep. She was relieved that none would be able to hear them, but frustrated by her own inability to monitor conversations below.

"Why do men always look for us, Mama?"

Mara raised her head. Sofya was sitting up and staring back at her with wide, luminous eyes. She deserved the truth but was too young to hear it, or, more to the point was too young to understand the need not to speak of it with anyone else.

"We're important, love," was all she could think to say. "And these men are a little bit afraid of us."

"I wouldn't hurt them," she said, earnest, kinder than her enemies deserved.

"I know you wouldn't. They don't understand that. And until they do, we can't let them find us."

This seemed to satisfy her. She lay back down and soon fell asleep. Mara remained awake, listening for any sounds that might tell her what was happening in the castle. At one point, she thought she heard voices outside and below, perhaps from the courtyard. But the sound was fleeting. Mostly she heard Sofya's slow breathing and the scratching of some small creature in the far corner of the room.

Time crawled past. Eventually, she realized that she had dozed off. She had no idea for how long. She tried to remain awake, but failed, starting awake again later. The pattern repeated itself several times more until she had no idea whether it was night or day, or whether the Sheraighs remained in the castle. She wanted to think she would have heard Corinne call for her from the stairway.

She feared for the duchess, for what might be done to her if the Sheraighs suspected her of treachery. And she wondered what would happen if Corinne was taken from the castle, or imprisoned in its dungeon, or...or killed. What if the soldiers took the castle and prevented Risch's return, and Tobias's? Their food and water couldn't last forever. What would she and Sofya do if no one came for them?

Orzili hadn't told Gillian where to begin her travels around the isle. She chose Duvyn because it was the one duchy that had declared itself in opposition to the new supremacy.

She understood what Orzili expected of her. She was no general. She couldn't lay siege to anyone's castle, or even threaten as much. But she could gather what information was there for the taking, and instill some fear in the duke.

She had some forty soldiers with her, most of them on foot. She rode, slept in a large tent, on a pallet that others packed and set up each morning and night. She ate well, was flanked at all times by four guards, was, at least nominally, in command of this company. Never had she imagined herself in such a position. She couldn't deny liking it.

A dozen armed men stood before Duvyn Castle's gate as they approached, lit by torches, all in uniforms of red, trimmed with blue. No torches burned on the battlements, but Gillian thought she saw shadowed figures atop the castle walls. Her soldiers, she understood, were vulnerable. Should fighting break out, the archers and marksmen above would have a distinct advantage—height and visibility.

She rode forward to Duvyn's guards, did not dismount. "I come from Hayncalde," she said, "as an emissary of the sovereign. I would speak with your duke."

"He's not here," said the Duvyn commander, a tall, trim woman with short yellow hair. "Perhaps you should withdraw and come back another time."

"My lady," Gillian said.

"Excuse me?"

"I am to be addressed as 'my lady' or 'minister.'"

"Forgive me. Perhaps you should withdraw, my lady." Her tone bordered on insolent, though her expression remained neutral.

"Your duchess is here?"

"She is, my lady."

"Then I will speak with her."

"Of course. You may bring four guards with you. If you would just have them leave—"

"No. All of them will enter, armed as they are."

"My lady, for the safety of our duchess—"

"As I've told you," Gillian said, her tone wintry, "I am here as an emissary of the sovereign. Surely you do not believe your sovereign is a threat to your duke or duchess. Unless there is some reason why the sovereign should feel threatened by them?" She raised an eyebrow, thinned a smile.

What could the woman say?

"No, my lady."

Gillian heard a shade more deference in the honorific.

"Of course you may enter."

The woman glanced at the soldiers behind her and nodded. Gillian rode through the gate, followed by her company of guards. Once within the courtyard, she told them to search the grounds and the structure, though with the duke gone, she doubted she would find Tobias, the woman, or the child within the castle.

Only then did she dismount and hand the reins to a castle steward.

"Have him groomed, fed, and watered."

"Yes, my lady."

Gillian surveyed the courtyard. It was a modest castle, small, plain in design, pleasant enough in adornment. As she completed her perusal of the structure, a woman emerged from the closest archway, accompanied by eight soldiers. As the woman neared, Gillian recognized her. The duchess. She and her duke had visited Mearlan in Hayncalde, had dined at a grand table with Gillian and Bexler. She and the woman had never spoken, but Gillian wondered if she remembered her.

"Welcome to Duvyn Castle," the woman said, halting before her. "I am Corinne, Duchess of Duvyn."

She remained as she had been at the time of that visit: tall, exceedingly pretty, with long, satiny hair of silver and black, and shrewd, dark eyes.

She didn't curtsy or bow. Neither did Gillian.

"Thank you, my lady," Gillian said. "I am Gillian Ainfor. I come as an emissary of the sovereign, in whose court I serve as a minister of protocol." Orzili's wording.

"An honor to see you again, minister." So she did remember. "We are pleased to name you as a guest of our house. I only wish you had sent ahead to let us know you were on your way."

"And here I assumed, given all those marksmen on your battlements, that you knew to expect our arrival."

"A company of soldiers? Approaching under cover of darkness so late in the night? Of course we took precautions. And of course we have scouts watching the road. Our castle may be small and far removed from Daerjen's great cities. But we're not fools."

"No, I wouldn't think."

Both of them kept smiles on their faces, but they might as well have faced each other with blades drawn. When the duchess offered her food and wine, she wished she had brought a taster.

They repaired to the castle's main hall, where platters of cheese, fruits, meats, and bread had been set upon a long table. A carafe of white wine awaited them. The duchess poured, gave a cup to Gillian, and raised her own.

"To unexpected pleasures."

Gillian drank, was embarrassed to see that her hand shook slightly as she set her cup on the table. She should have been better prepared for this confrontation. It might have been a mistake to begin her journeying here, rather than with a visit to a friendlier court.

"Your soldiers are searching our castle. I would know why."

"A precaution. Nothing more."

"And yet you eat our food, drink our wine, walk our corridors with only a small retinue of guards. Doesn't that seem rash? Or are you searching for someone in particular? 'Northisle instigators?' That's the phrase being bandied in the streets of the city, isn't it?"

"Yes, I believe it is. Have you seen any?"

The duchess's laugh sounded genuine. She appeared far more at ease than Gillian felt. Again, she feared she had erred in coming here so soon.

"Yes! The castle is crawling with them. Haven't you seen?"

"This isn't an occasion for jests, my lady."

"You're right," Corinne said, turning grave. "It's an occasion for shame, for all who love this isle to lament how far we have fallen."

Gillian had been reaching for her cup again, but she stopped, sat back in her chair, and regarded the woman.

"You did hear me when I said that I was an emissary of the sovereign? The new sovereign. Noak."

"Clearly."

"I could have you arrested this night. Your words are treasonous."

"You can *try* to have me arrested. You can even try to kill me if you like, though I believe you'll find that more difficult than you imagine. But you will not keep me from speaking my mind. And frankly, I don't think you're foolish enough to attempt either. You came here with forty soldiers. I command five times that number and more. You would not survive the night."

"Are you trying to provoke me? Do you seek war with the supremacy?"

"Of course not. I'm not stupid. I'm also not afraid. You know as well as I that Noak hates my husband, that he sees us as a threat to his authority. If I feigned friendship, I would fool no one."

"And yet—"

"I remember you, minister. You served as a protocol minister in the old supremacy as well. Which makes me wonder if you are lying to the present sovereign, or if you were a traitor to the old one. Either way, I would ask that you not speak to me again of what is treasonous and what is not."

Gillian drank more of her wine, placed the cup on the table, pushed back her chair, and stood.

"I had hoped our conversation would go differently."

"Surely you didn't expect it to."

She frowned, feeling again that she was beyond her depth. The truth was, she *had* expected it to be a different sort of encounter. She thought the duchess—or her duke—would dissemble, would seek to mollify. Instead, Corinne seemed intent on provoking her. Was she as inexperienced in this sort of diplomacy as Gillian, or did Duvyn's hatred of the Sheraighs truly run so deep? Gillian couldn't tell, and she took this as yet another measure of her own ignorance.

She was halfway to the chamber door when she realized that it was neither ignorance nor hostility that elicited these barbs from the duchess. It was desperation. Corinne sought to make Gillian and her men feel unwelcome in the castle. She wanted them gone. And Gillian was certain she knew why.

She faced the duchess again, her pistol drawn. The pistol with which she had already killed once in the past few days.

"The woman and the infant princess—where have you hidden them?"

Corinne dropped her gaze to the pistol, then looked Gillian in the eye again.

"You would draw your weapon on me in my own castle? And you call yourself an emissary?"

"You are harboring a traitor and a threat to the safety of our isle."

The duchess laughed. "A threat. You speak of an infant. Is the House of Sheraigh so weak that it can be brought down by a mere child?"

"You're not fooling me, my lady. Now tell me where they are."

"There is no one here—"

Gillian cocked the pistol, silencing her. "You think I won't kill you. You believe you're safe because there are soldiers wearing Duvyn colors in your courtyard and on your battlements. You're wrong."

"If you kill me, those men—"

"If I kill you, those men will be faced with a choice between following *my* orders or being hunted down and executed as traitors to their sovereign. Do you honestly believe that your corpse can inspire such loyalty?"

She backed to the door, the hand holding her pistol never wavering. She opened the door.

"The child and woman are somewhere in the castle," she said to the guards waiting in the corridor.

"We've searched, minister. We haven't found them."

"Search again. Check every room, every stairway, every corridor. They're here. I'm certain of it."

"Yes, minister."

The duchess glowered, the muscles in her neck and jaw tightening. Further confirmation of what Gillian already knew.

She could barely contain her excitement. Lord Orzili would reward her handsomely for delivering the princess. And if he had the woman, he would eventually have Tobias as well, which, she knew, he desired above all else.

Gillian closed the door and moved to the center of the chamber. She waved the pistol toward a chair. "Sit, my lady. We'll wait together."

Corinne didn't move until Gillian cocked an eyebrow and motioned more sharply with the weapon. Reluctantly, Corinne sat. Gillian reclaimed her cup and poured more wine.

CHAPTER TWENTY-FIVE

17th Day of Sipar's Ascent, Year 634

Her soldiers' search of the castle took far longer than Gillian anticipated. A bell passed, and then a second and third. In the small of night, there came a knock on the door to the hall. The duchess started awake. Gillian might have been dozing as well. She wasn't certain.

She stood and faced the door. "Enter."

One of the Sheraigh soldiers stepped into the chamber.

"What have you found?"

The soldier shook his head. "Nothing, minister. We've been in every chamber and hall, every corridor."

"What about the stairways and towers?"

"Nothing."

Gillian glanced at Corinne, who watched her, wary, anxious. "They're here," she said to the soldier. "Look again. Search for anything unusual, any door or passageway that might conceal...something."

The man's expression flattened, but he nodded and left them again.

"You're wasting your time," the duchess said.

"We both know better." Gillian tried to sound sure of herself but wasn't convinced she succeeded. Perhaps she had misread the woman's reactions earlier.

She reclaimed her chair, ordered Corinne to settle back into hers. And again, they waited.

Another bell passed. The same soldier returned, his bearing as it had been.

Gillian knew before he spoke what he would say. And still she remained convinced that Tobias's woman and the child were in this castle. True, she was relatively new to the sort of intrigue that Orzili had brought into her life. But she had always been clever, had always sensed truths that others missed. Bexler would have believed the duchess's denials. So would any number of ministers from Mearlan's court. She didn't, and she trusted her intuition.

Mostly.

"You found nothing at all?"

"Nothing, minister. There was... No, there was nothing."

She stepped toward him. "What? What were you going to say?"

"It's nothing. A tower stairway that goes beyond the castle's second level and ends at a wooden wall."

"A wall? Or a locked door?"

"A wall. There is no handle, no lock, nothing at all. It's solid—it doesn't give at all. It can't be opened, and the wood appears ancient. I would guess that whatever lies beyond it hasn't been seen in years."

As the soldier spoke, Gillian watched Corinne. The duchess barely responded. She sat unmoving, her stare fixed on the far wall, her mien placid. Too much so.

"That's it," Gillian said. "Did you leave someone there? Is someone watching that stairway?"

The man wet his lips. "No. Minister, I swear to you, it's nothing. An old stairway is all."

"And if you're wrong, would you care to be the one to explain to Lord Orzili how the woman and child escaped us?"

No answer.

"Go. Take ten men and stand watch at the bottom of that stairway. Let no one past you."

"Yes, minister."

The man turned smartly and left.

"Come along, my lady," Gillian said, aiming the pistol again. "We should be there as well. To greet your guests."

Corinne rose, graceful and grave, fear in her dark eyes. She said nothing—what could she say? Gillian followed her, the barrel of her pistol pointed squarely at the woman's back.

Mara woke to a noise she couldn't identify. Sofya slept on, and for a fivecount, Mara heard nothing at all. Had she imagined it? She rose slowly, carefully, so as not to disturb the princess, and crept out of the small room toward that slab of wood blocking off the stairway. She halted short of it, listened.

And heard it again. Someone was on the other side. Whoever it was hadn't knocked. Rather, they were scratching at it in some way. The wood creaked, as if those below were pushing on it. She heard a voice, and then a second. Men. Not Corinne. She took a step back, her heart abruptly laboring.

Sheraighs. It had to be.

They had been pursued for so long, had come close to dying during their fight with Orzili and his men. Somehow this felt...closer, more threatening. If they found a way through that piece of wood, she and Sofya were dead. The barrier seemed all too flimsy.

After another tencount, the scratching ceased, the voices faded, vanished. Still she remained where she was, listening, trembling, sweating.

Would the men move on and give up, or would they return with axes to break through the board? It could only be opened from above, but it could be rent from below.

She wheeled, hurried back to the small room and its pallet. Kneeling, she shook Sofya awake. The princess's eyes fluttered, closed again. At a second shake and the whisper of her name, Sofya opened her eyes, yawned, blinked, stared.

"Are you awake, love?"

The girl nodded.

"I need you to listen to me very carefully. We have to leave this place now. We can't make a sound, and once we're downstairs, I'll need to find a place to leave you for a short while."

Sofya scowled, bunched her face to cry.

Mara stopped her with a raised hand. "I need you to be really big now, and as brave as you've ever been. I need you to do exactly as I say. Please."

Sofya was smart and strong and, yes, as brave as anyone Mara had ever known. Maybe it was the "please" that reached her; Mara sensed her making up her mind to do what she asked.

"Aww wight," she said.

She retrieved her weapons, loaded her pistol. Sofya frowned at the weapon and then at Mara. But she didn't comment, and when Mara was ready, she held out her arms to be picked up. For the span of a breath, it was all Mara could do not to cry like a child herself. She had never felt such pride for anyone as she did then for the princess—her child.

She carried Sofya to the wooden slab, set her down, and motioned for the princess to be silent. Sofya nodded, wide-eyed and solemn. Mara went back to the room for the candle and placed it near the princess. After listening for a tencount and hearing not a sound, Mara removed the brackets that held the board in place and blew out the candle, plunging them into complete darkness. Sofya gave a soft cry. Mara shushed her gently. She ran her fingers around the edges of the piece of wood, grasped it, and lifted it away from the opening, taking care to do so noiselessly.

She picked up Sofya again and descended the stairway. The princess kept silent. At the bottom of the stairs, Mara eased out into the corridor, which was as dark as the stairway had been. She followed it to its end and paused, trying to recall the route she and Corinne had taken earlier in the night. Here, there was a bit of light—arrow slits on one side allowed in some glow from the stars and the moon, and on the other side the inconstant glow of torches burning in the courtyard. She heard footsteps, the jangle of steel and the scrape of leather. Men. A good many of them, headed in her direction, likely to try the stairway again. She had left their hiding place just in time.

She hurried to the left, reasonably certain the hallway would take her to the chamber of someone she could trust. She turned right at the next corner, and at the one after, only to backtrack the other way after a few steps. Along that last corridor, she came to the door she'd been seeking. She knocked.

She thought it must be late, and she assumed she would have to knock several times before she received a response. Instead, the door opened almost immediately, revealing Tarrod, the young healer, his hair in disarray, but his eyes alert.

"My lady," he said.

She held a finger to her lips, glanced up and down the hall.

His expression sharpened. "They're searching for you," he said in a whisper.

"Yes. For this one, really." She bounced Sofya in her arms, drawing a smile from the girl.

"Why?"

"I can't tell you that. I need you to keep her safe. Hide her if you can. Kill for her if you must. The future of everything depends on it."

He stared at her, then at Sofya. "Yes, all right."

"Nava, I need to leave you with Tarrod for a short while."

Sofya shied from him, clung to Mara more tightly.

"Remember what we talked about? What I asked you to do?"

"I have a wooden top," Tarrod said. "Have you ever played with a top?"

Sofya regarded him, curiosity warring with skepticism. She shook her head.

"Would you like me to teach you how?"

"I'll be back soon, love," Mara said. "You can learn how and then show me in a little while."

Still the girl hesitated. Mara begrudged every instant, but she sensed that to allow Sofya to cry would imperil them both.

At last she nodded and held out her arms to the healer.

Tarrod took her, offered a wan smile to Mara. "She'll be fine."

"Thank you." Mara kissed Sofya's brow and hurried away. She heard the door close and lock behind her.

She headed for Corinne's chamber, but long before she reached it, she had to duck into another corridor to avoid a company of soldiers, at least eight of them. They walked briskly, their footsteps and the jangle of their weapons and armor masking her breathing and her steps.

When they had passed, she continued on, only to have to duck out of sight a second time.

In this instance, she heard only two people. Peeking out from her place of concealment, she had to stifle a cry. Corinne was trailed by a woman Mara recognized. The traitorous minister from Mearlan's court. The one who once lured her to the Notch on the pretense that she was helping Tobias rather than trying to capture him. She couldn't recall the woman's name. Not that it mattered. She held a pistol, had it aimed at Corinne's back. That was all Mara needed to see.

As the women passed, Mara stepped out into the corridor directly behind them and drew her sword. The minister heard and whirled.

Mara gave her no time to shout or to fire. She plunged her blade into the minister's chest.

The woman gave a small gasp, and her eyes went wide. She grabbed at the blade, slicing open several fingers, then started to level her weapon. Mara slapped it out of her hand. It clattered to the floor. Corinne claimed it.

Mara pulled her sword free and blood blossomed from the wound, staining the minister's robes. The woman's mouth moved, but no words came out. Her eyes rolled back in her head and she fell to the floor.

Corinne and Mara eyed each other, both glum.

"I'm sorry," Mara said. "I was afraid—"

"She would have called for help," Corinne said, her voice low. "Or fired her weapon. You did what you had to. But now you need to get out of the corridor until I can summon my soldiers."

Mara knew she was right. She knew as well that she would pay a price for this murder. Yes, the woman had been her enemy. She had hurt Mara during their first encounter and would have thought nothing of killing her and Sofya this night. Still, there would be a cost. She had killed without hesitation, without giving her foe a chance to strike or defend herself. There had to be a cost for killing that way. Didn't there?

Shouldn't her stomach have turned at what she'd done? Shouldn't she have been shaking? She stared down at the woman's corpse, at the blood pooling on her chest, glistening in the torch light, so dark it almost looked black. The minister's eyes remained open. Her mouth as well. Shouldn't killing a woman bring tears or tremors or immediate remorse? Was there something wrong with her that she felt nothing but grim satisfaction?

Yes, she had killed before. She had fought humans and Ancients, had killed with a musket and a pistol. Her memories of the confrontation with Orzili and his men on the strand near the Notch had grown hazy. She wasn't certain why. But she thought she recalled killing assassins there with her blade. Perhaps Sheraigh soldiers, too.

This killing was different.

It was also necessary. Corinne had said so. Tobias would agree.

"Mara."

She looked up from the body, took a sharp, startled breath. Corinne watched her, concern creasing her forehead.

"Are you all right?"

"I'm fine," she said, and meant it.

"You have to go. The soldiers will return here before long, as soon as they realize we're not behind them. You should go to the healer."

"Yes. That's where...where Nava is."

"Good. Go there now. Have a care in the corridors. There may be more Sheraighs about."

"What are you going to do?"

"Summon my soldiers," Corinne said, impatience in the words.

Right. She had said that earlier.

"Are you sure you're well?"

"Yes. I meant, what do you plan to do with them? Will you have them fight the sovereign's guards?"

"We have no choice. We have to kill all of them. If any make it to Hayncalde, the men who are after you will know you're here. They'll know we killed their minister."

"They're going to know all eventually."

"Yes. Eventually. Not now, though. Not yet."

"All right. I can fight with you. You know I'm Windhome-trained." She glanced down at the minister. "Obviously I'm willing to kill."

"We outnumber them by a factor of ten, Mara. My soldiers don't need you. Nava does."

How could she argue with that?

She left the duchess there, navigated the corridors back to Tarrod's chamber. Along the way, she started to sheath her weapon, but thought better of it.

Reaching his door, she knocked. At first, she heard no response. Fear rose in her throat. She reached for the door handle. As her fingers brushed the metal, the door swung open revealing the young healer with a dagger in his hand.

Seeing her, he exhaled and let his blade hand drop.

"Mara," he said. "Come in."

Had she been a Sheraigh, the weapon he held would have heightened her suspicions. It also would have been next to useless against guards armed with swords or muskets. She didn't say any of this, of course. He was trying to protect Sofya, and she was grateful.

He closed and locked the door. "It's all right, Nava."

The princess emerged from the healer's wardrobe. She squealed happily and rushed to Mara. Mara hugged her with one arm, sheathed her blade with the other. She would clean the steel later.

"Is someone wounded?" Tarrod asked.

She met his gaze. "It's nothing urgent," she said with meaning.

His cheeks blanched.

"There are bound to be more injured before this night is through. Save your magicks for them."

"Awe the men stiww aftew us, Mama?"

"Yes, love. For a little while longer. We'll remain here, if Tarrod will let us."

"Of course." His voice had tightened.

Mara crossed to a chair beside the hearth and sat. Sofya crawled into her lap and curled against her. Mara started to tell her a story, but noises from outside the shuttered window and the locked door soon distracted them both. All three of them really. Tarrod stood by the fire, tense, listening. Sofya watched Mara, appearing to gauge her reactions to the shouts and screams, the clang of steel and the flat crack of flintlocks and muskets. Mara did her best to school her features, but she was afraid.

Duvyn had numbers. Sheraigh's soldiers, however, were likely some of the best-trained in all of Daerjen. Despite Corinne's confidence, the outcome of this battle was far from certain.

The blaring report of a firearm in a nearby corridor made Sofya flinch and bury her face against Mara's chest.

Tarrod eyed the door. Mara eased her loaded flintlock from her belt. She shifted the chair so that she had a clear shot at the door, cocked the weapon, and rested her forearm on the arm of the chair. She glanced down at Sofya, only to find that the princess was staring back at her. She turned to eye Mara's weapon, then settled against her again.

More weapons discharged in the hallways, but the sounds of fighting came no closer. Outside, the battle seemed to be ending. In time, the noises in the corridors receded as well. They all remained where they were. Sofya fell asleep. Tarrod still held his knife, Mara her pistol.

After another quarter bell of quiet, someone knocked at the

healer's door. Tarrod and Mara shared a glance. Tarrod stepped to the door, unlocked it, looked back at Mara again. She motioned him to the side with the pistol so she would have a clear shot.

He shifted and opened the door.

Corinne stood in the doorway, a number of soldiers behind her.

"It's over," she said. "Healer, we have a number of wounded. They require your attention."

"Of course, my lady," Tarrod said, stepping to a cabinet that Mara assumed held tonics, herbs, bandages, and other implements of his trade. "Please have them moved to the hall."

"We're doing that already," the duchess said.

"Very good, my lady. What of the sovereign's men?"

Corinne's gaze flicked to Mara. "There are no survivors among the sovereign's guards."

Tarrod turned at that. "None?"

"None."

He frowned. "I don't understand. How is that—"

"Healer," Corinne said, perhaps more sharply than she intended. "Tarrod," she went on in a softer tone, "our guards are dispatching the last of their survivors now. There can be no outside witnesses to tonight's events. Do you understand?"

Again, he had gone white. Mara felt badly for him. He was young, healer to a minor house. He had probably thought he was comfortably far from warfare and the questionable ethics that came with it. Then Mara, Tobias, and Sofya had come and thrown his safe world into turmoil.

He cleared his throat. "Yes, my lady. I understand perfectly."

"Good. Come when you're ready." She spoke Mara's name, gestured for her to follow.

Mara stood, slipped the pistol onto her belt, and shifted Sofya in her arms.

"Thank you for keeping her safe, Tarrod," she said. "And for giving us refuge."

"Of course." Was it disapproval that tightened his voice?

Mara left with the duchess, walked beside her in silence until they reached Corinne's chamber. The duchess issued orders to her soldiers and admitted Mara to the room.

"Wine?"

"Please."

Corinne poured, handed her a cup. Mara still carried the princess. She could have set her down and Sofya would have remained asleep. But Mara didn't want to let go of her. This night had been too fraught, too close to a bitter ending.

"What now?" the duchess asked. "It won't be long before Hayncalde wonders why they haven't heard from the minister. They'll send more soldiers, a larger company. You're welcome here—you know that—but I fear you can't stay."

"I know. As soon as Tobias and Risch return, we'll go. I'm hoping that by then we'll have heard something from Seris."

"It wasn't so long ago you left her ship. Now you would go back to it?"

"What choice do we have? Since we arrived here, you've been beset by Belvora and by Sheraigh soldiers. Obviously we're not safe here—and you're not safe as long as we remain. And there's no one else in Daerjen whom we trust."

They had little to say after that. Mara was scared, angry, weary beyond words, though she couldn't have slept even if she wanted to. She was desperate for word from Captain Larr. Mostly, she wanted Tobias here.

Corinne walked to her shuttered window and opened it. A faint shimmer of silver gray had seeped into the eastern sky. An end to an endless night. And yet...

Someone knocked at the door. Corinne called for whomever had come to enter.

The door opened, revealing a soldier. "My lady."

"What is it?"

"You'd best come and see. We're not certain, but we fear we might not have...have taken care of all the Sheraighs."

Corinne and Mara eyed each other.

"Blood and bone," the duchess said, speaking for both of them.

They followed the soldier through the corridors and into the castle courtyard, where a dozen more guards surrounded them in a tight, protective formation. They hurried out through the main gate, Sofya asleep and warm in Mara's arms, mercifully unaware.

The sky had brightened enough that they didn't need torches. They walked the main road away from the castle, past the now-empty camp the Sheraighs had established upon their arrival. Some forty mounts grazed on grasses near a small rill. Soon they entered a strip of woodland. The soldiers steered them onto a path that curved away from the road to the west. They wound among the trees for a short distance until they reached a small clearing.

The ground here was well-trodden, the brush flattened, branches broken. Charred and grayed logs still smoked in a fire pit. Discarded food littered the ground. Half-eaten bones from some fowl. A meal interrupted.

Corinne surveyed the clearing, her mouth a dark gash in an otherwise ashen face. "How many do you suppose?"

"Two or three," said the man who had fetched them from her chamber.

"How long ago did they leave?"

"We can only guess, my lady, but—"

"When the fighting began, yes? Bells ago?"

The man nodded. "Yes, my lady. We've sent riders after them, with orders to kill them on sight. But I fear they have too much of a head start on our guards."

"How many days to Hayncalde?" Mara asked.

"At speed?" Corinne said. "At most, three or four days. And then they have to ride back. We still have some time."

"No, we don't," Mara said. "Orzili doesn't have to ride back. He has tri-sextants. Or he will soon. For all we know, he can Span here within a bell or two of learning what's happened. And he can bring men and weapons."

CHAPTER TWENTY-SIX

21st Day of Sipar's Ascent, Year 634

Before Orzili left Fanquir to Span back to Hayncalde, the Lenna there told him that she would join him in Hayncalde. Their marriage was no more than a shell, a veneer intended to fool the rest of the world. Their love—or at least her love for him—was dead.

Yet they remained partners in this endeavor, their lives forfeit if they failed Pemin. And so she said she would come and help him as he circled in for the final kill.

He was still waiting for her.

The arrival of soldiers at his door late in the evening raised his hopes.

At first, when the men in the corridor told him that, no, Lady Stenci had not yet arrived, Orzili nearly flew into a rage. Why then, had they disturbed him so close to the midnight bell? What was so important that it couldn't wait for morning?

What indeed.

Two of his guards—not Sheraigh soldiers, but his own assassins—led the other two men into his chamber.

Sheraighs, both young, one with dark eyes, the other's pale. They shared the same haunted expression. They were dusty, their faces coated and streaked with grime. Their uniforms were stained, they stank of sweat and horse. Both could barely stand for their weariness. They bowed to him—one stumbled as he straightened. Orzili's anger sluiced away. What was this?

"Bring them chairs—wooden ones," he added as one of the others took a step toward the fine plush chairs near his hearth. He wished to offer the men some comfort, but he didn't want his chamber smelling of...of them.

After the two soldiers were seated and had been given water, they began their tale.

It was extraordinary.

They had been part of the company sent with Gillian Ainfor on her tour of Daerjen's duchies. Their first stop was Duvyn, where these two were selected to remain apart from the rest, on the off chance that some calamity befell the rest of the soldiers. A precaution often taken among armies of Daerjen, but almost never needed.

In this case, it had been.

"We heard fighting," said the one with light eyes. He met Orzili's gaze. The other man wouldn't. "We wanted to...it might have made some difference to have two more, but..." He broke off, his mouth twisting. "We listened for what we could, then...then crept forward to see the camp, to see if any were still there.

"There were none. Only the horses. By now we didn't hear anything more. No more fighting. I thought maybe they were in the corridors instead of the courtyard, but that didn't make much sense. What made sense was, they were all dead. That's what both of us figured. And when we saw the Duvyn guards come out their gate and start searching the camp, we knew. So we left."

"What of the minister?"

The soldier cast a quick look at his comrade. "I don't know, my lord. I assume she was taken prisoner or killed."

Orzili had assumed as much. "Were you followed here?"

"We don't know. We rode as if we were."

"That was wise."

He considered them. After a fivecount, he stepped closer to his fire. He had expected to have word from the Belvora, Glimik, by now. He'd heard nothing. He would have expected a missive from Gillian Ainfor after her audience in Duvyn. He would hear nothing from her, either.

This couldn't be coincidence.

And then there were the tidings from the north. It seemed that Duvyn's duke wasn't even in his castle. According to messages he had received from more than one of his many spies, Risch had sailed to Trohsden, though whether for trade or to foment dissent, Orzili didn't know.

Any one of these developments would have made him curious. But all three together?

Was Tobias truly this bold? Would he take shelter in a duchy less than fifty leagues from Hayncalde? Could he convince his hosts to declare themselves in open rebellion against the new supremacy, even to pit themselves against the Sheraighs militarily? And might he be clever enough, and influential enough, to bring other dukes into his fold?

The soldier's report, and the apparent failure of the Belvora, suggested that the Walker was all of these things and more. The last point confirmed that he had more than mere influence. He had the princess. No duke in his right mind would follow a court Walker who had no court. An exiled princess, on the other hand —the orphaned daughter of a beloved, lost sovereign—would be enough to win the loyalty of dukes from every corner of the isle. The question was, had Tobias taken the princess to Trohsden, or had he left her in Duvyn?

Events in the southern duchy suggested the latter.

"Did you have any warning?" Orzili asked the men.

"Warning, my lord?"

"Was there fighting from the start, as soon as you arrived? Were there skirmishes before you heard that last battle?"

"No, my lord. All seemed to be going as it should."

"Not quite," said the other man. His first words since they entered the chamber.

Orzili approached him. "Explain."

The young soldier's gaze flicked between Orzili and his companion. "Well, they were all in the castle, weren't they? And late into the night. There was no one in the camp at all. So somethin' must have happened. That's my thinkin' anyway."

"But you have no idea what it might have been."

"No, my lord."

Orzili nodded, faced his guards. "Get them food, put them in a chamber here in the castle for the night. They've earned a sound night's sleep."

"Thank you, my lord," said the first soldier.

He answered with a tight smile, indicated to his men that they should leave. Within a spirecount, he was alone.

He wanted to Span to Duvyn this very night, but he wouldn't go alone, and he didn't yet have his tri-sextants from the Binder.

The Binder, who might soon need to be told that his wife was dead.

He also didn't yet know enough to Span; even if he'd had the devices, he wouldn't risk the journey. Impatience had long been his enemy. His rashness, his lack of attention to every possible detail, had allowed Tobias to escape him twice. At a minimum. He would not allow this to happen a third time. He needed Lenna. More than her, he needed information, word from the Belvora. *Any* Belvora. Where did they sense magick—Trohsden or Duvyn? Or both?

That made the most sense. Tobias wouldn't risk taking the princess on a voyage north. What if Myles refused to help him? More, what if he chose to take the princess captive and present her to Noak? There would no better way for him to win the trust of his new sovereign. No, Tobias had left the babe in Duvyn. With the other Walker, no doubt. And Gillian Ainfor discovered the princess there. That explained all.

Impatience ate at him.

Qiyed had sent word through the Belvora—he was not to be summoned. He was under Distraint, whatever that meant. The Belvora had offered herself as a replacement.

Orzili stepped to his window and opened it. It was a cold night, raw. A fine mist fell over Hayncalde.

"Glimik," he said, the name swallowed by the damp and dark. "I would speak with you." He waited, scanning the sky, wondering if Belvora could hear a distant summons as could an Arrokad. After several moments, he repeated his summons. He called for the winged one a third time several spirecounts later, but by then, he had abandoned hope. She couldn't hear him, or she had no intention of heeding his call, or she was dead.

He shivered, wishing to close his window and return to his fire. He did lock the shutters again, but then he donned a heavy fur robe and left the castle for the shore.

Qiyed had warned him that he could only be summoned from within a league of water. The castle was closer to the gulf than that, but Orzili didn't think the Arrokad would enter the city or the fortress. Best he go to the strand and call to the Arrokad from there.

The Most Ancient would be angry. Glimik had conveyed his wishes most clearly. Had Orzili's need not been so great, he might have found another way. But Tobias was close, and he could not afford to fail again. Just one summons. Surely the Arrokad would understand.

Humans, he decided, were idiots.

Qiyed had no doubt that the winged one had delivered his message. The human, though... Likely he did not understand the gravity of Distraint. Maybe he had never even heard the word.

Certainly he could not know that a summons to an Ancient uttered once could be ignored, that a summons repeated twice could be resisted, but that a summons spoken thrice became compulsion. Qiyed had to answer, or at least make the attempt. This was a closely guarded secret. Ancients did not wish for humans to know that they possessed such power over their will.

The human would have known—the Belvora would have

explained—that other Ancients could hear summons such as this. If they listened for a name, if they sought to find a particular individual, they could use a summons as a sort of beacon.

Droë would be listening. So would her companion, the other Arrokad.

Qiyed swam toward Daerjen. He had no choice but to swim. He was not surprised when the two of them appeared in his path, Droë clinging to the back of the Most Ancient.

They were lovely, deadly. They hated him. Both had cause. He tasted his own death in the briny air. He tried to push past that last thought. *Someone* would die this night. At least one of them. Two, if he proved fortunate.

He had been in the waters around Preszir. They confronted him within sight of Brenth. Land of sweet wines and fine cloth.

"You are under Distraint, Qiyed of the Arrokad," Droë said by way of greeting. "You have failed to answer a challenge. You have violated agreements freely entered and fairly sworn. You are mine to command and so I compel you to make land on the nearest isle and vie with me in mortal combat."

She did not sound frightened. Not even a little. That boded ill.

"I have been called to a different land by a human. Summoned thrice."

"That does not matter, and you know it," Ujie said. "The exigencies of Distraint take precedence over all."

"You have no place in this," he said. "This is between the Tirribin and me."

"I have witnessed your violation, and like you, I am Arrokad. If I wish to make this my concern, I will. You are fortunate, though. Droë has demanded that I leave the matter to her." She smiled, exposing sharp teeth. "Well, perhaps not so fortunate. I would not wish to face her in combat."

"You will swim with us," Droë said. She pointed to a stretch of white sand. "There."

"I demand additional witnesses," he said. Another gambit that was fated to fail. He had nothing else.

"You are under Distraint," said the Arrokad. "You have no

right to make any demands. I will be witness. If you prevail, I will tell as much to the Guild."

"If I prevail, you will try to kill me."

Another smile. "Yes, but after you are dead, I will inform the Guild of your victory."

Had this been a chance encounter, had the two of them found him on their own, he might have fled. Carrying Droë would slow Ujie. Not a lot, though enough to make escape possible.

But humans were idiots.

He had to answer the summons, which meant Ujie knew where he would go. There was no escaping them. Best then to fight them here, without the human present to witness his potential humiliation.

He started toward the strand Droë had indicated, trying to come up with a strategy for their coming battle. She had, during their time together, discovered some method for resisting his power. Once, some time ago, he could have killed her with a thought. He had threatened to do so on several occasions, had been tempted to just as often. At the time, though, he resisted the impulse, thinking she was of value to him, expecting she would remain pliant and vulnerable. He had been a fool. Or maybe she had proven more canny than he imagined possible.

More recently, he had surprised her, and nearly succeeded in subduing her again. There would be no surprise this night. She would expect his assault, would be ready to repel it. And then he would be subject to her otherworldly speed, her unnerving strength.

An idea came to him. A gamble, but what did he have left? He had first accessed her thoughts in service to her wish to grow, to change, to know desire. Was this the key that would unlock her defenses?

They reached the shallows. Qiyed stood, walked onto land. Droë detached herself from Ujie and they both followed him.

"This is single combat," Qiyed said, directing the words at the Most Ancient. "Whatever else I have lost because of Distraint, that remains. I do not have to face both of you at once. Only her."

Droë offered no reaction to this—again he was struck by her confidence. Ujie scowled, appearing less certain of Droë's ability to fight. Was there hope for him after all?

"Only her," the Arrokad said.

Qiyed grinned, turned to Droë, and reached out with his magick.

He did not lash at her; he made no attempt to halt her breathing or land a blow. That was what she expected, and he was sure those attacks would fail. For the moment.

Instead, the touch of his power was as a feather over skin, a lover's lips on the base of the neck, a caress at the small of the back. Gossamer, tender, sensual, as if he sought to seduce. Because he did.

A flush spread across Droë's cheeks and neck. He touched her with magick again. The lightest dance of a tongue over her breasts, and then a more intimate touch, also gentle. He sensed her breath shallowing, her pulse quickening. He thought her knees might have weakened.

His next touch might have elicited a soft moan. With surf pounding the sand, he could not be certain. Ujie watched the Tirribin with apprehension. She might have understood what he was doing, but she was helpless to stop him.

One last brush of magick over her most intimate places, and her eyes fluttered shut. Only for an instant, which was more than enough for Qiyed.

Odd that power should give such tantalizing pleasure in one moment and inflict torment the next. Or perhaps not so odd, given his preferences in matters of sport.

Droë staggered, fell to her knees, clawed at her chest. Qiyed covered the distance between them in a single stride and kicked out. Her head snapped to the side, and she sprawled across the sand.

Magick again. Pain—it would feel to her that fire spread across her face and neck. She writhed, made a choked sound somewhere between a shriek and a gasp. Using more precious breath. He allowed her no new air, gave her no respite.

He loomed over her, kicked her in the side. He heard bone break. She folded into a ball. Qiyed reached down, took her by the throat, lifted her off the ground.

Grinning, he punched her in the face with his free hand. She went limp in his grasp. With a glance back at Ujie, he threw Droë to the ground. Kicked her once more. She barely responded. It had been some time since her last breath.

The other Arrokad had not moved or made a sound, as was proper in a challenge of single combat. Her fists were clenched, and she regarded the Tirribin with despair, but she kept her place. Nothing else mattered to him.

Qiyed prodded Droë with his magick. She lay still, like wreckage washed up on the shore. Killing an Ancient was never easy, and he was not yet ready to assume victory. And on the thought, the Tirribin stirred, justifying his prudence. He pushed at her with magick again but sensed nothing.

"Are you still with us, Droë?" he called, allowing himself this one taunt.

"Yes, I am."

Qiyed went still. He had not meant to release the pressure on her chest, had not intended to allow her to draw breath. He pounced on her again with his power, taking care to keep his distance. He denied her air again, seared her face. She stiffened at the touch of the heat but did not cry out or flinch. Her chest rose and fell.

Impossible!

She turned over, pushed herself to her hands and knees. He closed on her again, reared back to kick. Before he could, she scuttled away, like a crab over sand. Not quite at the speed one would expect from a Tirribin, but fast enough. He considered pursuing. Thought better of it.

She staggered to her feet and moved off a distance. Again, not at full speed. Fast enough, though, that he would have had to run to keep up with her. He did not.

"You flee," he said over the surf and the wind. "Do you yield?"

"I do not."

She remained where she was, breathing deeply, stretching her side and back.

"She has run away from me," he said, rounding on Ujie. "This is a violation of conventions. The contest is mine."

"A violation?" the other Arrokad said. "What rule in particular has she broken?"

"This is supposed to be combat, not pursuit!"

"I find no fault with her decision to retreat, so long as it proves temporary. Withdrawal for the purpose of marshaling forces is a recognized tactic in battle, human and Ancient."

"You would say anything to give her aid. I demand again that we summon other witnesses!"

"I have already ruled on this matter." Ujie bared her teeth in a cold smile. "Besides, she returns. I suggest you defend yourself."

He spun, stumbled back a step. Droë was beside him. Tirribin and their damn speed.

"Tell me, Most Ancient One, do you consider what you did to me at the start of this encounter to be combat?"

He didn't hesitate for long. "It was a tactic, yes."

"So was my decision to move away. But I'm back now. Shall we continue?"

Rather than answer, he approached her once more with his power. He tried arousal first. When that failed, as he knew it would, he struck harder. At her lungs, her throat. He lashed at her, attempted to burn, to slice, to bludgeon. He moved not a muscle. He was afraid to. The frenzied brutality of his magick should have been enough to overpower her.

She did not move either, not to cringe or buckle, not to flee or even to counter his assault. She weathered it all, amusement touching her full lips, that unnerving confidence brightening her pale gaze.

"How?" he whispered, relenting. "Three times now, I have had you in my grasp, and three times you have managed to resist me. I would know how you have done it."

"Before you die, you mean?"

He was not yet ready to capitulate so completely, not even to deceive. He had long been proud. "I would know," he said again.

"I learned your magick, Qiyed. During our time together. I learned its flavor, its strengths and its flaws. I learned to anticipate it, though I have not always been as vigilant as I should be. And I learned as well to let it pass through me without it doing harm. Strong as you are, without your magick, you're no match for me."

He itched to strike her, to prove her wrong. He kept his hands at his side—proof in his own mind that she was right. He would die this night. A strange thought for one of the Most Ancient. He had to admit that he never anticipated that such a night would come.

"Have I silenced you?" she said, clapping her hands. It was the most childlike thing he had seen her do since her transformation. "How delicious."

"You mock me."

"I do."

She blurred. By the time Qiyed thought to react, she was behind him, one arm crooked around his throat, the other pinning his arms to his sides. Gods! How could she be so strong? How could he have been so foolish as to create this creature?

Droë put her lips to his neck, just behind her arm. A creamy, multi-colored glow illuminated the strand. Qiyed knew a moment of light-headedness. His limbs grew heavy.

Real fear surged through him. He bucked, twisted, tried to flail, desperate to break free of her. He might as well have tried to push back the tide. The glow brightened, he labored to draw breath. His attempts to throw her off grew weaker.

"I will never bother you again," he said, gasping the words. "I cannot. You have taken too much. I will retreat, leave you to live in peace. I will... I will do anything."

She pulled her lips away from his neck. The strand darkened. "Will you leave Tobias alone? Will you call off the winged ones?"

"Yes." He must have faltered for too long.

The Tirribin put her mouth to his neck again. The glow rekindled. He fought her. Still she stole his years.

His body sagged. It occurred to him that this must be what it was like for a human to bleed out.

"The combat is yours. I surrender."

She paused, only long enough to say, "To the death, Qiyed. To the death."

Then she attached herself to him one last time. He had no strength to fight her. His limbs ached with fatigue. Even with the light of her magick his vision faded. *I surrender*. He could not give voice to the thought. He did not have to. She knew.

She had long since sated herself. Qiyed's years were rich and sweet, fuller than any human years. And they went on and on and on. But this was not a matter of sustenance.

Droë hated him as she had never hated any other creature. He had hurt her too many times, had sought to enslave her. And though she had submitted to his magick willingly, had in fact requested that he effect her transformation, she could not forgive him for making her into what she had become. He should have refused her. As Ujie had done.

She had been angry with Ujie at the time—a child's response. Now she knew better. It had been the response of a friend, an act of compassion and wisdom. Qiyed had seen only opportunity. Changing her had been an act of commerce, nothing more or less. Mostly, she was angry with herself, but she gladly took out that anger on the Most Ancient One.

So she fed, and fed some more, and, in time, drained him of his years, all under the avid gaze of Ujie.

When his years ran dry, when his struggles ceased completely and his body had shriveled to husk, she released him, allowed him to fall to the sand. He landed on his side, tipped onto his back. The serpentine eyes remained open, bulging from his hollowed face. Their silver had faded to gray, dull and lifeless.

Droë staggered, not from her injuries or from weariness, but like a drunken human. She had taken in too many years. She felt she would never need to feed again.

"Are you well?" Ujie asked.

She crooked a smile. "I ate too much."

Her friend laughed, sobered. "I wondered if you would spare him at the end. When you spoke to him of Tobias, I thought you might."

"So did I, but as soon as I asked the question, I realized that I wouldn't trust him no matter what he said. I knew I had to take all his years." She eyed the carcass, then met Ujie's gaze. "Do you disapprove?"

"Would it matter if I did?"

"Yes! It would... You're..." She turned away, fixed her eyes on the waves approaching the strand. "It matters."

"Then, no, I don't disapprove. You did what was necessary. You did what I would have done if I could feed on years."

She heard Ujie walk to her, smelled her near—brine, kelp, the memory of lightning, a storm wind in the warm turns.

"I would heal you, if you would allow it," she said, speaking softly.

Droë turned so that they stood face to face. Close enough to hold each other. Close enough that she sensed the coolness of Ujie's body. Close enough that they could kiss.

A corner of the Arrokad's mouth quirked upward.

"I can read your thoughts, Droënalka."

"Don't call me that. Please."

"Forgive me," Ujie said, grave now. "That was what he called you, was it not?"

She nodded.

"I am sorry. I would never hurt you. I would not seek to control you."

"But you would have me for sport?" Droë tried to ask it lightly, a jest. Only her voice shook, and she awaited Ujie's reply with a pulse that beat like the wings of a butterfly.

"Not sport, no. Love. I would have you as my love."

Which was the one answer she had hoped to hear.

No smile this time. They gazed for the span of another breath. Then Ujie leaned in and kissed her lips. A lingering kiss. Cool, slightly salty. As soft as a ripple in still waters. The Arrokad's tongue darted, touched her own, withdrew. Ujie drew back. Droë opened her eyes. She hadn't been conscious of closing them.

"I will heal you now," the Most Ancient One said. "Please sit."

Droë lowered herself to the strand. Ujie knelt beside her. Placed her long, delicate hands over Droë's side. Somehow she knew which injury hurt most.

Cool magick flowed through her shift and her skin, soothing, like water on a burn. She hadn't realized how much her ribs hurt until the pain began to recede.

Droë watched the Arrokad as she worked, abruptly aware of Ujie's body. She was naked. She was always naked. For so long now, since their first night in each other's company, Droë had taken this for granted. But that kiss...

The touch of the Arrokad's lips lingered on her own. And she couldn't help but admire Ujie's form, her hair, her grace.

"Where else?" Ujie asked, removing her hands.

Tentatively, Droë pointed to her temple, where Qiyed had kicked her. "Here," she said. She put her hand to her middle. "And here."

Ujie's smile was knowing, breath-stealing, as if she could read every nuance of thought in Droë's head. Likely she could.

"I wish to help Tobias and the woman," she said, blurting the words.

Ujie had raised her hands to Droë's head, but she stopped now, lowered her hands. "I believe you already have." She gestured in the direction of the dead Arrokad. "To do more would be unwise."

"Why?"

Ujie frowned. "I misspoke. It is not a question of wisdom, but rather one of commerce. There is a Hanev involved. And Belvora. We do not know what arrangements Qiyed made, nor do we know what other bargains have been made—freely and fairly. To involve ourselves, in the absence of commerce, as a matter of...of sentiment, would be irregular."

"Are you jealous of Tobias?" Droë asked, knowing she took a risk.

A long silence, and then, "Where you are concerned? Yes, I am. Then again, he owes me a boon, and so I wish to see him survive nearly as much as you do."

"Him you want for sport. I know you do. Perhaps I should be jealous."

To her delight, the Arrokad laughed.

"I will find another boon for him," she said. "And we will do what we can to keep other Ancients from intervening on behalf of his enemies. Would that be acceptable?"

"Yes," Droë said. "Now heal me, please. And then kiss me again. I liked that."

CHAPTER TWENTY-SEVEN

22nd Day of Sipar's Ascent, Year 634

Myles's Binder did good work and completed it quickly. Tobias had been slow to trust in her skill, and slower still to place faith in her duke's good will.

It seemed, however, that Risch had talked sense to the man. On the same day Tobias and the others left the dungeon, at the evening meal, Myles spoke to Tobias of his desire to overthrow the new supremacy.

"I will be regent to the princess," he said. "And regent only. Mearlan was... He was a brother to me. The girl might as well be my daughter. That's how I will treat her. And when the time comes, I will cede all authority to her. I swear this to you on my life and on the lives of my wife and children."

How could Tobias receive such assurances with anything other than grace?

"Thank you, my lord."

Myles shook his head. "Don't thank me yet. I have a good deal to prove to you, and I intend to begin as soon as possible. When you and Risch sail from here for Duvyn, you'll be accompanied by three ships from my fleet, each carrying fifty soldiers. We're past the time for concealing our intentions. Emella is our prisoner.

We've declared ourselves in opposition to the supremacy. So be it."

Tobias had to admit that he was both surprised and pleased.

Within three days, his chronofor had been repaired and a new one constructed. When the Binder presented them to him at that morning's breakfast, she appeared exhausted, her face haggard, her eyes red. But she smiled with pride and urged Tobias to try using them.

He retreated to an empty chamber—one that had also been empty a bell before—and Walked back twice, using both devices. His passages through the between, though brief in each instance, left him light-headed and breathless. It had been too long since last he used his talent.

Upon his second return to the present, he felt more hopeful than he had at any moment since his arrival in this time. At last, he had the means to combat Orzili, or, perhaps, simply to Walk back in time and prevent Mearlan's assassination. He would discuss their strategy with Mara before doing anything. If he did go back to stop Orzili from killing the sovereign, he and Mara would never again be together. History would be remade. She would have no reason to Walk back from fourteen years in the future to find him. And when he Traveled to his proper time, he would be nearly thirty years older than she.

He wasn't sure what would happen if they Walked back together. This was one of many questions he had for her. But now, they had options.

They set sail for Duvyn that very day, just after the tolling of the midday bells. As Myles promised, three ships bearing banners of gray and purple sailed with them. This time they did not intend to stop in ports along the way, nor would they keep their pace leisurely. They cared nothing for commerce—much to the consternation of the merchants who had accompanied them. Speed was all.

A strong northwesterly wind aided them. The sky remained clear, save for small wisps of cloud that scudded overhead. Sea eagles glided over the isle's western shores and whales breached to starboard, the spray from their spouts dissipating in the wind.

As much as he loved to be at sea, as fine as these conditions were for a voyage, Tobias begrudged every rise and fall of the ship. Now that he had his Bound devices, he itched to use them. And, of course, he desired nothing so much as to be back with Mara and Sofya.

They covered the distance from Trohsden to Duvyn in half the time it had taken them to sail north. On the evening of the fifth day, they entered the Firth of Rime and spied in the distance the lights of Duvyn and the dark mass of the pinelands fronting the shoreline adjacent to the city. The surface of the firth was glassy, reflecting the last light of dusk and the brightest of the emerging stars above. As they neared the city, Risch's captain ordered the lead ship onto oars. The crew furled the sails and went below to row. The other ships in their small fleet did the same.

Tobias intended to join the men below and take up an oar, but his eye caught on a small vessel coming their way. It was a skiff, oared with urgency by two men. Tobias called to Risch, pointed out the vessel when the duke and Ejino joined him at the ship's prow.

With the duke's ship headed in toward port and the skiff approaching from that direction, the two vessels were soon hull to hull. One of the oarsmen from the skiff scrambled up the lines to the deck, bowed to his duke, and presented him with a scrap of parchment. To Tobias's surprise, the man then handed him a second missive.

He unfolded it, recognized Mara's flowing hand.

On water with an old friend. – M

That was all it said. More than enough. Tobias closed his fist around the parchment and scanned the firth, searching for the familiar form of Seris Larr's ship. It took him a moment to remember that he searched not for the *Sea Dove,* on which he, Mara, and Sofya had voyaged for so many turns, but rather for the *Gray Skate*. The ship on which he sailed from Windhome, so long ago, so far in the future. For a dizzying instant, he had a sense of time's whorls, of life and history pulling him in a great arc, closing a circle that he wasn't sure he wanted closed.

"What does yours say?" Risch asked, voice flat.

Tobias continued to sweep his gaze over the water. "Mara is on Larr's ship. I assume they're on the firth somewhere. Yours?"

"Corinne has left the castle and taken up residence at my hunting cabin."

He did turn at that.

"Why would she go there?"

"An arrangement she and I first made many years ago. If ever the castle were in danger, and I was away, she would go to the cabin. It's deeper in my lands, safer for her in a way. Few even know of it, and fewer still know its location. She won't be quite as comfortable as she would be in the fortress, but if the castle is taken, she'll be hidden." He held out the message for Tobias to take. "What troubles me is the wording."

Tobias took the parchment. *I have your bow – C*, was written in a hand as neat as Mara's, and even more elegant.

"A code you've worked out?" he asked.

"No. I'm guessing at her meaning, and I'm confident that I'm right. But clearly she feared the note would be intercepted."

"So did Mara."

"I see no warships, but I would wager every round in my purse that the Sheraighs have come." The duke folded his missive and slipped it into a pocket. "Even if you spot the ship, we should ignore it, continue to the wharves. We may be watched."

Tobias's skin prickled. He checked the sky for Belvora. Seeing none, he nodded his agreement.

None of them spoke for the rest of their voyage. Tobias soon spotted the *Gray Skate*, but he didn't point it out, or even allow his gaze to linger on the vessel. She was anchored to the west of the city, at the point of a small promontory, her sails furled, her oars shipped. Other vessels bobbed on the swells near her. In the time he allowed himself to study her, he saw a few of the crew on the deck, but no one with long bronze curls and skin the color of his own, and certainly no child.

As the duke's vessel and those accompanying them made port, a company of at least two dozen men in Duvyn uniforms marched onto the wharf and positioned themselves before the ship. Risch's expression tightened further—it seemed this was not how he was usually welcomed home.

Almost as soon as the crew of the duke's vessel set a plank in place to disembark, a pair of soldiers boarded from the wharf, approached the duke, and bowed to him.

"What's happened?" Risch demanded.

"Fighting at the castle, my lord," said one of the men.

Tobias expected him to continue with a description of a siege, of Sheraighs surrounding the fortress, perhaps bombarding it with engines of war. The story he heard instead could not have been more different. It didn't take him long to understand that Mara had played an integral role in all that unfolded in the castle several nights back. He didn't know whether to be proud or horrified. A minister slain, soldiers massacred, bodies buried in an unmarked mass grave.

"Did we lose men as well?" Risch asked.

"A handful of wounded, my lord, but none killed. The Duvyn army acquitted itself well."

A frown flashed across the duke's features, only to vanish again. "Yes, of course. We will wait to leave the ship until all the soldiers from all the vessels are ready to march to the castle. Please marshal them into formation."

"Yes, my lord."

The two men left the ship. Risch and Tobias moved to the prow. Tobias begrudged the delay. He wanted to find Mara and Sofya.

"It sounds like it was a slaughter," the duke said, his voice low. He stared after the man who had spoken. "That's not— His pride bothers me."

Tobias considered what the soldier had told them. "They wouldn't have had a choice," he said, assuming this was so, hoping it was. "If the minister learned about Sofya, Mara wouldn't have hesitated to kill her. And once that happened—"

"I understand. And I don't blame her. Or the child. Or you. But my house is now in a state of war with the supremacy, and my wife and I will be considered traitors. Noak will hunt us down." He briefly met Tobias's glance. "I wasn't ready for this. Not so soon."

"I'm sorry, my lord."

Risch waved away the apology, but said no more. When all the ships had docked and the soldiers from Duvyn and Trohsden had mustered on the wharf, Tobias followed the duke off the ship and to the center of the company. They started toward the city, following the lane that led back to the duke's home. They hadn't gone far, though, before Tobias spied two men he knew: Moth and Jacq, members of Seris Larr's crew. Jacq was young, wheaten haired, tall, powerfully built, a fine marksman. Moth was older, bald, also good with a musket. They wore pistols on their belts, but neither carried a musket. That was probably wise, as larger weapons would have drawn attention. The two sailors eyed the duke's procession as it passed them; they weren't so foolish as to stare directly at Tobias.

"I see men from Larr's ship," Tobias whispered to the duke.

Risch stiffened, but didn't look. "Then you should go to them. Can you do so without being noticed?"

"I believe so, yes." The road curved some distance ahead of them. "Up there, I think."

"Yes, all right. Sipar keep you safe. Send word when you can. We're at your disposal should you need aid."

"Thank you, my lord," Tobias said, humbled by the duke's generosity in the wake of what had happened at the castle.

As they reached the bend in the lane, Tobias slipped away from Risch's side, stepped between two rows of soldiers, and ducked into a narrow byway. He didn't know if any had noticed, so he followed the alley to its end, turned away from the waterfront at that corner, and followed a circuitous route back to where Moth and Jacq waited.

He approached them from behind, on yet another byway, and cleared his throat loudly as a warning to them. Moth whirled, hand dropping to his pistol. Upon seeing Tobias, he relaxed, straightened.

"That's a good way to get shot."

Both sailors joined Tobias in the narrow street.

"I was in this alley for a tencount before you heard me. Who do you think would have been shot first?"

The bald man grinned and pointed at Jacq. "Him."

Tobias embraced both men. "It's good to see you. Mara is on the ship?"

"And the wee one," Moth said. He started toward the waterfront, but not in the direction of the wharves. "We've a pinnace waiting on the strand."

They walked quickly, saying little, watchful. At the strand, they pushed the boat into the firth, and the two sailors rowed them out into deeper water. Tobias held a fishing pole he found on the floor of the ship and pulled a straw hat—also on the floor —low over his face. In time, they rowed to the promontory and to the *Gray Skate* itself. It was possible they had been seen by enemies, but Tobias thought the men had done well to keep them inconspicuous. Reaching the ship, the sailors held it steady, and Tobias climbed the rat lines to the deck. Even in this, Larr and her crew had been careful, angling the ship so that the side he climbed faced away from the city and the more crowded waters.

Mara greeted him on the deck with a fierce hug and a hungry kiss. Sofya was on the deck as well, but had taken care to keep to the middle, away from the rails where she might be seen. She rushed to Tobias, nearly knocking him over when she threw her arms around his legs.

"I've been good," she said, sounding more mature than he recalled. He'd been away less than a turn, and he could see the changes in her.

"I'm sure you have, love."

"I don't wet anyone see me."

"Not anyone."

She shook her head, solemn, her blue eyes raised to his. "I'm impowtant."

He could only nod and say, "Yes, you are, love."

Seris Larr greeted him next, tall, grave, as formidable as ever. And after her, other sailors he had missed, including Bramm and Old Yadreg. Tobias felt like he had come home.

He and Mara sat at the ship's stern and spoke in low tones. He told her of his discussions with Myles. She described events at the castle, including her murder of the minister and Corinne's orders to the Duvyn army, all of which had unfolded much as he imagined. If Mara carried the weight of having killed the woman, she hid it well.

"We're back where we were in Herjes all those turns ago," Mara said, as Captain Larr joined them. "We're trapped on the ship. We have allies on land, but they may not reach us in time if Orzili can Span here with men and weapons."

"Then we should leave," the captain said. "I've seen no Belvora. We can sail for the Knot, or the Labyrinth, or anywhere else you might wish to go. The farther we are from here, the less likely he is to Span on board. Isn't that so?"

Tobias and Mara shared a look. Her reasoning was sound, but at this point, leaving Daerjen would be a betrayal of Myles and Risch. They had endangered themselves, their families, and their subjects, all in support of Sofya's claim to the throne. To leave them now would be to abandon them to charges of treason. They had set events in motion. They had no choice now but to see their plans through to the end.

"We can't," Mara said. "We've enlisted too many in our cause. It wouldn't be fair to them."

Tobias expected the captain to argue. She didn't.

"Then what will you do?" she asked.

Tobias watched Sofya totter around the ship's deck, as at home onboard as she had been before they left the *Sea Dove* so long ago. She appeared content, fearless, prompting a notion he would never have considered even a ha'turn ago.

"I have an idea," he said. He added to Mara, "I don't think you're going to like it."

Five mornings after the soldiers brought Orzili word of the uprising in Duvyn, Lenna finally reached Hayncalde. His Lenna, the one from this time. The only one he had left.

Her ship had docked late the night before, he was told. She chose to wait until morning to approach the castle. This annoyed him. He couldn't say why.

Yes, he could. Not so very long ago, she would have rushed to him from a recently docked ship. It would have been unthinkable for her to spend a night away from him if she didn't have to. One more barb in his heart, from a quiver he had thought empty.

Soldiers escorted her to his chamber and left them alone. She wandered the room, saying nothing for a long time. He watched her, unaccustomed to this younger woman. He hadn't been with the older Lenna for all that long—not in the context of their love, of their marriage—but he had been deeply taken with her. He had forgotten—again—how lovely this younger woman was, her skin smooth, her silken hair untouched by gray.

"This is impressive," she said, gesturing at the walls, the desk, the ornate rug.

He had to remind himself that this woman had never been in Hayncalde Castle.

"I don't know whose chamber it was," he said. "Some minister, I would guess. I've left the sovereign's chambers empty for when Noak comes."

Trivialities. A conversation for people who no longer knew how to speak to each other.

"Your voyage went well?" *Why in the name of the Two did it take you so bloody long to get here?*

"Well enough. Any word on the Walker?"

"Yes. I believe he's been in Duvyn, and in Trohsden. I think the princess is in Duvyn still. I intend to Span there today."

"Do you have tri-sextants?"

"I do now."

The Binder had finished them, at long last, two days before.

"So I can go with you."

That was more than he had expected.

"You'd be willing?"

"I want the princess dead, too, Orzili. We have a job to complete. *We* do. You might have forgotten that Pemin employs both of us, but I haven't."

He wasn't sure that was fair. He had been working with Lenna all along. Not this younger Lenna, but Lenna nevertheless. He kept these thoughts to himself.

"Thank you," he said. "I'll be glad to have you with me."

"Good. Where are my quarters?"

Another reminder that she wasn't his anymore, another slash at his heart. But this one he could avenge, even if she didn't know it.

He summoned a steward, had her escorted to the same chamber the other Lenna had used. A hollow victory, but he couldn't hope for much more.

Once he was alone, he tried summoning Glimik again. The Belvora hadn't come to him the previous night, nor did she now. Qiyed hadn't answered his call either. The Ancients had abandoned him, or had been defeated.

The possibility gave him pause, as did the realization, newly come, that Tobias and the woman had taken several tri-sextants from him. Enough to use as he did, if only they could find other Spanners to help them. He had to hope that they were so isolated, or so ignorant in the ways of tri- devices that they could not use the devices against him before he used his new ones against them.

This is your last chance.

The words came to him in Pemin's voice, utterly unwelcome. Yet, he couldn't deny the truth of them. Whatever advantages he had once held in his conflict with Tobias were nearly gone now. The tri- devices, the Ancients, his bond with Lenna. Soon, all he would have left would be the assassins he commanded. If he failed today, tonight, he would be defeated.

"Then don't fail," he whispered.

He strode to his door and told the soldiers in the corridor to have his assassins gather in the middle courtyard. He then gathered his Bound devices and his weapons, and walked to Lenna's chamber.

He knocked, entered, drawing a scowl.

"You haven't given me much time," she said.

"You took your time getting here," he said in a tone that, not so long ago, he would never have used with her. "We have no more time. We'll do this and you can leave; you'll have all the time away from me that you want. Until then, we're working on my schedule, not yours."

Her mouth tightened, but after a moment, she dipped her chin. "All right. Shall I bring my chronofor?"

"Yes. We might need it."

She joined him by the door. "Then I'm ready."

They hesitated, eyes locked. His heartbeat accelerated. He hadn't stood so close to her—to any one of her—in some time.

"You look...more yourself than you did in Fanquir," she said. She brushed a strand of hair back from his brow.

His breath caught and she smiled. He thought—hoped—she might lean in to kiss him. Instead, she fisted her hand in his hair, yanking his face closer to hers. He sucked air through gritted teeth.

"Don't ever speak to me like that again." She released him. "Now come along. We've a princess to hunt."

Tobias was right. Mara didn't like his idea at all. If she'd had a better one, she would have insisted on doing whatever it was instead. But she had nothing, and despite the risks, his plan had some chance of working.

Captain Larr allowed Bramm, Moth, Jacq, and three other

sailors to remain with Tobias and Mara. All of them were skilled marksmen. Mara sensed that Tobias had hoped for more support from the *Skate*'s crew, but given what they were asking of Larr and the others, he could hardly complain.

He also sent word to Duvyn Castle, and by midday, eighteen soldiers had joined them. A dozen were from Duvyn, and the balance from Trohsden. Twenty-six in their company in all, every one of them capable of shooting and fighting with blades. A small force, but a formidable one.

Tobias chose to position them near the wharves, assuming that Orzili would arrive there, be it by ship or by tri-sextant. They had a clear view of most of the city waterfront, and the lanes approaching it from west and east.

Tobias and Mara had enjoyed some success against Orzili's assassins, in part by aiming not only for the men, but also for the tri-sextants themselves. Mara suggested to the others that they do this again.

"If we can keep them from Spanning, it becomes a fair fight," she said. "And these are precise devices—it won't take a lot of damage to keep them from working."

They kept watch in shifts, unsure as to when Orzili might arrive. While Bramm and Moth scanned the coast, Tobias and Mara moved off some distance. He removed something from a pocket and held it out to her. It took her a moment to realize what it was.

A chronofor. She had known he intended to secure devices while in the north, but a part of her had doubted it would ever happen. They had been searching for them for so long.

"Is this for me?"

He nodded, pulled out a second device. *A second!* "This is mine, repaired now. It was given to me by Mearlan."

His was the more handsome of the two, not that this mattered. Hers was plain, but it shone brightly in the hazy sun and had a simple etched pattern of swirls on its back.

"Thank you," she said.

He studied the chronofor he held. "We've been after them for such a long time. I feel as though I should have used it already. I'm just not sure what I should do with it. Do I go back to the night Mearlan was killed and try to prevent all of this from happening?"

"It's been a long time. A lot has changed. Maybe too much."

"I know." He glanced at her, looked away. "And if I keep the assassination from happening, you'll remain in your time and we'll never be together."

She took his free hand. "You can come back to *our* time after you've stopped Orzili."

"I'll be old, at least compared to you. Forty-three? Forty-four after a Walk to the time of the assassination. And you'll still be fifteen."

Mara didn't say anything at first. The truth was, as much as she wished Mearlan had never been killed, she wouldn't have traded her time with Tobias for anything. As far as she remembered, they had never met before she came back to this time. That might change, of course, if he were to undo the entire misfuture. She might have memories of their friendship in Windhome, but that wasn't enough for her. How could she even contemplate a different life, one that didn't include this man?

"There must be other times we can go to, other ways to use the chronofors."

"I'm not sure there are," he said. "We've been fortunate, almost uncannily so. Yes, people have died—Gwinda and Ermond and too many others. But we've kept Sofya alive. We got her back from the slavers, and more than once we kept Orzili from taking her. Going back—doing any of this over—would be too dangerous. I know that we've been trying to find a chronofor for turns and turns, but there's a part of me that hopes we'll never need to use these. Because I can only imagine using mine to change something that we didn't want to happen. Something..." He shook his head, took a long shuddering breath. "I don't even want to think of what it might be."

Neither did Mara. She kissed him and put her arms around him. "It's better that we have them, even if we never use them.

Who knows when we might need to go back, even if just a single day."

They kissed again, separated. Mara slid her chronofor into her pocket, unwilling to look at it or feel it in her hand. She gazed out over the water toward Seris Larr's ship. Tobias did the same. She assumed his thoughts were similar to hers. Sofya was there, on that ship. Away from them and so, they hoped, away from the gravest peril. She hated the very idea of it, though, she had come to realize, no more than he did.

In all their earlier encounters with Orzili and those he sent in his stead, Sofya had been with them. Tobias was shot on the strand below the Notch. Mara was shot on Larr's ship outside of Herjes. And the Tirribin Aiwi almost managed to take the princess from them at Piisen's wharf, in the Knot. As Tobias said, they had been fortunate. He didn't want to take such a chance again, and neither did Mara. So they were on land, and Sofya was on the water, surrounded by an armed crew, in the care of a sharp-witted, courageous captain, a woman they both trusted above all other people in their lives.

Mara had never been so afraid.

CHAPTER TWENTY-EIGHT

26th Day of Sipar's Ascent, Year 634

Orzili wouldn't have allowed for the possibility a turn or two ago, but he grasped now that Lenna's mistrust had its uses. This Lenna didn't defer to him, didn't assume that he knew the best way to approach this latest attack on Tobias and the woman.

On the contrary. She viewed his past failures as proof that he had no idea what he was doing. Humiliating, yes, especially because he knew that her skepticism was warranted, but helpful as well.

She demanded that he describe for her every detail of his other confrontations with the Walkers, and soon came to a realization that had eluded him.

"Each time, you show up with all your men, all your weapons, and they see you coming," she said, explaining this as if he were simple. "Yes, the tri-sextants allow you to surprise them—I can see the value in that—but surprise hasn't done you much good, has it?"

When he admitted that this was so—and how could he deny it?—she continued. "The problem is, you give yourself no chance to figure out what approach might work best, and what won't. You're so taken with the advance, with the magick of tri- devices, that you've forgotten what made us so effective for so many years. There's a reason Pemin considers us his best assassins, and it has nothing to do with tri-sextants."

He shouldn't have needed her to tell him this. She had always been brilliant, but he'd long had faith in his own wit as well. As soon as she said this, however, he knew she was right.

He had the men trained in the use of tri-sextants take a company of soldiers to Duvyn Castle. Upon their return to Hayncalde, he sent a second group of soldiers to Trohsden.

Finally, he and Lenna Spanned with a third company to a spot near Duvyn city. Near it, not in it. They brought with them not only weapons and explosives, but also clothes that would allow them to draw as little notice as possible as they explored the city. They were Northislers, dark of skin, with bronze hair. They *would* be noticed, though no more so than Tobias and his woman. But at least they would have a chance to survey the terrain and learn something of their quarries' whereabouts.

The two of them left the assassins and Sheraigh soldiers who accompanied them—forty fighters in all—in the clearing to which they'd Traveled. Together, Orzili and Lenna entered the city through the north gate, posing as local craft workers. They had cloth with them. Lenna knew enough about cloth making—from long ago—to convince the gate guards that they were who and what they claimed to be.

Once in the city, they went to the marketplace and the warehouses by the water. They inquired about Lenna's cousin and his wife, Northislers like them, with a child. The family was said to be in the city, but they had yet to find them. Orzili remembered to ask about the merchant captain as well. A tall woman with a long face and dark hair. Well known in these waters, he thought. Her name might have been Larr.

It took some time, and several orbits through the market, but eventually his inquiries about the captain bore fruit. She was in these waters, another captain said, in the midst of haggling with a local peddler. She was in a new ship—larger than her old one, though not so much larger that the investment made much sense.

She had anchored to the west of the city, off the Duvyn promontory. The man knew nothing of Lenna's cousin.

As they left the market, Lenna asked him about the sea captain.

"She sheltered Tobias and the princess for several turns after he escaped Daerjen. She and her crew fought us in Herjes."

"So her new ship—"

"An attempt to evade me. Her old vessel was called the *Sea Dove*. I'm sure she gave it up because of the danger to Tobias. I'm equally sure that he's on board, or close by. Why else would a merchant captain anchor here rather than Hayncalde or Sheraigh?"

They made their way to the waterfront, this time asking no questions and keeping to narrow lanes. Soldiers in the blue and red of Duvyn patrolled the wharves and the coastal lanes. A cluster of them stood together in the distance, to the west of the waterfront.

Orzili and Lenna scanned faces, searching for other Northislers. Seeing none, they circled the market a second time, and then walked back to the piers. By the time they had walked the length of the city's coast, Orzili was convinced that Tobias and Mara must be on the ship. He looked to that promontory mentioned by the merchant, but saw no ship anchored there. Vessels dotted the firth, of course. There were dozens of them. Any one of them might have belonged to Captain Larr. It was also possible that none of them did. Could Tobias have left the isle already?

They halted. He sensed Lenna's growing impatience, shared it despite seeing the value in the time they had spent in the city.

"We should gather the men and attack the ship," Lenna said.

"If we can find it."

She regarded him, scowling, and looked toward the foreland. "There's no ship there!"

"No."

"A lie?"

"I don't think so. He believed what he was telling us. Tobias is too smart to remain in one place for so long. The ship could be anywhere."

"You think he's left Daerjen," Lenna said. She gave him no chance to answer. "I don't. He has allies here, and he wants to put the girl on the throne. He must, or else he wouldn't have dared return in the first place. He's still on Daerjen, and that ship is still nearby."

Orzili was inclined to agree and started to say so, even as he studied the shoreline again.

That group of Duvyn soldiers remained where they had been a bell before. Peering at them through narrowed eyes, he saw that there were others with them—some wore gray, the color of Trohsden. A few wore ordinary clothes. And the two figures standing a short distance from those in uniform—were they dark-skinned?

"Look west," he said, staring straight out over the water. "Don't be too obvious about it."

"The soldiers?"

"Yes, the two beyond them. Northislers?"

She didn't answer right away. When at last she said, "I think so, yes," her voice carried a new note of excitement.

"That has to be them. I'd wager they're looking for us." He cast a quick smile her way. "You were right. If we'd Spanned here, they would have been ready for us."

She replied with a smile of her own, and they started back through the city to the north gate, and then to the clearing where Orzili's men waited. There they made their plans. They would wait for late in the day when the sun was low, and they would Span to the strand west of where Tobias and his company waited. Tobias and the others would have to aim into the sun, while Lenna, Orzili, and their men would have a clear view of their targets.

They would bring the explosives as well, in case Tobias returned to their ship before sundown.

Their plans made, Lenna moved off on her own. In the past, Orzili would have followed. They would have chosen to be together, even if they spoke not a word, even if they didn't so much as look at each other. Now, he knew better. He let her be, moved away from the company in the opposite direction.

The wait was unnerving. He had pursued the Walkers and the child for so long. In a matter of bells, one way or another, it would be over. Or it wouldn't and Lenna would Walk back to earlier this day and tell him what he should have done. One way or another, Tobias and the princess would be dead by nightfall.

Tobias grew ever more unnerved as the day progressed. He had been so certain that Orzili would come, that he and his assassins would wink into view as they had each time before. He had marksmen with him, more than two dozen muskets. Orzili might have more, but they would arrive in a cluster—the one constraint to journeying by tri-sextant. By the time Orzili's men could take their formation, half of them would be wounded or killed.

That had been his thinking. As the day lengthened, though, and golden sunlight stretched shadows across the sand, his surety vanished.

"We should go back to the ship," Mara said, the fear in her voice echoing his own emotions. "I don't like this. Something feels wrong."

"He usually shows up at night," Tobias said. "He might still come."

"So you want to stay?"

Tobias shook his head. "Actually, no. I don't like this any more than you do."

He gave her hand a quick squeeze and started toward the soldiers. The Duvyn commander noticed him and strode in his direction, shielding his eyes from the sun with an open hand.

A musket went off behind Tobias, the report flat, too close. The commander fell, clutching at the base of his neck, blood darkening his fingers.

Mara screamed Tobias's name. He wheeled, gripped his

musket, dove to the sand, all in a single wrenching motion. Muskets crackled beyond where Mara had taken shelter behind a hulking, weathered tree trunk. She clutched her weapon but didn't dare expose herself to take a shot. A storm of bullets whistled above where Tobias lay.

He glanced back. The soldiers from Duvyn and Trohsden ran toward him, as did Bramm, Moth, and the other sailors. Several paused to fire, then ran on. Others fell and didn't move again.

Tobias faced forward as another musket boomed. A spray of sand stung his face from a few hands ahead. He couldn't remain here.

Gritting his teeth, Tobias scrambled for shelter. Farther from the water, among more driftwood. Musket fire chased him. Bullets sang in the air and struck the sand around him.

The soldiers and sailors had ducked for cover as well. They were pinned down. Five remained prone on the strand.

The sun was blinding, but through its glare, he could make out the forms of Orzili's company hiding along the edge of the pinelands fronting the shoreline. How could he have neglected to check the position of the sun at all times of day? How had he not considered the possibility that Orzili would flank him in this way?

He had mucked up everything.

Not everything. Not yet.

Eyeing the strand and the pine forest, Tobias thought he could work his way back to Mara. Then the two of them could join the others, maybe marshal them into some sort of formation.

He raised his weapon, peered over the wood protecting him, and fired. One of the figures ahead fell back. The stink of spent powder mingled with the smells of brine and pine and seaweed.

Tobias tried to get a better of count of Orzili's men, but another volley of musket fire sent up a cloud of smoke. He ducked down as bullets peppered the log in front of him. Chips of ancient wood rained down on him.

He dashed off the strand, in among the trees, and made his way back toward the others until he was even with Mara. He called to her, motioned for her to join him. She raised herself, fired in Orzili's direction, and sprinted toward Tobias. Halfway to him, she had to take cover again. She reloaded. Tobias took the opportunity to do the same, braced himself behind a tree. Mara looked his way, raised a hand, and silently counted off from three. On one, they both fired.

She ran the rest of the way, threw herself behind a tree near his.

Tobias waved his musket until he caught Bramm's eye. The sailor needed only to see where Mara and Tobias had gone. He and the others fired a fusillade at Orzili's men and took to the woods as well. Within moments, they were advancing on the assassins' position. Orzili and those he commanded took cover. The forest seemed to tremble with musket fire. Pale smoke hazed the air in the wood, and every tree appeared to have been gauged by bullets. But now that they were in among the trees as well, Tobias and the others struggled less with the setting sun.

Tobias could see now that Orzili's company included assassins in black, and also blue-clad soldiers from Sheraigh. They spread themselves deeper through the wood, trying again to flank Tobias and the others.

He couldn't tell how many Orzili had lost, but he knew he and his friends were still outnumbered. Orzili and those in black—and a woman he hadn't noticed earlier—were deadly with their muskets. The Sheraighs less so.

The soldiers Risch and Myles had given him were better than the sovereign's men, but no match for the assassins. Bramm, Jacq, and Moth, on the other hand, were outstanding. As Tobias watched, Jacq fired at an assassin who must have assumed he was concealed behind a pine trunk. Blood spurted from the side of the man's head. He was dead before he hit the ground.

Bramm shot another assassin in the shoulder. As that man went down, a golden object bounced away from him. A tri-sextant.

Tobias aimed for it, fired, missed.

An instant later, someone else snatched the device out of view.

Another consequence of Orzili's surprise attack: Tobias and the others had lost their chance to destroy any of the tri-devices. They needed to keep the assassins pinned behind trees so that they couldn't use the devices. A thin hope.

Their initial volley had killed a few of Tobias's allies but not the Walker himself, or his woman. Or the babe for that matter. Orzili hadn't yet determined where they had her hidden.

His own losses had been minor at first. Now that Tobias had led his force into the wood, however, the battle had taken a dark turn. The boy had some marksmen with him. Two of his best were down, one of them dead. Several of the Sheraighs had fallen, though that bothered Orzili less.

Lenna bore a cut on her brow from a sharp scrap of wood. When he expressed concern, she waved him away and fired again. It wouldn't keep her from fighting.

He had sent a small force—half his men, half the sovereign's—to cut off any escape Tobias might attempt, and to expose the Walker's force to a crossfire. He wasn't yet convinced that this would work.

"Where is the princess?" Lenna called to him.

Before Orzili could answer, another musket boomed. Fragments of wood exploded just in front of him, stinging his cheek, forehead, and neck. He dabbed at the spots but saw no blood on his fingers.

"They can't have her with them, Orzili. She must be on the ship."

A strong possibility. How then to find her? He surveyed the firth—what he could see of it from the wood. There were so many ships, he wasn't sure where to begin a search.

Fortunately, he had tri-sextants. He didn't have to study the vessels from a distance. He signaled to the nearest of his assassins—a tall dark-haired man named Sendil. The man sprinted from tree to tree, until he was close enough to hear.

"Gather the tri-sextants and five other men. Ours, not Sheraighs." Sendil gave the most fleeting of smiles. "Meet me back where we stowed the gear. Quickly."

"Yes, my lord."

Sendil hurried off. Orzili made his way back to where Lenna stood, her musket aimed toward Tobias's company. As he neared her, she fired, then cursed.

"I'm going after the princess."

"I'll come with you."

"You can't."

"I don't need your permission."

"Listen to me, Lenna. If I fail, we'll need to do this again, using a different tactic. The only way that can happen is if you Walk back and tell me what to do differently. We can't risk both of us."

Her expression soured, but she didn't argue.

"I need you to remain here and keep the Sheraighs in line," he went on. "Have a care. They're not as good as my men. Tobias and his soldiers may try to advance."

"We'll be all right," she said. He started away, but she stopped him with his name. "Get it right this time. I don't want to have to do this again."

Orzili tucked his chin and hurried back to where they had first arrived at the strand. There, he gathered the items he would need. He didn't have to wait long for his assassins to join him. Six, as he'd ordered. Three with tri-sextants, all of them armed with pistols and muskets. If this went as he hoped, they wouldn't need to fire more than a single round each.

Tobias and his allies couldn't see them from the forest. Orzili hoped the Walker hadn't noticed his retreat.

He and his men gathered in formation on the beach. He had the three with tri-sextants aim their devices at the nearest of the large ships floating on the firth. On his command, they activated the devices and jerked into the gap. Wind whipped his hair, scraped at his skin, drew streaming tears from his eyes.

It didn't last long. They emerged from the chaos of light and gale onto the deck of a merchant vessel. Orzili and the three men not holding the tri-devices leveled their weapons at the sailors aboard the ship.

"Who are you?" a man demanded. He stood at the stern, beside the ship's wheel. He might have been the captain.

"Stay still, and we won't hurt you. We're looking for a sea captain named Seris Larr. Do you know her?"

"No."

Orzili wasn't sure he believed the man. He pulled back the hammer on his musket.

"I don't know him. I swear."

Him. It seemed the man was telling the truth.

Orzili pointed at another ship, also large. "That one," he said to his men. "Now."

The gap again. It lasted less than a fivecount. This time the captain did know Larr, and even pointed them toward her ship, though he couldn't identify the precise vessel.

"She's one of those," he said, waving a hand at a cluster of perhaps a dozen vessels. "Now get off my ship."

Orzili saw no point in pressing the man. They were getting closer. They'd find her eventually.

The next captain proved no more helpful than the first had been.

Upon arriving at the ship after that one, Orzili and his men were met with pistol fire. One of his men fell, a bloody wound in his chest. A powerful impact spun Orzili. Searing pain in his left arm made him hiss. But he heard screams from belowdecks. A child. *The* child.

His remaining men fired at the armed sailors. Muskets, then rifles. Several members of the crew fell. Shouts from below told him that there were more armed sailors guarding the princess. That wouldn't matter.

Orzili crouched. His men loaded faster than the surviving sailors. More weapons fire, yowls of pain. He removed the two devices from the sack he'd brought with him. Not Bound devices this time. A different sort. The kind he had used against Mearlan.

He checked the fuses, motioned his assassins toward the ship's hatch. Reaching it, he ordered the men into formation, told them to ready the tri-devices for their return to land.

Then, with a flint and his steel blade, he struck sparks to the fuses. His first two attempts failed. His hands shook. He'd been so close so many times before. He couldn't allow this chance to pass him by.

A figure appeared on the stairway leading into the hatch. A pistol boomed from beside him. The sailor gasped, fell back out of sight. Orzili heard murmurs below, footsteps. He hadn't much time.

He struck steel to stone again. One of the fuses caught. He held this first fuse to the second. It lit as well. He straightened, threw both explosives down into the hold.

"Now!" he shouted to his men.

The gap swallowed them. Wind again. He squeezed his eyes shut.

They dropped out of the gap onto damp sand. Orzili stumbled, righted himself.

He wheeled, located that cluster of ships. From this distance, he couldn't make out which was Larr's. He would know soon enough. He watched, waited. Less than a fivecount.

Mara had just reloaded and taken aim when the ship exploded. And her world with it.

She stared out over the firth. A second detonation followed on the heels of the first. Flame and black smoke poured into the twilight sky. Burning debris rained down on the ships around the one that had been destroyed.

The *Gray Skate*. What other ship could it be? She took a step toward the water's edge. Halted. Swayed. Her stomach spasmed. She fell to her knees and heaved, emptying her stomach, her body convulsing.

"Sofya!"

Tobias's cry was like a spear through her heart. He screamed the girl's name again and again. She couldn't even bring herself to look at him.

Muskets crackled and a ball struck a branch less than a hand's width from her head. She forced herself up, fired, saw a Sheraigh fall.

Most of the others fired as well. Not Tobias. She forced herself to turn his way and wished she hadn't. He stood dumb, tears coursing down his face, his musket on the ground beside him. Forsaken, forgotten.

"Sofya," he said. Not a cry this time. Merely the name. He spun, was wracked by illness as well.

At length he straightened, eyed his weapon, and then the men they'd been fighting. He seized the weapon, raised it to his shoulder to take aim, and fired. In the distance, a man shrieked. He pulled his pistol and fired that. A woman's cry this time.

Tobias reloaded, not bothering to seek cover. Mara wanted to warn him, to beg him to hide, but she didn't dare. Nor did she have to. Bullets soared past in both directions. Nothing touched him.

He fired both weapons again. So did Bramm and Moth and Jacq and the soldiers from the two duchies. Mara should have joined them. She couldn't. She stared back over the water. The ship burned—what was left of it. Bitter smoke continued to pour into the evening sky. Most of the vessel's hull had been destroyed. The masts were a memory, the deck and rails gone as well. Only the bottom half of the vessel remained. No one could have survived. That was what her anguished heart told her. There was only one way to be certain.

First, she faced Tobias again. He already watched her, tears still running down his face, his eyes red.

"I love you," he mouthed without making a sound.

Her own tears blurred her vision. "And I love you."

They remained thus for a fivecount. She could guess at his thoughts, as he could at hers. She wondered if they would ever see each other again.

At the same time, they both turned, he toward the city, she

toward the shore. She paused to grab her sextant and continued on.

She pulled off her clothes as she neared the water, aimed the device, and thumbed the release as she took her last step to the water's edge, striding into the gap.

The distance wasn't great. Within a tencount she had fallen out of the wind and light into the briny swells of the firth.

She went under, surfaced, sputtered. When she could, she shouted Sofya's name. Nothing. She called for the child again and again, forcing herself to believe there was the smallest chance that she would hear the darling voice. She and Tobias had taught her to swim...

Not far from where she swam in place, the carcass of the *Gray Skate* continued to spew smoke into the sky. Wreckage surrounded her. Jagged scraps of charred wood, bits of cloth and food stuff. An adult human arm. There was more debris closer to the ship. She didn't dare look at it.

"Sofya!" She wailed the name.

No answer. The stillness of these littered waters shattered the last of her composure. Sobs shook her. She could barely remain afloat, but she refused to touch any piece of the ship, refused to rely on a spar of it for aid.

It was more than Sofya, though that wound cut deep to her heart. Seris Larr was gone, too. So were Starra and Yadreg, and so many others.

She raised the hand holding the sextant—her arm leaden. She recalibrated, aimed, and pressed the release. The gap dragged her from the surf, flung her through the cool evening air, dumped her on the strand near where she had left her clothes. She dressed in a sort of daze. Only when she felt the heft of the pistol on her belt did she remember that she should take cover.

But no. The shooting had stopped. Sofya was dead. What did Orzili care for the rest of them?

CHAPTER TWENTY-NINE

26th Day of Sipar's Ascent, Year 634

The force of the blasts surprised even him. He had known the explosives would destroy the ship. The sound, though—everyone stopped fighting for a moment. Tobias's force and his own.

Orzili had heard the girl crying below before he lit the devices. He had no doubt that he had succeeded at last. Tobias knew it as well. Hearing the Walker scream the girl's name had been profoundly satisfying. Only killing the boy would be better.

And he had every intention of remaining on this strand until the Walker and his friends were dead. All of them.

Then Tobias reclaimed his weapons and in quick succession killed Sendil and shot Lenna.

The assassin's truncated cry shocked him. Lenna's knifed through him like a toothed blade.

She fell back, blood welling from a wound to her chest. He ran to her, threw himself to the ground next to her.

"Kill him," she said, her voice a rasp. "End this, Orzili. Kill him now."

She needed a healer. Had she been hit with a bullet from a musket rather than a pistol, she would have been doomed. As it was, they had a chance, if they got her to a healer quickly enough.

"In formation!" he shouted. "Now! Tri-sextants! Back to Hayncalde!"

"Orzili, no. Listen to me! I'm dead—"

"You're not. You won't be."

His men appeared to be moving in slow motion. One had stopped by Sendil's body.

"Leave him! He's gone. But we can save her."

"Orzili—"

"Quiet!"

Even wounded, perhaps mortally, she glared at him.

"Save your strength," he said. Which is what he had meant in the first place.

Several of the others helped their wounded into the space defined by those with tri-sextants. Orzili resented the delay, but he could hardly deny these others transport while so intent on saving Lenna.

"Activate as soon as you can," he said.

"You're a fool." Lenna whispered the words, her eyes closed now.

If he lost her, he would—he would what? He couldn't go back and repeat this day. She was his access to the past. He would spend the rest of his life tracking down Tobias. That was all her death would leave him.

So she wouldn't die.

"Hurry up, damn you!"

"Yes, my lord."

"Orzili—"

The gap took them before she could finish her thought. He held her to him, aware of her breathing, her pulse, the warmth of her. And he prayed to the Two. He couldn't recall the last time he had invoked God or Goddess.

Their journey through the gap might have been the longest moments of his life. On and on the Span stretched, until he wanted to rail at his men for erring in their calibrations. Surely the Travel back to Hayncalde couldn't take so long.

His knees ached with the impact of their arrival in the castle courtyard. Lenna gasped at the drop from the gap. At least she was alive. So much blood, though. So much.

"Healer!" he called as loudly as he could. "We need a healer immediately."

This, too, took forever. Lenna said nothing, didn't open her eyes. Her breathing was too shallow, her pulse quick and weak. Yet she lived, which was all that mattered to him.

"Healer!"

"Yes, my lord. I'm here."

It was the same woman with short, steel-gray hair who had healed him more than once. She knelt on Lenna's other side and scrutinized the wound. Her expression tightened.

"My lord—"

"You will heal her. You will use every bit of magick you possess, and you will keep her alive. I don't care if you die in the process. You will heal her. And when you do, if you survive as well, I will give you more gold than you have dreamed of. Now, do it."

She exhaled. "Yes, my lord."

She put her hands over Lenna's heart and closed her eyes. Her glow kindled, pale and colorless as starlight. It surrounded her and Lenna, but was brightest under her hands, over the wound. Orzili watched them both, but mostly he eyed the healer, thinking that when Lenna's fate was determined, for good or for ill, he would see it in her expression.

The healer remained as she was for a long time, aglow, hovering over Lenna. Twilight faded to darkness. Stars emerged overhead. Her healing light illuminated the courtyard. Soldiers came and went, their shadows pale on the surrounding walls. Sweat slicked her face and dampened her hair. In time, her hands began to shake.

Orzili didn't move, despite the ache in his knees. He didn't know whether to be heartened or dismayed by how long this was taking. A part of him wondered if the woman really would kill herself trying to heal a mortal wound.

After a full bell and more, the healer shuddered and made a

small sound somewhere between a sigh and cry. Her glow faded, and she fell over onto the stone.

"Get blankets and pillows," Orzili said. He leaned close to Lenna. She breathed still. Her heart beat a strong rhythm. "The Two be praised."

He stood, wincing at the pain in his knees, and walked stiffly around Lenna to the healer. There he knelt again.

"Can you hear me?" he asked.

She nodded.

"She'll live?"

"Yes, my lord." A breathy whisper.

"And you will as well?"

She gave a weary smile. "Yes, my lord."

"Then you will be rich beyond all imagining."

"I have a good imagination, my lord."

He laughed and helped her to her feet. The healer ordered soldiers to set Lenna on a pallet and carry her to her chamber.

"She needs rest, my lord. Not a little bit, but a lot, and for a qua'turn at least. My power only goes so far, and she was nearly dead when you brought her here."

That sobered him. "Yes, all right."

He followed the soldiers to Lenna's chamber and remained with her after they left. For the next several bells, he dozed, took a much needed meal in the chamber, had a change of clothing brought from his quarters.

Through it all, Lenna slept. Her cheeks regained their usual color, her breathing was strong. The healer came to check on her and claimed to be pleased.

Early the following morning, as he paced the chamber, he heard a rustle from the bed.

He whirled, beamed to see Lenna gazing back at him, somber, but alive and awake. He stepped to his chair, sat, and took her hand. She didn't resist him.

"How are you feeling?"

"Tired. My chest hurts. How long have I been sleeping?"

"Several bells."

She settled back against her pillow, rubbed a slender hand over her sternum. "Tobias got away, didn't he?"

"It doesn't matter."

"Of course it does."

"Not as much as other things." He looked away as he said this, unwilling to chance gauging her reaction.

She tightened her hold on his hand.

"I'm grateful to you. I'm not sure I deserve what you did."

"That's not—"

"Listen to me. When I'm well, you should send me back. We can try this again, complete what we started."

"No. We did what we had to do. The princess is dead. I won't risk trying this a second time. What if we fail? What if you're killed?"

"Tobias won't let this stand, Orzili. You know he won't. For all we know, he's Walked back already to change the outcome."

"For all we know, he doesn't even have a chronofor. And correct me if I'm wrong, but if he were to succeed, we would know soon enough. Our memories would change, isn't that right?"

"Yes."

"Then he hasn't saved her yet. And if he does change history, we'll try again. Until then, I'm content with the outcome. I think Pemin will be, too."

She didn't argue. Nor did she release him. Rather, she caressed the back of his hand with her thumb, something she once did quite often. It had been a long time.

"You have good hands," she said. "You always have."

His cheeks colored.

"Tell me again about the night Mearlan died."

"Why?"

"Because I know what happened on the strand yesterday, and I should know this as well. In case."

He met her gaze. "You'd Walk to save me?"

He thought she might say something cutting, a jibe intended to lighten the moment. Another surprise.

"I would," she said. "I'd Walk to save us."

He made his way northward from the strand, bearing both his musket and his pistol. With each step, he felt the weight of the chronofor in his pocket. He couldn't bring himself to load his weapons. If he met up with Orzili or his men, they would kill him. Or at least try. He dared anyone to oppose him this evening.

His heart ached. For Seris Larr and her crew. For Mara, whom he loved so much, and who understood that he had to leave, had to do anything he could to prevent what had already occurred. For Sofya most of all. He could hear her voice, her giggle, her singing—sweet, slightly off tune. She haunted him. The blue eyes and silken black hair, the perfect features, the toddling steps across the shifting deck of the *Sea Dove*. Fresh tears streamed down his face. He wasn't sure he had stopped crying since the ship exploded.

He walked to Duvyn Castle. There, he stole to one of the sally ports, an entrance Risch had showed him, managing to avoid the Sheraighs positioned outside the fortress. The Duvyn soldiers he encountered inside the entranceway recognized him, though not before nearly putting a crossbow bolt in his chest. One of the soldiers asked if she should summon the duke. Tobias told her not to. He made his way to the chamber he had shared with Mara before he left for Trohsden, a voyage he might as well have undertaken in another lifetime.

He locked the door, peeled off his clothes, and set his chronofor for five nights before, when he knew from all Mara had told him that she would be there, and when he was certain he would not.

He pressed the center stem, surrendered to the between. Surely it was as noisome and harrowing as ever. He endured it without caring, without suffering. He had gone back farther, had survived worse. His world was desolated.

After a fivecount, or a bell, or a day, it was over and he stood in the middle of the dark chamber, his eyes adjusting to the gloom.

"Tobias?"

A whisper from the bed. He stepped to her, knelt. He wore no clothes, but what did that matter?

"What are you doing here?"

A sob caught in his throat. In the next instant he was bawling like a babe, as he hadn't since his earliest days in the palace at Windhome.

Mara put her arms around him, rested her head against his. "Tobias, what is it?"

For two spirecounts, he couldn't speak. By the time he raised his head to look at her, she was crying too. She knew. She had to know.

"Don't let me leave her on the ship," he said, his voice thick. "Don't let anyone stay on board. There has to be another way. Please find it. Don't let this stand."

They held each other, weeping, trying not to wake the princess who slept on the pallet beside them. An irony too bitter to contemplate.

"I have to go," he said after some time.

She clung to him.

"I love you," he said. "Never forget that. Never doubt it. No matter what happens, no matter what I do. I have loved you more than I can possibly say."

"And I you."

She released him, watched as he returned to the middle of the chamber. He didn't look at Sofya. He wanted to, but he couldn't. It would have broken him.

He reset the chronofor, pressed the release, and fell into the between.

26th Day of Sipar's Ascent, Year 634

He falls out of the between onto his knees, naked in his cold chamber, alone, bereft. Memories flood him.

Sofya is dead. That hasn't changed. As to the how...

Are these memories new or the same? He can't say for sure.

They thought it wisest to leave her in one of the warehouses near the wharves. Mara had argued with passion against leaving her in the care of Captain Larr and the crew of the *Gray Skate*, saying that he had begged her not to let him do this. He doesn't remember their conversation, but assumes it must have taken place during the Walk he has just completed.

It has made no difference. Explosives destroyed the warehouse, and those on either side of it. He and Mara and the others have done battle with Orzili and his assassins. Men and women have died and been hurt on both sides. All for nothing.

Sofya is dead.

His heart aching, his limbs heavy with fatigue and grief, he stands, sets the chronofor again. He has come forward five days, after going back that much. Now he will repeat the Walk. They will find another way. They have to.

He thumbs the stem. The between seizes him.

He sprawls to the floor of his chamber, chronofor held in a cramping hand, his legs too weak to support him. His passage through the between was not long, but he senses that this was not his first Walk of this night. Nor will it be the last. It can't be.

Sofya is dead, and Corinne with her. Hiding the princess at Risch's hunting cabin, deep in his ducal estate, was a terrible mistake. Also not the first.

Tobias recalls a prolonged battle with Sheraigh soldiers, a siege on all sides, a failed attempt to drive the soldiers away. Eventually, Orzili and his assassins Spanned to the forest. Their explosives obliterated the cabin.

Bramm and Jacq have been killed, along with most of Myles's men and several of Risch's. Tobias and Mara should be dead, too, but Tobias, in his rage and anguish, has managed to shoot a woman who was fighting by Orzili's side. He has known for some time that Orzili works with a woman, that he loves her. He can't recall her name. He hopes his bullet killed her.

As soon as the woman fell, Orzili ordered his forces into formation and Spanned away. In the confusion that followed, Tobias and Mara escaped the remaining Sheraighs.

He has told her, it seems, that they cannot leave Sofya in the warehouse. Now they know the cabin is not safe either. The castle then? All of these strike him as questionable choices. Why would they not put her on Seris Larr's ship? She would be protected, distant from the shore, difficult for Orzili to find, even with his tri-devices. They should leave her there.

This is so obvious to him that he falters. Somehow he knows that they have done this already, that this would have been the first choice of any version of himself, of any Mara. How many times has he Walked this night? How many times have he and Mara watched explosions kill their adored child?

More tears, more sobs.

The castle then. What else is left?

The mere thought of another Walk staggers him. But he is trying to keep Sofya alive. He is desperate to thread some path through time's whorls that will allow her to survive this night. One night. That's all he seeks. He will worry about tomorrow night tomorrow.

Another Walk of five days, based on what the settings of his chronofor tell him of the journey he has completed. Another conversation with Mara. If he fails again...

If he fails again, he will do whatever he must. He will not allow her death to become part of history.

He forces himself to his feet, enduring a wave of dizziness. Once it has passed, he depresses the central stem, falls back into the between.

The between tosses him to the floor of his empty chamber. He lands hard, rolls, slams into the wardrobe. His chronofor drops from aching fingers.

Memories.

Agony. Another failure. Sofya has died. Not the first time, certainly. An entire corridor of Risch's castle has exploded and burned. The duke is dead as well. And so many men and women. Only a fortunate shot that struck a woman in Orzili's company saved those who remained alive.

Tobias cannot think of what to do next. Mara has warned them away from hiding the princess in Risch's cabin. Intuition tells him that the ship and waterfront aren't safe either.

Where then? When?

He sits up, is overwhelmed by dizziness. He grips the edged of the wardrobe until the spinning of his vision eases. Retrieving his chronofor, he checks the settings. Five days.

Such a short Walk should not affect him so. How many times this night has he suffered the between?

And still Sofya is dead.

Orzili has won their war. None of the previous battles matter. He has prevailed this night, ending their combat on his terms.

"No."

The sound of his own voice startles him, but strengthens him as well.

"No." He says it again, and a third time. "No."

He first Walked back, so very long ago, to prevent a war. Why can't he do so again? What is there left for him to try but this?

He should sleep first, but he recoils from the idea. How can he possibly sleep? When this is over, he'll be dead, or he'll have time to rest. Until then....

Tobias dresses, reclaims his weapons and chronofor, and leaves the castle. He will need to find a way into Hayncalde Castle. He has a notion as to how he might.

CHAPTER THIRTY

26th Day of Sipar's Ascent, Year 634

"I love you," he told her earlier this day, the day their world crumbled and their life together was torn asunder. He hadn't managed to speak the words. His voice failed him as hers failed her.

Still, she knew a goodbye when she saw one. On the lips of the man she loved.

He also professed his love the night he came to warn her about the cabin. "No matter what happens," he had said five nights before in the dark of her chamber, "no matter what I do. I have loved you more than I can possibly say."

At the time, Mara was too overcome with terror for Sofya to understand what he was telling her. This continued to be true all the times since. She was certain they had relived that night again and again. He was trying to save Sofya, searching for the solution to a deadly puzzle.

Now though, she heard the words in her memory and she knew. She *knew*.

They hadn't found it.

They had been fated to fail. Sofya's death had been written in the stars, etched into history.

Which meant that Tobias was truly gone. He had given up on

changing this day's outcome in order to attempt one more Walk. A final gambit.

There was an ending in this, one she both dreaded and understood. She would have done the same.

She had to let him go.

Yet she had seen one other thing this day, and it kindled an idea. Something she could do. A solution of her own.

She wept as she prepared to leave Duvyn. How many tears had she shed this day and night? She didn't think she would ever stop crying. Sofya dead, Tobias gone. This very morning she'd had a family. Tonight she mourned.

Her grief, though, was tempered by resolve, by purpose.

Tobias had a journey to undertake. So did she. There was history at stake, a misfuture to confirm or correct.

He rode. He hated horses and would have preferred to make the journey on foot or by boat, but a mount would get him there soonest.

He took one of Risch's horses. Corinne wouldn't have denied him had he asked. The soldiers didn't try to stop him. They knew what he had lost, knew that he mourned their duke as they did.

They gave him powder and bullets, too. He didn't bother to tell them that they would do him no good. A Walker couldn't carry weapons or ammunition through the between.

After several bells in the saddle, he stopped to eat and drink and allowed the horse to browse and water itself. After the second leg of his journey, he allowed himself to sleep. He dreamt of Sofya, of course. He was running across a boulder-strewn strand, chased by Orzili and a host of Belvora. The princess slept in his arms, an infant again, as young as she was the night her father died. She bled from the cuts on her chin and temple that she suffered in the explosion that killed him. The sand softened as he ran, his feet sinking deeper with each step, his legs aching with fatigue.

He woke panting, soured by his own sweat. He wished he hadn't slept and vowed he wouldn't again.

When morning broke, he rode on. At midday he stopped in a small village and traded the duke's fine steed for a lesser mount, one that was fresh. He traded down again upon reaching Ysendyr, and traded one last time in the Faendor Highlands to cover the final eight leagues to Hayncalde. By the time he reached the gate of the great city, he was riding an old plough horse.

It was well past sundown when he arrived. He was hungry, exhausted. None of that mattered. He didn't enter the city, but instead made his way to the strand between Hayncalde and the Notch. Every step he took made him think of Sofya and of his dream. As if he needed to be reminded. As if the raw wound on his heart wasn't enough.

When he was far enough from the city gate, he said, "Teelo," and waited.

The Tirribin didn't take long to answer his summons. He looked pinched. His cheeks were hollow, the hair framing his face had grown long and lank. Tobias didn't know if Tirribin normally groomed themselves as humans did, but clearly Teelo had long since stopped caring how he looked. He wondered if the boy still hunted, or if sorrow had rendered him too empty to care for himself in even the basic ways. He could understand if this was the case.

"Tobias," the Tirribin said. His voice sounded the same. "I hadn't expected to see you again. There was an Ancient—she was a Tirribin once—"

"Droë."

"Yes. Did she find you?"

"We've spoken, yes. She told me... I'm so sorry about Maeli."

"You're kind to say so. Droë grieved for her as well. She wasn't kind to either of you."

Tobias shook his head. "That doesn't matter. She was... It wasn't in her nature to be easy. She was Tirribin. That was the essence of her. And I know she was everything to you."

He nodded. "She was. Thank you."

Teelo's voice had no inflection. Tobias couldn't tell if his words meant anything to the boy.

"You summoned me. Why?"

"I need your help."

Teelo canted his head. "With what?"

"I need to enter the castle, and I would like you to distract the gate guards."

"The human. The one who summoned the Belvora..."

"His name is Orzili."

"Droë spoke of him. You would kill him?"

"It's not quite that simple. He has..." Tobias's throat closed and for a moment he couldn't speak at all. "He killed Sofya. The baby. She's gone." Tears welled and fell.

"I'm sorry for you. Truly, Tobias."

He nodded. "I need to go back to when this misfuture began," he said, his voice cracking. "That's the only way to save her. I have to stop Mearlan from being killed. If that means killing Orzili, then that's what I'll do. But I need to Walk from within the castle. Trying to pass through the gates the night of the assassination is too risky."

Teelo stared at him, his expression sharpening. He had finally caught up with the implications of what Tobias had in mind.

"If you save the old sovereign, this misfuture will be repaired?"

"Possibly?"

"And Maeli—"

"I won't lie to you, Teelo. I can't promise you anything. Your kind—as I understand it, you're subject to some changes in history and immune to others. Isn't that right?"

The Tirribin dropped his chin ever so slowly. "Some folds of time pass us by. Others..." He flicked his thin hand in a sharp, circular gesture.

"Exactly. So we can't know if this would bring her back."

"There is a chance, though."

"There is a chance. I just don't want to give you hope where they may be none. It's possible that you'll help me, and you won't profit from it in any way. If you demand some other form of payment, even years, I would give it."

Teelo frowned. "You worry about commerce?"

"No. You're my friend. I worry about you."

The Tirribin's expression softened. "Since the day we met you, you have been...different from other humans. Kind, honest. I'm grateful for your concern. I'll help you despite the risks. I require no payment."

"Maeli wouldn't approve."

The boy actually smiled. "No, she would not."

They parted, agreeing to meet again in short order. Teelo's mention of Droë, however, had reminded Tobias of something. Once Teelo was gone, and he was again alone on the strand, he called for Droë.

Several spirecounts passed. Tobias grew impatient and wondered if this had been a mistake. He wished only to Walk and finish this, one way or another.

He called for Droë a second time and was contemplating a third summons when he spotted something riding the surf far out over the Gulf of Daerjen. As it neared the shore, Tobias recognized the transformed Tirribin. She clung to the back of the Arrokad, Ujie, much as she had the last time he saw them.

Before long, the Tirribin detached herself from Ujie, and together they waded from the shallows onto the wet sand.

To Tobias's surprise, the Arrokad spoke first and with concern.

"What has happened?"

His throat closed and his eyes stung. "The princess is dead," he told them.

"I am sorry for you." This was more sympathy than he would have expected from her.

"Thank you, Most Ancient One."

"If you summoned me to help you..." Droë began.

He stopped her with a raised hand and wiped tears from his eyes. "I summoned you because I wanted you to know that I'm going back to the night of Mearlan's assassination. If I can stop that..." He trailed off, unsure himself of what the result might be. "You've changed since that night. You've left Trevynisle, and become something...different, and you've forged a friendship with Ujie. I wanted you to know that it could all go back to what it was before. I don't know if your magick, or that of the Most Ancient One, can protect you from a shift in history. But it seemed...*polite* to warn you."

Droë nodded slowly but said nothing. Tobias remembered their encounter in Herjes and her cryptic responses to his questions about her transformation. At the time, he had thought her ambivalent about what she had become. He couldn't tell if she was still.

"This is why you summoned her?" Ujie asked. "The only reason?"

"Yes. Forgive me if—"

"There is nothing to forgive. On the contrary: You have done us a service." She considered him. "You are most unusual for a human. Most unusual indeed." The Arrokad drew herself to her full height. "Your debt to me is paid, Tobias of the humans. This is a boon, one for which I am grateful. For which we both are."

"Does that mean you can stop the change from touching you?"

She lifted a bare shoulder, let it drop. "I do not know. If we can blend Droë's time sense and my power, we might. Surely if any two beings between the oceans can do this, we can. You have given us...an opportunity. For that, I thank you."

"As do I," Droë said.

Ujie pivoted, took a step toward the water. Then she halted and held out a hand to Droë. The Tirribin faltered, but only for an instant. A smile lit her face. She took the Arrokad's hand and walked with her back into the surf.

Tobias and Teelo approached the gate to Hayncalde Castle together, Tobias keeping to shadows, Teelo walking down the center of the lane with brazen indifference. He threw a stone in the direction of the gate and its Sheraigh guards and yelled, "Long live House Hayncalde."

Then he ran, not at Tirribin speed, but like a normal boy.

One soldier pursued him, following him into an alley.

Teelo rounded on the guard, leapt onto him, and attached himself to the man's neck. Colored light, as slick as oil on water, lit the walls of the alley. The man screamed.

His comrades dashed in his direction, leaving only one soldier to guard the gate.

As soon as they were gone, Tobias approached the castle entrance.

"Who are you?"

"A friend of Orzili's," he said, walking toward the man. He didn't stop until he was directly in front of him. "I need to see him."

The guard gazed in the direction his friends had gone. After a moment, he glanced behind him, perhaps searching for someone who could carry word to his lord. He turned back to Tobias.

Who had already reared back to throw his punch. He connected with the man's jaw. The soldier stumbled back. Tobias followed. His second punch put the man on the ground. He took the man's musket and pounded it into the soldier's face. Blood gushed from the guard's nose. He didn't move again. Tobias thought it possible that he had killed him. He didn't care.

He assumed Teelo had gotten away from the soldiers. They would return soon. He hurried into the castle, stripping off his clothes.

CHAPTER THIRTY-ONE

21st Day of Sipar's Settling, Year 633

The between spat Tobias out like chewed gristle.

Naked in the cold and dark, he dropped to his knees, shivering, sucking at precious air.

He clutched his chronofor in stiff, frigid fingers and braced his other hand on the courtyard stone. Fear lifted his gaze, despite the droop of his shoulders, the leaden fatigue in his legs. Torches flickered in nearby sconces. Stars gleamed in a moonless sky. He saw no soldiers, no assassins. He heard not a sound.

Had he arrived too early? Too late?

He fought to his feet and turned an unsteady circle to get his bearings before heading to the next courtyard and the castle arsenal. No soldiers here, either. Panic rose within him like a spring tide. Within the armory he found a stained uniform in Hayncalde red, as well as a musket and ammunition. He didn't see any boots that would fit.

He pulled on the uniform and loaded the weapon. He took extra powder, paper, and bullets—habit. He had been on the run for too long. He knew he wouldn't have a chance to use them. This night would end in one of two ways. In neither scenario would he get off a second shot.

As he left the armory, he noticed what he had missed earlier. A body lay in the grass a few paces off the stone path. A woman with a gaping wound across her neck, and a bib of blood glistening on her uniform. A few paces on, he spotted a second dead guard on the other side of the path. Both from Hayncalde, both killed with stealth. Not too early then, perhaps in the very teeth of time.

He hurried on to the hall, bare feet slapping on stone. Nearing the archway that led into the back corridor, he heard the first explosion rock the west gate. Voices rose in alarm and anger. Bells pealed from the castle towers. Moments now. He stole through shadow and candlelit passages, only pausing when he reached the door.

Another explosion, not so distant, but also not the one he awaited. Inside the hall, men shouted.

A baby cried, a voice he knew so well. His heart folded in upon itself.

He gripped the musket, readied himself. One last explosion made the stone beneath him shudder and buck. His cue.

He kicked the door open, stepped through.

Bedlam. A haze of smoke. And the one he sought.

"Orzili!" he shouted, raising his weapon to fire.

Orzili had cocked his arm to throw the smoking explosive he held. He hesitated now, his attention catching on the sound of his own name.

Tobias didn't falter. He aimed, fired. Flame belched from the barrel. The report rebounded off the walls and ceiling, deafening. Through a mist of blue-gray smoke, he saw blood stream from the assassin's broken brow.

Orzili fell back. The explosive slipped from his hand.

"Get down!" Tobias cried. "Expl—"

The detonation shook the floor. Smoke suffused the hall. Debris flew in all directions, pelting down on Tobias and those around him.

He held on to his musket and kept his feet. Torches on the far side of the hall were extinguished by the blast; those closer to him flickered but burned on.

Through the ringing in his ears, Tobias heard men shout to each other. Some screamed in pain. Muskets boomed and flared through the smoke. A baby cried.

A baby cried.

She was alive.

Tobias started in that direction.

"Walker!"

He whirled. A woman stood in the same doorway through which he had entered. Bronze hair, skin the color of his own. She looked older than Tobias, at least older than he felt. She wore a tattered, stained gown of pale green. And she held a pistol, had it aimed at his heart.

"You think you've won," she said. "You haven't. He's dead now, but he won't be next time. With Walkers, history is never certain."

The hard crack of pistol fire made him flinch. He grabbed for his chest. But there was no pain, no blood. There had been no flame from her weapon.

The woman's hand shook. Tobias thought she was trying to maintain her aim. Blood trickled from the corners of her mouth. She twisted, her arm drooping. Her pistol went off, the bullet striking the floor to Tobias's left. She sagged, fell. Blood glistened in the center of her back. She didn't move again.

Another form appeared in the doorway. Also a woman, also bronze-haired, dark-skinned, armed with a pistol.

Mara.

She eyed the woman, even as she reloaded.

Tobias stepped to her, halted before her.

Mara met his gaze, grim as a warrior, as lovely as ever.

"You followed me back again," he said.

"I followed her back. She followed you. Again."

Of course.

He stooped, kissed her lips. "Thank you." He surveyed the wreckage in the hall. Weapons fire crackled in the courtyard beyond the hall, as it had the first time Orzili and his men tried to kill Mearlan. This time, though, Hayncalde soldiers within the hall had survived the attack. And Orzili and most of his black-clad assassins were dead from the explosion.

Mearlan's guards, led by the sovereign's minister of arms—alive but bloodied—gathered at the other end of the hall and fired from cover at the Sheraigh rebels. Mara and Tobias joined the fighting. It was a pitched battle, one that lasted well into the night. Orzili and the Sheraighs had subdued the gate guards and many of those atop the battlements. Still, with the leader of the attackers killed, and the assault on the hall thwarted, Hayncalde's guards gradually gained ground. When soldiers from the city walls and gates reached the castle, the last of the Sheraigh fighters were forced to surrender.

During the fighting no one bothered to ask Tobias and Mara who they were or why they had come. Now, the soldiers around them turned wary. Mara, Tobias realized, wore tired breeches and a torn shirt. His ill-fitting uniform and lack of shoes made him a curiosity as well.

"I would speak with the man who killed that assassin." Mearlan's voice.

Tobias started forward, only to be stopped when Mara spoke his name.

"You're there with him," she said. "You can't meet yourself."

He nodded, kept his eyes trained on the floor. "I'm here, my lord," he called. "But you must send your Walker from the hall before we can speak."

"Why?"

"Because I am him, and we can't meet."

Silence met this. After a tencount, Tobias heard steps and the open and close of a door.

"It's safe for you now, Walker. Come forward please."

Tobias held out a hand to Mara. She took it, and they walked together to where the sovereign waited, by a table littered with dust and broken pieces of wood and glass, stained with blood and spilled wine.

Mearlan eyed him, his gaze tracing the scars on his face.

"Your family is safe, my liege?"

"I assume they are, thanks to you. I have guards checking on them as we speak. They fled the hall and took shelter in another part of the castle."

"All of them? Even Sofya?"

Mearlan narrowed his eyes. "Yes, even Sofya. Your friendship with her in the future means much to you, doesn't it?"

Tobias tried to answer, found that he couldn't. Nor could he stop himself from weeping.

"What happened to you?" the sovereign asked. "Your scars—"

"He was tortured by the man he killed tonight," Mara said for him. "This is not the first time he's survived this attack. The first time...you were killed, my liege. You and your family. Except Sofya. He kept her safe. We both did. Orzili—the dead man—he tortured Tobias in your own dungeon, trying to make him reveal where the princess was hidden."

The sovereign, the young Mearlan whom Tobias recalled as arrogant and quick-tempered and too set in his ways, offered him a look of deepest compassion and gratitude.

"I am in your debt, Walker. And in yours," he said to Mara. "But there is more to your story, isn't there?"

"There is," Mara said. "But it's...it's lost history now. This is the thread of time that matters. Orzili is dead, as is the Walker who would have allowed him to try again to kill you."

"They worked for the autarchy, my liege," Tobias said, finding his voice. "I believe Pemin is behind all that happened tonight."

"And yet, you've told me—the other you—that I shouldn't go to war against him."

"That's right. This was his response to learning that you had sent a Walker back so many years."

"His response? He knew?"

"Yes, my liege. Gillian Ainfor and Bexler Filt are traitors to your court."

The sovereign's expression ossified. "Thank you, Walker. They will be dealt with." He summoned a guard and ordered the man to find the minister and Binder. "Imprison them if you can; kill them if you must." As the soldier hurried away, Mearlan faced

Tobias and Mara again. "My debt to you grows. How can I repay you?"

"I would see your daughter, if I may," Tobias said, his voice quavering.

Mearlan smiled. "Of course."

Accompanied by twelve guards, Mearlan, Tobias, and Mara left the hall and made their way to a chamber on a lonely corridor in the farthest, highest reaches of the castle. There, they found still more soldiers, as well as Keeda, the sovereign queen, the sovereign's son, Mearlan V, and the infant princess, who slumbered in her mother's arms.

Tobias was overcome again when he saw the child. Relief, love, loss. Together it was more than he could handle. Mara cried as well. Keeda appeared puzzled by all of this, but she merely looked a question at the sovereign, who shook his head.

Tobias wanted to hold Sofya, to kiss her brow. He didn't dare ask. This child didn't know him. She wouldn't squeal with delight at the sight of him. She wouldn't grab his shirt in her fist and smile at him around her thumb. She wasn't old enough to call him "Papa" or run to him headlong on her tiny, chubby legs.

He had to content himself with the surety that she was alive and safe and with people who loved her as much as he and Mara did.

He turned away. "Thank you, my liege," he said, his voice rough.

"Of course. We'll have quarters arranged for you. And we can discuss your future on the morrow."

Tobias couldn't help but smile at this. Mara caught his eye, and they began to laugh.

Mearlan frowned. "Did I say something funny?"

"No, my liege. It's just...our futures have been uncertain for some time now."

His explanation did little to ease the sovereign's expression. This only made Tobias and Mara laugh more.

"Forgive us, my liege. We're tired. And relieved that you and your family are well."

"Yes, all right." Mearlan still looked perplexed and, Tobias thought, a little annoyed. "Find them a place to sleep," he said to a soldier, eager, it seemed, to have them gone.

They were on the water, wrapped in a cocoon of magick. Ujie had shaped it. Droë had guided her, tasting the Arrokad's power as it formed and reformed, until at last Droë sensed that it had taken them beyond the reach of time.

Ujie swam them through the currents of the Inward Sea. Not quickly. They were waiting, both of them, wondering what would happen if Tobias succeeded.

"I feared that you would choose to go back to the way you were," Ujie said, ending a long, long silence.

I feared...

Droë felt her cheeks heat. Could Ujie tell?

"Not so long ago, I would have."

"What has changed?"

Unfair, that.

"I think you know."

"I would like you to speak the words."

She could hear her heart beating, feel the rush of blood to her face, her neck, her body. Everywhere. The places where she touched Ujie seemed to burn with the most delicious of fires. She pushed herself off of the Arrokad and swam in place as Ujie turned in the water to face her. A light rain fell. The air might have been cold. She couldn't tell.

"What has changed is that I have found love."

Ujie's lips curved into a smile.

After a tencount, Droë said, "It's rude not to respond in kind to a statement like that."

"Is it?" Ujie asked, playful. "Is the Tirribin now an expert in the ways of love?"

"No, like others of her kind, she's an expert in all things rude."

Ujie laughed, full-throated, tipping her head back in the drizzle. With a single stroke of her lovely, sinuous arms, she closed the distance between them.

She touched her lips to Droë's, the slightest brush. Exquisite and promising.

"I have found love as well, Droë of the Tirribin. It is most unexpected, and most welcome."

Before Droë could answer, she sensed a ripple in the world around them. She threw her arms around Ujie and clung to her.

Time shifted. History curved, skipped. Misfuture gave way to something else, something uncertain, but not necessarily wrong.

It was over as quickly as it began. A hiccup in the flow of bells and days and turns. Most—human and Ancient—would notice nothing, would continue their lives unaware of what had happened.

A Tirribin would not. An Arrokad might. An Arrokad sheathed in magick...

She remained as she was. In her grown form. Their magick had accomplished that much. Had it done all? She searched Ujie's silver eyes, seeking recognition. And finding more.

"You are still here," Ujie said. "Still transformed."

"And still loved?" Droë asked.

"Yes. And still that."

Droë kissed her, swam around her, and climbed onto her back. "Then take me somewhere. Somewhere I've never been before."

The Arrokad laughed. "Where?"

"Just swim, Ujie. The world is remade tonight. Everywhere is new."

Pemin woke to the tolling of morning bells, as he did every morning. Servants attended to him as he bathed and dressed. Later in the day, he and Deya would return to the range for another of their archery contests. The prospect of their play should have pleased him. Today it didn't.

He brooded, obsessed with Mearlan and Daerjen's interference with his ambitions in the Bone Sea to an extent he hadn't been in some time. Open warfare would have been preferable to this game they played, this advance and retreat, feint and feint again. It should have been easier to draw the man into conflict. Daerjen's sovereign had shown unusual patience. He was more canny than Pemin had credited.

His thoughts snagged on this realization, like a loose thread caught on a sliver of wood. Why hadn't he done anything about this? What had stayed his hand for so long?

The answer was both obvious and oddly unsettling. There was nothing he could do. Yes, he had assassins in his employ, but none he trusted with an attack over such distance, on a target so difficult to reach. Perhaps if he had a Walker...

Another snag.

His ruminations were disjointed this morning, his desires stubborn in their refusal to reconcile with limitations he knew to be insurmountable.

And yet...

He left his chamber, striding past the guards who stood outside his door. Without a word or gesture from him, they fell in step two paces behind and followed as he strode through corridors, down a flight of steps, along another passageway. He halted before a plain door. He wasn't sure why. This chamber... Pemin couldn't remember the last time he had been in it. He couldn't have said whom he expected to find within when he lifted the door handle and entered the room.

A bare pallet, an empty wardrobe, a dust-covered night table.

Why would a barren chamber bring such...disappointment?

One of the men behind him cleared his throat.

"Is there something wrong, Your Excellency?"

He shook his head. What or who had he thought to find here?

He stepped out of the chamber, closed the door behind him. The guards watched him, wary expectancy in their gazes.

Pemin was not a man given to explaining himself to anyone, much less lowly soldiers, but he felt compelled to say, "I had a memory of... It's been too long since last we had guests in our home. I will speak of this with the queen."

"Yes, Your Excellency."

Pemin pivoted and started back toward his chamber. The men walked behind him, swords jangling. At the first corner, he paused to stare back at that door. Something hovered in his mind, barely beyond the reach of knowledge or memory. He couldn't say, though, what it was. Likely a dream.

Yes, a dream.

Satisfied with this, Pemin walked on.

Tobias and Mara slept late into the morning. Their chamber was cold when Mara woke, their fire long since burned out. Tobias slept on. Mara rose, dressed, and left the chamber. There was a conversation she needed to have.

She asked a guard where she would find him, navigated the corridors with his instructions, and knocked on what she hoped was the correct door.

At a word from within, she entered.

Tobias stood near the hearth, dressed in ministerial robes. He looked younger than her Tobias. His face was smooth, unmarked by scars. He was beautiful, and yet she thought he looked...wrong.

"May I help you?" he said.

"I'm Mara," she said. "I'm here with the other you."

"You're Mara? How is that possible? Mara is a Spanner."

"And a Walker. It's me, Tobias. I swear to you."

After a brief hesitation, he nodded and motioned her into the chamber. She entered, closed the door behind her.

"I want to tell you what's happened. What the other you has been through. I think you should know before you go back to your time, if that's your intention."

"It is. But why? It seems to me there's risk in telling me these things."

She shook her head. "That future—that *mis*future—is gone.

Whatever follows from today will be different. And I believe you should know who you are, who you became in the darkest of times. You deserve to feel the same pride in you that I do, and that the other Tobias does, even if he doesn't know it yet."

He weighed this, looking young and beyond his depth. "All right," he said. He sat on his pallet. She sat in a chair by the hearth. And she related all that she could, sharing her own memories, and also things that Tobias had told her, that she hadn't lived through herself.

This Tobias interrupted her occasionally with questions. He was especially interested in his time in the Hayncalde dungeon. Mara said little about her relationship with the other Tobias. She didn't hide that they were in love, but neither did she dwell on that. For her purposes this day, other elements of the tale mattered more.

She spoke for the better part of a bell, and when she was done, Tobias kept still, clearly moved, perhaps troubled as well.

In time, he roused himself, met her gaze. "Thank you for telling me. I'm... I don't know what to say. This other me—he's done things I wouldn't dream of doing. Heroic things. And terrible things as well."

She bristled at this but tried to hide her anger. This Tobias was young, innocent. There was, to her mind, less to him than there was to the man she loved, though obviously the seeds of what her husband had become resided in this lad as well.

"He did what was necessary," she said, filling an uneasy silence. "*You* did what was necessary. Don't judge him or yourself too harshly. We kept Sofya alive for as long as we could, and when we lost her, we found a way to bring her back. Nothing else matters."

He nodded, no doubt sensing her resentment. For a spire-count, neither of them spoke. At last, Mara stood and left him. She didn't think they would speak again before he left for his future. She didn't wish to.

Mearlan granted Tobias and Mara an audience later that day. He offered them gold, positions in his court, residence in his castle.

They thanked him, asked him for time to decide, which he granted. As they prepared to leave his hall, Tobias remembered something he should have told the sovereign the previous night.

"You have a friend in Duvyn, my liege. You know this, of course, but I wanted to tell you anyway. In the future we experienced, Risch risked his life repeatedly to keep your daughter safe. So did Corinne. And, for that matter, so did the duke of Trohsden. They were as loyal to your memory and your line as they are to you yourself."

"Thank you, Walker. That is good to know."

That night, after dining with the sovereign and his family, Tobias left Mara in the castle and made his way to the waterfront. There, with more than a little trepidation, he said, "Teelo of the Tirribin, I would speak with you."

He didn't have to wait long.

A small figure blurred into view, halting a short distance from him, head canted, pale eyes wide. He looked as Tobias recalled from their first encounter—beautiful, mischievous.

"You're a Walker," the demon said.

"Yes, I am."

"There is a price for summoning a Tirribin, even for one such as you."

"I understand. But—"

"There is no but." A second voice. A girl's voice.

Tobias wheeled. Maeli stood at the mouth of an alley.

"Why would he summon you and not me?" She strolled to where her brother stood, hands behind her back, her steps as light as a dancer's.

Tobias smiled to see her. He nearly laughed aloud.

"I don't like the way he's looking at me," she said. "He's odd. Not rude. Not yet at least. But very odd."

"I'm— I'm glad to see you, Maeli."

"How do you know my name?" She flicked a slender hand toward her brother. "Or his, for that matter?"

"We met in a different future. You were my friends. I'd like to think you still are."

Maeli started to say something, but Teelo held up a hand, stopping her.

"I sense a misfuture," Teelo said. "More than one, actually. Layered upon each other."

"I believe this is the one that will go forward."

"And you summoned me because something happened to Maeli. You didn't expect to see her, did you?"

Tobias paused, shook his head. "No. I came back with your help to fix many things. This was one of them."

Teelo dipped his chin, solemn as a cleric. "Then the debt for your summons is paid."

"Thank you. I can offer a riddle as well. It's one I think you'll like."

They nodded in unison, eager as children.

"It goes like this:

Down I live, up I die,
In dark I thrive, in day turn dry;
Half of a whole, I mirror my twin,
But lack the glory, of her tresses and skin."

The Tirribin huddled together, hands blurring as they spoke in low tones. Tobias watched them, smiling, his heart full. The humans of Hayncalde, he was sure, would have preferred to have only one time demon in their midst rather than two. He understood, but he didn't care. Without Maeli, Teelo would have wasted away and died in misery. They belonged together. Anyone could see that.

Eventually, to their great satisfaction, Tobias gave them the answer to his riddle. The Tirribin thanked him, told him to summon them again with more riddles, and left him to hunt.

Tobias returned to Hayncalde Castle and the chamber he shared with Mara.

She sat in the glow of the fire, clad in a robe, her eyes and hair shining. She glanced up at him as he entered and locked the door.

"The other you is gone, back to our time. A guard brought word a short while ago."

"You weren't tempted to go with him? He's prettier than I am."

He smiled. She didn't.

"I wasn't tempted for a moment. And there is no one more beautiful to me than you are."

He crossed to her, knelt by her chair. She took his hand and raised the back of it to her lips.

"We can stay here if you like," she said. "Stay close to Sofya. This Sofya."

"This Sofya," he repeated. He bent close to her, his forehead pressed to hers. "I don't want to stay. I can't."

She pulled back, hazel eyes questioning.

"Sofya is safe and with her family. That's as it should be. And we made it possible. But you said it yourself. This isn't our Sofya. This Sofya will be raised as a princess, not as a fugitive." He smiled, his vision swimming with tears. "Or a sailor, or a warrior. And that's as it should be, too. I just can't stay here to see her grow up. It would hurt too much to be with her, and to know that she remembers none of it."

"For me, too," Mara whispered, her lips quivering.

He inhaled deeply, breathed out. "The future is ours now. Not Mearlan's or Sofya's, not Orzili's. It's ours."

"And have you thought of what you want to do with it?" she asked. "Where you want us to go?" He heard something in her voice.

"I haven't, but you have. I can tell."

A soft smile lit her face. "Yes, I have. I want to go back to sea. I want to find Seris Larr's ship and join her crew."

"She doesn't know us in this time."

"She doesn't have to. Two Walkers? One of whom can Span? Both of us with Bound devices? She'd be mad to refuse us."

He couldn't argue.

"All right, to sea it is."

"And then I think we should have a baby. Or two. Or even three."

He grinned again. This time they both did.

"I believe," he said, "that Captain Larr would tell us a ship is no place for one child, much less a brood of them."

"Yes, well that's the price she pays for adding Walkers to her crew." She laced her fingers through his. "Honestly, Tobias, I don't care what we do. I want a life and a family and a home, even if it's a floating one. And I want all of that with you. The rest is..." She shrugged, the smile warming, deepening. A moment passed. "So? What do you think?"

He leaned forward and kissed her. "I think that sounds perfect."

"Which part?"

"All of it. Whatever you want. You've followed me through time, through history. So now it's my turn to follow you across the seas."

They kissed again. He slipped into the chair beside her. And they held each other, and watched the fire burn, and listened as the midnight bells in the castle courtyard rang in a new day.

GLOSSARY OF TERMS

Aperture — A Bound device used by Crossers. An aperture is a golden circlet that expands and contracts according to the needs of the Crosser. When placed against a wooden or stone surface, it creates a portal that allows the Crosser to move through that surface.

Arrokad — Creatures of the sea, they are considered by humans to be demon-kind. They take human form and possess magicks that remain poorly understood. Capricious, sexual, powerful, dangerous, they can be reasoned with and bargained with, though their tolerance for human interaction is limited.

Bell — A measure of time equal to fifty spirecounts. There are twenty bells in a day.

Belvora — Also known as magick demons, they are winged predators, tall, muscular, lethal, but slow-witted. They are found mostly in Northern waters, near the Labyrinth and the Sisters, the isles from which Travelers and Seers hail.

Between, The — The space traversed by Walkers as they navigate from one time to another. A place of intense sensory stimulation, totally lacking in breathable air.

Binder — A crafter, usually employed in noble courts, who shapes and imbues with power the gold devices (apertures, chronofors, and sextants) used by Travelers.

Chronofor — A Bound, golden device used by Walkers. A chronofor resembles a chainwatch, but has three dials on its face, and three corresponding stems to set those dials, which represent turns, days, and bells. A fourth stem activates the device.

Crosser — A Traveler who can move through solid matter—stone or wood—with the use of an aperture. A Crosser who encounters metal or some other material created by humans during a Crossing risks injury or death.

Fivecount — A measure of time equal to the amount of time it takes to count to five.

Gap, The — The space traversed by Spanners as they navigate from one location to another. A place of significant sensory stimulation and stinging wind.

Ha'turn — A measure of time equal to fifteen days.

Kant — A small- to medium-sized merchant ship made in Kantaad.

Healers — Most similar in their magick to Binders, Healers can mend wounds and ease illness, though their powers are limited and they are not proof against death.

Kheraya — The Goddess, who represents birth, war, sexuality, water, the heat of summer.

Magi — Also known as Seers, they include those who can divine the future, perceive truth or falsehood in the words of others, and remember in perfect detail everything they see or hear. For their ability to manifest, they must constantly imbibe (through drink or vapor) tincture, a highly addictive spirit.

Marauder — A large warship made in Oaqamar and used by Oaqamaran navy.

Press, The — The traverse experienced by Crossers as they move through matter, which can include painful compression of the body, blindness, and deafness.

Quad — A square brass coin, the least valuable of Islevale currency.

Qua'turn — A measure of time equal to approximately seven days.

Round — A round, gold coin equivalent to twenty silver treys.

Seer — Also known as Magi, they include those who can divine the future, perceive truth or falsehood in the words of others, and remember in perfect detail everything they see or hear. For their ability to manifest, they must constantly imbibe (through drink or vapor) tincture, a highly addictive spirit.

Sextant — A Bound, golden device used by Spanners to cover great distances. A sextant includes an arc for plotting distance, an eyepiece for selecting a route, and a trigger for activation.

Shonla — Also known as mist demons, they only exist with clouds of vapor, though not all mists carry Shonla. They are vaguely human in form, smell of must, and bring cold. They are linked to one another and have knowledge of events occurring all through the world. They swallow sound and can be bribed with song. They disorient those at sea and even on land, feeding on screams. But they are not truly deadly.

Sipar — The God, who represents death, peace, love, land, the cold of winter.

Spanner — A Traveler who can cover great distance in a short period of time with the use of a sextant.

Spirecount — A measure of time equal to the amount of time it takes to count to one hundred. There are fifty spirecounts in a bell.

Tencount — A measure of time equal to the amount of time it takes to count to ten.

Tincture — An addictive and narcotic spirit used by Seers (Magi) to enable their talents for divination, perception, and remembrance.

Tirribin — Also known as time demons, they appear as children, beautiful, but smelling faintly of rot and decay. They are deadly, preying on humans and consuming their years. They have an understanding of time that goes far beyond that of humans, even Walkers. But they can be distracted by riddles.

Traveler — Often a native of the Sisters or Sipar's Labyrinth, trained on Trevynisle, and assigned to a noble court, s/he can be a Crosser, Spanner, or Walker. A Traveler expresses his/her talent through the use of a Bound device (aperture for a Crosser, sextant for a Spanner, chronofor for a Walker). Travelers using these traditional devices must Travel unclothed and unburdened by any objects save the devices themselves.

Trey — A triangular silver coin equivalent to ten brass quads.

Tri-Aperture — A Bound, golden device resembling an aperture, but constructed in three circlets that intersect to form a wedge. Three Crossers, standing in a triangular formation, can move themselves and any people standing in the space defined by their positions through matter, so long as one of the people within the triangle is also a Crosser bearing a traditional aperture. Crossers Traveling by tri-aperture can be clothed and can bear objects in addition to their bound devices.

Tri- Devices — Bound, golden devices developed in the 630s and used by Travelers. They enable groups of Travelers to Span or Cross together, fully clothed and bearing objects, including weapons. There are tri-apertures and tri-sextants. There are, as of yet, no tri-chronofors.

Tri-Sextant — A Bound, golden device resembling a sextant, but constructed with three arcs. Three Spanners, standing in a triangular formation, can transport themselves and any people standing in the space defined by their positions, so long as one of the people within the triangle is also a Spanner bearing a traditional sextant. Spanners Traveling by tri-sextant can be clothed and can bear objects in addition to their bound devices.

Turn — A measure of time equal to thirty days and corresponding to the cycle of the moon.

Two, The — Kheraya and Sipar, the Goddess and God, worshipped in some isles or cities in tandem, and in others individually.

Walker — A Traveler who can move through time with the use of a chronofor. For each day a Walker moves backward or forward through time, s/he ages a corresponding day.

The Year:

Each season is equal to three turns; each turn is equal to thirty days.

Spring:

(Kheraya's Emergence — Equinox, Goddess's day, first day of the year. Powerful, sensual day and night.)

Kheraya's Stirring — Storms and wind, the first hint of life's return

Kheraya's Waking — Warm, rainy, peaceful, plantings begin the northern isles

Kheraya's Ascent — Warmer, blooming, resplendent, plantings begin in the southern isles

Summer:

(Kheraya Ascendent — Summer Solstice, a day of feasts, celebration, gift-giving)

Kheraya's Descent — Hot, dry, northern crops begin to come in

Kheraya's Fading — Hot, stormy, southern crops begin to come in

Kheraya's Settling — Hot, languid days

Autumn:

(Sipar's Emergence — Equinox God's day, the pivot of the year. Powerful, sensual day and night.)

Sipar's Stirring — Stormy, windy, harvest begins in the southern isles

Sipar's Waking — Cool, clear, harvest begins in the northern isles

Sipar's Ascent — End of harvest, leaves changing, resplendent

Winter:

(Sipar Ascendent — Winter Solstice, a day of fasting, contemplation)

Sipar's Descent — Cold, snows begin in southern isles
Sipar's Fading — Cold, storms and snow in northern isles
Sipar's Settling — Cold, quiet, shortest days.

ACKNOWLEDGMENTS

Deepest thanks to Faith Hunter, A.J. Hartley, Edmund Schubert, Kate Elliott, Laura Willis, Virginia Craighill, Megan Roberts, April Alvarez, Patrick Dean, Adam Latham, and Brooks Egerton; my dear friend and wonderful agent, Lucienne Diver; John Hartness and the great folks at Falstaff Books, especially Theresa Glover and my wonderful editor Melissa McArthur; Marc Gascoigne, Eleanor Teasdale, Gemma Creffield, Penny Reeve, Nick Tyler, Lottie Llewelyn-Wells, and Simon Spanton-Walker, for their work on the Islevale Cycle, and a special shout-out to Marc for the map.

Lastly, I owe an incalculable debt to Nancy, Alex, and Erin—for their love, their humor, their patience. I will say this once more: The Islevale Cycle is a tale of family and the bonds that keep us safe and sane and content. Nothing I do as a writer or a person would be possible without the love I share with these three brilliant women.

ABOUT THE AUTHOR

D. B. Jackson is the award-winning author of more than two dozen books and as many short stories, spanning historical fiction, epic fantasy, contemporary fantasy, and the occasional media tie-in. His novels have been translated into more than a dozen languages. He has a master's degree and a Ph.D. in U.S. history, and briefly considered a career in academia. He wisely thought better of it. He lives with his family in the mountains of Appalachia.

Visit him at http://www.dbjackson-author.com.

ALSO BY D.B. JACKSON

The Islevale Cycle

Time's Children

Time's Demon

The Thieftaker Chronicles

Thieftaker

Thieves' Quarry

A Plunder of Souls

Dead Man's Reach

Tales of the Thieftaker

As David B. Coe

The Case Files of Justis Fearsson

Spell Blind

His Father's Eyes

Shadow's Blade

Blood of the Southlands

The Sorcerers' Plague

The Horsemen's Gambit

The Dark-Eyes' War

Winds of the Forelands

Rules of Ascension

Seeds of Betrayal

Bonds of Vengeance

Shapers of Darkness

Weavers of War

The LonTobyn Chronicle

Children of Amarid

The Outlanders

Eagle-Sage

Knightfall: The Infinite Deep

Robin Hood

FRIENDS OF FALSTAFF

Thank You to All our Falstaff Books Patrons, who get extra digital content each month! To be featured here and see what other great rewards we offer, go to www.patreon.com/falstaffbooks.

PATRONS

Dino Hicks
John Hooks
John Kilgallon
Larissa Lichty
Travis & Casey Schilling
Staci-Leigh Santore
Sheryl R. Hayes
Scott Norris
Samuel Montgomery-Blinn
Junkle